SMOKEJUMPERS SERIES OMNIBUS VOLUME TWO

BOOKS 4-6

EVIE RILEY

Smokejumpers Series Omnibus
Volume Two
Books 4-6

Copyright © 2023-2024
Evie Riley
ISBN: 978-1-77357-707-4
978-1-77357-709-8

Published by Naughty Nights Press LLC
Cover Art By Willsin Rowe

GAGE

GAGE

One stormy night could change everything…

Firefighter Gage Torres is currently certified to work the rescue squad and perform dangerous rescues on shift, but his adrenaline junkie side is always looking for more. Recently chosen for the coveted opportunity to become trained to work forest fires, he's excited to ship out to California and get started. Only thing is, he has to leave his younger brothers behind, whom he's never been away from, but they have some unexpected news of their own to share.

Aerial Firefighter Xavier Cruz is an instructor for the Sacramento Fire Division. Rough around the edges, Xavier prefers to remain a loner. He doesn't have close friends, his social skills are terrible, and even his sixteen-year-old son doesn't like him. A former fighter pilot for the Air Force, he suffers from PTSD and has turned to alcohol to fight the nightmares. But if he's ever going to mend his relationship with his son to protect him like a real father would, Xavier needs to find a way to get sober, and fast.

During a routine practice flight, their helicopter is attacked and they crash in the forest. With no map and no cell signal, the men must find a way to survive both a storm and crazy extremists with no supplies until they can get to safety. Forced to share body heat when they spend the night in a cave, things take an unexpected turn and survival becomes a night neither of them can seem to forget.

Will Gabe and Xavier make the connection between them work, or are they doomed from the start?

CHAPTER 1

GAGE

I SANK into the worn leather chair, the familiar creak echoing through the firehouse's morning haze. The room, dimly lit by the soft glow of emergency exit signs and flickering overhead lighting, carried the aroma of stale coffee and lingering solidarity. The worn wooden table before me bore the scars of countless debates, laughter, and the occasional game of poker.

Around me, my fellow firefighters sprawled in various states of fatigue, nursing mugs of coffee like lifelines. The room hummed with the low buzz of conversation, punctuated by the occasional raucous laughter. The worn-out radio crackled intermittently, its static-filled messages a constant reminder of the unpredictable nature of our calling. Captain Clarke's distinctive voice reached my ears, a steady undercurrent in the background as I waited for the morning check-in meeting to offi-cially commence.

I watched as every member of the group walked in and proceeded to approach Jase, welcoming him back into the fold with back slapping and a general happiness to have him return. The team spirit was palpable, a tangible force that bound us together in a brotherhood forged by flames and shared risks. The banter flowed effort-lessly, seasoned with firefighting jargon as my teammates described their recent call outs and the gallows humor that was our coping mechanism for the relentless stress of our profession.

I leaned back in my chair, absorbing the banter as the room gradually settled into a semblance of order. I drummed my fingertips absentmindedly on the tabletop, a silent rhythm mirroring the pulse of anticipation coursing through my veins this morning.

Captain Clarke strode to the front, his pres-ence demanding immediate attention from everyone in the room. His weathered face betrayed the countless battles he'd fought along-side us, etched with lines that spoke of both victo-ries and losses. The room hushed, the collective gaze fixed on the man who held our destinies in his calloused hands.

"All right, listen up, everyone," Captain Clarke's gravelly voice cut through the air. The room fell silent, every eye trained on our leader. "First let me say, welcome back, Turner. It's been quiet around here without you."

"Thanks, Cap," Jase responded. "It's good to be back. I'm sure you all had a difficult time around here without my bright and sunny disposition to keep you going." He flashed his pearly whites and then ducked his head.

Gaffaws and chuckles, and slow motion clapping rang out in the room before the commotion died down and the captain continued. He delved into the details of the previous day's incidents, the lessons learned, and the challenges faced. The air crackled with a mixture of focused attention and the shared understanding that each word could be a nugget of wisdom crucial for survival.

As Captain Clarke transitioned into the plan for the day ahead, my senses sharpened. The distant wail of sirens outside, the rhythmic thud of boots on the linoleum floor, the acrid scent of turnout gear—all familiar elements that composed the symphony of a firehouse morning.

And then, he dropped the long-anticipated bombshell.

"We've got an opening for the aerial firefighters division in Sacramento, California," Captain Clarke announced, and a hush fell over the room. My heart quickened its pace, anticipation and anxiety intertwining in a chaotic dance. My mind whirled and I sent up a quick prayer.

Please say it. Tell me I've finally been chosen.

"And," he continued, locking eyes with me, "Torres, pack your bags and make whatever arrangements you need to. You'll be wheels up tomorrow at oh eight hundred."

A stunned silence enveloped me, broken only by the sounds of the firehouse waking up to a new day. The weight of the announcement settled on my shoulders, a mix of exhilaration and trepidation.

My fellow firefighters erupted into cheers, clapping me on the back and offering hearty congratulations. The room transformed into a cacophony of laughter and excitement, and amidst it all, I felt a surge of pride. The coveted training, a chance to soar through the skies and battle blazes from above, was now within my grasp. Finally.

As the reality sank in, I couldn't help but crack a grin. I'd been chosen for a placement that transcended the routine of life here at the station, a chance to elevate my skills to new heights.

The room continued to buzz with excitement, and I found myself caught in a whirlwind of congratulations and well wishes. My fellow firefighters, Hawke, Jase, Johnson, Zander, Carmen, Mark, Cy, and Quinn, our weekly rotated paramedics Newt and Ellie, each one a brother or sister in arms, surrounded me, offering slaps on the back and words of encouragement. The air was charged with energy, and I couldn't help but feel a surge of pride and gratitude for the friendships that bound us together even beyond the firehouse.

Amidst the elation, I exchanged nods and smiles with my colleagues, their genuine happiness reflecting the tight-knit bond forged through countless shared experiences. Captain Clarke, his eyes crinkling at the corners with a rare smile, approached me with a firm handshake.

"Torres, you've earned this opportunity. Make

us proud up there," he said, his words carrying the weight of both expectation and trust.

"Thank you, Captain. I won't let you down," I replied, the gravity of the moment settling in.

As the room gradually quieted, Captain Clarke regained control of the meeting, transitioning into the nitty-gritty details of the day's assignments and ongoing projects. My mind, however, raced ahead, already envisioning the challenges and adventures that awaited me in the aerial firefighters division.

The morning sunlight streamed through the grimy windows, casting a warm glow on the firehouse memorabilia that adorned the walls. The familiar scent of old leather and fire-resistant fabric hung in the air, a comforting reminder of the home I was about to leave behind temporarily.

The next day flashed in my mind like a series of rapid-fire images—the airport hustle, the hum of the plane's engines, and the anticipation of stepping onto unfamiliar ground. I couldn't suppress the mix of nerves and excitement that surged through me. This was a chance to push my limits, to evolve as a firefighter, and to contribute to missions that transcended the boundaries of the firehouse.

As the meeting drew to a close, the room gradually emptied, each firefighter dispersing to tackle the day's tasks. I remained seated for a moment longer, absorbing the gravity of the moment. The journey ahead promised growth, challenges, and the opportunity to make a difference on a larger scale.

I rose from the worn leather chair, a sense of purpose coursing through my veins. The firehouse, once a familiar sanctuary, now felt like the launching pad for a new chapter. I exchanged more nods and encouraging words with my coworkers as I made my way toward the gear room to prepare for the day ahead.

The journey to California loomed on the horizon, a path filled with unknowns and possibilities. I couldn't help but reflect on the journey that led me to this point—the countless drills, the shared laughter and hardships, and the unwavering support of my firefighting family, and my reason for it all.

My younger brothers, Greyson and Asher.

With a deep breath and a sense of determination similar to the one that had seen me through many life challenges so far, I welcomed the new opportunities that lay ahead. I was so ready to soar into the skies and face the flames from a new perspective.

CHAPTER 2

Xavier

Beep... beep... beep...

I smacked my hand down on the annoying alarm clock next to my bed with a groan. I was not ready to be awake right now. I was not ready to face the headache that I knew would hit me the second my eyes opened.

I hated Mondays. I hated most days, but Mondays were the worst. I wasn't a morning person. Shit, I wasn't even an afternoon person. I was a night owl. I preferred to be up all night and sleep during any sunlight hour, especially if that meant I could avoid the hustle and bustle of people all over the place.

I didn't mind being around crowds when it was in a bar, when I could drink and find the next guy to have a one-night stand with. But when I had to be sober during the day and in a crowd, I always felt like my skin was crawling. Something as simple as walking down a busy street was difficult and the act of grocery shopping during peak hours, fucking forget about it. Being around people was hard, especially idiots.

There were times when I was at work and I had to go off and be by myself because I couldn't handle the stupidity and immaturity that some of the others have. I knew it was part of life, that at some point I was just as stupid as them, but I wasn't at that part of my life anymore. I couldn't handle most things that I used to be able to. And I knew that was from the PTSD.

Fuck, I'm so sick of hearing those four letters.

I had been in the Air Force since I was eighteen. I enlisted right on my eighteenth birthday and I didn't regret it, not for a single second. Yes, shit had been hard plenty of times and there were an endless number of close calls over the years, but my time in service had been some of the best years of my life. I had made some of the strongest bonds that could be possible. They were all dead now, which hurt, but I didn't ever regret knowing them, even if that meant I had to deal with the hurt of burying them.

I had been honorably discharged four years ago when I was thirty-eight. It was a bit by choice and a bit forced, but that's a story I try never to think about. The shrink that I was forced to see before starting my new job told me I had PTSD, but it would only affect my personal life and not my professional life so I was cleared to keep flying planes.

I didn't believe the whole PTSD thing at first. I

thought it was bullshit and just some fancy way to say I get nightmares.

Who the fuck wouldn't have nightmares after what I'd seen?

Turns out, she might have been on to something because as time went on, I started to notice different things. Like how life was so much easier if I was drunk for most of it. Obviously, I never drank when I was working or on call, but when I was free to do whatever I wanted, I spent most of it drunk. It also destroyed my desire to be social, which put my social skills down to questionable at best.

The thing was though, I didn't give a shit. I didn't care to be social and happy all of the time. I didn't care to listen to pathetic little problems that people complained about like they were something serious. I couldn't listen to people going on and on about their coworkers or being cheated on. I had to scrape my friends up off of the ground with a shovel and put them into buckets.

Why the fuck would I care about someone's boyfriend not being able to keep it in his pants?

If that made me anti-social, then I was more than happy to be. You couldn't tell that to a Shrink though, they'd just tell you that you had survivor's guilt and deep-rooted traumas that were masked by sarcasm. And maybe they were, or maybe I was just an old, bitter cat who wanted to be left the fuck alone.

What was so wrong with that?

Seriously, I wasn't hurting anyone with how I was. I wasn't in a relationship. I didn't bring any toxic behavior around people.

If I didn't want to be happy and social, then why did it matter to other people?

I was content with the way that I was and that should have been good enough.

There was one regret in my life, fuck many, but the biggest regret would be my ex-wife. Sure, most people felt that way about their ex-spouse, I knew she did about me as well. The thing was though, I regretted ever kissing her, let alone marrying her. At the same time though, it was a double edge sword, because if I hadn't kissed her, if I hadn't married her, I wouldn't have my son Dexter. He was the only pride and joy that I had. The only one who could truly bring a smile to my face.

When I'd discovered that Kate was pregnant almost seventeen years ago, I had never felt so happy before in my life. I never thought I would have children and then I found out I was having a son. I couldn't have been happier. I was there for everything. Every doctor's appointment, every ultrasound, all of the food cravings, the decorating, everything. I was hands-on and there for it all and when he was born, it was me who cut his umbilical cord. I was the one who held him first.

The very second that I held him in my arms I was in love. The feeling of seeing him, of getting to hear his cry, there was no other feeling like it in the world. There was no way to describe it. It was an instant tidal wave of love, a drive to keep him safe and give him the best life that I possibly could. Even if that meant I had to stay with his mother and continue to keep my true desires a secret. I would do anything that I could to give him the best life.

I grew up with amazing parents. They had been together since they were in high school and they were madly in love until the day they died. They never fought in front of me. They were always affectionate with each other. If one was sick or tired, the other was there for them. If one was sad, the other comforted them. If one was happy, they were both happy. Their love was pure and contagious and I wanted that for my son. I wanted him to grow up seeing love and happiness between his parents.

I had tried my best. I pushed down my desires and urges to be with a man. I continued to live a life in the closet and foolishly believed that I could be with my wife and be happy. That the sex could be satisfying if I only tried harder. I was delusional and that delusion was ultimately the end of our happy life.

The end of normalcy for Dexter.

For six years we were the perfect family. I was often gone from operations and deployment, but we made it work. I had to give it to Kate, she was the perfect military wife. She never complained about having to relocate with literally thirty days notice. She never complained when I was called away at any given time of the day or night, including birthdays, holidays, and anniversaries. She never freaked out if I came home a bit injured. She was the ideal military wife and the men all envied what I had. They envied not having arguments with their spouse. They envied the type of mother she was. They envied how easy it was.

What they didn't see was that I was dying inside.

I loved Dexter and I wanted everything for him, but every single kiss that Kate gave me, every time we touched, I felt like an enemy was touching me. It made my skin crawl. It made me sick just thinking about being with her sexually and it was wrong. I knew it was wrong to feel that way, to put her through it, but I couldn't help it. I couldn't tell her that I wasn't attracted to her, that I was attracted to men. She didn't sign up for that.

I knew I was gay when I first kissed her when I was sixteen. I knew I wasn't attracted to her, but back then there was no such thing as acceptable homosexuality. You didn't broadcast it and if you wanted to survive high school, you had to fit within a specific box. It was just supposed to be to get me through high school and then I would be in the Air Force and we would go our separate ways.

Only, she was supportive of my decision to be in the military. She was in love with me and the military was even less accepting of homosexuals, so I continued to play along. When we had been together for years, it was natural to propose to her and get married. If I had died in action, she deserved to have the benefits. She had been in my life long enough and put up with me, she had earned the widow benefits. Then Dexter came along and it all snowballed, all from a single kiss back in high school.

For six years after my son was born we made it work, but one afternoon, the one time I had given in to temptation, my whole life changed. It was an afternoon and Dexter was at school, Kate was supposed to be out with her friends until that evening. I was supposed to be alone, so when I invited a man that I had found on a sex app over for some afternoon fun, I figured we would be fine.

At that point, I had never been with a man before. I just wanted to see just once what it felt like. I wanted to feel like myself for just one afternoon and it was amazing. The second our lips touched, I knew exactly what I had been missing. It was like a dream come true.

Until Kate walked in on us having sex in our bed.

In that one instant my entire life changed and my son's entire life changed. I had hoped after Kate had calmed down that we could talk about it. That I could finally be honest with her and we would work through it. That we could have an amicable divorce and co-parent like civil adults.

Only that wasn't what happened.

Kate had grown up in a very religious family. I knew that and in hindsight she really was the worst girl for me to kiss or marry, but it was far too late to change anything. She demanded that I go to conversion therapy, but that wasn't something that I could do. I was gay, and despite not being out and proud, I wasn't going to sit and listen to someone telling me that I needed to be cured from a disease.

I didn't have a disease. I had a closet problem.

When I refused, she had left. I thought she would be gone for the night and then calm down. I was spun up that night and when I returned three days later, all of her and Dexter's things were gone and she had already filed for divorce and sole custody. I wasn't going to give her sole custody of Dexter. I wanted joint custody, at least, and I fought through court for it, but with being deployed and getting spun up at a moment's notice, the judge granted Kate full custody and left visitation up to her.

Kate had not calmed down over the weeks or months that followed her finding me in bed with another man. She often kept Dexter from me and refused to allow me to see him. She was convinced I would *infect* him.

What the fuck?

I had to watch as my son grew up through social media and photos. Whenever I called, she wouldn't answer. Whenever I sent gifts, they would be returned to me. She would move and not tell me where they were living.

On the rare occasions that I could see Dexter, it was hard. Dexter had grown distant from me, especially during his teenage years. I didn't blame him. I knew that Kate would often tell him that I didn't care enough to be there. She put it all on me and not on her own actions.

Now he was sixteen, almost seventeen, and he didn't really want anything to do with me. He was angry all the time and he didn't like me. I was the *deadbeat dad* in his life and that wasn't what I wanted for him.

This wasn't the life that I wanted for him.

I hadn't told him the full story. He believed that I cheated on Kate, which was true, but he thought it was with a woman. I was scared to tell Dexter the truth, because he grew up with Kate and her family. He went to church every week and she constantly pushed her religious beliefs onto him. I didn't know how he would react if he discovered I was gay. I didn't want to risk losing him and I was terrified that I would if he knew I was gay.

All I could do was try to be there for him and hope that in time he would see that I wanted to be there and it was his mother who had kept me from him.

Even after Kate discovered I was gay, I still kept it a secret. I would meet up for a quick booty call from a sex app, but I was very much in the closet. I couldn't come out, not with being in the military. The guys that I worked with wouldn't understand.

That did change though, once I was discharged.

I figured I was at a point in my life where I wouldn't have to keep that part of myself a dirty secret. I wasn't walking in any parade, but I wasn't hiding in a dark underground club either. I still hadn't dated anyone, just kept it to one night stands or the few fuck buddies that I had. Friends with benefits would be putting it a bit generously.

I didn't like hanging out with them, or even pillow talk. I just wanted sex and for them to leave, it was just that simple to me. I had problems, I knew that, and it wasn't fair to drag anyone into my problems. They were my problems that I got from being in war. I had made the choice to go, and it wasn't fair to make someone else take on my problems for decisions I had made.

My phone's alarm going off only reminded me

that I was supposed to be getting up. I let out a groan, as I reached over and finally opened my eyes to turn it off. The second my eyes opened, that headache that I knew would be hitting me, hit me.

That was the downside to drinking. The morning after when that hangover hits you, it was a serious bitch. I couldn't roll over and go back to sleep, even though I really wanted to. Just like I couldn't have a shot of whiskey for the hair of the dog, because I had to be prepared to fly if I should need to.

After I got out of the Air Force I didn't know what I wanted to do, but I knew I wanted to continue to fly. I had moved out to Sacramento, California, my hometown, and joined the fire department as an aerial firefighter. I was the guy who flew the planes or choppers to help when there was a forest fire. I would bring water with specialty planes and I would fly with firefighters or paramedics for search and rescue. It was different compared to flying over a war zone. There was a simplicity to it, but it still allowed me to utilize my skills.

There was also a personal connection to helping with stopping forest fires.

My parents had been killed in a forest fire twenty years ago in Northern California. They were on a camping trip when a forest fire broke out from a lightning strike during a storm. I had been on tour at the time and when the call came in, I didn't even know what to do or to think. I had lost both of them completely out of the blue. I didn't have any siblings and both of my grandparents were dead. They had died when I was younger.

Having to bury my parents, it was a surreal experience, one that to this day still didn't feel real. I was still waiting to see their name pop up on my phone when it rang. I honestly didn't think I would ever get used to them not being in my life. Not being on the other end of the phone. Losing them, it made me want to keep helping people and with being an aerial firefighter, I could do just that.

I had worked forest fires all over Northern California, Texas, and in Montana. Wherever it was needed, we went, and we did everything we could to help save lives.

Today, I was supposed to be helping to get ready for some new recruits to be here tomorrow. We ran different training courses to turn normal firefighters into aerial firefighters. We were always in need of more firefighters to help with the forest fires.

Forest fires were twice as deadly as a standard fire and they often took a lot longer to put out. When a fire was in a building, it could only burn as long as there was fuel for it. Eventually, it would run out of fuel once the building was gone. That wasn't the case with a forest fire, because there was always fuel for the fire. Whether that was the trees, the grass, the log cabins in the forest or the cities that were close by. There was always something the fire could eat to keep going that made it very difficult to completely put out. It was why some forest fires could take weeks to completely put out and it was grueling on the firefighters.

My job was to make sure they got in and out safely and I provided air support with the water bombers. I also had to keep track of the fire and predict which way it was going to move based on the destruction speed of the fire and wind direction. I was their eyes and it was a job that I took very seriously and I expected all of the firefighters on the ground to do the same.

I wasn't a fan of teaching, but I was one of the harder instructors and everyone knew that if I said one of the guys was good, that meant they were good and they could trust that person with their lives. It was why I was so hard on the cadets. A lot of lives rested on their shoulders and I would be the one to make sure they were ready to handle it.

The ding from my phone telling me I had a new text message only made me groan once again. We had a lot of work to get finished today before the new cadets arrived tomorrow and I wasn't looking forward to it.

I pushed myself up and instantly regretted it. Once again it felt like my brain was trying to escape through my eye sockets. Sitting up on my bed for a moment, I took the time to check out the damage to my studio apartment. I knew if a Shrink ever stepped foot in here they would immediately make me see them four times a week. I had empty beer bottles and whiskey bottles all over the place. Along with take out containers and pizza boxes.

The furniture in my place left something to be desired. I only had my bed, a double mattress and box spring on the floor, an old loveseat, an old coffee table that by some miracle was still standing, and my tv. Other than that, I had some clothes in a duffle bag and that was it. I didn't have any photos up, nothing personal at all. This was a studio apartment, not a home. I didn't know how to make it a home. I didn't know if I wanted a home.

I knew I should want more. I should want a nice place that was home to me. I knew that, I did, but I couldn't seem to bring myself to care to make it happen. Some days by the time I made it through work I was so exhausted that I couldn't even string two words together, much less figure out how to make my place look like a mentally stable person lived there. I knew I had to figure it out, but I couldn't bring myself to care enough to even get started on figuring out how to do that. I certainly wasn't going to start now. I had to get to work and maybe tonight I might have enough energy to think about it. I doubted it, though.

CHAPTER 3

"YOU'RE SERIOUSLY DROPPING this shit on me now?"

Holy fuck, I loved my brothers, I did, but they both had the worst timing for when they told me shit. Part of that was my fault, I was man enough to admit it, but in my defense I was young when I had to step up and raise them and they did not make it easy for me.

At eighteen, I should have been a free man. Free to explore the world and build my own life, but instead I found myself raising identical twin eleven-year-old boys. It wasn't our mother's fault, she didn't plan on getting cancer and she sure as shit didn't plan on dying a week after I turned eighteen. At least she hung on that long so the twins wouldn't end up in foster care, but sometimes I wondered if maybe they would have been better off if they did end up in a loving two parent household.

It wasn't easy growing up, far from it. I loved my mother, but she was a single mother for most of my life. My father took off the second that stick turned blue, and to this day I still had never met him. I wouldn't know him if he was standing right in front of me. It was just my mother and me for the first seven years of my life. Then my mother met the twins' father and he stuck around until they were five. He was the twins' father, but he wasn't mine. He wasn't even interested in being a stepfather. Shit, he wasn't all that interested in being a father to the twins.

When he took off I was twelve and had to take on a huge responsibility with taking care of the twins when my mother had to go back to work. It was on me to get the twins to school. It was on me to make sure they got home from school. It was on me to make sure any homework was done. It was on me to cook dinner for all four of us. It was on me to make sure they were bathed and in bed at a decent hour. At twelve years old, I was raising two five-year-old boys while our mother worked all day or all night long to make enough money to keep a roof over our heads or food on our table.

It was hard. There were plenty of days where I was exhausted and didn't know if I could do it. The days where all three of us had the flu and I had to still take care of them while being sick, because even one day off for our mother could mean we didn't eat one day.

That was our life until I was fourteen and she started to get sick. She was rundown all the time, not eating, losing weight, she always had a headache, and she woke up with new bruises with no idea of where they came from. One day, she collapsed at work and was taken to the hospital. We found out she had blood cancer; stage three.

I could still remember the look on the twins' face when I had to tell them that our mother was sick. When they asked me if she was going to die, all I could tell them was no, even though I was terrified that she was. She fought with everything in her. She continued to work as often as she could, even while going through chemotherapy and radiation.

I couldn't work until I was fifteen and then I picked up a part-time job at a restaurant as a busboy. It was incredibly hard though, having to balance working, school, and the twins. Plus being there for my mother during her treatments and taking care of her when she was sick.

I had to do it all though, because if anyone suspected that something was going on we would have been taken away from her. Child Protective Services would have been called and then we all would have been split up and placed in foster care.

That wasn't what I wanted.

I had friends at school who were in foster homes and it was horrific. I wasn't going to risk that happening to the twins or myself. So I pushed through and I raised them and took care of my mother. For four years we made it work, until she lost her fight against cancer.

When the social worker showed up after her funeral, she asked me if I was going to have custody of the twins, I hesitated. It wasn't because

I didn't love them, it was because I was exhausted. I had been going non-stop since I was twelve and I was just worn out and wanted to have the chance to have a normal life. I told myself they could go to a loving home together. That they would never split twins up. But then every story that I had heard from my friends popped into my head and I knew that I couldn't roll the dice on their lives. I had to take them, because they were safe with me.

It'd been just us ever since and I had joined the Fire Academy as a way to provide for them. At the time there was no waitlist to get in, and I knew it would be a good paycheck for someone that only had a high school diploma, and just barely. I would have health benefits for all three of us, plus dental. The dental was huge because they both needed braces at the time. Becoming a firefighter was all about giving the three of us a chance at a decent life.

Now they were eighteen and how were they paying me back for all of the years of sacrifice I'd made?

By surprising me with life-altering decisions two hours before I was supposed to be on a plane to fly out to Sacramento, California.

Fuck me.

"You asked us what we wanted to do once we graduated," Asher replied, shrugging a shoulder.

Asher was the older twin, by all of ninety-three seconds, and he never let Greyson forget it. Though, Greyson liked to point out that he was smarter, to which Asher always countered that Greyson was only smarter because he stood on Asher's head for a good three months before they were born. The two of them were identical by looks, right down to the fucking smattering of freckles on their faces. Honestly, sometimes I still got confused on who was who. In my defense though, they liked to switch places.

Asher was terrible at school, especially math, so Greyson used to go and sit in his math class to take his tests. The teachers either never noticed or they were too tired and overworked to care. Either way, the only reason Asher had graduated high school at all was because of Greyson. I knew I should've been angry about it, but I was more relieved than anything.

"I meant for the summer. I meant parties you wanted to go to or a vacation you were looking to take. Not that you wanted to go work at a horse ranch in Texas or for Thing Two to be enlisting in the fucking Army." I ran my hands over my face, forcing back the resulting nervous tension from the bomb they'd just dropped, even as my guts wound into a tight knot.

For fuck's sake, all they had to do was behave while I was gone for the aerial training in California. I was only going to be gone for a month. All they had to do was behave for the last two days of school, really. They'd both graduated and they did the whole walk across the stage and throw the hat thing. The school had done it a few days early because all of the Seniors were supposed to help with an end of school carnival and they didn't want to run the risk of leaving the graduation ceremony too late and some of the Seniors couldn't be there. It worked out great for me, because I got to see them graduate.

"I don't see how it's a big deal. You knew we were going to get jobs and start our own lives," Asher commented.

"I know and I get that you are both young adults now and want to start your lives. But you have never mentioned your desire to move to another state. To work with horses. Do you even know anything about a horse ranch?" I said to Asher before I turned to Greyson, who was supposed to be my smart brother. "And the Army? Seriously? You know that involves running right? You have to do push ups and sit-ups, you have to run with a hundred pounds on your back. You have to shoot a gun at people."

"I know what the Army does. I am well aware of the physical challenges, but Asher has been helping me and I already passed the physical qualification tests. I think this is more about you coming back in a month to an empty home," Greyson calmly alleged.

"Don't. Don't Shrink talk me. I'm pissed that you both have clearly known about this for a while now and you didn't tell me. You waited until I was just about out the door before you decided to inform me that when I come home you'll both be in different States. I had the right to know. I had the right to process it all and be involved in that decision making. We don't have secrets, that's the rule. It's been the rule since you were five years old. You tell me everything, even that you both dated the same guy at the same time without telling him. You can tell me that, but you seriously couldn't tell me this before now? Urgh."

And that is what it came down to. They kept

something that important a secret from me. As if I would be furious that they wanted to make plans for their lives. It wasn't even that they would be out of the house or in a different State, it was that I didn't get to be there for the planning stage.

We could have taken a trip to Texas to look at different horse ranches to find the right one for Asher to work at. Greyson could have been within ROTC to see if he did in fact want to be in the Army without the complexity of enlisting. I had always been supportive of what they chose to do with their lives. I had always walked that fine line between being a father and their big brother. It wasn't always easy, but I didn't want to give up being their brother in favor of being the parent.

Why leave me out now?

To be honest, it hurt, and I wasn't afraid to let them know it.

I deserved better.

"Look, we're sorry. We didn't know how you would react. It's all new to us, to all three of us and we didn't want what little time we had left living together to be filled with anger. We just wanted to have fun. But we should have told you," Asher said, his voice contrite.

"It's all new to us. Even Ash and me, we're gonna be in different States. The three of us have always been together and now everything is going to change. We just wanted some normalcy and we didn't want you to worry about us. I was also worried you would be disappointed in me for going into the Army and not medical school," Greyson confessed, his eyes downcast.

"All I want is for you both to be happy and

healthy. I thought you were going into medical school, because you're so smart and you've been volunteering at the free clinic for four years now. I thought you wanted to be a doctor. You applied for medical schools and received a full scholarship for Harvard." And that was what I couldn't get over.

Who in their right mind turned down a free ride at one of the best medical schools?

"I want to be an Army Medic. I want to help other soldiers to return alive. I want to be able to help protect people and serve this country. You have been a firefighter for seven years. For seven years we've watched as you risked your life to save other people. I want to do that too, just in a different way."

Fuck.

Leave it to Greyson to guilt trip me without even trying. I rubbed the back of my neck.

"Okay, okay. You both know I love you and you know I will always support you and your decisions. If this is what you both truly want to do and what you want your careers to be, then I will support it and I will always be there for you."

It terrified me that Greyson wanted to join the Army. I had no idea what I was supposed to do with that. How to handle knowing that he would be going into war zones and being shot at and there was nothing I could do to protect him.

I was a protector through and through. It didn't matter if I knew a person or not, if they were in trouble I was going to be there for them. I had been in dozens of fights at the bar for defending a guy who was being harassed for being gay. I was gay myself and I had been out and proud since I was fifteen. I didn't care what other people thought, I was going to be myself and if they didn't like it, then they could kick rocks. I didn't care.

When the twins told me they were gay at fourteen, I was a bit surprised.

I mean, what were the odds?

But it did make things a lot easier in terms of giving them the sex talk. Helping them with their relationships was a hell of a lot easier.

Now they were both going to be starting their own lives in two different States and I would have to deal with not seeing them every day. I was going to be alone for the first time in twenty-five years. I wasn't going to have to come home from work and help with homework. I wasn't going to have to make breakfast or dinner for all of us every night. There wouldn't be any movie marathons on the weekend. No more nights where we would sit outside and barbecue and go for a swim. No more birthday parties or pool parties. Even Christmas or Thanksgiving, if they both couldn't get time off it was just going to be me. I had no idea how I was going to handle that. How I was going to handle the quiet.

"We know you will and we love you too," Greyson said, flashing me a warm smile.

"How come you didn't think I would be a doctor?" Asher said, effectively ruining the sweet moment between us all.

"Seriously?" Greyson asked with a smirk.

"You know I love you, but you are the farthest thing from book smart, Ash. I honestly thought you were never going to move out. That you would be an unemployed model until you gained too much weight and started to work at a burger joint," I teased, following with a slight chuckle.

It sounded wrong, I knew that, but he wasn't book smart. Greyson was the book smart brother and Asher was the street smart brother. He knew people, he knew how to survive in the world. I teased him all the time about being a pretty face, but he knew that I loved him and I was only joking. I figured he would actually work in construction or be a personal trainer. Him going to work on a horse ranch fit him perfectly, in fact, and I truly hoped he had an amazing time doing it and it was something he loved.

"You're such an asshole," Asher said, flashing me a warm smile.

We all laughed at that. I could sometimes be an asshole. I was hardheaded and anyone who knew me would tell you that. It was a result of having to grow up so fast. I wasn't used to asking for help. I was used to being the one that had to give help. A lot of that was because we couldn't ask for help growing up because then the authorities would come knocking and we all risked being split up. I had to handle everything myself, no matter how hard things got.

The guys at work called me the Reckless Brother. I loved riding my motorcycle, skydiving, bungee jumping, anything that had to do with adrenaline, I was all for it. It was why I wanted to learn how to be a Smokejumper and fight forest fires. I loved being a firefighter. Something that I started because it was my best chance at providing for the twins. I never expected to fall in love with it, but I did and I fell hard. I couldn't imagine doing anything else with my life and that's what I wanted for the twins. I wanted them to love their job and be excited to go to work every day.

"I love you too. Do you both have everything you need? Do you know where you're living?" I had to leave to go to the airport soon, but I needed to make sure they were both set for their new adventures or if I needed to help them get things figured out before they left.

"I'll be staying on the horse ranch. It's Moonlit Horse Sanctuary, so they take in horses that have been abused and they get them healthy and socialized again. They have a bunkhouse for ranch hands," Asher answered.

"I'll be going to Fort Moore in Georgia and staying on base there for Basic training. Afterward, I might be stationed there or moved to another base. I won't know until after Basic is completed."

I wasn't too worried about Greyson finding a place to live. The military always had dorms or places for their soldiers to live in every town they were in. It was Asher who was my main concern, as usual, but he'd found a ranch that had a bunkhouse so he wouldn't have to worry about finding a place or even paying rent. All he had to do was pay for his food, cell phone, and gas for his truck. At least they were both going to be fine and taken care of.

"All right, good. I have to get going so I don't miss my flight. I want you both to text me every day and let me know when you will be leaving. I mean it, no more secrets, no matter what."

"We promise," Asher said on their behalf, both of them dragging me in for a backslapping hug.

I would have loved to be home to see them off, but I couldn't put this training course off. If I wanted to be a Smokejumper, I had to take this course and with them now being legal adults, I didn't have to worry about leaving them alone for a month. I'd waited a long time for this opportunity and I wasn't about to blow it.

This was my chance, my time, to be my own adult, my own person without obligations or responsibilities to other people. It was different and it was going to take some getting used to, but it was something that I had to do. It was something all three of us had to do. We had been living for each other for so long and now it was our time to be our own individuals and live our lives.

I just hoped it wouldn't be too terrible of an adjustment period for the three of us. Only time would tell. I prayed they got everything they wanted out of life, because they deserved it and I couldn't be more proud of them.

CHAPTER 4

XAVIER

I HATED the first day of a new training class. The students were always filled with so much joy and excitement that it was like trying to teach a group of thirty puppies how to sit and shut up. Most of them were in their mid-twenties and older, all of which were younger than mid-thirties. The simple fact was there was a point where a body couldn't handle the physical requirements of being a Smokejumper. That and normally it took a young buck to be stupid enough to do this job. I, of course, was the exception, but I came from a war zone, so this was nothing to me.

I could see they were all feeling pumped and ready for this, but I also knew that would quickly change. The first few days were the honeymoon period. Where they all thought it was easy and they were going to graduate and get their certificate. Normally, on day five was when reality would hit them and they would feel how exhausted and sore their bodies were. They would learn that they couldn't be a complete idiot if they were going to be able to understand all of the weather graphs and be able to predict how a fire would move. There was a lot more book smarts to it than people expected. They figured they would ride on a chopper, repel down, and then fight a fire, but that simplicity of it all was how you got yourself and others killed. You had to be able to understand the weather side of things to properly save people's lives.

"What do you think?" Jackson came up beside me and asked.

He was one of the guys that I worked with often. I wasn't really based out of a firehouse because what I did required me to be up in the air for the most part. Jackson did search and rescue, so whenever someone was lost in the woods or hurt, he went in to save 'em. He was talented at what he did and he was double certified for search and rescue and also medical. If that wasn't enough, he had a beautiful golden retriever that would go with him on his searches.

"I think they're all idiots," I said with zero humor in my voice.

I did like Jackson. He was one of the good ones to be around. He was older like I was, and still going strong. You would never know he was forty-five, he looked ten years younger, and he acted like a horny twenty year old. Jackson was the guy that your parents warned you to stay away from. He was the guy you didn't bring home to your parents, because he would never be there two weekends later. He was the type of guy that I would never want Dexter to be with, not that Dexter was gay, but my point still stands.

"There's those people skills again," Jackson said, flashing a smirk before he continued. "Some of them look delicious."

"There's those people skills," I countered with my own smirk that caused Jackson to laugh.

That was one of the nice things about Jackson, he didn't try to change me or judge me. He understood that I was damaged and he accepted who I was. Some of the others were always trying to get me to go out or to see someone. They wanted me to find a hobby and all that bullshit. Jackson didn't, he was just there and I really appreciated it. That was probably why we were good friends.

He was actually the only person that I would call a friend. It helped that his father had been in service and he had an older brother that was in service. Both were killed in action, but he understood the toll the job took on people. So he never gave me shit or looked at me with pity when I was drinking. He never tried to drag me out during the day to busy places. He was perfectly happy to hang out at his place or go to one of the smaller gay bars.

"Come on, you have to admit that some of them are looking very sexy."

"How many times do we have to have this conversation? You aren't supposed to sleep with any of the cadets."

"It's not my fault there's always one gay guy or

bi-curious guy in the group. I bet you there's at least one here right now."

"Weren't you interested in that other guy? The one you met at the strip club."

Jackson didn't date in the traditional sense. He tended to have the guys he was with believing that they were special and could make him change. That they were the ones that would change his ways and make him fall in love. He didn't advise them against that belief. He would be sleeping with them, but also sleeping with others. He usually had a few guys on the go at the same time, most of which didn't know about the others. He was a dog, a dirty down dog, but he had his reasons, I'm sure. We'd never talked about it, but I was certain there was something in his history that made him that way. I respected him enough to not press, just like he had never pressed me for more answers.

"I was and we were hooking up for a few months before he found out that I was also seeing three other guys," he said with a small shrug.

"How did he find out? You're normally more careful than that."

"He's got a younger brother that walked in on me with one of my other honeys at the club. He told Devon and apparently Devon felt like we were exclusive and he wasn't looking for an open relationship."

"I'm surprised you weren't trying to get with the younger brother. You always like them young and dumb."

"He's eighteen, but he's not dumb, and he's

not your typical eighteen year old, at least according to Devon. He's got a good head on his shoulders and doesn't like meaningless sex. He's like a seventy-year-old man trapped in an eighteen year old's body."

"The horror of responsible sexual activity," I said sarcastically. The kid sounded smart and like he knew what he wanted out of life and he wasn't letting anything get in his way.

"It's the worst thing in the world. But enough about my very active sex life, we have to get started before the natives get restless."

I gave a slight hum in agreement before we both made our way toward the front of the classroom. Everyone was in different groups and talking, they didn't even notice us at the front ready to go.

"That's enough! Take your seats!" I called out.

"These poor cadets have no idea what they are in for," Jackson mumbled next to me and I knew he meant about my attitude. I wasn't the friendliest teacher, but I was the one that would give them the best chance at living.

All of the cadets turned their attention to me and I could see it registering in their mind that it was time to get started. They all made their way to their seats and I could see they all had a small notebook and a pen with them. They really were expecting this to be more hands-on and it would be, eventually, but there were a lot of classroom hours and an exam as well.

"My name is Xavier Cruz, I will be one of your main instructors for this course. I will also be your pilot. This is my colleague, Jackson Hall. You will see him for the medical side of things for the course. He is one of the best search and rescue firefighters in the country. When they have someone they can't find, they call for Jackson. He's been all over the country searching for people who have gone missing in complex forestry locations. This course is a month long, six days a week. In order to qualify for your certificate, you must score eighty percent or higher on your final written and practical exam. Anything under, even by one decimal point, and you will not receive your certificate. Any questions so far?"

I was hoping not. I hadn't gotten into anything technical so there shouldn't be any questions right now. Thankfully no one raised their hand.

"Today, I will be taking you up in groups so you can see the area that this course will be about. You will get to have aerial views in class, but seeing it in person helps you to visualize the area. Those who are not up in the air with me, will be meeting with the head doctor to go over your medical history. We need to know everything so there are no surprises that come up. When every group has had a turn, we will then be doing class work for the next week."

"A week?" One of the cadets said.

I had no idea who he was. It wasn't like they were wearing nametags. I nodded and moved on.

"Half of this course is done in the field and the other half is done in a classroom. Something you all should know if you actually read the course program before you applied to be here. You have to be able to read weather maps, understand wind speeds, wind structures, and how it can all change based on the weather forecast that is moving in. All of that helps you accurately predict the path of the fire. Being able to predict how the fire is going to move will allow you to evacuate the cities that are in the destruction path. It also allows you to try and contain the fire to prevent it from spreading further. Every firefighter, whether on the ground or in the air, has to be able to read the fire. You can't rely on someone else to be able to do it because you could be separated and your very life depends on it. If you are not going to take this seriously, then leave. Do not waste our time."

That was something I was not going to tolerate. I didn't have a problem teaching those who were willing. You didn't have to be the smartest person in the world; I just needed you to try. If they weren't going to try, then they could get the hell out of here and make room for the people that were committed to being here and learning.

"This isn't going to be easy for you. We know that learning a new skill in the classroom can be very difficult for people. We have no problem taking the time and working through it with you. But we're not going to put that time in if you aren't committed to learning. If you thought this was going to be you repelling out of a chopper for the next four weeks, you were wrong. Just like you have to be able to read a fire in a building, you have to be able to read a fire in the forest. But like I said, we will help you as long as you are willing to learn," Jackson added.

I could see a mixture of reactions within the group. Some were annoyed that they would have to be stuck in a classroom. They completely thought this was going to be fully hands-on. Others were content to learn what they had to so they could get through this course.

However, a couple looked excited for it all.

They were excited to learn a new skill and it was those that I was looking forward to teaching. It was refreshing and more enjoyable to teach someone who wanted to learn. Someone who literally loved to learn. I had come across a few firefighters who just wanted to learn new skills so they could help more people. It made for a great learning experience and I was hoping the ones who wanted to learn made it through the course.

"All right, I need you four right there for the first flight up." I pointed at the four in the first row. "The rest of you will be meeting with our Doc one at a time. When you are not with the doc, we have a workbook for you to start going over. It covers basic information that you most likely learned in the Fire Academy, but you don't utilize it every day on the job. It's important to remember the basics so we can build up on it. Jackson will be here to answer any questions that you have."

They were getting busy work today, but we really did need to make sure they knew the basics so we could build on them. If they didn't remember all of the basics we had to cover that real quick, otherwise they were going to be confused down the road.

"Have fun," Jackson said with a short wave to me before I headed off and gave a nod to the four guys who would be coming with me on the first trip. It was going to be a long ass day for me and all I could do was hope that I didn't snap at any of their questions. I was still hung over from last night so I just needed this to go smoothly today.

CHAPTER 5

GAGE

WELL, today hadn't gone like I thought it would. When I first got here, I was excited and filled with so much energy at the prospect of learning a new skill. I'd always loved to learn something useful.

I didn't care too much about school when I was younger, because I had to focus on taking care of everyone. School growing up took a backseat in my life, a very far backseat, like the nosebleed section. Being in the Fire Academy allowed me to learn all these different skills and to be able to utilize them in real life. I loved every minute of it and I was hoping that this would be similar.

I had read the course outline before I decided to take the course. I didn't just jump in like some of the others had based on the name alone. I wanted to make sure it was what I thought it was going to be and it was, but also with a lot more technical aspects than I had initially expected.

I would be lying if I didn't say I wasn't a little bit worried about the class work. It wasn't that I wasn't smart, I was, but I was also a lot like Asher in that sense. I didn't have the fancy math or science classes that Greyson took, but only because I had to take what I could just barely get away with in high school. I honestly didn't know if I would be able to understand half of the course work, but I was willing to do everything in my power to learn it.

Meeting with the doctor hadn't been a big deal. I had always been a healthy guy. I didn't have any previous surgeries or any bad breaks. I'd only broken a couple of fingers and my wrist once since being on the job.

I took my job seriously, especially because I had two kids at home who were counting on me to come back alive and in one piece. I was always anal about safety and making sure that I was aware of my surroundings to reduce the risk of injuries or death. It had still been a long process though, to cover everything from my birth practically until now.

I hadn't been picked for a group yet, so my group was last and I was hoping the previous group hadn't gotten back yet. I didn't know what would happen if I missed my chance to go up there today. It was getting a bit later in the afternoon, almost five o'clock, and I wasn't certain how long Xavier would be flying with it being closer to winter and it getting darker out earlier.

The second I walked back into the classroom

my heart sank. The other three that I was to be going up with weren't there. I had missed them. I saw the other teacher, Jackson, coming toward me and I hoped he wasn't going to tell me to just go to the dorms for the night.

"Hey, he took them up about thirty minutes ago. He didn't know how long you would be so he is flying them around and then he will take you up for a solo flight. Afterward, you can head back to the dorms and grab some food and rest up for tomorrow."

"Thanks. I'm assuming that is where everyone else is."

"Yeah, they left thirty minutes ago. They all seemed very thankful to be leaving. I guess we don't have any bookworms in the group," he said, flashing me an easy smile.

I had noticed that Jackson seemed to be the friendlier instructor. I didn't know if Xavier was really that unfriendly or if he was just serious. I had known a few instructors in the Fire Academy who were hardasses in the classroom, but once you got outside of it they were the life of the party and all smiles. It just depended on how they taught. Some found it easier to be friendly the whole time and others found it was better to keep the two lives separate.

There was also the chance that Xavier was like that all the time, in which case, he would be terrible to go for a beer with. Only time would tell. The good news was, if he was an asshole all the time I only had to deal with him for the next thirty days and then I would never have to see him again. Most likely, anyway. The odds of him being my chopper pilot going into a fire were pretty slim. Even if it did happen, I would only have to see him in small doses.

I made my way over to my seat and continued on with the booklet. I knew most of the guys weren't taking it very seriously. To them the basics were already instilled in their minds and they didn't need the refresher. I got it, we were all Alpha males, practically. To me though, I wanted to make sure there weren't any areas that I had forgotten about or maybe I wasn't that good at something. If there were areas that I needed improvement on, I wanted to know before things in the classroom got complicated. Besides, working on it was better than staring at the walls waiting for the chopper to land. I was relieved though, to know that most of the basics had stuck with me and maybe that was because I wasn't too many years out of the academy. It had only been seven for me, compared to seventeen for some of the guys here.

It was a good hour later when I heard the thumping of the chopper propellers coming down. It was getting pretty dark out now and I was starting to question if I was going up tonight or not. I knew Xavier would have flown at night, you can't exactly only fight a forest fire during the day; however, that was when he had to and technically he didn't have to take me up tonight. I was hoping we would be, but at the same time I could understand why we wouldn't go. It certainly would be easier to go during daylight hours so I could see the ground and different land markings. I couldn't exactly do that at night.

I watched as the guys came in and I could see they were excited and talking about what they had experienced. I wished I could have gone up with them, because something was telling me that going up one-on-one with Xavier wasn't going to leave me feeling that excited.

I watched as Xavier walked in and he looked the opposite of the others. He looked very annoyed and just done with life. I guess I couldn't blame him. He didn't seem like the type who would enjoy teaching others or being trapped in a tin can ten thousand feet in the air with no escape. It wasn't making me feel good about my turn with him.

He went over to Jackson first, not even looking in my direction, and I could see them talking but I couldn't hear them. The look on Xavier's face didn't change, but I wasn't certain if that was a good thing or not. After a minute, Jackson gave a nod and headed out before Xavier finally turned his attention to me. I could have sworn he grew more annoyed that I was still here.

"Let's go," he ordered before he headed out the door, not even checking to see if I was following him. I wanted to be annoyed, but he was at least taking me up so I wasn't going to push my luck.

I grabbed my jacket before I followed him out. By the time I got there, he was already in the pilot seat. I quickly jumped into the passenger side and put the headphones on so I could hear him. He didn't speak though, not a single word, as he got the blades spinning and took us into the sky.

I suddenly felt like I was sitting outside the

Principal's office waiting to find out how much shit I was going to be in. A situation that had happened a good dozen times in my life in both grade school and high school. It was never because I had bullied someone or gotten into a fight, it was always about my school work or missed days. Apparently, their sympathy for my sick and dying mother could only go so far. Not that I expected it to work for me the whole time, but it would have been nice for it to last a bit longer.

"How do you see the land markings at night?" I asked, breaking the silence between us. I wished I could say the silence was comfortable. It was more like animosity and I had no idea why. It wasn't like I had done something to him.

"There is a light on the bottom of the chopper that will allow you to see. When there is a forest fire, it lights up the sky and makes it easy to see. If the smoke gets too thick, every chopper's lights are able to penetrate the fog."

I knew the lights on the chopper were powerful, but I also knew it wasn't as easy as Xavier was making it sound. I knew the smoke from a fire could choke up the engine and cause the whirlybird to go down too. That was the deadly balancing game that every pilot had to face every single time they went up in the air. If they stayed too long, they risked the chopper going down and hurting or killing everyone inside. On the other side of the coin though, if they stopped too soon, then the fire spread and they risked the people who were trapped inside dying. A pilot really had to know their helicopter and how its engine was feeling. It wasn't easy and I had serious respect for every pilot, because it wasn't something I would be able to handle. That was too much stress and I would be a ball of anxiety before I even got the thing off the ground. I'd stick to fighting fires.

"And I'm going to be able to see this during the day too, right?"

"Assuming you make it that far."

Wow.

I knew he didn't know me and he had no reason to believe that I would be able to get through this course, but come on. He didn't even know me. I don't even think he knew my name. He could have at least a little bit of faith in me. I was a firefighter, had been for seven years, so I obviously knew what I was doing to still be alive. I wasn't a novice, but it felt like I was this annoying teenager Xavier had to deal with. Before I could even comment there was a bang right before the chopper shook and I knew that wasn't normal.

"What was that?" I instantly asked, but Xavier didn't say anything. I wanted to be annoyed, but I was more worried about the look of confusion and worry that overtook his face. For a man who seemed to have one hell of a poker face, his really sucked right now.

Another bang echoed off of the metal walls of the chopper. Whatever hit the chopper was stronger this time, because it wasn't even a second later when we were in a full tailspin.

"Fuck!" Xavier yelled as he fought to get the helicopter to stop spinning and level us out again. "Hold on, we're going down."

"What?" I grabbed onto the metal bar attached to the door, but I knew it wasn't going to be doing much if we were going to crash. This was insane. My first time in a chopper and we were going to crash.

Fuck my life.

Xavier didn't elaborate, but I didn't think he would. He was too busy trying to level out the chopper and, hopefully, land us down smoothly. I knew it wasn't going to happen though. We were over ten thousand feet and whatever hit us, they got our tail, which is what Xavier needed to keep the chopper leveled out.

I kept my gaze on him. I was too terrified to look out any of the windows to see the trees and ground getting closer. So I kept my eyes glued on him, on his face and his arms, as his bicep muscles bulked out from the sheer strength he had to use to try and keep the chopper leveled out so he could attempt to land us. It wasn't going to be a smooth landing, even though the main propellers were working. Without the tail there was nothing to keep us balanced while in the air. The chopper would be useless to get us back to the training facility.

My body jerked around as we finally hit the thick trees and we both thrashed around as we rolled and free fell down the rest of the drop until we finally crashed into the hard ground.

My head was pounding. It had smacked against the passenger door window and I could have sworn there was blood going down the right side of my face. We landed on the side, my side, and I could feel the ache in my head, but also my entire right side as it smashed into the door. I could see the front windshield was a mess of spiderweb cracks and I could have sworn I smelled smoke.

I managed to turn my head to look at Xavier and I was relieved to see that he was awake. He was hanging above me, thanks to his seatbelt. I knew we couldn't stay here though. If I could smell smoke that meant the chopper was smoking and there was a good chance it would go up in flames. I really didn't want to be here if that should happen.

I moved my left hand up and hit the middle clip for the seatbelt and released the multiple parts that clicked together. I was already on the ground, but my body still jerked forward slightly. I pushed myself up to my knees as I spoke.

"Xavier, we gotta get out of here. Can you unclick yourself?"

"Yeah, once you move out of the way I can drop down. Kick out the windshield and crawl out."

I didn't need to be told twice.

I climbed down to the front of my seat and kicked at the windshield. Even though it was already cracked all to hell, it was still difficult to get it to detach from the frame of the chopper. I didn't have much room to pull my legs back to give myself some real power behind each kick. After a good five times, I was able to get it off and I crawled out.

I immediately looked back at the chopper to see if I could pinpoint where the smoke was coming from. It was coming from the tail and the engine of the chopper. There were no flames yet and I hoped that maybe we got lucky and nothing explosive was compromised from the crash.

A bang sounded and I turned to see Xavier had gotten out of his seat and landed in a crouch just in front of the passenger seat. He didn't come out right away though, but went into the back of the chopper looking for something.

I hoped it was a radio or flashlights. It was dark as shit out here and I knew it was going to be getting worse before the sun started to rise. Just like I knew it was only going to be getting colder out. This was supposed to be a fun and easy trip around a designated area and now we were stranded in the forest with next to no supplies. This was not how I saw this course going.

Not even fucking close.

CHAPTER 6

Xavier

Fucking shit.

All I had to do was take one more trip around the training area, just one fucking more, and then I could go home and get drunk in peace. Just a quick fly around the training area and then back to base. Simple, but no. Nope, I couldn't possibly be that lucky, not me. No, instead we got shot down by some fucking rebel survivalists that are more paranoid then a dozen schizophrenics in a nut house.

I didn't even need to think about who could have shot at us. We had been getting threatening letters for months now from the extremists who seem to believe we are some Government agency spying on them. They had threatened to shoot at us before, but we, *I,* never took it seriously because any idiot could see that the chopper was bright orange with the fire department insignia on it. Clearly we were not spies or the Feds looking to invade their encampment.

Apparently, they didn't fucking care though.

I guess it was a good thing that I only had the one cadet with me, whatever his name was, and not a full group. The last thing I wanted to deal with was four cadets all shaking in their boots because we crashed. This wasn't my first crash. It was the first since I had left the military, sure, but at least when I crashed overseas there were gunfights afterward. I wasn't going to have to worry about that here. The biggest threat to us was getting hypothermia out here.

I searched the back of the chopper for what little supplies it had. It wasn't really stocked for a trip through the woods. I didn't even have blankets because this wasn't a rescue mission, it was just a quick tour. I grabbed the two flashlights and the radio that I had. I also went to grab for the radios, but they were all smashed from the trip down to the ground.

Fuck.

It looked like we were walking back whether we wanted to or not. I knew the area, but it was still going to be a couple of days before we made it back. At least come morning when we both didn't show up Jackson would know something was wrong. But without any flares and no way of getting word about our location, it was going to take Jackson some time to find the chopper. Hopefully, the black box was still intact and he would be able to pull up the GPS.

I knew it would make the most sense to hide

out here and wait for the rescue chopper to show up. With some luck, we would be able to find a place that would block some of the cold wind and it would keep us warmer until the sun came up. The last thing I wanted to be doing right now was wandering through the fucking woods, and hopefully the universe would give us this break.

I headed back out and turned the flashlights on. I pointed them in the direction of where I thought the cadet was and I was pleased to see he was at least standing. He had blood trickling down the side of his face though, and my initial concern was a potential concussion. If he was concussed, it would make the night a hell of a lot longer. I went over to him and held out the other flashlight for him before I turned my attention to his head.

"Does it hurt?"

"I'm fine," he said, but I wasn't in the mood for his macho bullshit.

"I'm trying to determine if you have a concussion. Answer the questions."

I knew I was snapping at him. I knew this wasn't his fault. He missed his turn with his group because he was with the Doc. It wasn't his fault we were out later than I wanted to be. It wasn't his fault that we got shot down by rednecks. Still, he was the only one here and my anger didn't care about any rational thoughts.

"It's tender, but I'm not dizzy or nauseous. And your obnoxious flashlight in my eyes doesn't make it hurt any worse. Now, get your hands off of me and tell me what the fuck just happened."

He had every right to be just as angry as I was and yet hearing it directed toward me only fueled my own anger. We were both victims of circumstances, but my mind refused to remember that every time he opened his mouth. I had to get a grip on my emotions. I was the senior man in charge here and I needed to take control with a rational mind.

"Survival extremists within the area have been sending threatening letters to the Station about the choppers. They seem to believe we are the Government and spying on their land. They have threatened to shoot the choppers out of the sky, but we didn't think they would actually do it. Our choppers don't exactly blend in and scream Federal Agents."

"Great. Fucking great. Radio?" he asked as he started to pace around. I was getting the feeling he wasn't used to just standing still for very long. Because that would make my night even more complete; an ADHD cadet in the fucking woods.

I was getting too old for this shit.

"Broke on the crash down. We don't have much. I was only supposed to take everyone around the training area. Wasn't exactly planning on a midnight stroll. The black box is most likely still intact. Our best bet is to find a place to hunker down for the night. Once we're not there in the morning Jackson will know something went wrong and pull up the GPS on the helo. He'll come out and we will be back at the station before lunch."

This wasn't going to be up for debate, we were going to hide out and just wait. Thankfully he gave me a nod and I knew we were at least in agreement.

I stood where I was and turned in a circle as I

moved the light around the area. I knew what it looked like from above, but I hadn't seen this place on the ground. It looked different when it wasn't from ten thousand feet.

I didn't want to go too far away from the crash site. Jackson would come to this area first and with the trees being so thick it was going to be harder for him to see us from the sky. There wasn't a place for him to land so we would have to be repelled up to the chopper. We had to be close by and in some type of clearing, even a small one so we could be spotted. All of that was not easy when it was so fucking dark out though.

"What about there?" the cadet asked and I went and looked at where he was pointing his flashlight. It was a set of large boulders, but the way they were positioned it created a man made cave in a sense. It would be a tight fit, but we would be able to manage and it would help to prevent the wind hitting us from three sides. It was roughly five hundred feet from the chopper, close enough that we would be able to hear Jackson come morning.

"That'll work," I said, before I started to walk over there. I could hear him following behind me and I was glad that I didn't hear him stumbling.

The second I was at the little cave, I went in first and I was not surprised to see that it wasn't all that deep. We would just fit and it was going to be tight, but it would work for the night. This wasn't the first time I had to sleep rough or not sleep at all. I didn't know about him though, and I really hoped he wasn't the bitching type. The last thing I wanted to deal with was listening to someone whine all night about being cold or the hard ground.

I sat down on the ground with my back against the cold rock. The cadet sat across from me on the other rock wall and he had his knees up to his chest. There was only enough space in the cave for us to sit down with our legs kept close to our body. I was sitting with my legs crossed; I was too big to sit with my legs up against my chest. I was actually surprised that he could because he wasn't much smaller than I was.

He kept his eyes locked on the outside of our little cave and he didn't seem to be in the mood to talk, something I was relieved about because I wasn't in the mood to make small talk all night. I had to admit though, now that I was getting the chance to just sit and look at him, he was good looking. Even with the shadows from the flashlight playing across his face, he was attractive. He wasn't man-pretty like Jackson liked, but he was handsome, rugged, the type of guy that I found attractive. Though, they weren't normally his size. I tended to go for smaller guys, the type where I knew they were a bottom. If this cadet was gay, I wouldn't even know if he was a top or bottom.

Our pleasurable silence came to an end when the cadet decided to open his very sexy mouth and ruin it.

"Will the black box work if the chopper blows up?"

"Yeah, it's designed to handle fires and being submerged in water."

It was a reasonable question so I had no problem answering it. The black box was our only hope of being found; it was logical that he would be concerned about it. I was just hoping that the smoke was nothing more than the engine being overheated and not the sign of something seriously wrong with it. The chopper itself was a write off, there was no fixing it, but the last thing I wanted to worry about was it blowing up and accidentally starting a forest fire. That wasn't the hands-on experience I was looking to offer for this course.

"You got any kids, a wife?" he asked next.

"We don't have to talk," I instantly said. The last thing I wanted to do was make small talk with this guy for the next twelve hours.

"You want to sit here in the dark and cold all night long and not say a single word?" he countered as he looked over at me. I could tell he wasn't too happy with that idea, but it sounded perfect to me.

"You want to share your darkest secrets around the campfire?" I countered sarcastically. Maybe if he was annoyed enough he would shut the hell up.

"There's no campfire and I wouldn't consider having children or a wife being a dark secret. Unless it's actually a husband and you are too ashamed to admit that you like cock over pussy," he countered, flashing me a cocky smirk.

I wanted to punch it off his face.

It was none of his business if I was gay or straight. It was none of his business if I had kids or not. My life was none of his business, just like his life wasn't any of mine. We were not friends. We were not colleagues. I was his instructor and he was my cadet. It was a professional, barely, relationship and that was all it would ever be.

"I'm your instructor, your superior, it would be best that you remember that when you speak to me. I can send you right back to whatever State you came from for insubordination and being disrespectful to the chain of command. Do you understand me, Cadet?"

Maybe that was harsh, but he needed to learn his place. He needed to learn that I was not his friend, nor did I want to be. I had done the whole friends thing. It always ended with me having to bury them and I wasn't about to bury another friend, another person I cared about. It was better to be alone. If I got lonely, fuck, that's what whiskey was for.

"Yes, Sir." His tone was borderline disgusted and I could tell he wasn't happy with me.

In my opinion, there were three types of people in the world. The type who always gave someone respect because they were their superior and they respected the chain of command without question. The second type never gave the other respect regardless of their rank, because they were little assholes and their mommy and daddy didn't teach them about respect. The third type though, they were the ones that had no problem giving respect, but you had to earn it. This cadet was either the second or third type and my gut was leading me toward the second type. We were never going to get along and I highly doubted that he would make it through this course. If he couldn't respect me, then he was never getting in my chopper again.

He turned his attention back out toward the helicopter and I was glad that he was keeping his mouth shut this time. I'd had some pretty long and horrible nights in my life, but I was getting the feeling that this night was going to be right up there with them.

CHAPTER 7

WHAT AN ASSHOLE. If he wants to sit here all night and not say anything, fine. Two can play that game. I once played the silent game with the twins for four days and won. A night in a makeshift cave, shit this was nothing.

A quick glance over in his direction and I saw that he had his eyes closed. I didn't know if he was asleep or just looking to rest his eyes. I honestly didn't care which option it was, it was better than him staring at me. Not going to lie though, there was a large part of me that wanted to just start singing the most annoying song I could think of.

Was it childish?

Absolutely.

Did he deserve it?

Fucking yes, he did.

Apparently, Xavier was the type of leader who

demanded respect without earning a shred of it. I knew there needed to be some level of respect at first. He was my superior and I knew that meant I had to respect him; however, I also knew that full respect was not freely given. He had to earn it. He had to show me that I could give him that respect, that he was worthy of it and so far, he hadn't shown me he deserved that level of respect from me.

I knew most people would have freely given it, but that wasn't who I was. That wasn't something I was capable of doing. I had been screwed over too many times to trust blindly, to give full respect blindly. It might seem silly to others, but not to me.

A small flicker of light caught my eye and I turned my full attention into the darkness within the woods. I knew we weren't around any roads, so it wouldn't have been the headlights of a passing vehicle. I knew it was possible that my mind was playing tricks on me, but I could have sworn I saw a light. Another flicker behind the trees proved me right. Someone was out there.

Part of me wanted to be happy, excited, that someone was out there. Someone who might have seen the crash or was out for an evening stroll. People camped in these woods so it wouldn't be that far of a stretch to think they heard or saw the crash. They also could have been a camper looking to take a leak. They might have a radio or a phone that had a signal that we could use to call Jackson and get out of here before sunrise.

"Hey," I said as I lightly hit Xavier's calf.

"What?" Xavier responded and I could see that he didn't even bother with opening his eyes.

"Someone's out there."

That seemed to get his attention. His eyes snapped open and he instantly looked out of our little cave. I wasn't certain what I expected his reaction to be, but I was surprised to see that he appeared to be more worried than anything else.

This was a good thing, right?

We could get out of here tonight and sleep in an actual bed.

More lights started to appear and now I was starting to worry, because there shouldn't be a dozen people in the woods. It was the end of fall; it would be too cold for a large group to go camping. One or two, sure. People camped in the winter, but they were dedicated campers and they had the proper equipment they needed to survive the weather. A dozen people didn't just decide to go on a camping trip together in this weather. We could hear voices, but I couldn't hear everything they were saying. It was clear though they were looking for the chopper.

The sound of movement next to me made me turn my head slightly to see that Xavier had moved and he spoke softly into my ear. "It's the extremists. They think we were Feds and they want to hold us hostage, get news coverage. We have to move. Don't turn the flashlight on and stay close to me."

Holy fuck.

As if this night hadn't been bad enough, now we were going to have to play hide and seek with the gun-toting extremists.

Xavier moved before me and he stepped over me before he grabbed my hand and pulled me. I just managed to get up without falling over and being dragged by him.

I knew we had to be quiet; we couldn't risk them overhearing us. What was difficult though, was walking through the woods without the use of the flashlights. I couldn't see anything and it was very difficult to not trip on any of the tree roots that were sticking up. We were trying to be quiet, but that wasn't all that simple when every step we took made a crunching sound of dry leaves and twigs under our feet.

We didn't even make it fifteen feet when a light hit us followed by a loud male voice. "There they are!"

I didn't know what I had been expecting to happen next, but the sound of a bullet hitting a tree by our head was not one of them. Before I could even process what was happening Xavier was pulling me as he started to take off at a run. I had no choice but to run with him or risk getting my arm pulled out of the socket.

I ran as fast as I could, trying to keep up with him. I wanted to pull my hand out of his, but not only did he have a death grip on it, but I also had no idea where we were going. Xavier knew the area, even if it was from the sky, he knew the area better than me and if we separated right now, there was a high risk that I wouldn't be able to keep up with him and then we would really be separated and the last thing I wanted to do was be lost in the woods alone with the rednecks.

I had no idea how long we kept running for. All I knew was that my lungs were burning and my legs felt like jell-o, but we kept going. The gunfire had stopped at least. I suspected that the rednecks were unable to track us right now with it being dark, but I highly doubted they were going to pack up and go back home. They thought we were Feds and they wanted a show. They wanted to parade us out front of cameras to prove their point to the world. We were too valuable to them and their beliefs to just let us go.

And because this night hadn't fucking sucked enough, it had started to pour rain hours ago. We were both soaking wet, exhausted, and I was starving. Not to mention we both were filthy from slipping in the mud. We needed a break. We needed a chance to catch our breaths. We needed a chance to get out of this rain.

"Xavier, stop," I managed to get out. Fuck, even talking was taking me a minute.

To my utmost pleasure, he did stop. He was breathing just as heavily as I was and I knew he wouldn't be able to go much longer, much like myself. It didn't matter that we were both fit and weren't ones to shy away from cardio day, this was a lot of running on rough and uneven terrain and it was fucking pouring out. Plus, it was so dark we couldn't see our own hand in front of our face. This was far from an ideal environment, but we had made it work. Now we needed to find a place to wait out the storm, something I was hoping the extremists were doing.

"We have to find a place to bunker down. We can't keep going, not like this."

I really hoped he wasn't going to disagree and tell me to suck it up, that we had to keep moving. I honestly didn't think I could keep moving. My whole body was sore and my legs were seconds away from giving out. It was going to be a miracle for me to keep moving while we looked for a place that we could hide out in.

"I know. If I'm right on our location, there is a cave about ten minutes just north of here. We should be far enough away from them to hide out for the rest of the night," he said with a heavy breath and I could hear him gasping for air in his overexerted lungs.

"Okay," I managed to get out, grateful that he at least agreed easily. What I wanted to say was *thank fucking god*, but I didn't want him to know just how much I was struggling.

I kept my hand in his as we started to lightly jog this time. It wasn't any better than running, but it would at least get us to the cave faster and then we could rest. It was not lost on me that going from running to just nothing wasn't good on your body. It would cause our muscles to spasm and tighten up. Something as simple as walking tomorrow would be hilariously painful. My mind couldn't help but conjure up the image of the Tin Man without his oilcan. It was really funny when I put Xavier's face on that mental image. I guess the good thing was that we were too exhausted and out of breath to even speak to each other.

By the time we made it to the cave, I felt like I was going to pass out. It took every last ounce of energy that I had to make it inside the cave. This time it was a legitimate cave and there was enough room for both of us to stand and move around. I was worried about bears, but apparently Xavier wasn't.

"How do we know if we're alone in here?" I couldn't help but ask.

"The migration patterns don't have any bears in this area right now. A few more weeks and there will be. We have to get out of our clothes."

"What?" My sluggish mind couldn't seem to follow that train of thought.

Why would we be getting naked?

"Hypothermia. We have to get out of our wet clothes and use each other's body heat to get warm. Strip, Cadet," he said with a bit of an edge to his voice that I didn't particularly appreciate, especially given he wanted me to get naked for him.

"Gage," I said as I tried to get my brain to tell my hands to move.

"What?" It was his turn to be confused and I couldn't help but smirk.

How do you like it?

"My name isn't Cadet, it's Gage. And considering you want me to get naked for you, the least you could do is bother to remember my name."

He was right, we had to use each other's body heat but that didn't mean I was going to make it easier on this asshole.

"Fine, take your clothes off, *Gage*," he said with a snippy attitude.

I would let that go, for now.

I got my coat off and was about to get my shirt off when I heard him let out a groan. It wasn't a sound of discomfort, but pain. I wished I could see him better, but it was too dark to see anything.

"Where are you hurt?" I really hoped he wasn't going to pull some macho bullshit and tell me he was fine. I was not in the mood to play that game.

"I'm fi—" Before he even had a chance to finish that bullshit statement, I cut him off.

"I swear to fucking god if you tell me you are fine I am going to punch you. And considering it's dark, I have no idea where that punch will land. At the rate our luck is going, I'll end up punching you in the nuts. So unless you would like to play Russian roulette on your balls, give me a goddamn fucking honest answer. It's been too long of a night for this shit."

Now, I acknowledge that I could have been a bit nicer about it. But in my defense, this had been the longest night of my life and I didn't even think it was half over. He was not my superior right now. He was some guy that I just met and got stranded in the woods with. That's all wc were, just a couple of guys trying not to get our heads blown off by some fucking radicals with riffles. Like we were in a Steven King novel. It wouldn't surprise me if there was a bear in this cave with us, because that is how my luck had been going since I left Baton Rouge. So yes, I could have been nicer, but at the same time I didn't have any fucks left to give tonight. Completely sold out until I got a hot shower, a double bacon cheeseburger, and about eight hours of sleep in a warm and soft bed.

He let out a sigh, a fucking sigh, like I was the impatient child on a road trip asking if we were there yet, before he spoke. "A bullet grazed my right bicep. I will be fine."

Right, because getting grazed by a bullet was a completely natural thing.

Oh, Jesus fuck.

Okay, medically getting grazed isn't really a big deal. A few stitches and the wound would heal itself, but we had been running and falling down in mud, so chances were that the graze on his arm was now a mess of blood and mud.

"We need to clean it out before it gets infected. We can use the rain to wash it out, but we'll have to turn on one of the flashlights for a minute or two." He wasn't going to like that idea.

"Absolutely not."

Yup, called it.

Couldn't actually agree on one thing, that would make this way too easy and who wanted an easy life?

Sigh.

"I can cover it with my hand to reduce the brightness, but we have to use the light long enough for you to clean that wound. The last thing we need is you getting an infection. If those guys show up, we both have to be able to fight and run. Two things that can't happen if you are fighting off an infection."

I just needed him to agree with me on this. I didn't want to argue about this for very long, but I couldn't let it go because the threat was still real out there.

"All right," he growled. "Cover the light with both of your hands. We can go to the entrance of the cave and I can wash it out." He'd caved and I was so fucking thankful for it.

"Okay," I said, knowing he wouldn't be able to see me nod.

We both wandered over to the entrance of the

cave. I placed the end of the flashlight under my armpit and turned it on before I cupped my hands around the outside of the light. It made it dimmer, but bright enough that we would be able to see the injury. It looked deep to me and my gut said he needed stitches. We would have to try and keep it as clean as possible until we got back to the station.

Xavier had already pulled his shirt off and he quickly used the rainwater to wash the blood and mud from his cut. It was down and dirty, but that was all we really had right now. With it cleaned, I turned the light back off and we made our way back into the cave and further away from the wind and rain.

We both removed our clothing and I felt like an idiot standing there naked, not really sure what I was supposed to do. If I had been with a guy that I knew was gay, I wouldn't think twice about it, but I had no idea if he was gay or not. I suspected he was straight, making this even more awkward.

"Come here, we have to lay down and go chest to chest," Xavier said as he took my hand.

I knew we had to do this, but that didn't make it any less awkward and I knew I was going to be feeling weird about this when we got back to the classroom.

I went to my knees and then lay down with my chest against his. I couldn't help the hiss as his cold skin touched mine. I knew we would get warmed up soon enough, but until that happened it was going to suck. It also sucked because we were on the hard, cold ground. Typically, we would have a blanket or sleeping bag over us to help trap the heat, but we didn't have one. Which meant it would take longer for us to get warmed up, but it would help to fight off the risk of hypothermia at least. We might not get very warm, but it wouldn't kill us and that was really all I could hope for.

Xavier wrapped his arms around me and pulled me tight against his chest. Something I also didn't account for was the fact that we were the same height so we were chest to chest, but we were also cock to cock. And I didn't care how cold someone was, when they were naked and pressed up against another sexy naked person, their body notices.

Not good.

"I guess this would be a bad time to mention I'm gay," I said, letting out an awkward chuckle. It was a defense mechanism for me. When I was uncomfortable, I made jokes and said things I knew I shouldn't, but my brain/mouth filter didn't kick in to keep those words in my head.

"So am I."

Son of a bitch.

CHAPTER 8

Xavier

"I guess this would be a bad time to mention I'm gay," Gage said with an awkward chuckle.

Yup, it would be a bad time to tell me the sexy naked man I was pressed up against was actually gay. It was fine when I thought he was straight. I survived the military without anyone discovering I was gay. I was very good at telling myself that everyone was straight and not allowing my body to respond to any touches or situations. All of that self-control went out the window though, once I knew they were gay.

I was also a bit annoyed that once again Jackson was right. He did say there was always at least one gay guy in the group. Of course, with my luck, it would be the guy that I was snuggling up with.

I had two options, either admit to being gay or

tell him it was fine and play straight. The biggest issue with playing straight was the fact that I swore I wouldn't hide in a closet after I got out of the military. I swore I wouldn't live that life and even though it might be simpler to play straight right now, I didn't want to have to be back in that closet. Telling him I was gay though, could have also added to the awkwardness of the situation. I was an asshole, but I wasn't as much of an asshole to make it so that only Gage was the one that was feeling uncomfortable.

"So am I."

Short and simple.

I wasn't going to tell him to not worry about it. I wasn't offering him any comforting words. I was simply letting him know that I was gay too and to not think about it. It was easier said than done though, because as every second that ticked by I was becoming painfully aware of his body pressed up against mine. I couldn't see it, but he felt very impressive to me. He was all muscle, hard muscle, and normally I liked my guys a bit smaller and leaner, but I had to admit he felt very good against me.

He moved his leg and it caused his cock to rub up against mine and I had to bite the inside of my cheek to keep the moan from escaping.

"Sorry, leg cramp," Gage said, and I had a feeling if I could see I would see a tint of red to his cheeks. I hated the flash of arousal that image brought to me. I was never going to get through this without getting hard. There was just no way.

"How old are you?" I asked. Maybe if we

talked we would both be able to ignore the situation we were in.

"Twenty-five, you?"

Fuck, he was young. I thought he was closer to thirty. Most of the guys who come through this course are at least thirty. He had to be one of the younger ones that I'd had in this course.

"Forty-two. You start at eighteen?"

"Yeah. What about you?"

Eighteen was too young to be a firefighter, in my opinion. I knew it was a bit silly considering I went to war at eighteen, so why not be a firefighter that young. Still, having to run into burning buildings seemed a lot braver than going off to war to me, but that might have more to do with my feelings toward fire. I could do a lot of things, but the idea of running into a burning building made my chest tight. I had to give it to him, he had been doing this for seven years and he was still here, that's not easy.

"Four years now."

"Since you got out?"

"What?" I asked, confused.

Did he mean when I came out of the closet?

"The military. I can feel your dog tags, which are freezing by the way."

Oh, right. I forgot I had them on. I was so used to their weight that I didn't even recognize them anymore. "I was an Air Force pilot. When I got out I started working for the fire department."

"What was it like? The military, going to war?" he asked, and I could have sworn I heard a bit of worry and fear in his voice, but I wasn't certain why it would be there.

"It wasn't what I thought it would be. When you enlist everyone tells you what it's going to be like. Every recruiter, veteran, Boot Camp instructors, they all tell you that you are at risk of being shot, blown up, losing a limb or more, being captured and tortured. They don't hold anything back and even though I had been given plenty of warnings I still believed it wouldn't happen to me. I still believed that I was going to war and I would be fine. That I could come back home like nothing had happened. We all believed it. We were all stupid; young and stupid. The reality was that we were at war. I saw my friends being killed, some right next to me. I saw the worst that humanity had to offer and all the warnings in the world didn't prepare me for it."

This was the last thing I wanted to talk about and I shouldn't have been talking about it with him. He was a complete stranger and I didn't owe him the truth. I should have told him that it was fine and just like the media says, be all you can be, and all that shit. But for some reason, maybe it was our current position or the fact that we had deranged rednecks hunting us down, but I didn't want to lie to him. I didn't want to sugar coat the experience, even though I probably should have.

"That had to be extremely hard. I don't think extremely hard even covers it. I'm sorry you had to go through all of that," he said, and I could hear the sincerity in his voice. I also could have sworn it shook slightly, but I chalked that up to the shivers that were wreaking havoc throughout his body.

"I got through. A lot of guys didn't and I even

made it out with all of my parts. I got nothing to complain about. Have you always wanted to be a firefighter?"

I was fully expecting him to give me the same answer I had received hundreds of times. *'Yes, I have always wanted to help people.'* It was the politically correct and acceptable answer, but I also knew nine out of ten times it was complete bullshit. Most people had a deeper reasoning for becoming a firefighter. There had to be a real reasoning behind choosing a career that involved running into burning buildings and it wasn't because you wanted to help people. I'm not saying they didn't want to help people, but that wasn't what drove them into the career.

"I hate that question. In the Fire Academy we used to get asked that all the time. All of the other cadets always had this profound reason behind their decision. They came from legacies, or they had experienced a fire growing up, they volunteered in the burn unit at the hospital and wanted to help people. Everyone had something that was special that drove them. Whenever it got to be my turn, I always felt like an idiot because I didn't have some profound, life altering event that drove me to the Fire Department."

That was surprising to me, because I really expected him to tell me the same line. I doubted he didn't have a reason, everyone had a reason, it just might not have sounded that important to him. Still, I wanted to know.

"What was it?"

A strong shiver went down his spine and it once again forced our cocks to rub against each other and neither one of us could hold back the soft moan that escaped from our lips. At least I wasn't the only one who was struggling with our proximity.

Despite my better judgment, I held him closer against my chest, putting our hips closer together as well, but I was hoping it would help to produce more body heat between us. I was ignoring the warmth that went through my chest when Gage curled up closer into me.

"My brothers," he said, but it was slightly muffled with his face being turned into my chest.

"They were firefighters?" I asked, hoping for some clarification.

"No, they were eleven. Our mom got blood cancer when I was sixteen, stage three. They told her she was most likely going to be dead within the year, that it was a highly aggressive strand. She held on though, even when the doctors all told her she wouldn't make it, she would just tell them she had to make it for two more years. To do whatever they had to do, because she needed me to get to eighteen before she could leave this Earth. She made it though, one week after my eighteenth birthday she died."

The pain was clear in his voice. This wasn't an easy topic for him to talk about. It was still painful to him and I didn't blame him. I lost my parents in a forest fire, but I was an adult. I had been raised by them for the majority of my life. I was lucky in that sense. But Gage didn't get that luxury or privilege.

"Where was your dad?"

"Me and the twins have different fathers. Mine

was never around, took off the second he discovered my mom was pregnant. The twins, their father stuck around until they were five before he took off. It was just us."

"Jesus, there was no one else to help. Grandparents, aunts or uncles?"

"Nope, just us. I did what I could. I made sure to help with the twins, get them meals, get them to school, and help with homework. I was old enough to work, so I would work as much as I could while trying to go to school and act like everything was fine. We were always worried about Social Services being called if anyone suspected anything was going on. The last thing we wanted was for any of us to be put into foster care. They would have split us up, including the twins, not to mention the horror stories we had heard about foster care. It was hard, but we made it work."

Holy fuck.

I never in a million years would have figured he had a troubled past. He didn't come across as someone who had struggled. I knew I shouldn't be judging people, but often I was right. My gut instinct was usually right on the money, but this time around it was wrong; so very wrong.

"So you went into the Fire Academy for them?"

"Yeah. I barely made it through high school. I'm not book smart. I missed a lot of school and I didn't do well on tests. I just barely made it through and I'm fairly certain some of my teachers gave me a passing grade just so they wouldn't have to deal with me again. I knew I needed a really good job though, to take care of the twins properly. Without it, we were still at risk of them being taken away from me. The Fire Academy was in need of recruits. It was good pay, better than minimum wage at some fast food joint. Plus there were health benefits and life insurance so the twins would have been taken care of if I died. It made the most sense to sign up."

As a father, I understood exactly why he signed up to be a firefighter. It gave him the financial stability that he needed to properly take care of his brothers who were more like his sons. I got it and I would have done the same thing. What bothered me though, was the fact that he shouldn't have had to do that. He shouldn't have had to care for his sick and dying mother and take care of his brothers. He didn't really get to be a kid himself and that was sad.

"I think you doing that for your brothers was the best reason anyone could have. And you must have enjoyed it, you've been in for seven years."

"I do enjoy it. I wasn't certain at first if I would, but I do love the work. I love the guys that I work with. I feel good about what I do at the end of the day and that's what I want for the twins."

"That's all any parent can hope for."

I was hoping that Dexter would find something he was passionate about later on in life when it was his turn to get a career. I was hoping he could do whatever he loved and be proud and happy to go to work every morning. I just wished I would get to be there for him, to experience it with him.

Gage was quiet for a bit, long enough that I couldn't help but wonder if he fell asleep. He proved me wrong though, when his muffled voice hit my ears.

"Though, when I signed up for the Fire Academy, I had no idea that one day I would be snuggled up naked to one of my instructors stranded in the woods being hunted by extremists. They should probably have put that on the welcome brochure."

I couldn't help the small chuckle that escaped. He was annoying and frustrating, but I had to give it to him, at times he was funny.

"You should have read the fine print."

"That fine print can be a bitch. I have to say though, out of all of the instructors that I have laid naked with, you are by far the biggest," he said and I could feel his smile against my chest.

I was surprised by the spark of jealousy that shot through my chest for a moment before it disappeared. I had no reason to be jealous. I didn't see Gage like that. He wasn't even my type.

"And exactly how many instructors have you laid naked with?" I shouldn't have asked. The answer wasn't going to be one I wanted to hear, but I needed to hear it. I needed to hear that it was just one other instructor, that it was a reasonable number. It was irrational, because he meant nothing to me, and yet I needed to know.

"Five. I guess I don't have to tell you how many closeted men there are in the Fire Department."

"No, you don't."

Five. I guess that wasn't as bad as it could have been. I had slept with roughly twenty other instructors and Captains within the Fire Department. That also didn't include the dozens of random hook ups to go with it. It wasn't like I was a virgin either. We all had a past.

"You are definitely the coldest too," he added, and he wasn't wrong.

"So are you. We need to generate more body heat, but outside of doing some jumping jacks, I'm not sure what we could do."

I had a lot of fun ideas that we could do, but I wasn't about to suggest any of them to him. I felt his hips moving forward and our cocks rubbed against each other once more as he spoke.

"I can think of something that could generate body heat. Strictly in a life saving sense, of course."

He placed a kiss to the center of my chest and I knew exactly what he was thinking and I would be lying if I said I wasn't tempted. He was sexy, and it would generate some body heat, but we were also exhausted, our bodies were pushed to their limits, not to mention we had nothing for lube. Even though I knew all of that, my body was still responding to his, to the idea.

"If we did, and I'm not saying we are, but if we did it would be purely for medical purposes." It was a ridiculous statement, but it might be the only way I would be able to say no later if this was really good.

"What happens in the cave, stays in the cave," Gage easily agreed, and that was all I needed to hear.

I rolled us over so his back was against the cold ground. If he cared at all he didn't show it, because he opened his legs and made space for me between them. I covered his body with my own and the second our cocks touched we were both moaning.

It was cold, very cold, but I knew soon enough we would build up a bit of body heat.

We couldn't have sex, I had no lube and I was not about to have sex without it. That didn't mean we couldn't dry hump like teenagers.

I rolled my hips and started to rub our cocks together. We both moaned and he tangled his hands in my hair, pulling me down toward him.

The second our lips touched I took control of the kiss. His lips were freezing, but they were also soft. He felt amazing against me and I knew if I wasn't careful I would become addicted to him and that was something I couldn't allow.

I felt his tongue against my lips and I opened my mouth, allowing him to enter. The second his tongue touched mine though, I was right back in control and he simply submitted to me. I rolled my hips once again and our moans were swallowed up by the other.

I didn't even care if we got warm. All that mattered now was how incredible he felt underneath me. I could have frozen to death right then and there and been happy.

I switched from just rolling my hips against him to thrusting, a breathless moan escaping my lips at the pleasure that shot through my balls and up my cock.

Gage pulled back from the kiss and let out a deep moan too. He arched his back and it gave me perfect access to his neck. I trailed kissed all along his skin as I felt his legs wrap around my hips.

"Fuck, Xavier."

I could hear the desperate need in his voice and I felt the same. There was nothing I wanted more than to be buried inside of him. My body and my mind were screaming for it and it took every ounce of self-control that I had to keep myself from slamming into his tight hole.

"You feel so good," I said into his neck as I picked up the pace.

I could feel that we were both painfully hard and I knew it wouldn't be long before we were both coming. Under normal circumstances, I would have taken him into my mouth, but that wouldn't generate the body heat that we needed to try and stave off the cold until morning. I was going to have to settle for rubbing up against him.

I wished I could see him, could witness the look of pleasure all across his face. I was betting he looked beautiful when he came.

I felt his hands trailing down my back and squeezing my ass, trying to pull me even closer to him. I captured his mouth once more and he joined me by thrusting his hips up to meet mine, causing us both to give a deep moan as we edged even closer. If I had been more focused on our surroundings, I would have thought about the noise we were making and that it could alert the men currently hunting us.

Currently though, I wasn't thinking about that or anything other than the pleasure that was scorching through my body. I could feel Gage's breathing becoming hitched and I knew it wouldn't be much longer, which was good because

I didn't know how much longer that I could hold on for.

After a few more thrusts against each other, I felt Gage's cock swell and pulse and he arched back with a deep moan, breaking the kiss as he came. Feeling his cock pulse sent me over the edge and I held still as my cum shot out and landed on his stomach. The fact that he had our cum mixed together on his stomach only made my cock pulse more. I would have loved to see it.

I placed my forehead down against his as we both fought to catch our breaths.

Holy fuck, holy mother fucking god.

That should not have felt that good. That felt better then most of the sex I'd had and we didn't do anything but rub against each other. My heart was racing. It was pounding so hard against my chest I thought it might actually break it.

"Fuck, I gotta start carrying around a packet of lube in my wallet for emergency purposes." I could hear the goofy smile across his face and he was definitely not wrong.

"I would have loved to feel you wrapped around my cock." I placed a few kisses along his neck and he leaned his head back giving me better access.

"Wrapped around your cock; try wrapped around my cock."

I pulled back and looked down at him. I wished once again that I could see him, for him to be able to see me. I had a feeling that should have been a conversation we had beforehand and outside of the darkness. It never even occurred to me that we could have both been tops. It made sense, though. He wasn't that small, certainly not a spinner, but he also wasn't that large either.

"I only top," I stated.

"I only top," he mimicked.

Well, fuck me.

"Maybe you're a switch and you don't know it."

I had no idea why I was even trying right now. Despite how amazing this short time was I was never going to be doing it again with him. It was no concern of mine that he was a top as well. And yet, I couldn't get my mind to tell my mouth to shut the hell up.

"I've never bottomed. That's just not something I've been interested in. What about you, I'm sure you could be a switch."

"Nope. I tried it once and hated every second of it. All I will ever be is a top."

"Looks like what happens in the cave really will stay in the cave."

I couldn't tell if he was disappointed or not. It really would have helped if I could see his face and gauge his reaction.

Was he disappointed?

Was he secretly considering trying to be a switch so we could fuck?

Or worse, was he relieved?

The self-doubt was sinking in now and I knew if I didn't shut it down soon, I would go down the rabbit hole and that was the last place I could be right now. We were still at risk and I needed to be focused on that and not my fucked up head.

"We should try and get some rest. Once it's first light out we need to get moving," I said, looking to try and get the conversation off of what would never happen between us.

"How do you want to sleep?" I could hear the slight exhaustion seeping into his voice. We had exerted ourselves, had been all day, and now his body was starting to recognize just how tired he was. I was tired as well, but I was used to being tired and staying awake for days straight.

"We'll have to sleep chest to chest to keep our body heat up. Hopefully come morning our clothes will be somewhat dry and with any luck the sun will be out and the rain will stop."

"I didn't check the weather, but I didn't think it was supposed to rain much this week," he said as I rolled us so we were on our sides once again chest to chest. "Do you think they will still be looking for us?"

"Jackson will look for us come morning, he might already be looking for us now with the Park Rangers. As for the rednecks, it depends how determined they are."

I really didn't know if the rednecks would give it a rest or not. I didn't know what their goal was, if they thought we were spies or the military, they might keep searching for us so they had a totem they could hold for everyone to see to get what they wanted.

As for Jackson, I knew come morning when class started and we weren't there he would know something went wrong. He would start to search for us. He might know something was wrong already, it just depended. Sometimes he would text me to check in on me, but I didn't always respond. If he sent me a text and got nothing back from me he might not worry right away. He might assume I was getting drunk and not in the mood to chat.

We just had to make sure we made it through the night and then get to a Ranger lookout tower to the radio. We should be able to reach it tomorrow and be sleeping in our own beds tomorrow night. We just had to make it through the rest of this night first.

CHAPTER 9

GAGE

THE SOUNDS of birds chirping brought me slowly back to the living. I was no stranger to lack of sleep, but I didn't want to be awake right now. I was exhausted and my whole body was sore. Not to mention I was cold as fuck.

For a moment, just a moment, I wondered where my blanket ended up, before my brain kicked back in and reminded me that I was currently laying naked, on the hard ground, in a cave, because a bunch of fucking insurgents with guns shot the helicopter down and tried to kill us. This right here was why I didn't *do* camping. Why I didn't go hiking. Because leave it to me and my shitty luck to find the only serial killer in the woods. Sure, they weren't serial killers, but they weren't friendly campers either.

I let out a soft groan as I started to move away

from Xavier's chest. I wanted to spend a lot more time pressed up against him, but I knew we needed to get moving. Plus, we were both tops and that wasn't about to change. At least we would always have our time in the cave to remember.

My movement caused Xavier to wake up and I felt his arms loosen around me. I slowly pushed myself up into a sitting position. My whole body was aching from the cold and hard ground. Not to mention the chopper crash and running through the woods for hours. It was going to be a few days before I would be able to move without feeling stiff.

I turned slightly so I could look out the cave and I was pleased to see that it was sunny out. The rain had stopped and based on the shadows the sun wasn't very high, just past sunrise I would imagine.

I forced my body to move as I stood and went over to my wet clothes. We had tossed them into two piles and looking back on it now it might have been better for us to lay them out flat. It was too late now though.

"Tell me it stopped raining." Xavier's gravelly voice echoed against the cave walls.

"It has. The sun is out and hopefully it helps to dry our clothes the rest of the way."

He gave a groan as he sat up and looked over at our clothes. I could see that he had already figured out they weren't very dry, but walking around the forest naked wasn't an option.

I dug out my cell phone from my pocket, but I couldn't get it to turn on. I was really hoping it was dead and not that the rain had caused water damage.

"Is yours working?" I asked as I held my phone up.

Xavier moved over to his clothes and dug his phone out. "There's no service and I only have twenty percent on it. We need to head out and start making our way toward the Ranger Tower. They'll have a radio and I can get in contact with Jackson."

"How far do you think it is?" I asked as I started to get dressed. My jeans were damp and cold and they were not comfortable at all, but I had to put something on.

"I'm not too sure, but I'll have a better idea once I get my surroundings," he commented, getting dressed now as well.

I was hoping we weren't too far. We were both exhausted, sore and hungry, the last thing we needed was to be wandering aimlessly around in the forest.

Once we were dressed we headed out and the warmth of the sun felt good against my cold skin. I knew we also had to be careful with the sun. If it got too hot out we risked getting heat stroke. We didn't have any water and there was no guarantee we would come across a freshwater stream to drink.

"Okay, I think we're about six hours away from the tower. I know that ridge," Xavier said, as he pointed in the direction of a large rocky hill off in the distance.

Six hours, fucking great.

CHAPTER 10

THE PAST THREE hours had been anything but pleasant. Our only saving grace was the fact that it hadn't started to rain again and so far there weren't any gunshots following us. Still, with nothing but walking to do for hours my mind was constantly racing with 'what if' scenarios.

I still wasn't over the bombshells that my brothers dropped on me just hours before I was set to fly to California. I wasn't too worried about Asher. He was going to a horse ranch in Texas. As long as he didn't get kicked in the head by a horse he should be fine. He was physically fit and could handle the physical labor that came with a horse ranch. He wasn't that book smart, but he didn't need to be. He was great with animals and he was good with people and reading them. He was very social and a place like a horse ranch made a lot of sense for him.

It was Greyson that concerned me the most. He wasn't very physical; he didn't really have muscles. He was very book smart and that was a good thing, but it also made it harder for him to understand social situations. I suspected he was kissing the autism spectrum, but it wasn't anything we had tested growing up. The only reason he had come such a long way was because of Asher. They had compensated for each other. But now Greyson was going to be surrounded by alpha males who wouldn't appreciate him being gay, nor would they tolerate his slight lack of social skills. He wasn't that bad, but he didn't read social cues very well. He didn't know when to stop talking or that a rant about something scientific wasn't as enjoyable for the other people as he thought. And all of that was before you factored in him learning how to shoot a gun and going into a warzone. It wasn't going to end well. I could feel it in my bones.

"Army medics, they just stay on base right?" I asked, breaking the silence between us for the first time since we left the cave.

"No, the doctors stay on base. Medics are more like a hybrid of a paramedic and ER doctor. It's on the medics to keep the soldiers alive long enough for them to get to a doctor. They go out with their unit, they are trained to shoot and they help with the operations."

That was not what I wanted to hear, not even close to it. I had been telling myself that at least Greyson would be safe on base working in the infirmary. Only now that dream was just blown up. I wanted to talk Greyson out of it, but I knew I couldn't. It wasn't my place to convince him to choose a different career. Just like it wasn't anyone's place to convince me to not be a firefighter and even if someone tried to talk me out of it I wouldn't have listened. I would have still done what I felt was right and I knew Greyson would do the same.

"Why the interest?" Xavier asked as he looked back at me.

I hadn't been walking beside him this whole time. I needed some space to get my thoughts and emotions in order. Plus, being next to him, having his arm lightly brushing against mine, it was not going to help me keep my hands to myself.

"Thing One and Thing Two decided to drop a bombshell on me just before I left for the training."

"Thing One and Thing Two?" he commented with a small smirk and I couldn't help but roll my eyes.

"Yeah, I know, but in my defense when they were younger they acted a lot like them. Even dressed up as them for Halloween one year. It stuck," I said with a small shrug before I continued. "They are identical twins, but they couldn't be any different. Asher, he's ninety-three seconds older than Greyson, and he's not too great at school. Greyson had pulled double duty on tests and exams a few times and he's the only reason Asher even graduated. But Asher, he's got a great heart. He loves people and animals. I figured he would go to a trade school, but instead he got a job at a horse ranch in Texas."

"What's wrong with that? I knew an Army buddy who retired and took over his family's horse ranch in Montana. It can be peaceful working with the horses."

"There's nothing wrong with it, it just came out of left field. He had never mentioned being interested in it. I had no idea he was even doing research and going on interviews for it. I was set to leave believing that I would be coming home in a month to two eighteen year olds and a messy house from all the house parties. Now Asher will be in Texas and Greyson, the smart one, the one who could be a surgeon and got a full scholarship to Harvard Medical School, he's going to be an Army medic."

"Ah," Xavier said with complete understanding to his voice, but I wasn't certain if he related to my position or Greyson's.

I stopped walking and placed my hands on my hips as I tried to catch my breath. We had been going up the side of a little rock mountain for roughly an hour now. I knew we needed to get to the top to reach the Ranger tower, and normally I would be okay with the physical work, but I was so exhausted and sore from yesterday that this hike was taking everything in me. At the sound of my footsteps faltering, Xavier turned to face me and I felt a bit of pleasure to see he was fighting to catch his breath as well.

"It's not that I have a problem with the military life. If Asher told me he was going to the Army, I would be worried, but it wouldn't be surprising. Greyson though, he's smart, too smart, to the point where social situations aren't always clear to him. And that's fine; he's always had Asher next to him to help guide him through the murky waters. But now he is going to be the skinny, smart guy, who is out and proud surrounded by alpha males. And he's not going to have Asher there to protect him, to shield him from the potential hurt."

And that was my biggest worry. Greyson was going to be tossed all alone into a world I didn't think he was fully prepared for. He wasn't going to have his protector. He wasn't going to have the one person who just understood him fully. He was going to be seeing the worst humanity had to offer and he would have to do that knowing he was an outcast. I highly doubted he was ever going to be one of the guys. He was too different and in a world like the military, that wasn't a good thing.

Xavier walked over to me and took my hand in his. The physical contact surprised me, because Xavier wasn't much for touching. Sure, we did plenty of touching last night but that was for survival. Ever since this morning, he'd gone out of his way to avoid any physical contact with me. I understood it. He had been through war and he was my instructor. It wouldn't look good for anyone to see us together, or even make assumptions about us. He was trying to go back to how things were before the cave and I understood it. It would be best for us to go back to how things were. It would just be simpler, plus he was never going to switch to a bottom and I knew that wasn't something I could do either. I had never done it before, but I had never had an interest in it either. So going back to being an instructor and student seemed like the best plan for both of us.

"I'm not going to lie, Boot Camp is going to be hard for him. If he survives though, he'll be placed in a unit and they will protect him. Medics are like royalty over there. They all go out of their way to protect their medics, because they are the rest of the unit's lifeline if shit goes wrong. They'll teach him everything they know in and out of the field. He'll be their kid brother and they will love him. He'll see horrific things, but you can help him learn how to deal with it in a healthy manner."

It was a nice thought. He painted this really nice picture, but I also knew that coming back after seeing war, it wasn't a pretty picture. I didn't know any veterans personally, but I did see the homeless on the street. Alcoholics and drug addicts, barely able to function all so they could forget about the horrors that they had seen. The fact that any veteran was able to hold down a job and have a somewhat normal life was beyond impressive to me. The fact that Xavier was able to continue being a pilot after being at war was impressive. I didn't doubt for a second though he had demons lying underneath the surface. And it was those kind of demons that I didn't want for my sweet baby brother.

"I don't know if I can handle him being over there," I softly admitted.

"Not a lot of people can. My parents had a really hard time with it. My mother worried, but my father was angry with me for a long time. At first, I didn't understand why he was angry with me, but after I had Dexter I got it. I don't think I would be able to handle it if Dexter told me he wanted to be in the military. To know that he was overseas at war and I couldn't be there to protect him. It took my father a very long time to accept my decision and I made sure that I never talked to him about what I saw or went through over there. I kept my injuries hidden as best as I could from both of them."

That was exactly how I felt. Greyson would be going off to war and I would be left behind, unable to be there to make sure he was protected from physical and mental dangers. I didn't know how I was going to be able to focus on my job while he was overseas at war. I knew I didn't have a choice in the matter though. It was Greyson's life and I had to accept it and I was going to have to figure something out that allowed me to function at work, but I highly doubted I would ever be okay with his decision. I also didn't know if I wanted Greyson to keep injuries from me or if I wanted to know about them. I really wasn't sure which would be worse.

"We should, ah... we should get going," I managed to say.

I didn't like the idea of being vulnerable around Xavier. I needed to stay strong. I was always the strong one and I was not about to let that change. My brothers needed me, now more than ever, to stay levelheaded and be there for when they needed me. I couldn't do vulnerabilities and weakness, too much was riding on me staying stable and able to handle anything that came my way.

Xavier just gave me a small nod and I could

tell he understood my need to move forward, both physically and from this conversation. I appreciated that he didn't try and push the subject.

He released my hand and continued on climbing up our rocky mountain. Letting out a sigh, I started to follow after him. We were hopefully halfway there and I was really wishing tonight I would be able to sleep in my own bed. For a course that was supposed to be fun, so far it had been anything but. I was really looking forward to continuing on with this course and hopefully, getting to the fun part. All I knew was that after all of this, if I didn't pass this course, I was going to lose my shit.

CHAPTER 11

Xavier

Finally! Thank fuck.

It had been closer to seven hours since we left the cave and I was starting to second-guess myself about the location of the Ranger tower. The trees kept it hidden from the ground and I had to use my memory from being in the sky. I had been confident, but the longer it took us to reach it, the more my confidence started to waver.

We both started to climb up the endless number of stairs. I took pride in my physical abilities, but even I was exhausted at this point and I doubted if I could even make it to the top. I knew Gage was feeling the same, but I also knew we both wanted to get the fuck out of this forest and back to the station.

I could hear Gage's heavy breathing as he climbed up behind me. At least I was hoping that was his breathing and not my own I was hearing. I knew I hadn't stayed as fit as I had been while I was in the Air Force, but I didn't think I was this out of shape, not that hiking uphill for seven hours and climbing five hundred stairs was out of shape exactly, but at one point in my life this would have been nothing.

I also couldn't ignore that I felt like shit. My stomach wasn't too happy with me right now and I knew that had nothing to do with the lack of food and water. Ever since I left the military I had been drinking every night and on my days off. I hadn't had anything to drink for two days now and my body was feeling it. I didn't want to think about what that meant. I kept telling myself it was from exertion and not something worse.

By the time we reached the top and opened that door, neither one of us could have defended ourselves if we needed to. I heard Gage groan at the sight of us being alone, I knew he had been expecting for there to be a Ranger here, but I wasn't worried about it being empty.

"The Rangers rotate within the areas to keep watch. The radio will still work and that is all we need," I barely managed to say as I crossed the short distance over to the desk.

I knew there wouldn't be much there. The Rangers brought what they needed, so nothing was left behind. There was no food or water, no cot to rest on, just two chairs, a radio and some binoculars. The radio and chairs were all we needed to get the fuck out of here.

I collapsed down into the chair with Gage doing the same to the other as he gulped air into his lungs. I turned my attention to the radio and switched it on and tuned it into the frequency for the station.

I pressed down on the mic button and spoke. "Mayday, Mayday, this is Captain Xavier Cruz with aerial station nineteen. Over."

"Will it only reach Jackson?" Gage asked as he continued the war against his breathing.

"Anyone on the frequency."

"Where the fuck have you been, Cruz?" I couldn't help the smile at hearing Jackson's voice.

"Decided to take the scenic route with the rookie. We're held up at Ranger Tower two-three-five."

"I got Bird Eleven already in the air. They've been searching the area once you didn't return last night. They found the crash site by the last ping on the black box, but no sign of you. Is there a spot for landing where you are?"

"Negative, we're surrounded by thick trees and uneven ground. We'll have to do a repel extraction." There was no way that the chopper could land in this terrain. They would have to drop a line and pull us up.

"A scenic tour and a repel extraction, you sure know how to keep a first date interesting," Jackson teased and I knew he was loving this.

"Do we really need to talk about some of the first dates you've been on?" I knew he was teasing me. I had saved his ass plenty of times when he was trapped by a fire. It was time he saved my ass. I was doing my best to ignore how my time with Gage ended last night. From some of the stories

Jackson told me about his first dates, this didn't even hit his top ten.

"Are you guys injured?" Yeah, it was probably best that he changed the subject.

"We're fine. The bear only ate part of the rookie's leg," I said with a smirk as I glanced over at Gage. He didn't look impressed.

"It coulda ate something worse. Bird Eleven is going to meet you in thirty minutes just east of the tower. They'll drop a line down for you. Try not to get into a crash this time."

"Over and out," I said, before I pushed the mic back. I knew I was going to need to give him a full rundown on what happened, but that could happen later. I wasn't exactly in the mood to rehash shit.

"We have to repel up?" Gage asked, and I couldn't tell if he was worried or not over the fact. I doubted he had done something like that before. I knew it wasn't typically taught in the fire academy.

"It'll be fine. They'll lower down a harness and the rigging brings you back up. You'll be on the chopper within two minutes," I answered as I sat back and rubbed at my temples, trying to stave off the growing headache.

"I've taken the repelling course."

Of course he had.

It seemed like he was very interested in taking any course that would make him more skilled. He might not have had the typical reasoning for being a firefighter, but he took it very seriously all the same. He was dedicated and hard working, I had to give him that.

"We need to leave in twenty to make sure to get to the pick up location," I said as I closed my eyes, hoping that it would help ease my headache. I was starting to feel a lot worse now that I was sitting down and no longer moving. I just needed some sleep and then I would feel better, that's all this was.

"How old is Dexter?"

It took my mind a minute to even realize how he knew about Dex. I almost never talk about him. It wasn't because I was ashamed to have a child. Dexter was the one thing I was most proud of. I didn't talk about him with people because it hurt. It hurt knowing that my only child hated me.

Dexter didn't know the truth and part of me wanted to tell him. I wanted to sit down with him and explain what had transpired between his mother and me. I didn't want him to hate me, but at the same time, I didn't want him to hate her either. I didn't want to take away the only parent he'd truly ever known.

I'd been with Kate and my son for the first six years of his life, but I was deployed for half of it and on operations in between. He barely saw me when I was there.

After the divorce when Kate was granted custody, I was devastated, but I also understood it. Part of me had started to doubt if I should be in Dex's life at all, and not because I was ashamed of being gay, but because he was so used to me not being there. Maybe it would have been better for me to step away completely, so if I did die in the line of duty he wouldn't miss me as much. It wouldn't be such a devastating blow to him.

I'd made it a whole week before the pain of not speaking with him became too much. It didn't matter though, because Kate made sure we didn't get time together. The result was a soon to be seventeen year old who didn't know me and hated my guts because of what Kate had said to him about why I wasn't around.

I was trying to gain some footing with Dex and I was really hoping that once he turned eighteen and became an adult it would be easier for us to communicate. I would be able to reach out to him without having to go through Kate. All of that was assuming he would even take my calls after his mother's brainwashing.

I knew when I was discharged from the Air Force I could have taken Kate back to court, but I was so screwed up, still am, and I didn't want to dump that on Dexter. And once again, Kate was the only parent he knew and I didn't want to take that from him by giving him the truth.

"He'll be seventeen in three months," I answered as I kept my eyes closed.

"Sixteen, I remember being terrified for the twins to be that age. Mostly for Asher. I could always count on Greyson to be level headed and logical, but when Asher got going he was able to drag Greyson into some pretty wild shit."

I cracked my eyelids open just part way so I could look at him as I spoke. "It couldn't have been easy. Having to be a parent, but also a brother."

"It wasn't easy. There was a balance to it and I'm not too sure I even have that balance figured out now. Now though, it'll be a bit different, I guess. They are legal adults so I don't have to be a parent any longer, but I doubt I can just switch it off. I tried to remember growing up, especially once they got older, that they didn't always need a lecture. That sometimes they needed an older brother to bitch to or admit to doing something they shouldn't have done, but they wanted to brag about it."

"What was the worst thing you let them get away with?" I didn't have any stories of my own for Dex, but I did like hearing them about other children. Some of the guys I worked with in the military used to show off pictures or videos of their children and for a little while I could pretend that it was my own son I was watching. I was well aware that it was pathetic and sad, but on those extremely hard days and lonely nights it was all I had to push me to keep going.

"I guess that depends on your definition of horrible. They did the typical teenager thing, the typical twin thing. Greyson would pretend to be Asher, mostly for tests or exams, like I said. There had been a few assignments when Asher was close to failing out that I would ask Greyson to write it. I know that counts as cheating, but I never put too much stock in grades. I knew Asher would find something he loved to do to make a career out of it. I didn't need them both to be lawyers or doctors."

"I knew a lot of guys who had the biggest heart and yet were dumb as rocks. Book smarts isn't everything."

That was also something Kate and I disagreed on. She came from a family that expected you to get the highest grades every time. I remember one time she got a B+ on a math test and she cried, almost had a panic attack at just the thought of showing her parents. I never wanted that for Dexter. School was supposed to be fun, a chance for you to learn, but also discover different pieces of yourself. It wasn't supposed to be about turning children into stressed out freaks and ticking time bombs.

"I've always told them that they didn't have to be the smartest person in the room, they just had to be in the room. They snuck out a couple of times, went to parties, came home drunk, typical teenage rebellion. I guess the biggest thing they pulled was when they were seventeen and both dated the same guy without telling him."

"What?" I couldn't have heard that right.

Gage smiled at the memory and I could tell he was slightly proud of it. "The twins are gay. We used to joke around about how our mother must have had this special gene that she passed onto us or something. Asher has always been a social butterfly and by the time he was sixteen he had already had sex and multiple boyfriends. Greyson was the exact opposite. They liked the same guy though, Matt, and he liked a bit of both of them. Asher went out on date with him first and when he got home he told Greyson that he should go on the next one. From there, it snowballed into them both dating Matt and Matt having no idea. It lasted about six months before Matt started to date the head cheerleader."

"High school has gotten far more complicated than I remember." None of that shit certainly happened when I was in school. Apparently it was a good thing that Dexter didn't have a twin brother, because I couldn't imagine what they would have done together.

"Well, that makes sense. You didn't even have the Internet back then."

There was that fucking smirk again. I didn't know if I wanted to slap it or kiss it off his face. Neither were going to happen, so I changed the subject.

"We should start making our way to the pick up location. We're both sore and exhausted, so it might take us longer to reach the extraction point than normal."

I didn't really want to get up and move, but I knew we needed to. Staying here definitely wasn't an option. Whether we liked it or not, we had to start making our trip to the extraction point and that would bring us one step closer to the station.

One step closer to my apartment where I could shower and sleep.

Gage just gave me a nod and I could tell he wasn't happy about it either, but if we wanted out of this forest we had to move. Pushing my sore body up and out of the chair was not easy, but I forced myself to ignore the stab of pain. Just like I forced my mind to not think about how the room spun slightly or how my head pounded more fiercely as I stood.

Far more slowly than I would ever admit, we climbed down from the Ranger tower and arrived at the extraction location. I could hear the *whomp whomp whomp* of blades of the chopper in the near distance. It was a sound that brought a great deal of comfort to me, because the thumping sound indicated safety. Usually when I heard it, I was going to help rescue good men and women. I was in control, even though I couldn't control everything within my surroundings. I couldn't control how the enemy troops would react, but I could control how I responded to them. I could control my landing, my flight path, and rescue maneuvers. When I was in that cockpit, I had control and there was a great sense of safety in that.

I knew that wasn't how all veterans felt. A majority of them hated the sound because it triggered painful memories. I could also understand why they felt that way. Often when troops on the ground needed air support it was because everything was going to shit. People were hurt, shot, blown up, you name it. It only made sense that the sound of propellers could send someone into a spiral.

The wind picked up around us as the chopper hovered above. I could see the side panel being opened and I knew it would only be a minute before they started to send the repel gear down.

I glanced over at Gage to see how he was handling all of this. It was one thing to do it in a class and another to do this in real life. He was holding strong though. I wasn't seeing any fear in his eyes. He appeared to be calm and steady, a good sign. Once the harness was close enough I reached up and grabbed it, looking over to Gage as I spoke.

"You're going first." He went to argue, but I wasn't having any of it. I was the instructor and he was the cadet. "That's an order."

He wasn't happy about it, but I didn't care. We were going back to the station and that meant we were going back to how things were supposed to be. I was his instructor, his superior and he was the cadet. I needed to put that defining wall back up between us and there was nothing that he could do or say to bring it back down.

Gage easily hooked the harness onto himself and I waved up to let the guys know to start bringing him up. I stood there and watched as Gage ascended into the late afternoon sky. It was getting hotter out and I could feel the exertion within my body. There was a slight tremble now and I knew I needed to get some water and rest soon before I couldn't fight it off.

I watched as Gage was secured within the chopper and the harness was lowered back down to me. The second I could reach it, I was slipping it on and the ground beneath me started to disappear. I kept my eyes up on the chopper. Looking down never bothered me before, but I knew today would be different. With the way my body was feeling, the way my stomach was feeling, I wasn't going to risk a dizzy spell or losing what little was left in my stomach. The second my feet touched down on the metal floor of the chopper, I felt like I could take my first real breath since the crash.

"You all right, Cruz?"

That was Smith; he was one of the older pilots. He had been working for the fire department for close to twenty years now. He always said he wouldn't retire unless he lost his sight or hearing. The guys often joked around about having to pry the stick from his cold dead hands. They had no idea how accurate that was though. Losing your ability to fly was a lot like a biker losing his ability to ride his motorcycle. It wasn't something that any pilot wanted to experience.

"Fuckers shot my bird," I answered as I made my way over to the other seat in the front. If I couldn't fly, then I damn well was still going to be sitting in the front.

"We gotta do something about those assholes."

"Jackson will make the call." I didn't know what Jackson was going to do. I doubted the police would do anything and then that fell to the Feds, but what they were going to do, I had no idea. They were in a tight spot, because they couldn't go in guns blazing and end up on the five o'clock news. The survivalists had every right to defend their property. The issue came when they believed everyone flying over them were spies. I didn't know what the procedure was in that situation, but I knew it would be on Jackson to figure it out.

"Anything feel broken?"

A quick glance over to Gage told me he was still holding strong. He was sitting with his back against the back of the chopper. He had his eyes closed and his breathing was even. I wasn't too sure if he was asleep or just resting. I was leaning toward resting based on the slight furrow of his brow, presumably from the pain he had to be feeling.

I turned my attention back to the windshield and spoke. "We're fine. Just banged up. I was able to control the crash landing as well as could be expected."

"No one was too badly hurt, that's the best

outcome you could hope for. We'll be back soon and then you can get some grub and sleep."

That was all I wanted right now, sleep and a shower. I knew I should eat something, but the queasiness of my stomach was telling me it wouldn't be the best idea. I needed some water and then I could always eat later after getting some sleep. We just needed to get to the station and then I could get the fuck home.

CHAPTER 12

Xavier

THE SECOND we touched down I was climbing out of the chopper and making my way toward Jackson as he stood on the outside boundary of the designated chopper pad. I could see a mixture of anger and worry over what happened to us. I didn't need him to worry about me though. I was more than capable of taking care of myself, even in the forest.

"Something has to be done about the survivalists. Nothing tragic happened this time, but it was close. They didn't just shoot us down, they came to the crash site and started to shoot at us," I said, before he had a chance to open his mouth.

"Graze or a through and through?" he asked with a nod to my arm.

"Graze, I can take care of it myself. The cadet is fine, just banged up a bit."

"I'll make sure he gets looked at before sending him to the dorm. Go get yourself taken care of. I'll make the calls to see what can be done about the survivalists."

That was all I needed to hear. Without looking toward Gage, I made my way toward the side of the station so I could go around to get into my truck. The second I was sitting in it, I couldn't help but close my eyes and rest my head back. I could feel my whole body trembling and I knew I had to get to my apartment before I wasn't able to drive.

"You're just tired, that's all," I told myself, not ready to admit what was really going on. I knew the signs, fuck, I had seen them myself in other soldiers and vets, but this wasn't that. Nope. I was just tired after everything that happened, that's all.

Turning my truck on, I pulled out of the station and started to make the drive to my place. Thankfully, it was only a twenty minute drive away.

The second I arrived home, I stumbled out of my truck and headed for the door. Sweat was starting to run down my face and I felt like I was going to hurl any second. Once I made it to my door, I pulled out my key and had to fight to get my hand to stop shaking long enough to get the key into the hole.

Slamming the door behind me, I didn't even think, I just went into my kitchen and grabbed the half drank bottle of whiskey sitting on my counter. I unscrewed the lid and took a drink right from the bottle. I knew it wouldn't be instant, but I also knew within a moment or two I would start to feel a bit better.

I took another swig before I sank down to the floor and placed my head against the cupboard. Closing my eyes, I decided to ride it out and see if my theory was right or not. I was praying I was wrong, that it wasn't alcohol withdrawal, because that meant I had gone and gotten myself addicted to the booze.

I knew I drank a lot, and frequently, but I didn't think my body was becoming dependent on it. I had been foolish to think I could drink for years straight without a single issue. I had fooled myself into believing there wasn't a problem because I didn't need to drink to get through the day, I just did it at night. After all, people have a beer or two after work; it was natural.

I liked getting drunk; it helped me sleep. It helped me keep the nightmares at bay. It was either drink or take a sleeping pill and those were addictive, so surely a drink was better.

But as my body started to feel better I knew just how stupid and naive I had been, because I got addicted to alcohol all the same and now that I knew about it, I had no idea what I was going to do.

CHAPTER 13

Gage

I SHOULDN'T HAVE BEEN SURPRISED that Xavier left without even saying a word to me, but I was. And I hated that I was a little hurt by it. I knew we had to go back to being instructor and cadet, but I didn't think he would be able to forget about the night we spent together that easily.

Again, I knew it was foolish, because what we did was out of necessity. We had to generate body heat and that was the best way. Still though, with how amazing it felt, I thought he felt it too. I thought he felt the same connection that I did, but apparently not. That was fine. We both had different lives. We both lived on opposite ends of the country. Not to mention we were both tops and I would never switch. Xavier was right. It was better to pretend like it never happened.

I immediately went and walked down toward the dormitory. I knew technically I should be heading to class, it was my second day and there was still work I needed to pick up that I had missed, but fuck it, I could catch up tomorrow. Today was going to be about me and that meant a shower, water, food and sleep. Everything else was tomorrow's problem.

The dormitory for this station was not connected to the actual station, but rather in its own building roughly a hundred feet from it. I had only been in the dormitory for a few minutes yesterday, just long enough to drop my bags off and head to the station. I will say it was much nicer than I was expecting. There was a large cooking area with some standard food in it, coffee, milk, eggs, cereal, bread, hamburger buns, frozen burgers, and hot dogs. If we wanted something different we could head into town, roughly a fifteen minute walk, to grab it. According to Jackson, there was some great pizza in town that I was going to have to try tomorrow.

As for my room, I was in a double room, but I didn't have a roommate. The dormitory was often used for a full fire academy and specialized courses in between seasons. It meant we were all lucky enough to be able to have our own room and our bathroom. The bathroom was connected to each room and it was designed to help with the flow when the dormitory was full. It was nice, almost like a hotel room. There was even a desk to do work at. Until tomorrow though, my room would be very much a hotel room. I was planning on doing nothing but eating and sleeping.

I went over to the fridge in the kitchen to see if there was anything I could grab to eat real quick. I snagged a water bottle from the shelf in the door and took a long drink from it before I turned my attention to the food. I saw a styrofoam to-go container with a note sitting on top of it. My name was written on the folded piece of paper. I picked it up and saw some pretty shitty handwriting, but I was able to make it out.

We figured after the long night you had you could use some real food. Hope you like Chinese.

-The Guys

Okay, that right there was exactly why I loved being in the Fire Department. It was a brotherhood that reached from one end of the world to the other. It didn't matter what you looked like, who you dated, where you lived, rich or poor, none of it mattered because you were a brother to millions, it was just that simple. We all looked out for each other and we all wanted to ensure that everyone was taken care of. It was this simple act that made everything that happened within the past twenty some odd hours better.

I grabbed the food and opened it up to see that it was rice, honey garlic chicken, and cooked vegetables. It smelled amazing, even though it was cold. I wasn't picky when it came to food. We didn't always get to have much growing up, so I never turned any down. Asher and Greyson were the same, but Greyson was starting to get a bit picky. He didn't want to eat things he didn't enjoy or appreciate the taste. I could understand that though. If you didn't really get to eat the foods you liked growing up, it only made sense to seek them out as an adult. Thankfully, Asher was like a garbage disposal and ate anything that was in front of him.

After warming my food up, my mouth watering as the smell hit my nose, I grabbed a fork before I made my way toward my room. I needed to shower, but I was planning on eating first.

I sat down at the desk and took a bite. I couldn't contain the groan that escaped me at the taste that flooded my mouth. Fuck, this might be the best thing I'd ever eaten.

I pulled my cell phone out and tried to see if it would turn on, but it didn't. I couldn't remember what battery percent it was at when I got onto the chopper so there was a chance that it had just died and it wasn't water-logged. I would have to put it into some rice just in case before I plugged it in. If there was water inside of it, trying to charge it could short circuit the system. It would be better to play it safe.

I got up and grabbed my laptop from my bag. I needed to check in with the twins and make sure they were okay. They were going to text me last night to let me know that they were okay but obviously I didn't get that text with a dead phone. I knew they would be packing up their stuff and getting ready to leave shortly. I hated that I wouldn't be there for them, to see them off. I wanted to be there. I would have taken them to the airport. Hell, I would have taken them all the way to their new lives if they had let me. I understood it was bad timing on all of our parts, but if I knew that they weren't going to be home when I got back, I wouldn't have left. I could have taken the course another time and at least been there for what little time we had left. Instead, now I was going to be returning to an empty house, for the first time in my entire life, and I had no idea how I was going to handle the quiet when I got home. There was normally always noise in the house. Sometimes it was Asher's country music blaring and other times it was the sound of their footsteps as they walked back and forth to each other's room.

It took about a year after our mother's death before I moved into her room so they could each have their own. They appreciated the privacy, but often you could find them together in one of their rooms. The house had never really been quiet and after a bad day it was nice to come home to the noise.

There had been plenty of times where I would crawl into bed with them and hang out. Being around the twins helped to calm the demons that a job like mine could bring. And now I was going to have to find a new way to deal with those demons, a healthy way.

I couldn't risk becoming dependent on alcohol to get me through the day. I had seen that plenty of times with guys that had been on the job a long time. They got drunk the second they could when their shift was done. I didn't want that life. I was going to have to figure it out.

I opened my email and ignored every one that didn't have one of my brothers' names on it. They hadn't sent me an email. I figured they wouldn't have. They would have just texted me, but if I didn't reach out to them they would worry that something had happened to me.

I quickly sent them off an email letting them know my phone got wet and I was drying it out. I wasn't going to be telling them about what happened, it would only make them worry and that was the last thing I wanted.

With that done, I browsed around online while I ate before finally grabbing some clean clothes and headed into the bathroom. I turned on the water as hot as it could go without burning my skin before I stripped out of my dirty clothes and stepped under the spray.

The second the water hit my skin I was in heaven. It felt amazing against my cold and battered body. I could have stayed here for hours, but I knew that wouldn't be possible because I would get light-headed and potentially pass out, something I didn't want to happen. I allowed the water to wash over me for a few minutes longer before I started the process of getting all of the dirt and grime off of me. I swear it felt like there was actual slime on my skin.

After a thorough cleaning, I washed my hair and when the struggle to keep my eyes open became too great, I turned the water off and quickly dried off. I didn't bother with much of my clothes outside of my boxers before I headed over to my bed. The curtains were pulled back over the small window so I didn't have to worry about the sunlight shining in. I was hoping by the time I woke up it would be tomorrow morning or at least close enough to it.

I pulled the covers off and collapsed onto the bed. It was so incredibly soft, especially compared to the cave floor that made my bed last night. I had to admit though, I missed the cold body that had been pressed up against me.

CHAPTER 14

Xavier

"Come on, pick up," I whispered to myself as I headed down the hallway toward the classroom.

The sound of an endless ring was something I had come to associate with my son. Every time I called Dexter that was the only sound that greeted me. I knew he was never going to answer, he never did. I would leave him voicemail after voicemail, but he never returned my calls.

I wished I could get through to him. I felt like if I could just talk to him, then I could start to repair the damage that had been done. I knew Kate had told him a shitload of lies about me and I wasn't going to be able to start to disprove them until I could get Dexter to speak with me.

I wasn't blaming everything on Kate. I had made plenty of mistakes myself where Dexter was concerned. I shouldn't have given up fighting for him. I should have changed career paths in the Air Force so I could be home more and would have stood a better chance at getting joint custody of him, or at the very least a set visitation schedule instead of it being left up to Kate. It would have been messy and frustrating at the best of times, but I would have had a better relationship with my son. It was a regret that I was going to have to carry with me for the rest of my life and it was time I tried to correct that wrong.

"You have reached the voicemail box of Dexter Cruz. Please leave your name and a brief message and he will get back to you as soon as possible."

I knew it was irrational to feel hatred toward an automated voice messaging system, but every time I heard that bitch's voice I wanted to punch her in the face. "Dex, it's your Dad. I would really like for you to call me back so we can talk. Please, Son, call me back."

I hit the end button before I pocketed my phone. I had no faith that Dexter would call me back, he never did, but it was a call I was going to make every day until I could finally talk to him. If there was one good thing that came from the shit-show that was the past forty-eight hours, it was that I needed to make things right between Dexter and I. I could have died in those woods and I never would have gotten to tell my son that I loved him. I wouldn't have gotten to hug him one last time, to hear his voice. I had to make this right, no matter what it took.

I walked into the classroom to see that the cadets were already there. They were talking amongst themselves and I instantly scanned the room and found the one person I wanted to see more than anything. Gage. He was speaking with a couple of the guys around him from where he sat in the front row.

I don't know why, but him sitting in the front row surprised me. I knew he hadn't done well in school and I had assumed that meant he would naturally place himself in the middle or at the back of the room. Out of the way so he could blend in and go unnoticed like I was certain he had done growing up.

I was a man that could admit when I was wrong and I was wrong in my assumptions of Gage. I thought he was too young to be here, that he would be too immature. When in reality he might be more mature than I was. It took a special person to step up at a very young age and raise not one but two children. He gave up the rest of his childhood for his brothers and that was one of the most honorable things I had ever heard of. There was depth to Gage and I shouldn't be interested in him, but I couldn't stop thinking about him.

I'd never done anything with any of the cadets that I trained. I'd always kept it professional and kept a wall up between us. Shit, I was like that with people I worked with each and every day. For a couple of reasons; one, I didn't like to bring any unnecessary drama into my life. Sleeping with someone that you worked with had the potential for disaster. And two, firefighters got killed all the time. Every single time we went out for a call it could be the one that took our life. I had enough loss in my life. I couldn't handle having another one. I couldn't handle losing someone that I potentially could care deeply for. It was easier for me to keep things simple and without emotions. Gage had the potential to stir up emotions within me and that was dangerous. Thankfully, we were both tops and he had no interest in bottoming. We weren't compatible, making it an easy clean break between us.

Or so I tried to convince myself.

Jackson nudging me with his elbow brought me out of my thoughts and I snapped my eyes away from Gage's radiant smile. Looking over at Jackson, I could see the smirk on his face and I already knew what he was going to say before he even opened his mouth.

"Found the one gay guy in the group, eh?" he teased, and I had to fight down my irritation.

"He is gay, but that wasn't why I was looking at him. I was making sure he looked ready to be back. A night in the woods with gun-toting extremists after you might have been what broke him. I don't need an unstable cadet up in the air with me."

I was not about to give Jackson the satisfaction of seeing me checking anyone out. And he was never going to hear about what happened between us in the cave. That was going to stay between Gage and me. At least I hoped it would. He could have already spilled the beans to the other cadets, but I was hoping he would have enough respect for himself as well as me to keep it quiet.

"Eventually, you are going to have to accept that you are capable of caring for someone. That being attracted to a guy doesn't automatically put a target on their back," Jackson countered without any malice to his voice. I knew he was trying to help, but right now I was not in the mood for it.

"Says the man who sleeps with multiple guys at once and doesn't take any relationship seriously. You are the last person that gets to give life advice." I couldn't keep the edge from my voice. I was still too raw from not being able to talk to Dexter, plus my discovery about myself last night.

I was still in denial about my dependency on alcohol. My mind knew the signs. My mind understood what my body was feeling, but I still refused to believe it. I couldn't be addicted to alcohol, that just wasn't possible for me. Lots of people drank every day. It would be natural for me to feel sick after exerting myself for two days in the woods. We didn't have any water or food, we barely slept and we were freezing. It was perfectly natural for me to have felt like shit last night. There was nothing more to it than that. I continued to give myself every excuse in the book, determined to believe at least one of them.

"Maybe I just haven't found the man that can hold my attention long enough to change my life," he countered, slightly offended, which I wasn't too sure as to why. This wasn't the first time we'd talked about his man-whoring ways. It had never bothered him in the past; it didn't bother him three days ago. I couldn't help but wonder what had changed.

I didn't ask him though, that would have taken our friendship to a more personal level and that wasn't something I was looking to achieve. Friends also get killed and I had buried enough friends to last me three lifetimes. The only way to avoid having to bury someone else that I cared for was to make sure I never cared for anyone ever again.

"You hear back from the police about our woodland rednecks?" I asked, looking to change the subject to something we were both more comfortable with.

Jackson gave a snicker at that. "I put the call in to the Sheriff's office and they were going to work with the Park Rangers to try and come to some sort of a solution. Obviously, they don't want to cause open season on each other, but the Sheriff can't let them shoot down choppers and go on a hunting party for survivors. If they aren't able to come to a peaceful solution, then they won't have any choice but to bring in the Feds. It's something they are avoiding though, for obvious reasons."

The Feds getting involved would turn it all into one epic clusterfuck. The extremists would take it as an act of terrorism against their people and their beliefs. They would start shooting and trying to kill as many Feds that they could. They would make a show of it and demand to have news reporters there to watch as the Government tried to take away their rights and put their women and children in harm's way.

"Their encampment is in our training flight path. I'm going to have to change the training area to ensure we don't fly over them and risk getting shot down again. We got lucky this time around."

And that was really what it came down to.

Fucking luck.

If the impact to the chopper had been on the engine and not the tail, we could have blown up before we even reached the ground. If I hadn't been able to control the landing as well as I did, we could have blown up on impact. We got lucky and I wasn't foolish enough to believe that we would get lucky a second time. I would need to change the training area to ensure that the cadets were safe when we were in the air.

"Agreed. You can map that out today while I go over the weather forecast with them."

I gave him a nod and we both moved over to the front of the class so we could get it started. I would need to find the best place in the opposite direction of the extremists encampment where we could safely do the training. The original flight path gave us the most level and open ground, making it safer for the cadets to repel down and get used to repelling people up, but it wasn't an option any longer and I might need to change how we did things moving forward.

"Good morning," Jackson started. "We are going to focus on reading forecast maps this morning and getting you guys used to predicting the wind direction. This will help you to have a better understanding of how a fire will move, but also if you are going to be repelling victims up to the chopper, you need to know how the basket or harness is going to swing."

One of the cadets further in the back raised a hand and Jackson gave a nod, indicating for him to speak. "Are we still going up in the chopper after it was shot down?"

"Yeah, what is stopping that survivalist group from doing it again?" another cadet added.

It was reasonable for them to be concerned

with being shot down. They didn't sign up for that and it wouldn't be something that they would be used to experiencing. It pissed me off that they were worried about their safety when they were up in my rig. I had always worked my ass off to make sure that the people who go up with me are as safe as they can be. And now the people that were supposed to put their lives in my hands were scared about getting back onto my rig.

It was bullshit.

I couldn't help but glance over to see Gage's reaction. I wanted to pull him aside and talk to him, check in to see how he was feeling after the last two days, but I knew I couldn't do that. Any alone time with him would be dangerous and far too tempting.

Gage's eyes locked with mine and I felt a wave of heat overtake me. This man had the potential to be dangerous and I really needed to keep the distance between us. Something that wouldn't be easy with us being up in the air together again. I had to make sure my walls were up around him, that I didn't let my body and desire blind me from the reality of the situation.

It wasn't even that he was much younger than me. It was the fact that our lives were on two different paths. He had a whole career back in Baton Rouge and I had a life here that I couldn't walk away from. Dexter was here and even if we weren't speaking with each other, I wasn't going to leave and abandon him here. Even if I was willing to entertain the idea of starting something with Gage, I knew the relationship would be doomed before it even got off the ground.

I broke the eye contact with him and turned my attention back to the cadets who had voiced their concerns. "I will be creating a new flight path that we will use for any training, one that will take us in the opposite direction of the encampment. The Sheriff and the Park Rangers are also working together to try and resolve the issues that the survivalists have."

"We are doing everything within our power to ensure your safety while you are in the air," Jackson added.

I could see that they were still worried about it all, not that I could blame them, but they were at least relieved to hear that we had a plan and things were being done to prevent this situation from happening again. With no further questions, Jackson got started on the lesson and I headed out to work with the maps to try and find a safe route that would work for the course. Somehow, I knew it was going to be a long ass day.

CHAPTER 15

GAGE

THE MUSIC from the bar was blaring even through the closed door.

The day had been pretty long with nothing but class work. I couldn't even count the number of forecast maps that I had seen today and my mind was in desperate need of a break. It had been a long time since I had to sit in a classroom for eight hours straight. Even in the academy we had time outside of class while we worked on the practical aspect of the job.

I hadn't realized until today how desperately I had needed that time outside of the classroom in order to make it through the class work. I was fairly decent at reading a forecast map, but as each one grew in difficulty it was harder for me to see what Jackson was talking about. It was harder for me to not let my insecurities about my intelligence seep in and I wasn't confident that I had managed to fight them off fully. When the guys had suggested that we go and let off some steam at one of the few local bars, I jumped on it.

It was nearing ten o'clock at night and I knew it would be too late to call Greyson over in Georgia, but I figured it wouldn't be too late for Asher in Austin. He was normally a night owl to begin with and I doubted the last couple of days had changed that. I hadn't been able to talk to them since I left and I was going through a sense of withdrawal without hearing their voices. They had emailed me back just letting me know they were still alive, but they didn't get into any details about how things were going with them and I was very anxious to hear all about it. I was going to have to try and find some time tomorrow to speak with Greyson, even if I had to leave class for fifteen minutes to catch him.

I pulled out my phone, very thankful that it was working, and called Asher. After a few rings he answered, but the tired-sounding voice did not go unnoticed. "You know it's almost midnight here and I have to be up at six, right?"

Hearing the sound of his voice instantly had me smiling. I knew I should have said that I was sorry and that he could call me tomorrow so he could sleep, but I just needed to talk to him for a few minutes. To hear the slight rough tone to his voice that always told me it was Asher. They were identical twins, but there was a slight difference to their voice. Asher had a slight gruff to his tone whereas Greyson's voice was smooth like silk.

"Sorry, I just wanted to hear your voice. It's been five days since I've seen you guys."

To some I knew five days would be nothing, but to me it felt like years. I had been around them their whole lives. Every single day I was there, taking care of them, and now I had been away from them for five days and I felt a great sense of loneliness. I had no idea how I was going to adapt to living alone once I returned. I knew I could get a roommate or something, but that would take one of the rooms away from the twins when they came home for visits and I didn't want to do that. I wanted them to know that no matter how much time had passed or where they were in life, that they could always come home. That they always had a place to live with me.

"You miss the insanity already?" Asher asked, sounding a bit more awake.

"I'm always going to miss you guys. How have you been? What has it been like working on a ranch? Are the guys you work with treating you right?"

I knew what it was like to be the youngest in a group of men. It usually went one of two ways. Either they were protective of you and took you under their wing or they were complete assholes. I was really hoping that Asher wasn't getting the second option.

"The ranch has been amazing. It's hard work and I tend to be sore by the end of the day, but the guys have all been awesome. They are showing me everything that I need to learn and they have been teaching me how to ride a horse. They are all really great, you don't have to worry about me."

"I'm always going to worry about you, but I am happy to hear that you are liking it so far and the guys are treating you right. Do you feel like you made the right decision?"

I knew it was easy at eighteen to think that the job you were choosing was going to be your career. There was that honeymoon period where everything felt great and exciting before reality hit you and you realized that that was going to be your life every single day for the next fifty years. I had been lucky that my honeymoon period hadn't ended with me feeling like I made a huge mistake and I was hoping that Asher and Greyson felt the same. As terrified as I was that Greyson would be in the army, I wanted him to feel like he had made the right decision. I wanted them both to find a career that they were in love with. A career that didn't feel like they were going to work every day, like I had been lucky enough to have.

"Completely. I mean, I'm sore as shit, but soon that won't be an issue as my muscles get used to the work. I like being here. I like being around other guys who aren't geniuses. Guys who are good people and want to help animals. And these horses, oh man, they are the sweetest animals I have ever been around. Some of them have been abused and you can actually see their ribs. It's terrible and sad. But then when you start to earn their trust, it makes you feel this warmth and all of the effort and hours that go into building that trust is worth it."

I couldn't help but smile at hearing how much he was loving his job and it wasn't just the words that he said, I could hear it in his voice. It was a good sign and it was sounding like he was in the right place.

"I'm really happy to hear that, Ash, truly. It's a huge relief to hear that you are loving it there and feel like it's where you want to be. Have you heard from Grey?"

Asher gave a chuckle before he spoke. "Oh yeah, he texts me all day long, mostly emojis of someone dying."

"So, it's not going well for him?" That was my biggest concern with Greyson. I knew he could handle anything in a classroom, but the military cared more about your physical health and strength over anything else, especially in Basic Training. It was going to be a lot on his body for those first six weeks until he graduated and then could move onto more specific training to be a medic.

"He's holding on. I did a lot of training with him beforehand so he's able to keep up. It's just a lot. The good news is that everyone is too exhausted by the end of the day to give him a hard time about any social cues he might have missed."

"I guess I should be thankful that you both have practice being the other. If nothing else, he could rely on how you act to get him through. Let me know though, if he tells you something bad happened. I don't want to be kept in the dark."

"I will, but you also can't go all papa bear and try to fix it either. He has to figure out how to be around normal people, you know that."

I did know that, but that didn't mean I was happy to accept it either. I was trying to remember that Xavier said that Greyson's unit would look out for him once he arrived in one. That they would make sure he was protected and help with any shortfalls in the social aspect of his personality. He just needed to make it through Basic Training and for Greyson's sake, I was hoping he would.

"I know. I just don't want to be blindsided. The same for you. I want to know if something happens, good or bad. You are both eighteen now, adults, and you don't need me to be your father anymore. Now I can be just your big brother and I don't want to lose the connection that we all have." Which was one of my greatest fears. Losing the special connection that the three of us shared. I had relied on it for so many years and I couldn't imagine not having it in my life.

"You're never going to lose that connection with us, Gage. We're always going to need you, no matter how old we are. I know this is hard on all of us, but especially you. So much of your life has been dedicated to taking care of us and making sure we had everything we needed, even going without just so we didn't have to. Our situation is new and it's scary, but we can all adapt to it and we can keep our connection to each other. And now when we do get to see each other, it will be even more special."

Fuck, leave it to Asher to go and say something deep and profound.

That was exactly what I meant when I told people that Asher was good with people. He knew what to say to them to help ease their worries. In a lot of ways, he was the voice of reason in my life and I was really going to miss having that.

"Well, now that you are going to make me cry, I'm going to let you go. You sound exhausted and you need proper sleep so you don't get hurt. I love you."

"I love you too. I'll let Grey know to call you when I talk with him tomorrow."

"Yes, please. I don't care when he calls me, I'll answer."

"I'll let him know. Be safe."

"You too. No standing behind a horse, I paid a lot of money for your teeth."

For both of their teeth. They both had to have braces from the age of twelve until seventeen. In hindsight, it was my fault they both needed it. They both sucked their thumbs when they were little in order to fall asleep, but they didn't stop until they were eight. The act of sucking their thumb after all of their teeth came in and even some of their adult teeth in the front had caused them to push back into their mouth. The result was two sets of braces and many dentist appointments. It was all worth it though, because now they both had perfect smiles and that helped a lot with Greyson's confidence.

"Worth every penny though," Asher teased.

"Yes, they were, but if you get them kicked out of your mouth, you will discover just how expensive teeth are."

"I promise not to stand behind a horse. Now, I gotta get some sleep. I love you, brother."

"Love you too. Good night."

"Night," he said, before he ended the call.

I felt a lot better now that I had gotten to speak to one of my brothers and I got an update on Greyson. I was hoping that I would be able to speak with him tomorrow at some point and I could hear for myself that he was doing okay and still feeling like he made the right decision.

With that stress and worry off of my mind, I turned my attention back to the reason that I had come out tonight and made my way back inside the bar. It was pretty busy for a Thursday night, but apparently it was Thirsty Thursday so the drinks were cheaper. That was fine by me, because I hated spending a lot of money on liquor.

I wasn't much of a drinker, but I figured that was connected to the twins. It was hard to be drunk at night when I might have to take care of them. I was always overly aware how easily things could take a bad turn. They could get sick or hurt and I needed to be able to care for them or, in the worst-case scenario, be sober so I could drive them to a hospital. Now that I was technically free to go crazy, I didn't have any interest in it. I think that was why I got along so well with some of the older guys at work. I didn't hold any interest in partying and making reckless mistakes. Though, they would argue that my motorcycle and love for skydiving was reckless and worse than a few drunken nights.

I made my way over to the bar to grab a beer. Afterward, I scanned the bar to see where all of the guys were. They were pretty spread out, some were playing pool or darts, others were talking with various women. I felt my heart beat faster as my gaze landed on the one person I never thought would be there.

Xavier.

Fuck, he looked good. He was wearing black,

straight-cut jeans, with a black t-shirt underneath his black leather jacket that was unzipped. The man was sex on a stick and I hated that my entire body wanted him. It was insane, because I knew we would never work. It should have been clear cut, and yet my body was craving to feel him against it again. I didn't understand what it was about him, because I had been attracted to other tops before. I'd fooled around with other tops in the past and I had never had a problem walking away from them.

What the fuck made Xavier so different?

Xavier's eyes locked onto mine and once again I felt a wave of heat overtake my entire body. Everything in me wanted him and I could see the desire burning in his eyes too.

Our one time in the cave was not enough for either of us and I knew it was affecting him as well. I could see it in the way he avoided eye contact with me during class. The distance he placed between us, almost as if he was worried about being unable to resist touching me if we were close enough.

I couldn't resist giving him a sexy smirk and that seemed to trigger him. He made his way over toward me and my gaze couldn't help but travel down his body to his noticeable bulge. I didn't get to see his cock yet in some form of light, but I could remember clearly how impressive it felt. I would have loved to see it, to get to taste him.

"I'm surprised to see you here," I commented once he was close enough.

He leaned his arms against the bar top as he

spoke, keeping his gaze on me. "Old people need a drink every once in a while."

The richness to his voice told me he'd already had a couple. Not that I could blame him, it had been a pretty shitty week so far.

"Isn't it past your bedtime?" I teased as I moved closer.

Fuck, this man was like a magnet.

"I don't know; you looking to tuck me in?" he countered with quite possibly the sexiest smirk I had ever seen.

"I could be persuaded into it." I ran my gaze up and down his body, lingering on his glorious ass. It really was a shame that he didn't bottom, because I had a feeling his ass would feel amazingly tight around my cock.

"I can think of something else I would rather persuade you into doing." He took a drink from his beer before he continued. "You should walk me to my truck out back."

"You shouldn't be driving and I'm already buzzed." I wasn't too certain if he was planning on driving somewhere with me, but I couldn't let him drive with him being this buzzed.

"Who said anything about driving?" he countered before he moved back and started to head toward the back door. The logical part of my brain was telling me this was a bad idea, but the buzzed part of my brain was much louder.

I took a quick drink from my beer before I followed behind him. We headed out into the back parking lot and I saw that his truck was parked in the back, furthest away from the back door to the bar. It was also away from any overhanging lights.

I caught up to Xavier as he unlocked his truck and opened his back door. Without any hesitation, I hopped inside and was surprised at how clean it was. It was a really nice truck with soft leather seats.

The second he closed the door my mouth was on his. He hungrily kissed me back, instantly slipping his tongue into my mouth. Our tongues fought for control and dominance, neither one of us wanted to submit and it should have annoyed me, but it only turned me on even more.

My hands went to his coat and I started to pull it off. I needed to feel him, all of him. He followed my lead and we started to quickly divested each other of our clothes, only breaking the kiss long enough to rid each other of our shirts. He let out a deep moan as I took his bottom lip between my teeth.

"Fuck, I need to taste you," I moaned as I pulled back from him.

He ran his hand through my hair and gripped it slightly as he spoke in quite possibly the sexiest voice I had ever heard. "Then get your mouth on my cock."

He pushed my head down and I didn't resist. I was normally always in charge, but right now my whole body was tingling with need. It was dark, but there was enough light from the evening sky that I was able to just make out his cock and it did not disappoint. It was long and thick and it was already dripping with precum making it look very juicy.

I ran my tongue along his tip and moaned at the delicious taste that exploded along my tongue.

I was instantly taking him within my mouth and he continued to push my head down until his tip hit the back of my throat. It wasn't enough for me though, because I was only getting half of him in my mouth. I relaxed my throat and continued to take him all the way down to his base and I was pleasantly rewarded with a deep moan from him. It was pretty clear that he wasn't used to being with a guy that could deep throat his cock.

"Fuck, you look so sexy with my cock down your throat and your ass up in the air."

I couldn't contain the moan of appreciation as he lightly thrust up and started to fuck my mouth. Usually I was always in control, in every aspect, but for some reason right now I wanted nothing more than for him to fuck the hell out of my mouth. I wanted my throat to be a bit sore come the morning. I couldn't stop moaning and whimpering at the feel of his cock sliding along my tongue and down my throat. My own cock was rock hard and I could feel my precum dripping down my tip. For the first time in my life, I thought I might come without even being touched.

I could feel his need building as his cock hardened and his thrusts became more erratic. He was getting close and I was in desperate need to feel him pulsing within my throat. To feel his cum running down it. I already knew he was going to taste amazing and my mouth was watering just at the very thought of it.

With a final snap of his hips, Xavier gave a hiss followed by a long groan as his cock pulsed and his cum shot down my throat. I gratefully swallowed every last drop that he had for me. His taste did not disappoint and I knew if I wasn't careful, I could become addicted to it, which wouldn't go well for me considering I was leaving after this course.

Xavier grasped my hair and pulled my head up off his cock and immediately was capturing my mouth with his own. His hand left my hair and both of his hands went to the back of my thighs and before I even had a chance to register what he was doing, he was flipping us so my back was on the seat and he was laying on top of me. His hand traveled up my thigh to my ass as I pressed my knees against his hips. I could hear him rummaging around for something, but I was too focused on his lips against mine, on the closeness of his half-hard cock to my own pulsing one. Far too soon for my liking, he was breaking the kiss and he spoke as he started to kiss along my neck.

"Trust me."

I had no idea what he was asking me to trust him on, but right now my mind could barely function and everything felt way too good to even care enough to figure it out. All I knew was that he was kissing his way down my chest, toward my cock and that was the only thing that I needed to know.

The second he reached my cock, he didn't even waste a single second before he was taking me into his mouth and quickly moving down to my base, something I knew wasn't an easy task given my large size. The sudden heat that engulfed my cock had my back arching, pushing my cock just a bit further down his throat. I couldn't stop moaning at the sensation of his mouth as it moved over my hardness.

I briefly struggled with where to put my hands. Normally, I would have my fingers tangled in the guy's hair and I would be controlling them, but I knew that wasn't something Xavier was going to be content with. Given no other choice, I raised my hands above my head and gripped the door handle.

Xavier's mouth worked my cock like he was born to do it. I was so consumed, so lost in the pleasure that was coursing through my body that I didn't even notice that Xavier had ulterior motives until his lubed up middle finger was pushing past the muscles of my very virgin hole.

I blinked my eyes open and looked down to see Xavier looking right back at me as he continued to suck my cock and slowly push his finger inside of me. Every intention of telling him to stop, to ask what the fuck he thought he was doing, completely died on my tips at just the sight of his mouth wrapped around my cock. I couldn't do anything but moan and whimper as I watched my dick disappear down his throat over and over.

Suddenly, the foreign finger inside of me became unimportant. I had to admit, it felt odd, but it didn't bother me as much as I thought it would. Though that could just be because Xavier's experienced mouth was devouring my cock at the same time.

What I couldn't understand before was why my partners loved being a bottom; it didn't feel overly good to me. All of that went right out the window when Xavier's finger hit something inside of me and my involuntary sharp cry echoed off of the walls of Xavier's truck. I quickly followed that with a whimper as Xavier removed his glorious mouth from my cock. He started to kiss up my stomach once again as he spoke.

"That's the sweet spot. That spot that sends electric pleasure waves all throughout your body. You've hit it in other people, I'm sure, but you've never felt it before. Not until me."

He started to rub a circle all over my sweet spot and I couldn't contain the repeated deep moans that escaped my body. I had never felt that kind of pleasure before and if that was what I made all of my partners feel like, then I completely understood why they loved sex so much.

Xavier leaned down even closer, his lips almost touching mine as he moved his finger even faster inside of me.

"Feels good, doesn't it, baby? Imagine just how good it would feel to have my cock sliding back and forth over it."

The sound that came out of my mouth couldn't have come from me. It was a mixture of a mewl and a whine. It was needy and not something I would ever associate myself with. I couldn't help it though. My whole body was being consumed with pleasure. Xavier was taking me to new heights, heights I had never thought would even be possible. My need to come was growing too great.

"Please, I need to come. Please," I begged, panting even harder as Xavier picked up his pace once again.

"Begging already, now you really are sounding like a bottom. Whose bottom are you?"

"Yours," I quickly caved. "Please."

"You're so close. You're gonna come any second now. I can feel your walls tightening. I'm going to make you come without touching your cock. I'm going to milk you for every last drop."

My mind was spinning and I felt completely out of control. Not a normal feeling for me but one I wondered now if might just be able to get used to. I couldn't stop moaning and panting. My whole body was tingling and my legs were trembling from my need to come. None of that had ever happened to me before and I thought if I knew that it was possible, I would have tried it a hell of a lot earlier.

I didn't know what it was about Xavier that made it so easy for me to submit to him. I had been with other tops before and if any of them had tried something like that, I doubt I would have let them. And yet there I was whining and begging Xavier for more. It was like he had this power over me and instead of being scared over it, my whole body was loving it.

A sudden heat exploded within my stomach and quickly traveled all over my body. My cock pulsed and my whole body went rigid as my walls clamped around his digit and I was finally pushed over that cliff. An extensive, deep moan filled the truck as I squeezed the door handle with every ounce of strength that I had within me. The orgasm was unlike anything I had ever felt before. I wasn't shooting out cum, but rather it was running out of me and it kept me at my peak the whole time. Every time Xavier's finger went over my sweet spot, more cum would come out. I was completely powerless under his hand. All I could do was moan and writhe at the pleasure that was scorching through me.

"That's it, come for me, baby," Xavier said as he started to kiss down my chest once more.

I felt his tongue licking up my cum and every couple of licks he would run it over my still leaking tip, sending electric shock waves down my cock. I was in a complete fog. I couldn't function. I could barely breathe. All I could do was pant and ride out the longest orgasm I had ever had in my life. I don't even know how long it went on for before I felt Xavier's finger slipping from my hole and I couldn't stop the whimper at the sudden loss of him inside of me.

I shouldn't have wanted him to have any part of himself inside of me and yet now I couldn't help but wonder what it would have felt like to have his cock buried deep inside of me. I was so lightheaded and even my teeth felt like they were tingling. I knew that was just from the lack of oxygen, but holy fuck.

"I told you I would make you feel good."

I didn't even have to look at him to know that he was smirking, the fucking asshole. And had I been able to have the brain function to form those words, I would have said them. Instead, all that came out of me was a breathy groan, which he promptly chuckled at.

"I'll call you a cab while you try and get your brain to work. You're gonna need your rest for tomorrow."

I knew he was right. I had another long day in class and I was going to need to be awake for it. At the same time, the thought of moving was really unappealing, let alone having to get dressed in the back of his truck. I had to do it, I knew that, but not just yet. I just needed a few more minutes to come back down from the best orgasm I had ever fucking had in my life.

Part of me couldn't help but wonder though, what would happen between us now?

Would this just be a one-time thing again, like the cave, or would it become a more regular occurrence?

I didn't dare vocalize my question for one very simple reason, I was too afraid of what his answer would be. And more disturbingly, I was too afraid of what my reaction to his answer would be. Those were emotions that I didn't need to unpack right now. Right now, all I had to do was keep breathing so I could eventually manage to get dressed. That was all that mattered tonight.

CHAPTER 16

Xavier

It was finally Friday and class was wrapped up.

I had managed to make it through without pushing Gage up against a wall and kissing him, a personal achievement that at times, I wasn't certain I would actually achieve today. I didn't know what it was about him, but I couldn't stop thinking about him and how fucking amazing his body felt against mine.

I knew we shouldn't have done anything last night, especially not in my truck where someone could have seen us. We had both been drinking, me more than him, and I knew it would be a terrible idea, but my body wanted his and it wasn't taking no for an answer. Now, I had no idea what was going to happen between us.

I knew what Jackson would say, to go for it and just enjoy the meaningless fling. I knew logically that would be the best course of action, but part of me didn't want a meaningless fling with Gage. There was something special about him, maybe it was because he was young and had sacrificed having a proper childhood to raise his twin brothers. Maybe it was because he was genuinely a good person and wanted to do what he could to help people and be the best role model that he could be for his brothers. He was different and not like anyone I had ever met or interacted with before.

My head was so screwed up over this, but I had to push Gage aside, at least for now. Tonight, I had a different battle to forge through.

I pulled my truck up to the street parking for the basketball court. I knew every Friday night after school Dexter would come here to shoot some hoops first before heading home for dinner. He hadn't returned my calls and I had decided to be more proactive. I couldn't leave it up to him to see me any longer. I would respect his space, but I couldn't go any longer not speaking to my son, not knowing him. I knew I had screwed up plenty of times when he was younger, but I was human and it was time that he saw me as such. It was going to take work, but I was no stranger to hard work or for a challenge that everyone said I would never be able to succeed with. I had gone off to war and faced the worst that humanity had to offer, speaking with Dexter and getting back into his life was going to be easy compared to all of that shit.

I glanced over at the basketball court and saw that Dexter was there alone just shooting some hoops. The basketball court was in really good shape thanks to the very high-end neighborhood that Dexter and Kate lived in.

Kate had remarried a handful of years ago now, to a doctor, and she had finally achieved the life she always wanted, the life that a military man couldn't ever give her.

Even from my spot in the truck I could see that my son was tall. He was a decent size as well, he had clearly been working out. I had no idea how well this was going to go over, but I was hoping that when I left this conversation it would be in a better position than when it started. I wasn't going to get anywhere if I never got out of my truck though.

Letting out a long slow breath from my nose to try and calm my nerves down, I climbed out of my truck and made my way across the street. I was relieved that he was alone, because the last thing I wanted was to make him feel embarrassed in front of his friends. I also didn't really want an audience for the rejection I was confident would be coming my way.

"Dex," I called out shakily as I walked onto the basketball court.

At the sound of my voice, his body stiffened, he stopped dribbling and the ball bounced off. He was clearly not expecting for me to be there or quite possibly to ever hear my voice in person again. His back was to me and I was praying that he would at least turn around. Very slowly he did turn around and I was finally able to lay eyes directly on my son for the first time in years. Seeing his face so clearly, it felt like I was being punched in the gut. He looked so much like me when I was his age.

My hands itched to be able to reach out and touch him, to pull him in for a hug and just feel him against me again. I didn't dare move though, too scared that it would snap Dexter out of his shock and he would dismiss me.

"What are you doing here?" Dex asked, with a hard voice. No *Dad*, no *hello*, just straight to the point. I guess I shouldn't have been too surprised, that was how I always acted when I didn't want to have to interact with someone.

"I came here to see you. You don't ever answer your phone when I call and you never call me back. I wanted to see you. I wanted to make sure you were okay and be in your life. You're my son, Dex."

I didn't even know how to start the conversation. I didn't know how to word how I felt or what my expectations were. I was completely at his mercy and I could only imagine what his mother had been putting into his head. He was my son, but he was a stranger standing in front of me and I hated it. I hated every second of it.

"And? Being a parent isn't a right, it's a privilege. A privilege that you haven't seemed to care about all that much. I know you were there for the first six years of my life, but you haven't been there for me for the past eleven, almost twelve years."

"Your mother," I started, but he cut me off before I could even start to defend myself.

"No, you don't get to do that. You don't get to blame it all on mom. I know she isn't easy to deal with, to live with. I've lived with her every single day for the past seventeen years, you think I don't know that she has extreme beliefs? You think I like going to church three times a week?"

"Three? Shit, it used to be once," I couldn't help but say. Kate had always been very involved with the church thanks to her parents, but I didn't know she had increased her involvement that much.

"Yeah, well, I guess when you find out that the man you have been in love with for the majority of your life is actually gay, it makes you go to extremes to be able to deal with it," he said with a small shrug, but there was no malice in his voice.

I was surprised that he knew I was gay and that was the reason for the divorce though. I had expected for Kate to make sure that never got out.

"You know?" I couldn't help but ask.

"Since I was twelve. Mom didn't tell me, I overheard her and Dan talking about it one night. She was worried that I would turn out to be a deviant like you, hence all of the church. She doesn't know that I know, it's not a conversation that we've ever had. She prefers to pretend that you don't exist, which is pretty accurate."

I was shocked at how well this conversation was going. I knew it wasn't very warm and fuzzy, but I had expected for him to act his age, to yell at me and tell me to go fuck myself. Instead, he was being relatively calm and rational and it actually pissed me off. I had left a six-year-old boy who always wanted one more bedtime story. Who would stomp his feet and pout for hours if he didn't get what he wanted. And now, standing here before me was a young man, a soon-to-be adult who was levelheaded and well spoken.

I had missed those formidable years where he grew into the man that he was today and that pissed me off. I wasn't mad at him, I was mad at myself, because I shouldn't have allowed for things to get to this level. I should have put a stop to all of it years ago. I wanted to ask him if he was gay as well, but that would have been too personal and honestly, I hadn't earned that level of honesty from him.

"Things were not black and white back then, Dex. I tried to fight for custody of you, but my job made it impossible to get joint custody. The judge left all of the visitations to your mother and she did everything she could to keep me from you. If I could go back in time I would change everything. I would have changed my career so I could be home more and have had a chance at joint custody. I made a lot of mistakes where you were concerned and I have to live with those regrets. I know it will take work, I have a lot to make up for, but I just want the chance to be in your life now. You are my son and I love you."

All I could do was lay everything down on the line and hope that he would be open-minded enough to try to form a relationship with me. I knew it wouldn't be as strong or as deep as it would have been had I been there for him growing up. But that didn't mean we couldn't have something real, something stable with each other.

"I know things with mom weren't easy. I know you tried. I found all of the court documents in the attic. That's not why I won't call you back. It has nothing to do with mom and everything to do with you."

I took a few steps closer to him as I spoke in a calm voice. "What about me? What is it that is keeping you from calling me back?"

"Come on, Dad, you really don't know?" he asked with a shake of his head.

The problem was, I didn't know. I didn't know what it was that I had done that was preventing my own son from reaching out to me. I didn't think I had done anything wrong that would warrant him not wanting to ever speak with me. The voicemails were polite and welcoming, I thought. I had never demanded to know why he wouldn't talk with me. I had never gotten angry or threatened him in any way. I had always left the ball in his court, despite how difficult it was for me to do that. I had no idea what the problem could be.

"No, I really don't know. I don't think I've done anything wrong with reaching out to you," I said, not even bothering with trying to hide my confusion.

"Almost every time you call and leave a voicemail you're drunk. Only one out of ten phone calls will you be sober. I don't want to talk to you if you are going to be drunk all the time." I went to speak, but he held his hand up and stopped me as he continued. "I'm not judging. I know you were in the Air Force. I looked up your unit online, so I know the type of places you were sent to, the things you would have seen. I understand why you would struggle, but I can't handle your problems on top of my own and mom's. I know that doesn't sound fair, but I have to deal with mom and her insane rules and her fucked up head. On top of that, I have to try and deal with my own anxiety and mental health problems. I can't handle anyone else's demons. I'm sorry, but I can't."

The deep hurt and pain radiated throughout his voice and it instantly sent a wave of pain through my chest to hear. I hated that he was hurting and I didn't even know why. That he was having his own mental health problems and I didn't even know what they were. I should have been there for him. I should have been someone that he could call when he was having trouble, and instead I was someone that he couldn't call because he couldn't handle more than what was already on his plate. I knew there had been times that I had called him drunk, but I didn't think I sounded drunk. I didn't think he would have an issue over it. That was my fault though, because I should have thought more deeply about it.

"Dex, I'm so sorry. You never should have to deal with any problem that either of your parents have. I didn't realize that I had called you that many times when I was intoxicated. It wasn't fair to you and it won't happen again. I want to be there for you. I want to help you with whatever you are going through. I'm always going to be there for you."

I couldn't keep my hands to myself any longer. I reached out and placed my hands on his biceps and I could feel the slight tremble within his body. He was trying to hold in his own emotions, his own demons, and all I wanted was for him to let them go, to give them to me. I could take them on and then he would be free from them. Only I knew it didn't work that way. I couldn't take his demons from him; all I could do was be there to help him fight them. All he had to do was let me.

"Tell me what is going on. Let me help you," I practically begged. There was so much hurt within him, he couldn't carry it alone anymore.

"You can't. You don't get it, Dad, you can't help me because you can't even help yourself. You're getting drunk all week long just to deal with your own demons. You can't help me because you aren't healthy yourself. Mom can't help me for the exact same reason. I'm on my own with this," he said, tears starting to build in his eyes.

I felt like my heart was being ripped right out of my chest. I had failed him on so many levels and I couldn't keep failing him.

"No, you aren't alone. You don't have to deal with this on your own. I'm going to be there for you. I'm going to stop drinking and get help for my issues, so I can be stronger and be what you need to help you with your demons. You are my son, I love you, and there is nothing in this world that I wouldn't do for you," I said as I wiped the tear that rolled down his cheek with my thumb.

It was time that I got my head out of my ass and started to get healthy again. I didn't think I was causing anyone any pain with my actions. I'd thought I was only hurting myself, but that was me being blind and selfish. My actions were hurting my son and that wasn't something I was ever going to tolerate again. He needed me, he needed my help, and in order to be the man that he needed I had to get healthy. I had to get my shit together so

I could help him heal from whatever trauma that he had endured.

"I feel so alone in this world," Dex admitted, and it only cut me deeper.

Fuck, how could I have screwed up so much?

"You aren't anymore, Son, I promise you." I pulled him in for a hug and he easily wrapped his arms around me. "I love you," I said, and I had to fight back my own tears. I was finally hugging my son; after eleven years I was hugging him.

This meeting had gone a lot differently than I had been expecting, but it was also good. I had one hell of a fight ahead of me, it wasn't going to be easy, but it was a battle I was going to be fighting to win with everything inside me. It wasn't just my life on the line this time around, but Dex's as well and I was not going to allow anything to happen to him. I didn't care what it took, I was going to be getting him healthy even if that meant I had to fix my fucked up head first. There was no war that I wouldn't go to if it meant protecting him. He was my whole world and I was never going to lose it again.

CHAPTER 17

GAGE

WHEN I WOKE up this morning I was actually looking forward to class. So much so that I wasn't even bothered by the fact that it was Monday and typically Monday mornings sucked. None of that bothered me today though, because I was going to get to see Xavier.

I had no idea how he was going to interact with me, if he would acknowledge me or ignore me like he did the last time we fooled around. So far, there hadn't been any time for either of us to interact with each other.

Once we got into the classroom, Jackson had immediately started on different word problems for various scenarios that could cause a forest fire and ways it could spread. We needed to determine the best course of action and how much time we would have before the fire spread given a wide degree of variables. The first few weren't too bad and we did the work together; however, now that we were working on our own the problems were increasing in difficulty level.

Now it was nearing the end of the day and I still had a few more scenarios to work through and everyone but one other cadet had completed their work and left. Jackson was currently helping the other cadet, leaving me on my own. I could have gone over there, but I hated feeling like an idiot, something that was left over from my high school days.

I knew I had missed a lot of school for a good reason, but that didn't make it any easier when I had to sit in class and not understand anything that was going on around me. To be the one kid who was confused when everyone else had long since got it. Teachers would always say there was no such thing as a stupid question, but I knew that was a lie, because when you had to ask for the same thing to be explained a dozen times, that question started to look pretty stupid.

I'd wanted to take this course so I could better my skills and be more useful in the future, but now it was looking like I was only going to fail, which meant returning home to the firehouse a failure.

The sound of a chair being pulled out drew my attention away from my paper to see Xavier had come over. I had been so lost in thought that I didn't even notice him coming back into the room or making his way toward me. He turned the chair around before he straddled it just to the left of me as he spoke. "You know there is nothing wrong with asking for help."

"You've clearly never been the kid who hides in the back of a classroom begging the universe for the ground to open up and swallow you whole." I tried to make it sound like I was joking, but I couldn't do it. My insecurities and disappointment in myself were coming through too much.

To my surprise, Xavier reached over and placed his hand over top of mine as he spoke. "You sacrificed a lot growing up for your brothers. Having to work to pay the bills and to take care of your dying mother, school would have been the lowest priority you had. The system failed you, Gage, not the other way around."

I wanted to believe him, I did, but sitting there and being one of the last people to leave was only making the voices in my head louder, repeatedly telling me I couldn't do this.

"The guys back at my firehouse think I took this course because I'm an adrenaline junky. And yeah, I do love to get my heart pumping. I skydive and bungee jump at least once a month, but that's not why I'm doing this. I just want to be useful. The more skills I can learn, then the more useful I can be to the department and the more people I can help. I knew there was going to be class work for this course, I just didn't expect for the material to be this hard. I don't think I'll be able to pass the final exam."

I hated that my insecurities were bubbling up, especially in front of Xavier. I was supposed to be strong and dominant, and yet here I was sounding every bit my age.

"You're not going to fail. I don't care if I have

to tutor you every night and on the weekends, you are going to pass this course. Out of all of the guys here, you are the only one who is doing this for good reasons. You're not doing it to show off or to brag to some guy in a bar. You genuinely want to help people and that is something worth fighting for. You can do this. I believe in you."

The pure strength in his voice had an instant calming effect on my nerves. I wasn't doing this alone and that reality hit me like a ton of bricks. I had spent so much of my life having to handle things on my own. Having to be the strong one, the one who could handle anything, the one who never complained.

I hadn't really had anyone that I could rely on, not since my mom got sick. Xavier's offer of support left me with mixed feelings, because as desperate as I was to have someone in my corner, someone who I could be vulnerable with, I also knew that it wouldn't last. Sooner than I would like, I would be leaving and going back home and Xavier would be here. I would have to go back to being on my own, even more so now that the twins were both gone. Allowing myself to rely on Xavier's strength here could devastate me for when I returned home.

Picking up on my inability to speak, Xavier thankfully changed the subject. "We'll take it one step at a time, it'll get easier the more you do."

I highly doubted it was ever going to get easier, but I appreciated the offer.

CHAPTER 18

GAGE

THREE HOURS. Three of the longest hours of my fucking life, but the worksheet was finally done. I wasn't too certain that the questions had gotten easier, but I had managed to get through them and I suppose that was the best I could hope for.

I did enjoy spending the past three hours sitting next to Xavier and getting to be close to him. I was struggling with not leaning over and just kissing him, even after Jackson and the other cadet left two hours ago. I had never felt this level of attraction to someone before, not even when I had discovered that I was gay and this whole world opened up to me.

The whole weekend I couldn't stop thinking about him and about our time in his back seat. I'd spent most of the weekend trying to keep my cock from getting hard and even that I wasn't successful at. I had jerked off six times in the past two days. I didn't masturbate that much when puberty hit, for fuck's sake.

It was like something had awoken within me, which made no sense because I had been having sex since I was sixteen, for close to nine years now. I was a top, I knew I was a top, I had loved being a top and not once in those nine years had I ever thought about being a bottom. And all it took was one fucking time in the back seat of Xavier's truck to make me question everything. What added to my confusion, I had thought about what it might be like to have another guy touch me like that, to be submissive to another man, but I couldn't do it. It left me feeling uninterested and unsatisfied. It was only when I thought about Xavier did it have any positive affect on me. It made no sense, but at that point I was just over trying to understand it. All I needed to know was that it felt good and I wanted more. I didn't have to over-analyze it to death.

"Thank you for staying here and helping me," I said, flashing him a genuine smile as I started to pack up.

"It's fine. With some more practice, you'll be able to do them easily. I know Jackson and I are on everyone's ass to be able to do all of this work, but the reality is once you are working on a team there is always someone that does something better and you naturally allow them to handle that stuff. You mostly need to know how to do this as a precaution in case you end up somewhere alone."

That was comforting and I knew from being at my own firehouse that lots of people had specialties and you rely on them within the field. Not everyone could be an expert at everything.

I was getting concerned about Xavier right then though. His hands were shaking, progressively getting worse as the minutes ticked by. He was starting to become pale and he just looked like he was getting sick. Xavier stood from his chair, but he leaned and I was just able to grab his arm to keep him steady.

"Hey, you okay?" I couldn't keep the concern from my voice. He really wasn't looking too good.

"Yeah, just coming down with a bug. I'll see you tomorrow." He went to move away, but I was not going to let him get away that easily. He was trembling and shaky on his feet. There was no way in hell that I was going to let him drive himself anywhere.

"Slow down, hot stuff, there's no way you can drive like this. Come on, I'll drive you home."

"I'll be fine," Xavier protested and I might have taken it seriously had he not sound like complete shit right now.

"No, you're sick and you are in no condition to be driving. Don't argue with me on this." I wasn't going to tolerate his macho bullshit. He was clearly not in any shape to drive and would be a hazard on the road.

I kept my hand on his arm to make sure he didn't collapse as we headed out of the station and toward his truck. He reluctantly passed me the keys before I helped him get into the passenger seat.

I tossed my bag into the back seat before jumping into the driver's side. My mind was instantly conjuring up what we had done in this truck just forty-eight hours prior and my body was immediately responding, but none of that was going to be taking place right now. A quick glance over at Xavier told me that he was not doing well at all.

After getting his address, I punched it into the GPS so he wouldn't have to give me directions and we headed out. I didn't talk on the drive, I knew personally that when I didn't feel well the last thing I wanted to do was answer all sorts of questions or have to hold up on my end of a conversation. Based on how pale he was looking, he was definitely having a personal battle with his stomach and talking meant a greater chance of throwing up.

Once we arrived at his address, I parked in the first spot I found on the street. I had to admit that it wasn't the area I had been expecting. There wasn't really a gang or ghetto area in the city, but this was as close as you were going to get to one. Which was surprising that he was living here because I knew he made more than enough money for a decent place. I climbed out of the truck and went around to his side as he started to get out. The trembling was overtaking his whole body at this point though, and he could barely walk. I tossed his arm over my shoulders as I spoke.

"I got you. Come on, let's get you up. What number is your apartment?" I was really hoping he was going to tell me it was on the first floor.

"Three-ten. It's on the third floor," he said with a tight voice and I could tell it was taking everything in him to not throw up right that minute, which I appreciated.

Of course though, his apartment was on the third floor and with how old these buildings looked, I knew there was no chance in hell there was an elevator. And even if there was one, I doubted that was a place you wanted to be in.

We worked together, getting into the apartment building and going up the stairs. It was not easy by any stretch of the imagination, but we finally made it to his apartment.

I took the keys from his shaky hands and quickly unlocked his front door before we stumbled inside. I didn't spend much time looking around, because I knew he needed the bathroom before his will power failed us both. I quickly took him to the right and down the very short hallway to the bathroom. I brought him in and helped to sit him down on the floor right next to the toilet.

"Let's get this off real quick," I said, as I bent down and started to remove his jacket. It was more comfortable to throw up without a leather jacket on, and, yup, knew that from personal experience. With his jacket off, I then turned my attention to his black boots.

"I got it," Xavier's shaky voice filled the silence of the bathroom.

"You can barely function while shaking so badly. Just relax. Do you need anything? Water, a pillow or a blanket?" I had no idea how long he was going to be stuck in the bathroom and I knew from experience that sometimes it was nice to just curl up and try to sleep it off on the cool bathroom floor. I knew some would find that gross, but when you were constantly fighting with throwing up, it was also nice knowing that if you did need to puke, you only had a few inches to reach the toilet and not twenty feet.

"No, I'll be fine. Just hit the lock on the front door on your way out."

"All right, call me if you need anything though. And thank you for your help tonight," I said, flashing him a warm smile as I grabbed his boots and his jacket to bring out into the living area.

"Thanks for driving me."

"I hope you feel better soon," I said before I headed out, closing the bathroom door behind me.

I brought his items out into the living area and for the first time I was able to see what his place looked like. I placed his boots down by the front door and draped his jacket over the back of a chair. It certainly wasn't what I had been expecting for his place. It was a bachelor apartment, one that was not very clean or organized. There was nothing personal in the whole place, nothing on his walls, nothing that would indicate who Xavier was. There was a bed that was on a box spring on the floor and the sheets were a mess. There were take out containers on an old coffee table and spread over the kitchen counter. There were empty liquor bottles and a huge pile of empty beer cans to go with it. A quick look in his small fridge and cupboards showed me that there wasn't any food in this place. Now it was all making sense. Xavier didn't have a stomach bug. He was going through alcohol withdrawals.

Fuck.

That was a completely different level of seriousness. I had once helped a fellow firefighter going through alcohol withdrawals and they were horrible on his body. For the first week it was the worst and then it would get easier during that second week. Even after the withdrawals, you had to deal with the reasons behind the drinking.

For Xavier, that meant him having to deal with his trauma from going to war. It wouldn't be surprising for him to have PTSD. Most veterans returned home with it and Xavier was functioning, but it appeared that he had been functioning with alcohol. For some reason though, he was trying to quit, and I couldn't help but wonder why. Regardless of the reason, he was trying to stop and I wasn't about to leave and let him go through this alone.

I removed my coat and started by making the bed. I'd get out here cleaned up before I would go and check in on Xavier. He didn't have to go through this alone and he was going to need all of the help that he could get until the withdrawals were over. I was just hoping that Xavier would be able to hold on and fight long enough to make it through the withdrawals and then he could start to work on healing from the trauma.

CHAPTER 19

Xavier

I was dying.

That was the only way I could think of to describe what I was feeling. It felt like my insides were trying to escape my body. Every time I threw up, I kept waiting to see if my kidney would be in the toilet. I knew withdrawals were going to be bad. I had done the research so I was mentally prepared for what was to come, but I didn't expect for it to feel as bad as it did.

I couldn't stop shaking, my stomach was cramping, I was throwing up things I had eaten when I was twelve at this point. I was freezing, but sweating at the same time, and my skin felt like there were millions of bugs crawling underneath it. I felt like complete shit and I knew it was only going to get worse as each day passed for the next week. I had been through a lot in my life, but detoxing was looking like it would be the hardest thing I had ever gone through and that included my time overseas.

If I was just doing this for myself, I would have said fuck it. I wouldn't be going through it. I wouldn't be putting my body through this torture. But I wasn't doing this just for me.

I was doing it for Dexter.

He needed a parent. He needed someone who could be strong for him so he had the freedom to work through whatever trauma he was holding on to. He needed me to be healthy and I wasn't going to let him down.

Not ever again.

I was curled up into a ball of misery on the cool bathroom floor when the sound of my front door closing caught my attention. I should have been alone. Gage should have left long ago, and considering he was the only other person who knew I lived here, that meant a stranger was in my home. It would be just my luck to be getting robbed right now, though I didn't know what they'd think I had that would be worth stealing. I didn't own shit.

I opened my eyes when I heard footsteps coming toward me. To my surprise though, it wasn't a burglar, but Gage. He had left earlier, I knew he did because I heard the door close, but for some reason he was back.

"What are you doing here?" I managed to get out, but it was a struggle with my stomach.

He had removed his coat and he was standing there with one of my pillows and a blue Gatorade in his hands. He approached me as he spoke.

"Here, putting your head elevated, even a bit, will help with any lightheadedness or dizziness. I also got you some Gatorades to help get some electrolytes into you. I know you are just going to throw it up, but some will still be absorbed through your stomach and that can help reduce the nausea."

I let him help me raise my head just enough for him to get the pillow underneath it. What I couldn't figure out was why he had come back. I wasn't his responsibility. He had class in the morning. He should have been back at the dorms getting a proper sleep. He was going to need his brain fresh to survive the class work. I'd meant what I said; I would tutor him and make sure he was able to pass the written exam. Gage had heart and the desire to help people, and that was worth the time and effort I would have to put in so he would be able to pass the exam.

"What are you doing here?" I asked again, because he clearly ignored my question last time.

"I know you don't have the flu. Alcohol withdrawals are serious and you shouldn't have to be going through them alone. I've done this before with one of the guys at my firehouse. I'm not an expert, but I at least know a few tricks. I got rid of your empties as well, by the way, and I double-checked that there wasn't any left in the apartment. I also cleaned up a bit."

"OCD?" I teased, that was easier than me having to face my feelings about someone being here and actually helping me. I was used to doing everything on my own ever since my parents died. I didn't exactly know how to handle

Gage's willingness to help without me even asking for it.

He gave me a rich smile as he spoke. "No, not even close. I'm just used to cleaning. Between the twins when they were younger and my mom being sick, taking care of people is something I am really good at."

He got up and grabbed a washcloth from my bathroom stand before he wet it and rang it out. It only made sense that Gage would be a natural when it came to care giving. He did have a lot of experience with it and I had to imagine while his mother was going to radiation and chemotherapy that she was sick often.

I had a lot of respect for the woman. To be told that she was going to die no matter what treatment was done, but to still go through it. To put herself through that pain and added sickness just so she could get a couple more years on this Earth. And not for herself, she did it for her children, so Gage could get to a legal age where her children could stay together. It was one of the more honorable and courageous things I had ever heard.

Gage bent back down and he placed the cool, damp cloth against my forehead as he spoke. "This can help settle your stomach. Something about the cold against your body that kinda calms everything down."

"Thank you, but you don't have to stay. I'll be okay. You need to sleep for class tomorrow." I could admit that I was not very good at having people around me when I was sick and vulnerable. It had been like that my whole life and after the

Air Force it did get worse. I was miserable, but that didn't mean I needed to make others miserable around me. Gage should be back at the dorms, sleeping and focusing on the course. He didn't need to worry about me.

He went and shuffled over so his back was against the wall and he was sitting with his legs stretched out in front of him by my head as he spoke. "This is far from my first all-nighter and it won't be my last. The first day is always the hardest and I know I have to go to class come morning, but the least I can do is be here for you during the first part of the twenty-four hours from hell. I'm not leaving, so you might as well accept it. It's not exactly like you can strong-arm me out of here. You might as well use me as a distraction."

I could keep arguing, but it wasn't going to do me any good. He wasn't going to leave me alone and if I was honest with myself, I didn't want him to. I closed my eyes as I spoke. "Can you text Jackson from my phone and tell him I won't be in? Just tell him I have the flu. He'll know it's bullshit, but he won't call me out on it." Another reason why I loved that man, he was perfectly fine to leave you in our own ignorant bubble.

"Got it," Gage said as he reached for my phone that I had placed on the counter by the sink. "Can I ask why the sudden desire to quit drinking?"

The first thought that came to my mind was that it was none of his fucking business. However, if he was going to be here for me and help me get through the withdrawals, he deserved to know my reasoning behind it. He deserved to know what I was fighting for so if there did come a point where I wanted to give in, he would be able to remind me.

"Friday night I went and saw Dex. It had been years since we'd talked. My ex-wife didn't handle it very well when she discovered I was gay. She comes from a highly religious family and she saw it as a sign from the devil. She took Dex and I had to fight to try and see him. I went through the court process, but I was in the Air Force and my job came with an unstable schedule. The judge didn't grant me joint custody and left visitation rights up to her. I almost never got to see him and as he got older, Dex started to grow distant with me, angry with me. He wouldn't take my calls, wouldn't return them. He didn't want to see me."

"I'm sorry, that couldn't have been easy. I can't even imagine what I would have done had something like that happened with the twins," he said with complete understanding to his voice, and part of me knew that was why I was telling him any of this to begin with. He would understand where I was coming from. He would understand the pain that I had been going through.

"Friday night, I decided to just show up at the basketball court by his house. He likes to play and I knew he went there after school. I wanted to explain myself, to tell him that I was gay and that I had fought for him. He already knew though. This whole time I thought he didn't want to speak with me was because of the lies his mother was telling him. Turns out, he didn't want to speak with me because I called him when I was drunk more times than sober. He said he understood that I would have seen horrible shit overseas, but he had his own problems and struggles with mental health, he couldn't take mine on." It still hurt to know that my own son was struggling and he wouldn't tell me about it because he didn't think I was stable and healthy enough to help him. I knew I had been a shit father, but I didn't know that was the reason I had been.

Gage let out a low whistle before he spoke with concern in his tone. "That's deep and fucked up. Did he tell you about his struggles?"

"I asked, but he said I wasn't able to help him, because I couldn't help myself. I promised him that I would get healthy again, so I could be strong and stable, so I could be able to help him carry his problems. I think something happened to him, but he's not willing to talk about it with me. Not yet, at least. I have to get better for him, so I can help him get better. I started to wean myself off from the booze, but when I ran out last night, I couldn't bring myself to purchase more just so I could quit. I wasn't planning on doing this cold turkey, but maybe it's better to get it over and done with."

I wasn't really all that certain on what the best way to do it was, but I was in the thick of things now and I was not about to change course. I was going to quit cold turkey and just hope for the best at this point.

"It's not going to be easy. You are going to feel like shit for about a week, but then you will start to feel more human by the end of it. Quitting drinking is only one part of it though. You'll need to speak with a therapist to correct the trauma, otherwise you will slip right back into the bottle."

"I know and I will once I get through the withdrawals."

I hated the idea of speaking with a shrink, but I also knew that I had to otherwise I wouldn't be able to get through the cravings once they started. I had to take this seriously if I was going to be able to help Dex. He needed to see me working hard and doing things the right way in order for him to start as well. I was doing this for him and there wasn't anything I wouldn't do for my son. The first step was getting through these withdrawals then the real work would start.

CHAPTER 20

XAVIER

GUNFIRE WAS COMING at me from all directions. I was fighting to hold the chopper steady as I picked up the SEAL Team that were in desperate need of an exfil. The situation was a serious clusterfuck that was only getting worse as each second ticked by. Landing had been difficult, but we couldn't have them repel up with this much gunfire. They would just have been moving targets dangling in the air. The pings of bullets off of the metal of my chopper were echoing all around me. I knew it was going to be a difficult take off, but staying here would be suicide. The SEALs started to fire back as I lifted up off the ground. I knew I just needed to get us high enough to where the tangos' bullets wouldn't be able to reach.

As we continued to climb, I started to head off toward the mountains directly in front of us. I had to get around the mountains and then we would be in a safer airfield and I could get these guys back to the base.

"*RPG! Take 'em down!*" one of the guys, Parker, I believe, called out and I was instantly swearing.

Of course they had RPGs, because that was the one piece that we were missing to turn this mission into a complete fucking disaster. RPGs could travel a lot fucking farther than a bullet, and they also had the power to bring this chopper down and kill us all.

I couldn't focus on that though, I needed to trust that the guys would be able to shoot the tangos down before they could get one of those RPGs released. All of my hope went right out the window though, when I rounded the mountain and was just able to make out the tango standing on the side of it with an RPG launcher aimed right at us.

I didn't have the time to maneuver us out of the direct path of the RPG as the second we rounded that corner, the tango had released the RPG and it was heading directly toward us.

"*Hold on, we're going down!*" I shouted before the RPG even hit us. I couldn't avoid it, but I could give the guys behind me the best chance they had to brace themselves for the impact of the RPG and the spinout I was going to have to fight against if I wanted to land this bird down without getting us all killed.

I gripped my stick with everything that I had as the RPG hit the tail of my bird. The second the tail was blown off, we were spinning out of control and heading for the ground at a rapid descent. Alarms were going off from the dash, as if I didn't fucking know we were going down.

The guys were all banging around in the back and I was hoping that they had managed to strap in to prevent them from being sucked out of the two sides. I couldn't think about that right now though, I had to focus all of my energy to keep us from impacting the ground at the wrong angle that would cause the engine to blow up.

As the ground rapidly approached, it was getting harder for me to hold onto the stick as the whole chopper shook. When the left side of my bird hit the ground we bounced before skidding across the rough desert ground. When we finally came to a stop I was frozen in place. My head was pounding and it felt like my heart was going to break through my chest. There was smoke coming off of the engine and I knew we had to get moving before the diesel in the engine blew up.

Forcing my body to move, I unclicked the seatbelt as I looked over to see that my co-pilot was dead. His empty eyes were looking out the front windshield with his neck at an unnatural position. The impact to the ground had killed him.

Slowly and carefully, I moved out of my seat to see some of the guys had survived. They were all injured, and three were missing, which meant they had gotten sucked out during the descent.

"We gotta move," I said as I went over to the first guy that I could to help him get up and out. It was only a matter of time before those tangos started to make their way toward us to finish what they started.

Out of the ten of them that I had picked up, only four were alive. I knew they wouldn't want to leave their fallen brothers, but we didn't have a choice, we had to move.

We were all injured, but we didn't let that slow us down. The second we got out of the chopper, we were moving toward a series of hills. We needed to get to high ground so we could pick off the tangos while we waited for help to arrive.

I looked over to my right to make sure the guys were all still moving, only to see the SEAL closest to me getting shot in the head and dropping to the ground.

"Xavier!"

I looked around, trying to see who was calling my name, who needed help, but all I could see were the bodies of the SEALs bleeding out.

"Xavier! Wake up!"

There was that voice again, but wake up?

I wasn't asleep, who the fuck could sleep through this?

I had to get to higher ground; it was my only chance at survival. I took off at a sprint, but the ground started to shake and each step I took threatened to bring me down to my knees. A sharp pain through my lower left side of my stomach caused me to drop to the ground. I could feel the wetness of my own blood soaking through my shirt. Black spots started to dance before my eyes and before I even knew it, the darkness overtook me.

"Xavier!"

My eyes snapped open at the sound of my name. There was someone touching me, a tango, he was on top of me. Instantly, I was wrapping my hands around his neck and flipping us so I was straddling his hips with him underneath me. He might have been the tango who shot me and I was not going to allow him to get another chance in.

He squirmed underneath me, his hands going to my arms, hitting my forearms trying to break my hold on his neck. When that didn't work, he started to move his left hand around on the ground, but he wasn't going to find anything in the desert that he could use as a weapon.

The side of my head exploded as I heard glass shatter and it was enough for me to loosen my grip for a moment. The blow to my head was quickly followed by a swift kick to my gut, pushing me back off of the tango and into a boulder, a smooth and cold boulder.

Wait, what was a boulder doing in the desert?

It was cold underneath my arm, it shouldn't be cold.

"Xavier? Baby?" A rough voice broke through my confusion, a voice I knew, but it didn't sound right.

Gage.

What the fuck was Gage doing here in the desert?

"Baby, are you with me? You're in California. We're in your apartment."

No, that didn't make any sense. I was just in the desert. My bird had just been shot down. I had been shot. They were coming for me. I couldn't be in California.

I blinked a few times to try and clear the fog that had invaded my mind. My head was killing me and my stomach was not too happy. My whole body hurt and I felt clammy and gross. I opened my eyes and I was no longer surrounded by desert, but in my own bathroom.

My hand wandered over to my left side where the bullet had torn through it, but there was no blood, no pain. I looked over to where Gage was and instantly my heart dropped to my stomach. He had bruising already coming through on his neck.

Bruising I had put there.

Fuck.

It wasn't a tango that I was attacking, it was Gage.

"Gage, I'm so sorry," I immediately said as the tears started to build up in my eyes.

I could have killed him.

He slid over to me without any hesitation and reached out and pulled me against his chest as he spoke. "It's okay, you didn't know it was me. It's okay. I'm okay."

This wasn't okay. I had put my hands around his neck; I had tried to kill him. None of this was okay and he shouldn't be trying to comfort me right now. He should be horrified and running out of here and never looking back.

"I'm sorry," I said again as I fought with the tears. I was normally able to control my emotions better, but I couldn't right now. Maybe that was because of the withdrawals, but either way, I couldn't seem to lock my emotions back up.

"You don't have anything to be sorry for. I'm okay. You didn't know it was me." He placed a kiss on the top of my head as he ran his hand up and down my back.

The fact that he was trying to comfort me after my hands were just wrapped around his throat only cut me deeper, because he genuinely was a good man and I had hurt him. I had almost killed him. I knew I had demons. I knew getting sober and working through them wasn't going to be easy, but I never suspected that I could attack someone who was trying to help me. That I could dream so deeply that I thought I was back there. It all felt real. I remembered everything with perfect clarity, as if I went back in time and was reliving it again.

How the fuck was that even possible?

"I don't know what happened. I thought you were a tango. I don't know what happened." I shakily pulled back from Gage's embrace. I was feeling waves of heat overtaking me and I was worried that my stomach was going to flip on me again and the last thing I wanted to do was throw up on him.

"You had a flashback. It's common with PTSD. The withdrawals most likely triggered it. It's why when you go through the process of getting sober it's important to speak with a therapist afterward to help reduce and eliminate triggers," he calmly explained, but his voice was still rough.

"It's never happened before."

Why would I have a flashback after all of this time?

I knew some vets had flashbacks or even locked in memories, but that had never happened to me. It was part of the reason why I never believed the Shrink I had to go and see after I got out when he said that I had PTSD. I had no signs, at least none that I would consider to be connected to PTSD. I knew I was fooling myself, but at the time it was just easier to believe that I was fine, that the shrink didn't know what they were talking about. Now I was getting a dose of reality slapped right across my face.

"That's not uncommon. Your drinking most likely has been treating your PTSD symptoms and now that you are not drinking they are starting to appear. I know it doesn't feel like it, but it's actually a good thing."

"How the fuck is almost killing you a good thing?" I couldn't help but snap at him. For fuck's sake, I had my hands wrapped around his throat, squeezing the life out of him. None of this was okay. None of this was a good sign.

"It means you are finally on the road to healing. I'm not saying it won't be hard and it will get worse before it gets better, but now there is a real chance that it will get better. You just need to remember that you are doing this for your son. So you can help him overcome his own demons. If you can get through to the other side of this, then everything that happens will be worth it."

I wished I had even a fraction of the strength and belief that he had, but right now I couldn't get the image out of my head over what happened not even five feet from where we sat. I knew going through withdrawals would be dangerous for me, but I didn't think I would become dangerous to other people.

What if I was in class or worse, in the air, when a flashback hit?

How could I trust myself not to cause harm to someone else?

It was my job as a pilot to ensure the safety of everyone on board my bird and right now, I was the biggest threat to their safety.

How the hell was I going to be able to trust myself with their lives while in the air again?

"Don't, don't do that. I can see it all over your face that you are doubting yourself. That you are already thinking worst-case scenarios and you need to stop. Right now you are sick, in pain and exhausted, everything is going to appear so much worse than it truly is to you right now. The best thing you can do is focus on the next two weeks and getting your body physically healthy again and recovered from the withdrawals. Then you can start to worry about everything else that comes after it. Starting with a shower. It will help with your withdrawals and it might make you feel a bit more human." He offered me a warm smile and I still couldn't believe he wasn't running out of here. A shower did sound good though, and maybe it would help to make me feel a bit better.

I gave a slight nod and Gage helped me to get my sweat-soaked shirt off. The second the air hit my damp skin, I felt goosebumps overtaking every inch of my bare body. I still couldn't understand how I could be hot and cold all at the same time.

"You know, this is vastly different to what I thought the first time I would be able to actually see you naked would look like," Gage teased as stood up.

"You have seen me naked," I countered as I slowly pushed myself to my feet.

"No, I've felt you naked. I've never actually seen you in the light. We were naked in the cave and then under a damn bar parking lot light, I barely could see anything. I had hoped the next time would be sexy ripping each other's clothes off type of naked and less Nurse Ratched."

"You don't find nurses sexy?" Despite how horrible I was feeling, the fact that he had been thinking about being with me again had my blood pooling down to my cock.

"No, and I don't understand what makes them so sexy? I mean, if you need a nurse it's because you're in the hospital either sick or seriously hurt. The last thing I'm thinking about while laid up in a hospital bed is having sex," he commented as his hands went over to my belt and started to open it for me, which I was thankful for because I couldn't get my hands to stop shaking.

"I don't know. You are looking pretty sexy right now." I couldn't help but flirt.

"And you have looked much better. Once you are feeling more human, then we can revisit this discussion on what is sexy," he easily countered, flashing me a warm smile and I couldn't help the light chuckle that slipped from my lips.

He was right about that. I was far from sexy right now, but I was looking forward to getting to do something more x-rated with him in the future. If nothing else, that was one hell of a motivation to reach the end of these two weeks so I would be healthy again physically and we could hopefully move forward and have sex this time around. Our last time opened his eyes, at least I hoped it had, that being a bottom with me could bring him to a whole new level of pleasure. Now, I just needed to be able to handle giving him that experience.

One thing was for certain, these next two weeks were going to be some of the longest weeks of my life.

CHAPTER 21

GAGE

"WE'RE ALMOST at the drop zone, everyone get ready."

Hearing Xavier's strong, gruff voice bark out orders was like music to my ears. It had been a long two weeks with balancing between my course work and Xavier's withdrawals. He never let me miss a single day in school, but every night I would go over to his place, usually with soup, and make sure he was doing okay.

I knew withdrawals from any substance were brutal on your body and I wanted to make sure that he was recovering properly. I was very relieved after four days when he started to make a turn for the better. He was able to eat more than soup and he wasn't throwing up as much. After a full week, he had a bit more energy and he was coming back to life. All were good signs.

Today he was back to work and I was very happy to have him back, because not only did I get to look at his sexy ass all day, but we were back up in his chopper and getting to make up for the lost time with our practical training.

If Jackson suspected he had more than the flu for the past two weeks, he didn't give any indication. I had a feeling he knew, but he seemed to care for Xavier and he wasn't about to report him to the Upper Brass.

I strapped myself into the repel harness as we neared our drop zone location. Today, we were practicing going up and down the repel line, plus picking up a dummy and using the basket to simulate a real life rescue. All of the guys were excited for it and couldn't wait to get started.

We could only go up in groups of five and this time I got to be in the first group. I wasn't certain how Xavier would feel about flying so soon after his withdrawals, but he seemed ready for it. We hadn't really talked about his flashback and I knew he was still feeling guilty about trying to kill me. I had meant what I said, it wasn't his fault. He wasn't aware of his actions. He thought I was someone who was trying to kill him and his body did what it was trained to do. I wasn't about to hold that against him, even though I knew others would have.

Getting to class the next day was an interesting time. It wasn't like I had a turtleneck or makeup that I could use to hide the fact that there was bruising all around my neck. There were obviously questions and I had lied and said I stepped in to break up a fight at a bar and got hurt for my troubles. It was believable enough, or the guys were at least nice enough to allow me the privilege of the lie. Either way, I was relieved that it hadn't turned into a big deal.

"All right, we're at the drop zone. I will hover here. You are going to go one at a time all the way down and wait until everyone else has gone. Then you will come back up one at a time. Mick is going to control the rigging for you. Remember to go at a steady pace," Xavier advised.

Mick was one of the firefighters from the station house up here. He had come by to help us with the repel gear so all of us could get to go down without one of us having to always work the rigging gear.

I hooked myself into the line and turned around before stepping down onto the landing skid. Grabbing my line with both hands, I bent down before pushing off from the landing skid and started to lower myself down to the ground. I had about a hundred feet before I would reach the ground and I knew from my repelling class that I couldn't go too fast on the way down or I risked landing wrong and breaking a bone in my foot or leg. I also didn't want to go too slow, because if this was a real forest fire, I couldn't be dangling above the fire in the air.

I kept an eye on my pace and once I was close enough to the ground, I put my feet down and landed perfectly. I unhooked myself and then stepped back to allow the next cadet to come down.

This was the type of stuff that I liked to do. The chance to utilize my skills and to be able to use the same skills for various situations to help more people. This was making up for all of the long hours sitting in a classroom feeling like a moron. And to make this day even better, Xavier was taking me out for dinner as a thank you for helping him through his withdrawals for the past two weeks.

He didn't need to thank me. I had enjoyed spending the time with him, even if it was while he was sick. Not only had I gotten to get to know him a bit more on a personal level, it had also helped to take my mind off of Asher and Greyson being out in the world on their own. And if all went well tonight, we would be going back to his place after dinner for quite possibly the best sex of my life.

CHAPTER 22

GAGE

I MADE my way down to the parking lot of the dorms. It was nearing seven at night and Xavier was coming by to pick me up.

We had worked all day long doing practical drills and we both wanted to take a shower and get changed before heading to dinner. I was really hoping it would be a quick dinner followed by a very sexy dessert. I also had no idea where he was taking me, but this was his town and I trusted that he wasn't taking me to some vegan restaurant.

As excited as I was to be going on this date, I was also nervous. It had been a long time since I had gone on a date. Actually, if I was being honest, I'd never really gone on a date, not an official one. There had been times I'd had sex with a guy and then we were both hungry so we went out for a burger, but I wouldn't count that as a date.

I'd never really had a boyfriend. There was no time growing up with working and taking care of the twins. Then when things got easier with the twins, I discovered sex and dating didn't seem important. Now, I was twenty-five and going on my first real date, which was pretty sad.

I spotted Xavier's truck pulling up and ambled over to it, quickly jumping into the passenger seat. The second the door was closed, he reached over and placed his hand on the right side of my face and pulled me in for a kiss. This was what I had been dying for. We hadn't done anything since that night in his truck and I was in desperate need to feel him against me again. To be able to taste him.

I felt his tongue against my lips, seeking entrance, and I simply granted it to him. Our tongues fought for control, for dominance, and this time around I wasn't going to give it up to him that easily. He could be in control later.

I moaned as he deepened the kiss and I briefly thought to say fuck it to dinner and just go back to his place for some very delicious dessert. All too soon for my liking, Xavier pulled back and broke the kiss.

"Hi," he said, flashing me a smirk. He was clearly proud of himself for getting me all hot and heavy.

"I'm suddenly starving for something much more fun than food."

He let out a deep chuckle before he spoke. "Oh, trust me, what I have planned for you is going to require you to fuel up first."

"Or we could go back to your place, have

some fun, then fuel up before having more fun," I counter offered.

"Now that is very tempting, but the second I get you into my bed, I'm not letting you out until morning," he said with a wink, before he moved away from me and shifted his truck into drive.

I was really hoping that was a promise. Hell, I would be happy to be late tomorrow if it meant some morning delight first. I put my belt on and sat back as Xavier drove us to a restaurant. With this being my first real date there was one thing I needed to know first.

"Are you out?"

"What?" he asked, glancing over at me with his brows slightly furrowed.

"I'm out as gay. I'm not hiding who I am. I just wanted to know if you were also out."

I was terrified of what answer he was going to give. If he wasn't out, then that meant we would have to hide this growing relationship. That shouldn't bother me considering in two weeks I was going to be back home and he would be here. We wouldn't really get to see each other again. I didn't even know if Xavier wanted something more than just a month long fling. At the same time, if he said he was out, I was worried that would make me like him even more. Out and proud firefighters were not very common, although more recently they were finding the courage to come out, be true to themselves, and it spoke volumes about the type of men they were.

"I guess I'm out. I don't know. I've never stated that I was gay, but I've never said I wasn't. Jackson knows and most of the guys that I work with know.

I'm not screaming my status from a rooftop, but I'm not hiding either. It certainly wasn't instant. I had kept my orientation a secret all through high school and then in the Air Force. When I got to the fire department, I still kept quiet about it at first, but then Jackson caught me with a guy in an alley, then another guy that I worked with did. There were never any problems over it, so I stopped worrying about someone catching me."

I couldn't stop the smile that spread across my face. He was like a lot of the other guys that I knew that were gay in the department. They were more focused on being themselves than trying to pin a cape to their shoulders and be a spokesperson for homosexuality in first responders. It was good though, it meant we wouldn't have to pretend to be friends if someone spotted us at dinner. It also meant another small piece of my heart was lost to him.

"That's good to hear. I'm out too."

He gave me a rich smile in return. "I figured. When did you come out?"

"I knew when I was a young teenager that I was gay and I told my mom pretty quickly. The twins grew up knowing I liked guys so I didn't have to come out to them. With the department, technically the first day in the academy when I gave my PT instructor head after a very rigorous workout."

"What?" he asked, shocked, but there was also a mixture of jealousy that I detected in his voice.

"You know that I've been with other instructors and firefighters. He was very much in the closet and it was only a one-time thing. I felt very dirty when I discovered he had a wife and three children at home. I've never hidden that I was gay and there have been problems that came up over the years with bigoted assholes, nothing ever serious though." I had lucked out that I ended up in a firehouse with other gay firefighters and my Captain was also gay. It made being true to myself a lot easier.

"I'm glad that you haven't had any problems with anyone, at least not any major problems. Though, I don't like the thought of you with any other instructors, or another man for that matter."

The slight jealous tone did not go unnoticed. Now would have been the perfect time to speak up and ask him about when I went back home in two weeks, but my fear of his answer had won out over my curiosity. I knew it was a conversation we were going to have to have, but it didn't need to be tonight.

When we arrived at the restaurant, a gourmet burger joint, Xavier parked his truck and we headed inside. I loved a good burger so I was really looking forward to getting our food. We grabbed a spot out on the back patio and I was pleased that it wasn't all that busy right now. I wanted to be able to talk freely with Xavier without having to worry about someone over-hearing us.

The second we sat down, the hostess took our drink order, both of us getting water.

"You know you could have ordered a drink. I have to get used to people drinking around me," Xavier said, flashing me a warm smile.

"I know, and yes, you do need to get used to

being around alcohol and not have any. But I just watched you spend the past two weeks feeling like shit and getting healthy again. I'm not about to test the waters. I don't need to drink to have a good time, not to worry. Plus, I have a feeling I am going to need the hydration for later," I added with a flirty smirk and I was rewarded with a rich smile for my effort.

"Before things go much further between us, there is something I wanted to talk to you about," he started with a serious tone, and I couldn't help but worry about what he wanted to talk to me about before we even got to have sex.

"It's about the flashback."

"I already told you that it was okay. That it wasn't your fault," I instantly cut him off. I didn't want him worrying that I would hold it against him or that I would be scared of him. I didn't really have much experience with PTSD, but I knew the signs and a little about it from work. With Greyson going into the military, it was something I would be doing more research on so I could be better prepared should Greyson develop PTSD himself.

"I know. I did some research and the best way to prevent a flashback from happening again is to talk about it. I have an appointment with a shrink tomorrow, but I hoped to talk to you about it, if you were interested in hearing it," he explained, and I could hear the self-consciousness slipping into his body now. It was obvious he expected me to tell him I didn't want to hear it, but that couldn't have been further from the truth. I wanted to know everything about him and if he was willing to share with me, then I was more than happy to listen to him all night.

"I will always be interested and willing to hear about anything from your past, present, or future." I *really* wanted to know about his plans for the future.

"Being in the Air Force, it was different compared to the on the ground troops. We had our own dangers, but you could also fool yourself into thinking you were in a safer position than on the ground troops. There had been a lot of operations where someone was bleeding out in the back of my bird. A lot of close calls with RPGs and heat-seeking missiles. There had been times where I couldn't go in and pick up the troops, when the area was too hot, and I couldn't get clearance to go in."

"It had to have been hard for you though, to know that people needed help and you couldn't help them." I couldn't even imagine what it must have felt like to be told that you couldn't go in and rescue people. I was thankful that so far in my career, I hadn't had a fire where I had been ordered to stay out of the building. It happened though, sometimes the fire was just burning too hot and moving too fast that sending anyone in to rescue the people trapped inside would only bring more casualties. I knew some of the older guys that I worked with had been in that position and it had destroyed some of them. A few were able to continue working, but the majority couldn't handle the guilt that ate away at them. I suspected that Xavier was living with survivor's guilt and that was making his PTSD worse. It was something that his therapist would have to help him work through.

"It was. We had always been taught that you didn't leave a brother behind and I was right there and couldn't help them. But if I went against my orders, then I was putting more people at risk. There was one operation that stands out the most to me and that was what the flashback was," he admitted with some pain starting to edge into his voice.

I reached over and took his hand in mine as I spoke, "What happened, baby?"

He sucked in a shaky breath before he spoke. "I was sent to pick up a SEAL team that was pinned down with enemy combatants surrounding them. I wasn't even able to land to load them on, they had to repel up, but it wasn't a typical repel line like you've been on. It's one line with multiple hooks along it so a whole team can hook on and everyone gets brought up while you fly away."

"That sounds dangerous for everyone involved." I couldn't imagine being on a line, just dangling in the air with gunshots going off all around me. I didn't even want to think about Greyson doing any of it.

"It is, but sometimes it's the only option we have. We can't always land a chopper where the troops are, especially the Black Ops guys." He let out a sigh before continuing. "That day everything was going wrong. What pissed me off though, was I got them all on board. We were feet away from being in the clear when the RPG hit. I did my best to land us without the chopper going up in flames, which I did, but not all of the guys had the chance to get strapped in before we got hit. I lost a couple on the way down. They flew right out while we were spinning. By the time we landed, most of the guys were dead. I was able to get out with who was left. We were in a valley in between a couple mountains. We needed to get to higher ground if we were going to stand a chance. We never made it through. The insurgents were ready for us. I got shot; you've seen the scar. It gets a bit fuzzy, but an insurgent reached me and it all went black."

He paused again and I could tell that what he was going to say next was still extremely painful for him and I suspected it was the cause of his PTSD. At least what pushed it into overdrive. I didn't doubt for a second that he didn't have some level of PTSD before the event. He cleared his throat and finished his story.

"When I woke up, I was in this cave with a couple of the other guys. They beat me up pretty good and waterboarded me. They didn't do anything too extreme, they knew by the patch on my uniform that I was just a pilot. I was the guy sent in to pick up the SEALs. I wouldn't have been briefed on their mission. But because of that, I had to watch as the few remaining SEALs that I was tasked to rescue, to get them safe, were tortured and killed. It took about three weeks before we were rescued and by then, it was just me. The Upper Brass had already filed the paperwork for me to be discharged before I even hit the hospital."

My heart hurt for him. I knew war was horrific. Everyone had heard the horror stories; it was why I was terrified of Greyson going over there, even in a medic position. No one was safe and I would be left home hoping that my phone didn't ring or I opened my door and saw some stranger in a suit standing on the other side. I had no idea how I was going to get through any of it.

"I'm so sorry. I know that doesn't really help or offer much comfort, but I am sorry you had to experience it. I don't know how you came back from something like that and yet you have. I know it might not feel like it to you, but look at where you are, baby. You have a job. You're still able to do the thing that you love, flying. You can still help people. I have to imagine that most people who have gone through what you did, have seen the things you have, they wouldn't be able to hold a job, an apartment, getting sober. I know it might not seem like a lot to you, but it's huge, baby."

I didn't want him thinking that the strides he'd made to get better were nothing. It was everything to him and I knew it would be everything to Dexter as well. It takes a strong person to get sober and start therapy all with the hope of getting healthy. He should be proud of himself.

"I don't have a choice, I have to be there for my son. I think if I didn't have Dex, then I probably would have given up long ago," he said, before he paused and I could tell he was getting his thoughts and emotions back in control. "How are your brothers?"

"They are doing really good, surprisingly. I wasn't too certain how long either of them would last, but Asher is loving the ranch, though I think he has the hots for his boss. As for Greyson, he's hanging in. He's acing his in-class work and he is passing the physical aspects. I guess a few of the guys are helping him with it. They both are in good spirits," I said with a small shrug. I still hadn't gotten over the idea of them not being home when I got back. I also was still trying to process Greyson being in the Army. At least they were happy though, and not regretting their decisions.

"Good for them. It's not easy to start a new life and they have both embraced it. Not many kids at eighteen do that anymore."

"A huge part of me wishes they were still tucked away safe at the house. I know I can't keep them forever, but it's hard to let them go."

"I wish I could tell you it gets easier, but it doesn't. But it will become normal."

I wasn't certain that was something I wanted, but I knew I would have to adapt regardless. They were growing up and there was nothing I could do about that. All I could do was be there for them when they needed help.

Pushing all of that aside, I focused on our date and what was hopefully going to come tonight.

CHAPTER 23

Xavier

I OPENED my front door and allowed Gage to walk in first.

The rest of dinner had gone great and I would have been happy to take Gage back to the dorms if he wasn't certain he wanted to do anything tonight. He had assured me though, that he did want to come back to my place, and I was so happy, I could have done a dance.

"Do you want a drink?" I asked.

He strolled over to me, placed his hand on my chest, and pushed me back against the door as he spoke. "You don't have to treat me like a delicate flower. The only drink I need is from your cock. Though, I would prefer for it to be in my ass. So why don't you shut up, and fuck me already?" He flashed me a sexy smirk.

That was all I needed to hear.

I flipped us around and slammed him against the door. I spoke as I slid my hand up his chest and lightly placed it over his neck. "Oh, I'm going to fuck you. I'm going to show you exactly how much of a needy submissive bottom you truly are."

"Only for you." He let out a soft, breathy moan.

"You're fucking right only for me."

I slammed my lips against his in a dominant and rough kiss. He quickly melted against me and effortlessly submitted to my authority and power. This was something we had both been waiting for and I didn't want to drag it out any longer.

We both quickly worked on divesting the other of their clothes. I guided Gage back toward my bed and we both collapsed down onto it. I broke the kiss and started to kiss and nibble my way down Gage's chest, stomach, and when I reached his hard cock, I ran my tongue along it from base to tip, gathering the pearl of precum from the slit. Gage let out a deep moan, writhing under my ministrations.

I took Gage's cock into my mouth all the way down to his base as I reached over and grabbed the lube and quickly coated three fingers. I slowly pushed my index finger into Gage's hole and he relaxed his muscles for me.

Gage's hands moved to the bed sheets and clenched them tightly as I added a second finger and really started to work his ass open for my cock. I knew he wasn't going to last much longer. He was too worked up and he wasn't the only one.

My cock was rock hard and pulsing with the need to feel him wrapped around me.

"I'm gonna," Gage started, but when I hit his sweet spot, he couldn't manage to get the rest of the words out when he gave a deep moan, more slick precum trickling from the head of his shaft.

I hummed my appreciation over Gage's hardness, sending vibrations down his cock as I took him down to his base and hit his sweet spot once again. I felt his whole body tense up as his cock pulsed in my mouth and his sweet cum flooded over my tastebuds. I swallowed everything that he had for me and I didn't stop even after he finished pulsing.

I slipped a third finger into his channel and truly started to stretch him out. By the time he was ready for me, he was a writhing and moaning mess on my bed, but that was exactly how I wanted him. The moans that were coming from Gage were driving me insane and I wasn't going to be able to last much longer.

I reluctantly pulled my mouth off his dick and removed my fingers from his sweet ass. He gave a whine at the loss of contact, but I knew shortly he was going to be screaming for more.

I reached over and grabbed a condom, quickly slipping it down over my dick. I then grasped the latex-covered hardness with my lube-covered hand and slicked it up just to make sure that this didn't hurt at all for him. I lined my tip up with his ass as I spoke. "You ready?"

"Fuck, yes," he said, need dripping from his voice. He might not have bottomed before, but he was confident in what he wanted and that helped to ease the slight nerves I was having. I didn't want Gage to regret this.

I gently began to push inside him, pushing through the first tight ring of muscle and breathing heavily with my effort to remain in control. I wanted to pound the hell out of him, but I knew I had to go slow at first. I had to make sure Gage adjusted to my size as my cock finished stretching him out.

Gage panted as each glorious inch of my cock was pushed inside of him and I had to fight with everything in me to stay at my slow pace. When I finally bottomed out, we were both breathing heavily and I could see that Gage was doing his best to adjust to this new sensation of having my cock in his ass.

"You okay, baby?" I asked as I bent forward and started to kiss along his neck.

"Fuck, you feel good, but also weird," he said with a slight huff of a laugh.

"That weird feeling will pass once you're used to it. The question is, do you want it slow and sweet or hard and fast?"

"I don't want you to hold back. I want to feel all of you and I want to feel your desperate need and passion."

I could see the desire burning in his eyes and I knew he meant every single word he said. And that was all I needed to hear before I pulled out almost all of the way and quickly slammed right back inside. Gage let out a soft scream as my cock nailed right into his sweet spot. I didn't go all out on speed, not yet, he did need to get used to the feel of it first, but that didn't mean I couldn't go hard.

"Oh fuck." Gage whimpered, thrusting his hips even as his back arched up in pleasure. He wrapped his legs around my hips and held on tight. I could feel his legs trembling from the pleasure and I knew he would already be getting close to coming again. I loved how responsive he was to me. It had been a very long time since I had been with anyone who was this desperate with desire and need. As I felt him loosen up, I knew he was ready for me to stop holding back.

I quickly pulled out of him and Gage whined at the loss of pleasure. Before he even had a chance to say anything, I flipped him over and he instantly got down on his hands and knees and put his ass out on display for me. The second his knees touched the mattress, I lined my cock up and slammed right back inside of his perfect ass. Gage gave a long moan as the pleasure overtook his body and his arms gave out and he collapsed onto the bed.

"You like that, baby?" I asked with a smirk.

"Fuck, don't stop. You feel so good," Gage mewled.

I placed my hands on his hips and started to pound into him with everything that I had, nailing his prostate with each thrust. Gage couldn't stop moaning and whimpering, his hands fisting the sheets, and I knew it wouldn't take long before he was coming without me even touching his cock.

I kept my pace hard and fast, making sure my cock was fully buried deep inside of him with each thrust. I could feel his walls tightening around my cock as I continued to pound into him. It was only moments later when he gave a loud scream, calling out my name as he came.

"Fuck, Xavier!"

I couldn't help but growl softly as I felt his ass squeezing my cock. I knew with each thrust it would cause him to pulse out more cum, milking him for all he had, and I wished I could have seen it as well. It only took a few more thrusts before I snapped my hips forward and buried myself completely inside of him as I erupted inside the condom.

"Gage," I moaned through clenched teeth as my body was rocked with scorching pleasure. Black dots danced before my eyes and for a second I thought I was going to pass out from the sheer pleasure alone.

I placed my hand on the wall to help hold myself up as we both were breathing very heavily. I managed to look down at Gage and he was struggling to keep his eyes open. His legs had given out on him from the intense pleasure he had just experienced and had flopped to the sides.

I had just enough strength to slowly pull out of him and toss the condom into the garbage can by my bed before I pulled Gage over to me and we were both out before my brain could form a single word.

CHAPTER 24

XAVIER

I HAD BEEN in a lot of uncomfortable situations in my life, but sitting there in a therapist's office might actually be the most uncomfortable place I had ever been. I needed to do it, but I didn't know how I would get through it. The only reason I still sat on the couch was because Dexter was counting on me and there was nothing I wouldn't do for him.

"I'm sure you would rather be in a hundred different places right now," Dr. Heath began.

"You aren't wrong."

"And yet, you are here. Care to tell me why that is?"

"My son, Dexter, means the world to me. He'll be eighteen soon and I don't have much of a relationship with him. It's a complicated story that I'm sure we will get into. Recently though, I tried to reach out to him, to make amends for missing out on so much of his life," I started to explain.

"And how did that go?"

"Not how I expected it would. I thought he would be angry and want nothing to do with me. I expected the hurt, but I wasn't expecting the type of hurt that he was in. He looked in pain and lost. He said he couldn't have me in his life until I got better. That something horrible happened to him and he couldn't handle my shit along with his own. I asked him what happened, but he wouldn't tell me. He doesn't think I'll be able to handle it. My own son is hurting and I couldn't help him because I'm too screwed up. I have to get better so I can help him."

I knew it probably wasn't the healthiest reason, but it was honest and if this doc didn't like it, well that was too bad for him.

"Sometimes we don't start getting better until someone we love forces our hand. Typically, a therapist is supposed to tell you that you can only get healthy when you choose to. That you can't do it for anyone else. However, sometimes it takes fighting for someone you love to make you want to get healthy. I think fighting for your son is a great place to start," he said, flashing me a warm smile.

That was unexpected, but I was glad that he understood where I was coming from and wasn't trying to give me a lecture about getting healthy for *me* and all of that shit.

"By the look on your face, I take it you've been in therapy before and it didn't go well for you," Dr. Heath said, a small smirk gracing his lips.

"Went through it when I got out of the Air

Force before starting at the Fire Department. Got diagnosed with PTSD," I answered with a shrug.

"I take it you don't agree with that diagnosis."

I let out a sigh before answering. "I guess it's not that I don't agree with it, it's that I don't like it. I know guys who have come back missing body parts, their life completely altered and they can never recover from it. I got to keep all of my parts. I get up and go to work every day and still get to fly my bird. What right do I have to complain?"

"I understand that you feel that way; however, PTSD doesn't discriminate. It's not about who had it worse, it's about trauma and how our brains handle it. If I were to send you for a CT-Scan, we would be able to see the PTSD in your brain scan. It's a real injury that can be healed with time and therapy. PTSD can develop from any trauma that someone goes through. You went to war, that comes with a lot of trauma. Can you tell me a bit about your time in the Air Force?"

"I was in for twenty years. Enlisted right at eighteen and left at thirty-eight. I've done hundreds of missions, most of them turned out okay. A few close calls, but nothing that I couldn't handle," I answered with a shrug, but Dr. Heath apparently wasn't buying it.

"Why did you leave?"

That was what I didn't want to talk about, but I knew I would have to. But I didn't know if I wanted to talk about it so soon.

"How does this work? I tell you about the worst things that happened to me and it magically makes me better?" I couldn't help but be skeptical. I couldn't understand how this was going to help me. I was doing this because I had to, but that didn't mean I believed in it.

"It's not magic. It takes a lot of work on your part. There is no magic pill that will make it all better. You have to want to be better. You have to put the work in and you have to be open and honest with me and yourself. You survived war, multiple times, you have the strength to survive this. As for how it works, we can do this one of two ways. We can start with the small traumas that are easier to talk about and work our way up. Or we can start with the biggest, it'll be hard, but once you work through it, it will give you the biggest relief. It's completely up to you. You have the control and power here. You dictate what we talk about and how fast we move."

I had no idea how I wanted to do this. Talking about some of the smaller shit would be easier, but then it wouldn't tackle the main reason I kept drinking and I needed to deal with that so I could help Dexter. As hard as it would be, I had to jump into the deep end and just hope I could remember how to swim.

"Since I was discharged, I've been drinking. I drink a lot when I'm not working. What I didn't realize was that I would often call Dex while drunk and leave him a voicemail. It's one of the reasons why he hasn't spoken to me and why he won't tell me what happened to him. I've been sober for two weeks now, but I've had a couple of flashbacks, always the same thing," I began to explain. I knew that I could tell him about the drinking and not have to worry about my job. He wasn't allowed to report anything like that, especially if I was sober and not drinking at work. I hadn't put anyone in danger and I never would.

"First, congratulations on getting sober. Even if you feel like two weeks is nothing, I assure you it's not. I have a bunch of information on AA support groups within the city if you want. I highly recommend that you go. You can't stay sober without a support system and sometimes the best support system is the one with people who are like you. With people that can understand what you are going through in terms of the battle you are fighting."

"I'll take the info. I've already been looking into it."

I had no interest in sitting around and talking about my problems to a group of strangers, but I also knew I couldn't foolishly just assume that I would be the exception and stay sober without putting in any effort for it.

Dr. Heath gave a nod before he continued. "Second, it's not uncommon to have flashbacks with PTSD and the only way you can prevent them from happening again is by talking about what you saw. If you are having a flashback about the same event repeatedly, then that is a major event that is strongly connected to your PTSD. Would you be willing to tell me about it?"

"I've only told one person about it. It's why I was honorably discharged. Most of it is classified, but the down and dirty version is I was picking up some SEALs to get them out of a hot zone. My chopper was shot down and not all of them survived the crash. While trying to get into a safer area, I was shot and we were captured. I spent three weeks trapped in a cave being tortured and the SEALs who had survived the crash were with me. By the end of the three weeks, I was the only one alive when the rescue team arrived. The drinking started when I got home after two weeks in a German hospital before I was cleared to be discharged."

"I'm terribly sorry you had to endure that. I think it's safe to say that traumatic experience is at the core of your PTSD. I would really like to speak to you about it, if you are comfortable with that as your starting point."

"No offense, Doc, it's not really about being comfortable. None of this makes me comfortable. I highly doubt that is going to change. I'm here because I have to be, because my kid needs me to be. If my last operation is what is standing in the way of me being healthy, or me helping my kid, then let's go."

Talking about those three weeks wasn't something I ever wanted to do, but I would do it. For Dexter, I would do it. I was just hoping that I could get through this so I could come out of it stronger and be there for Dexter again. He was relying on me and I was not going to fail him again.

CHAPTER 25

GAGE

"OH FUCK." I moaned as I leaned my head back against the wall.

I'd arrived a bit early to take my final exam this morning. I wanted some time to pace around and try to work off some nervous energy before I would need to sit down and focus on the exam. Only, Xavier appeared to have a different idea to work off my energy.

He'd pulled me into one of the supply closets and took my cock deep down his throat. My hand was threaded through his hair and my eyes were locked on him. I still couldn't believe he could take me all the way in his mouth. His throat felt so fucking good, so tight and hot. It was just like fucking someone's ass. I was going to miss that, but I wouldn't trade the feeling of Xavier's cock in my hole for anything.

He locked eyes with me as he took me deep and moaned his appreciation. The vibrations sent a shockwave of pleasure right up my spine and I couldn't help but thrust my hips forward just slightly. I didn't want him to choke, but I also wasn't willing to give up my complete control either. I watched as he reached down and started to jerk himself off as I fucked his throat.

"You feel so good. So tight and hot. You look so fucking sexy with my cock down your throat. Fuck, you're gonna make me come soon."

I couldn't help but pick up my pace. Xavier kept moaning and the vibrations were driving me up the wall. I loved seeing him like this. I loved knowing I could get him this wound up. That I could make him this needy. I could tell he was getting close as his moaning picked up and I could see his hand moving faster. He wasn't the only one who was close.

"Come for me, baby." I grunted as I fought to hold off. I wanted him to fall off the cliff first. I wanted to watch as he came with my cock down his throat.

It only took a few more seconds before he let out a long and deep moan around my cock as his own exploded with his orgasm. The sight of it pushed me over the edge and I thrust my hips forward once more before I came hard down his throat. I hissed at the sensation of his throat constricting around me as he swallowed everything I had for him. We both continued to pulse as we rode out our high and after a moment Xavier pulled back.

"Well, that's one way to start the day," I said with a slight huff of a laugh.

"I had to make sure you were relaxed for your test," Xavier said as he kissed his way back up my stomach and over to my neck.

"I hope you aren't doing this with all of your students," I teased, but in reality I was now back to being stressed and worried about the final exam.

I still couldn't believe it had already been a month. It felt like time had zoomed past me. I wasn't ready to leave. I wasn't ready to leave Xavier or face all of the unknowns about our relationship.

Was it even a relationship?

Maybe this was more like a summer fling and we would go our separate ways now and never connect with the other again. I really hoped that wasn't the case, but that wasn't something that only I could decide. I hadn't brought it up to him, yet, mostly because I was scared of what his answer would be. He was going through a lot and he had to focus on his mental health so he could be healthier for himself and for his son. I completely understood that needed to be his priority and I wanted him to make it a priority. At the same time though, I really still wanted to be in his life.

"Only you. Though, it wouldn't surprise me if Jackson had someone else in one of the supply closets." I felt his smirk against my neck as he kissed me one last time before he pulled back.

"Jackson gets around, I take it?" I asked, as I started to pull my pants back up.

"It's safe to call him a manwhore. He's a forty-five year old who is trapped in the mindset of a horny twenty year old. He tends to date multiple guys at the same time. One time, he even dated brothers. They weren't twins, so your brothers still take the cake on that, but Jackson has broken a lot of hearts. And he has a gift at sniffing out the gay guy or bi-curious guy in every class."

"I guess it's a good thing it was you flying that chopper and not Jackson. I couldn't imagine being cuddled up with him in the cave and not you."

I didn't have a problem with Jackson. He was a good guy and he was a very patient teacher. He looked good, especially for his age, but he wasn't Xavier and I couldn't imagine a scenario where I would want to be with him. Where I would want to feel his body against mine. Xavier on the other hand, now he was a man I wanted to do nothing but lay naked with.

"It's hard to believe that was only a month ago. It's hard to believe that in two days you are going to be gone," he said sadly as he moved back and righted his own clothes.

"This course has definitely not gone how I expected it to. It's going to be weird going home to an empty house, going back to work again. I've basically seen you every day for the past month, how am I going to survive not seeing your face every day?" I asked with a teasing smile, but the reality was I hoped he would tell me that I would get to see him again. That he didn't want this to end and we could work something out.

"I know what you mean. Especially this past week. I've gotten used to feeling your body against mine while I sleep. I know we live on opposite ends of the country, but I would like to keep seeing you. If you think you could handle the long distance thing."

I couldn't help the smile that instantly spread across my face. I had never done a long distance relationship, but for Xavier I was all for trying. I didn't know what the future would hold for the two of us, but I was willing to put the work in and see what we could make of this relationship.

"For you, I'm willing to try anything. I think we could make it work."

I had no idea how truly hard it would be, but I was hoping it wouldn't be too hard to adjust to the distance. Once I got back to Baton Rouge, I would be working at the firehouse again and it would hopefully make the days go by faster until I could physically see Xavier again.

"It wouldn't be forever. Maybe six months, a year at most. I have to try and get transferred over to Baton Rouge or close to it. I need to keep going with my therapy right now and start building up a relationship with Dex again."

"Take as long as you need. Your therapy and your relationship with Dex are more important than anything. We can survive off texts and phone sex," I said as I wiggled my eyebrows and it put a smile on his face.

"As much as I would like to explore more about our phone sex options, you have an exam to write in fifteen minutes."

"And now I am back to being nervous, thanks for that," I grumbled as we both headed out of the supply closet.

The exam was not one I was looking forward

to. I hated exams to begin with, but anything that had to do with the fire department always made me more nervous. This wasn't some stupid history exam; this was an exam that would dictate what happened with my career. If I failed, I wouldn't be able to take the course again and I would be going back home as a failure. That wasn't something I could handle happening. I had to pass, but I was truly worried about different parts of the exam. Xavier had been working with me in class and after hours to ensure I understood the material and I would be able to handle any tests. Still, that nervousness seeped into my bones and all I could do at this point was hope for the best.

Xavier grabbed my hand and stopped me from continuing down the hallway. I turned toward him as he looked me dead in the eyes and spoke. "You are ready for this. You know the material. All you have to do is trust yourself. Don't second guess your answers or the process. You're ready, I promise you."

A deep sigh escaped my mouth before I could contain it. Xavier knew about my lack of high school success, but he never judged me for it. He never saw me as stupid, not like I often viewed myself as. He believed in me, even when he had no reason to. I didn't feel ready, but the fact that Xavier told me I was ready did ease my nerves slightly.

"Tonight is our last night together for who knows how long and I plan to make sure it is a very memorable one for you. So whenever you feel stressed or anxious during the exam, just think about me and how good it feels to have my cock pounding into you."

I let out a soft moan before I managed to find my voice. "Now that's all I'm going to be thinking about."

I still couldn't believe how amazing it felt to be a bottom. I never thought I would ever submit to any man, but there was something special about Xavier that made it so easy to do just that. I suspected he was the only man I would ever submit to, but that was just fine by me.

"I'll see you tonight. Good luck."

I could tell he wanted to kiss me, but we couldn't do that out in the open. The last thing either of us needed was someone seeing us and assuming Xavier had shown me favoritism. Any celebrations would have to wait until tonight, but it would at least give me something to look forward to.

Letting out a long breath I turned and started to head back down the hallway to reach the classroom. There was no going back now.

CHAPTER 26

Gage

My brain was mush. That was the only word I could manage to think of to accurately describe how I felt right now. I had to imagine this was how Asher felt after every exam he had in high school. I was able to finish the exam, but I had no idea how I did on half of it. I didn't need a perfect score, but I hoped I had managed to at least pass it. Honestly though, I wasn't feeling too confident about it.

I collapsed down onto one of the picnic tables out back and pulled my phone out. I sent a quick text off to Xavier letting him know I was finished and I followed it up with a gun emoji and the brain exploding emoji. I knew Xavier would want to talk about it, but right now I wanted to try and reach out to Greyson. I had spoken to Asher a few times over the past month, but I hadn't been able to speak with Greyson. The time shift was killing me. We were literally on opposite ends of the country and by the time I got done in class, Greyson was usually getting ready for bed. It was just after four my time, so I hoped that meant I could catch Greyson before he got ready for bed.

I hit his contact and put the phone to my ear, listening to the endless number of rings, and just when I thought I was going to be getting his voice-mail again, I got the sweet sound of his voice.

"Hey, I was hoping you would call. Asher said you had your final exam today. How did it go?"

Just hearing his voice helped to put my fears at ease. He sounded good. A bit tired, but he didn't sound like he was ready to fake his death just to escape.

"Well, about halfway through I was hoping someone would run in and pull the fire alarm. I have no idea if I passed or not, but now all I can do is wait."

"I'm sure you aced it. You've always been good at these fire courses," Greyson said with complete confidence in me. Too bad I didn't feel that way.

"I'll see. I don't want to talk about me though; I want to know how you are doing. I've been getting second hand intel from Asher and I love your brother, but he sucks at telephone."

Greyson gave a chuckle at that before he spoke. "He hears what he wants to hear. I've been doing good though. It's not what I expected, but truthfully, I didn't know what to expect. The guys here are really good. I haven't told them much about myself other than I have a twin and older brother. I've been keeping personal details out of it."

"Like that you are gay. Any reason why?"

"I want my skills to speak for themselves. I don't want to be the token gay guy or used as a rung on some political ladder. I want to be like everyone else. Plus, I think it might be easier in the long run to not get too close to anyone. At any given moment they could be killed overseas and it'll hurt less if I don't develop any emotional attachment to them."

"I can understand that would appear to be the easier route, but I don't know how healthy or possible that would be. The one instructor for my course, Xavier, was in the Air Force. He told me that the teams are like a family. Everyone gets close and protects each other. Being part of a team, you're gonna have to open yourself up to the others. You're gonna have to know them to help build trust. I don't think you should shut yourself off to the possibility of a deeper connection to people."

I knew logically what Greyson was saying made complete sense. It would be easier to lose people if you didn't know much about them. If there was no emotional connection to them. However, in practice, that didn't really work out the same way. You couldn't be on a team with a group of people and not know them. Even if you didn't ask them questions, you would still gain information from conversations they had around you. Unless Greyson planned to walk around with noise canceling headphones on, he was screwed.

"I understand what you are saying, but I'm not

looking to mourn any losses. As a medic, my job is to keep the patient alive until I can get them to a doctor. It's just like a paramedic getting the patient to the hospital."

"Yeah, but you don't spend weeks or months, hell even years, with that patient as you take them to the hospital. You will be training with your team and doing team bonding exercises and living together when you are overseas. It's a lot more than just patching 'em up." I was worried that Greyson was setting himself up for more heart-break and failure with how he was planning on handling his connection to his team.

"I'll be fine. You don't have to worry about me," he said in a tight voice and I could tell he was not in the mood for the conversation. I had to let it go and just hope that he would meet his new team once he graduated Boot Camp and it would change his mind.

"I'm always going to worry about you. How has the physical aspect been?"

"It was tough at first, but now I've gotten into a routine with it. My mathematical skills have come in handy with the shooting. I'm at the top of my class in that sense."

"Good... I think," I said with a slight chuckle. I was glad he was doing well, but I didn't know if I wanted a first place trophy in shooting to come home.

"It is good. It means I will be better able to protect myself and my team in the field. I heard Asher is doing well and loves being on the ranch. He's got the hots for his boss. I told him to keep it to his wet dreams and not be stupid."

"Yeah, I practically told him the same thing. Hopefully, he listens to us, but that is a decision only he can make. Are you sure you are okay there? No regrets?"

"I'm sure. I like the work and I know it will be good once I can focus on the medical aspect of my training. I can do that here, so I won't have to relocate until after my training."

"And how long does that take?"

"Anywhere between sixteen and sixty-eight weeks. It all depends on how much specialized training I want to do. I'm not sure yet, but I might go for the full sixty-eight weeks. That way when I eventually leave the Army, I can get a job as an ER doctor or even a trauma surgeon with additional training."

I was not about to tell him not to do sixty-eight weeks. That was just over a year of me not having to worry about him being in the middle east. Another year where he would be safe.

"I think you should get as much training as you can. I mean, you are getting paid to learn, you might as well take advantage of that."

"I will most likely do the full program. It will give me more skills to have when I am out there and a greater chance of saving someone's life. I gotta get going though. I need to shower and then turn in for the night. I have to be up at oh-five hundred."

"Five am, no fucking thank you." I hated mornings and everyone at the firehouse knew that. "I love you and be safe."

"Always. I love you, too and I'll talk to you

again in a couple of days. Let me know when you get back home."

"I will. I'm proud of you, Greyson."

"Thanks, big brother. Talk soon."

He ended the call and I let out a long breath. I felt better now that I'd spoken to him, but at the same time I was just as anxious. I knew I had to get used to it. It was Greyson's decision to be in the Army and I had to respect it, even if it made me feel like throwing up.

I scrubbed a hand over my face and forced my body to move. I had to go and pack up my room so I could be ready to leave in two days. I already knew I would be spending the day tomorrow with Xavier so this was truly my only chance to get this done, because there was no way I would be leaving Xavier's to pack up my room. I hoped tomorrow I wouldn't even be wearing clothes. With that happy thought, I headed off for the dorms.

CHAPTER 27

Xavier

I MADE my way to the park once again where I knew Dexter would be. He had a half day today and I knew he would be at the park playing ball.

I hoped he was alone, because it would be easier to speak with him. If he was in the middle of a game, it would be harder to get him to stop playing and speak with me. Who the hell was I kidding, it was going to be a small miracle if I could get him to talk to me at all.

I knew I wouldn't be able to get him to trust me right away. It was going to take some time and a lot of work to earn his trust back. For him to see that I would be there for him, no matter what happened in the future or what had happened in the past. I desperately wanted to know what demons he was fighting. I hated that he was going through this alone.

I knew he had his mother, but given what little he had told me about her behavior since the divorce, plus what I had experienced with her, I knew she wouldn't be much help at all. Most likely she would send him to church more and pretend like nothing was wrong.

I rounded the corner and I easily heard the sound of a basketball dribbling. I was also pleased to see that it was only Dexter there and not a group of people. It was still early enough in the afternoon that others hadn't arrived yet. I waited until I was closer before I called out.

"Dex!"

At the sound of his name, he turned around and stopped dribbling. He didn't give me a smile, but he also didn't appear to be annoyed by my presence and I took that as a win.

"What are you doing here?" he asked, but there wasn't an edge to his voice. He actually sounded exhausted.

"I wanted to check in and see how you were. I know I could have called, but I like seeing your face. How are you doing, Dex?"

"Okay, I guess. Shouldn't you be at work?"

"The new round of cadets are doing their final exam today for the course I teach. I don't have to be there. My partner, Jackson, he watches over them. I mostly teach them up in the air. I got the whole day off. We could play a bit of ball if you want."

"Just because you show up here doesn't mean anything has changed," he simply said.

"I know, and I know I have a lot that I need to

make up for. I've been sober for just over two weeks now. I know it's not much, but it's a start. I've also started therapy to deal with my drinking and PTSD. I'm working on getting better so I can be the father that you need. So I can help you with everything you are going through. I want you to feel like you can talk to me. That you can depend on me and know that I'm always going to be there for you."

"And all of that sounds great, but it's only been two weeks," he said with a small shrug. He had every right to be skeptical. I hadn't been there for him and given how much hurt was radiating off of him, he needed the protection of a father and he had been denied that. He was going to need a lot more than two weeks sober before he felt like he could trust me, but I would prove to him that he could.

"I know. And I know it's going to take a lot more than just a couple of weeks, but I am not going to relapse. Those weeks will keep adding up and I will earn your trust back. There's no rush though, Dex. I'll go at your pace." The last thing I wanted was for him to feel like I was pressuring him.

He looked down for a moment, rolling the ball around in his hands before he finally looked up and spoke. "Do you play?"

"I have in the past. Basketball was one of the few activities we could do overseas on base. I'm out of practice though, so you might have to go easy on me," I said, flashing him a warm smile.

"I guess I could." He gave me a small one

shoulder shrug, but I also saw a hint of a smile and it warmed my heart to see it. I had a long road to go with him, but I had managed to finally take my first step on that road and it felt amazing.

CHAPTER 28

THE SECOND THE door was closed, I pulled Gage in for a heated kiss, one he easily returned. I guided us over toward my bed as we both worked on removing the other's clothing. We only had tonight and tomorrow to spend together and I was not going to waste a single second of it.

The second we were naked I pushed him down onto my bed. He instantly spread his legs and the sight of him spread out and ready for me, made me moan. I started to place kisses along the inside of his left thigh as I spoke.

"You look so fucking delicious, baby."

I ran my tongue along Gage's thick shaft, causing him to let out a hiss at the contact. We were both so wound up tight and I doubted either of us would last very long at this point. That was okay though. We had plenty of time to take things slow later.

I took Gage's tip in my mouth and sucked on it, moaning at the sweet taste of Gage's precum hitting my tongue, his flavor flooding my mouth. I pulled back and spoke as I reached over to the bedside table and pulled out some lube and a condom.

"Fuck, you taste so sweet. I'm never going to get tired of it."

"I swear I am going to explode soon if you do not get your mouth around my cock," he said with a slight growl.

"So needy, baby," I teased. I lightly licked at his cock, tonguing the slit and lapping up more of his delicious essence.

"Xavier, please, no teasing, not tonight. I just need to feel you," he whined.

I knew he had been stressed out over his final exam and I knew he needed to shut off his mind and to just allow his body to feel what it needed to feel.

"I got you, baby," was all I said, before I took his hard cock all the way into my mouth and I didn't stop until I was completely down to his base. His cock was already rock hard and I knew he was in desperate need to come.

I worked his dick in my mouth as I got three of my fingers slicked up with the lube. I inserted my index finger and I groaned around his cock at how tight his ass was. Gage moaned at the pleasure that I knew was scorching through his body.

I pushed my index finger all the way in before I slowly pulled it out before moving it back in. I felt Gage's hand moving to my hair and he grabbed a chunk of it as he thrust his hips slightly and began to lightly fuck my mouth.

I moaned as I added a second finger and really started to work his hole. I couldn't believe how amazing Gage tasted and how good it felt to feel his cock sliding over my tongue and down my throat.

I focused on stretching him, but I knew he was getting closer to coming. I added my third and final finger and started to search out his sweet spot. I knew it would make him fall off that cliff and I desperately wanted to feel his cock pulse in my throat. I knew I hit it when his back arched off the bed and he let out a sharp cry.

"Oh fuck, Xavier."

I could feel his legs starting to shake with his need to come. I picked up my pace, making sure to take all of his cock down to his base as I rubbed fast circles over his sweet spot. Gage was a writhing, moaning mess on the bed and it was only a moment later when he gave a small scream as he came hard down my throat.

I moaned as his sweet taste flooded into my mouth and trickled down my throat. I greedily swallowed everything that Gage had for me. I continued to work his cock in my mouth as he continued to pulse. I didn't remove my mouth until he finished pulsing, softening slightly, only then did I start to pull off and I gave his tip a hard suck to get every last drop from him. I removed my fingers from his ass as I spoke.

"Fuck, I could drink you all day, baby."

"I'd die a very happy man if you did," he said with a big smile on his face.

I picked up the condom and quickly slipped it on, before I positioned myself at Gage's hole. I placed my hands on the underside of Gage's thighs and held his legs up slightly as I slowly started to push my tip into his stretched hole. I couldn't stop the deep moan that escaped my throat as my tip was engulfed with the heat of Gage's tight ass.

Gage couldn't stop moaning as my cock slowly slipped inside of him, inch by inch, until I was fully buried inside of him. Once I bottomed out, I had to close my eyes for a moment and allow myself to feel the pleasure coursing through me. His ass felt amazing around my cock and I had to really fight with myself to not pound into him.

"Fuck, baby, you feel so good," I moaned as I fought to control myself.

"So deliciously big. I'm good, move," Gage begged.

"It's not going to be slow," I warned. I couldn't go slow, not right now, not when it felt this good. The next time, I would go slow then.

"Good, I don't want it slow. Fuck me hard, babe. Make me yours."

I didn't need to be told twice. I pulled out almost all of the way and then I slammed right back into Gage's needy ass until I was balls deep once again. The aggression of my thrusts caused him to let out a keening moan and I didn't waste any time before I angled my hips, pulled out and slammed back in, hitting Gage's sweet spot dead on. Gage gave a small scream as the pleasure shot through him once more.

"Oh, I love that sound," I moaned as I picked up my pace. I could listen to Gage's moans and pleasure for the rest of my life and never get tired of it.

Gage wrapped his legs around my hips and it allowed me to pound even deeper and harder into him. His hands made their way to my back and he ran his fingernails down my back, leaving scratches in his wake I was sure.

I continued to pound into Gage hard and deep. I didn't want this to end, but I could feel myself getting closer. I moved my free hand down to Gage's hard cock that was already dripping with precum once again. The second my hand made contact, Gage let out a whimper as I started to jerk him off in time with my thrusts.

After I hit his sweet spot one more time, Gage screamed my name as he came hard all over my hand, jet after jet of thick white ropes covering my fist and his belly.

The tightening of his walls was enough to push me over the edge and I came hard and deep inside of Gage's ass with a deep moan. We were both breathing heavily as we fought to come down from our high.

I placed my forehead against his as we both fought to catch our breaths. This was only round one and before Gage would need to leave in the next thirty some odd hours, I planned on having as many rounds as humanly possible with him.

EPILOGUE

Six Months Later...
Gage

My whole body radiated with excitement and pure horniness. I stood in the airport with my cock half hard because after six months Xavier was finally coming to visit.

He had been sober for six and a half months and he had been going through intense therapy, but he had a solid grip on his drinking and his PTSD. We'd been talking every day and having a lot of video and phone sex. He planned on moving to Baton Rouge soon, but he wanted to wait until Dexter graduated high school before he made the move. I completely understood and supported his decision.

Things between Dexter and Xavier were still more shaky than not, but they were making progress. We still didn't know what had happened to Dexter, he was keeping that in a very heavily locked box. I knew it was driving Xavier crazy not to know, but he had to wait until Dexter was ready to give that up. I just hoped that it wouldn't be anything too devastating to either of them.

Asher and Greyson were doing great. Greyson had graduated Boot Camp and was focusing on his medical courses. They were both having a great time and I couldn't be more proud of them. It was hard coming home to an empty house. Even something as simple as sleeping was hard. Not falling asleep to the faint sound of Asher's music or hearing them moving around from their room to the bathroom. Even just knowing that I was completely alone made it difficult for me to close my eyes. I had gotten used to it now, but that didn't mean I liked it. Maybe I needed to get a dog or something. That was something else I could figure out another day.

I pushed those thoughts aside as people started to come through the gate. I couldn't stand still as I waited to see Xavier come through the gate. I knew the guys at work all wanted to meet him, but I took today off for a reason and that was not so we could be around a bunch of guys. I wanted my man in my home, naked, and moaning.

The smile was instantly spreading over my lips as I finally saw Xavier coming toward me. I walked toward him and his arms opened for me. I practically flung myself into them and they were instantly closing around me in a strong hug.

Fuck, he felt amazing.

"Fuck, I missed you," Xavier growled into my neck.

"Me too. Come on, let's get the hell out of here and to my place," I said as I moved back.

"Straight to your place, eh?" he said, flashing me a sexy smirk.

"Would you prefer I take you on a tour of Baton Rouge?" I asked, but I already knew the answer.

"My cock in your tight ass is the only tour I need, baby," he whispered into my ear and it sent a shiver down my spine. Fuck, now I was fully hard in an airport full of people.

We quickly made our way to my car and after tossing his duffle bag into the back seat, we climbed in and headed off for my house. We had been driving for a few minutes when Xavier reached over and began to undo my jeans.

"What are you doing?"

"My mouth is bored," he stated, as if we were talking about the weather. Before I realized what was going on, my pants were open and he was bending forward to run his tongue along my half hard cock, causing me to let out a deep moan.

"You do know I'm trying to drive? And it's broad daylight, right?" I asked, as he ran his tongue up and down my now extremely hard cock.

"I'm not stopping you," he countered playfully.

Xavier sucked on my tip and moaned his appreciation as the taste of my precum hit his tongue. I did my best to focus on the road as Xavier took my cock into his mouth. I had done a lot of things in my life, but I had never gotten my cock sucked while I was driving. That wasn't something I ever thought I needed to experience and now all I wanted was for Xavier to suck my cock dry the whole way to my place.

Xavier took all of my cock into his mouth, burying his nose in my pubic hairs and sucking in a deep sniff. I moved my hand over to his head and threaded my fingers through his hair. Xavier moaned at the tight grip on his hair as he worked his mouth all up and down my hard cock. Every time he took me down to my base, I gave him a deep moan as my tip hit the back of his throat.

"Fuck, babe." I whimpered as I thrust my hips up slightly.

Xavier sucked hard and the pleasure shot through my whole body. My balls pulled up tight and I felt my orgasm coil in my belly.

"Babe, I'm gonna…"

After a few more seconds, Xavier let out a long moan as I came hard down his throat. Xavier swallowed everything that I had to offer him and when I finished pulsing, he continued to suck my cock. I hissed at the sensitivity, and grabbing a fistful of his hair, I pulled Xavier's mouth off my cock.

"It's sensitive." I said.

"Are we there yet?" Xavier countered.

"No, half way roughly."

"Then I'm not done playing yet," he said with a playful smile as gave my shaft a long lick.

"Oh my god. Fuck," I hissed.

Xavier took my tip into his mouth again and sucked on it, his tongue penetrating my slit and gathering the slick there. I did my best to focus on the road as Xavier worked my cock all over again, getting it just as hard as before. Xavier moaned as he moved up and down my cock before he pulled his mouth off.

"I love how your cock feels against my tongue," he growled before he took my cock back into his mouth.

"Fuck. I'm thinking you have an oral fixation, babe," I whined as I rested my head against the headrest as I pulled up to a red light. I took a moment to look down and watched for a moment as Xavier worked his mouth all the way down my cock. "Fuck, you are so sexy like that. I could watch you suck cock all day and night long."

I pulled out my cell phone and opened up the camera. I turned the video camera option on and placed my phone on the door handle so I could record Xavier sucking my cock.

"I swear, it'll just be for me," I promised.

Xavier looked right at the camera and gave a deep moan right before he took my cock all the way down to my base. I moaned, ecstatic that Xavier had no problem being recorded. I decided then and there that we would need to make a lot of videos during his visit.

I continued to focus on the road as we got closer to my house. I wanted to come again down Xavier's throat before I would get to feel his massive cock in my ass. I was getting close to coming, but I wanted to do it once I was parked so I could lean back and really feel Xavier's throat around my cock.

Once I finally pulled onto my driveway, I turned the truck off and leaned back in my seat, shifting my hips upward. Xavier could now get a better angle on my cock.

He looked right at the camera as he pulled off my cock and ran his tongue over my tip. He moaned his appreciation as he took my tip into his mouth and sucked on it hard. I moaned as Xavier played it up for the camera. I knew this video would be what I used at night to jerk off to once he went home, along with many others hopefully.

I watched in anticipation as Xavier ran his tongue up and down my shaft slowly before he took me back into his mouth, all the way down to my base. I tightened my grip in his hair once more and started to thrust my hips up, pushing my cock further down his throat.

"Fuck, I'm gonna come down this sweet throat of yours," I hissed as I picked up my pace, marveling at the gagging sounds coming from my lover.

I was so close. I needed to come and then I needed to take Xavier inside and have him fuck the living hell out of me. After another moment, I came once again with a growl as I shot my load down Xavier's throat. Xavier moaned and hummed as the taste of my cum flooded his mouth. He swallowed every last drop that I had to offer him.

Once I stopped pulsing, Xavier moved back off my cock and made sure to suck and lick at my tip, getting every last drop before he gave the camera a wink and then reached over to turn it off. He looked over at me and smirked at seeing how wrecked I was.

"I hope you're not too tired. We're just getting started," Xavier said, flashing me a playful smile.

"I'm never going to be too tired to feel your cock pounding into me," I promised.

I opened the car door and stumbled my way to my front door. I heard the other car door opening and I knew Xavier was right behind me. I headed inside, leaving the door open, and made my way up the stairs to my bedroom with Xavier's footsteps following right behind me. I would give him a tour later.

I removed each piece of clothing as I made my way down the hall to my bedroom, dropping them as I went. By the time I reached my bedroom, I turned around and saw that Xavier was already naked too. He grabbed me by the back of my neck and pulled me in for a deep kiss. I willingly allowed Xavier's tongue to enter my mouth, moaning at the taste of myself all over Xavier's tongue.

I continued to kiss Xavier as we moved back toward my bed and once my knees hit the bed, Xavier carefully lowered us down. I crawled backward on the bed to grant us more room, opening my legs for Xavier to fit between them.

Xavier pulled away from the kiss and slowly began to kiss and nibble his way down my neck, down my chest, nipping at each hard nipple, and then over my stomach, all the way down to my hard cock once again. I reached over to the bedside table and pulled out the lube and placed it down on the bed.

Xavier took my hard cock into his mouth and he didn't stop until he was all the way to my base. I gave a hiss as the pleasure shot through me and my sensitive cock. I highly doubted he was going to be able to make me come for a third time right now, but I was more than happy to allow him to give it his best shot.

Xavier worked my cock as he slicked up three of his fingers. He ran his left hand up my stomach, my chest, and finally to my throat where he grasped my throat in a light grip as he used his right hand and inserted his index finger into my needy ass. I whimpered, thrusting back against his digits and I couldn't help but roll my eyes back as my body was wracked with pleasure. I loved when Xavier took control over me and he fucking knew it. Xavier pushed his finger in all the way before he slowly pulled it out.

I clenched the bed sheets in my fists as Xavier added a second finger quickly. I couldn't believe how amazing this felt. Xavier worshiped my body like no man had ever done before. The pleasure was so intense I couldn't help but wiggle my hips to try and get more friction from his fingers. After a moment, he added a third finger and started to look for my sweet spot.

"Xavier," I moaned deeply as I felt that shock-wave of pleasure as he hit my sweet spot dead on.

Xavier picked up his pace on my cock, making sure to take all of me down to the base as he rubbed fast circles over my sweet spot. I was a writhing, moaning mess on the bed and it was only a moment later when I let out a small scream as I came hard down Xavier's throat for the third time in the past hour.

Xavier moaned as he greedily swallowed what I had for him, though I had no idea how I still had cum to offer him. He didn't remove his mouth until I stopped pulsing and then he pulled his fingers from my channel as he moved back. I whined at the loss, my hole fluttering on empty air.

Xavier kept his grip on my throat as he moved up and kissed me roughly. I happily allowed him to dominate the kiss and when he slipped his tongue into my mouth, I ran my own tongue over his and moaned at the taste of myself.

I loved that Xavier could be sweet and gentle, but also that he could take charge and be dominant and aggressive. This was exactly what I needed, especially because it was going to be a long time before we would get to be together again once he went back home. Xavier pulled back from the kiss and moved his free hand to snag the bottle of lube as he spoke.

"You sure?" he asked.

"Fuck yes. I want to feel your cock. I want to feel your hot cum shooting into my ass."

We had talked about the possibility of not having a condom the next time we had sex. We were both only seeing each other and we had both gotten tested and the tests came back negative for everything. Not that we had expected to have any surprises with the fact we were both tested regularly as part of the firefighter's health initiative.

I had dreamed about feeling his cock inside of me without any barrier, using the thoughts as jerk off fodder many nights since I'd last seen my lover, and I couldn't wait to finally make that dream into a reality.

Xavier positioned his hips so his cock was notched against my hole. He slowly pushed his tip into my already-lubed hole and I couldn't stop the deep moan that escaped my throat as his tip was engulfed within the tight heat of my ass.

We both had never had sex without a condom before and now that we were finally getting to experience it, together. I knew after this, condoms were something we were never going to want to go back to.

Xavier pushed in a bit more until he was buried all the way into my ass, his hips tight against my cheeks. Xavier closed his eyes for a moment and I knew he was fighting the urge to pound the fuck out of me.

"Fuck, baby, you feel so good," he groaned, his breaths coming heavily.

"I'm good, move." Fuck, I needed him to move.

"It's not going to be slow. I'm too worked up for that. I need you so bad," he warned.

"Fuck me hard and deep. Make me yours." Slow and gentle was the last thing I wanted right now.

Xavier didn't need to be told twice. He didn't waste any time before he pulled back a little, angled his hips, and slammed back in, nailing my sweet spot dead on. I gave a small scream as the electric jolt of pleasure shot through me.

"Oh, I love that sound," Xavier moaned as he picked up his pace.

I wrapped my legs around his hips and my hands made their way down Xavier's back to his ass. I dug my fingernails into his butt cheeks, and was rewarded with a deep moan. He continued to pound into me hard and deep, hitting my prostate with every thrust.

I could feel that he was getting closer as his cock was getting harder. Xavier moved his free hand down to my hard and leaking cock. He started to jerk me off in time with his thrusts. I was a moaning mess as the pleasure soared through me. I felt like I was floating on air and I didn't want it to end.

After another direct hit to my sweet spot, I screamed his name as I came hard all over his hand. The tightening of my walls was enough to push Xavier over the edge and he exploded deep inside of my ass.

I moaned as I felt Xavier's hot cum filling me up inside. The heat from his cum coating my walls was unlike anything I had ever felt before. I could feel Xavier's cock pulsing and it caused my own cock to twitch a couple more times, dripping more beads of cum down Xavier's hand.

Both of us were breathing heavily, but I reached down and grabbed Xavier's hand and brought it up to my mouth. I ran my tongue along his hand, getting my cum off of it. Xavier moaned as he watched me lick my own cum off each and every one of his fingers until it was all gone.

Xavier bent down and pressed his lips against mine in a heated kiss. He shoved his tongue into my mouth, sucking on my tongue to get the sweet taste of my cum in his own mouth. I moaned and easily gave myself up to Xavier.

Xavier broke the kiss when the need for oxygen became too much for the both of us.

"Fuck, I'm never letting you get off this bed," he growled.

"I got some handcuffs in the bedside drawer,"

I said, flashing him a playful grin. We had a lot of time to make up for and I planned to take advantage of every single second he was here.

Xavier reached over and pulled out the cuffs. He had them dangling from one finger as his eyes found mine and he spoke. "Fuck, I love you."

"I love you too."

I had no idea what was going to happen in the future, but I didn't care. Because as long as Xavier was in my life, then I knew we would work it out. We loved each other and I couldn't wait to see what the future had in store for us.

Thank you for reading Gage and Xavier's story.

For more in the Smokejumpers series, click now to read Jackson.

If you enjoyed this book, please return to your favorite retailer and leave a review. Even a few words could mean the world to an author.

Hey everyone!
I've a new series for you to check out next!
If you enjoy small town yuMMy man love—and let's face it, who doesn't?—be sure you snag your copy. This one is a little less gritty and dark than my other books have been, but it has more of that delicious gay male romance we all love to fall into. Join me and find your favorite book boyfriend in Cade, Book 1 in the Jasper Springs series.

Home is where the heart is…

Life in Jasper Springs may look perfect, but for Cade Green there's one thing still missing… a hunky billionaire to whisk him away, just like in the movies he can't stop binge watching after his latest break up. But life isn't some romantic tale for guys like him. That is, until the man of his dreams shows up at the local bar's karaoke night.
Can Cade's small-town heart handle the whirlwind that Weston brings?

Famed bachelor Weston Rhodes reluctantly returns to his hometown, planning on nothing more than a fleeting visit. The last thing he expects to find is a reason to stay. However, after one intense night, he soon discovers himself falling for the small town's adorable veterinarian.
Can Weston, used to city lights and endless possibilities, embrace a fairy-tale romance in his quaint hometown?

Readers seeking a small town good boy/bad boy billionaire, opposites attract romance set in a cozy little town may find this story hits those buttons.
While Cade and Weston may have cameos in future stories, each book in this series can be read as a standalone.

Grab <u>Cade</u> here: https://books2read.com/ JasperSprings1

JACKSON

JACKSON

**A convict. A firefighter.
A chance to slay the past and heal a
wounded heart.**

Firefighter Jackson Hall is content with his work in search and rescue with the aerial division in California. He also heads up the Cal Fire Inmate Program.

With his faithful golden retriever by his side, and the animal charities he's dedicated to, he needs nothing else to make him happy.

Preferring life with no-strings-attached entanglements, Jax avoids anything more than hook-ups. That is, until one timid prisoner catches his eye and he finds himself doting on the inmate in ways he never expected.

Ayen Gonzalez was convicted of the attempted manslaughter of his husband, despite the brutal circumstances surrounding his marriage. His past is far less than ideal, and now he just wants to do his time and get out.

As a reward for good behavior, he is given the opportunity to work for an inmate program to be trained to fight forest fires. Ayen is more than happy for the opportunity to escape the prison walls.

Then he meets Jackson and his heart stutters whenever the striking older man comes near.

Thing is, Ayen can't quite figure out what he has to offer a man like Jax.

When the program ends, will Jackson be able to set things in motion to right the wrongs of the justice system in Ayen's case? Or will he be stuck waiting three more years for the man he's fallen in love with?

Trigger Warnings: Violence, abuse.

CHAPTER 1

AYEN

FINALLY BEING able to breathe in the fresh air after being crammed inside of a SAC funded bus had me relaxing almost instantly.

Trees surrounded the training camp in a wide arch, acting as a barrier between us and the rest of the outside world. Not even the cars passing by from the freeway, just a quarter mile from where we'd gotten dropped off, could be heard through the treeline.

After the past two years, this all felt like complete paradise.

"All right, gentlemen! Listen up now," Barlow, one of the four COs that had come with us today, called out. "You're going to be taken into the back of the facility for a safety training course. After that, you're going to be fitted for gear. Do *not* make me have to cuff you and put you back on the bus. Let's be on our best behavior today."

Next to me, another inmate, Tyson, snickered quietly. "Looks like our Newjack is feeling a little twitchy today."

As much as I hated to admit it, I found the comment funny even as I actively fought my smile.

There weren't many COs that came through our unit that didn't feel like they had something to prove—especially the newbie ones that many of the other inmates, including Tyson, liked to call 'newjacks' for some reason.

A lot of insider slang typically went over my head, and back when I'd first gotten sentenced, I'd questioned practically everything, wanting to learn as much as I could about my new home for the next half decade. I'd learned pretty quickly, though, that asking questions got your ass kicked and soon stopped opening my mouth as much.

Officer Barlow was a lot different, though, in the sense that unlike most newbie COs, he had a tendency to baby us. I understood why, but I had a hunch that since all of us—in this program in particular—were the least violent offenders currently in California State Prison, Sacramento aka SAC, and that his preternatural 'mama bird' instincts tended to kick in.

Today, though, Tyson was right. Barlow seemed unnaturally twitchy and more harsh than usual.

But honestly, I didn't really care. I was just happy to be outside of those fifty-foot barbed wired walls for once.

We were ushered to the back of the property,

behind the large main cabin where I assumed our COs and the firefighters for this program would be staying. We had our own cabins, quadruple bunked, right across from that—all of which faced directly toward the mess hall.

I never intended on coming with Tyson, my cellmate, on one of those work release programs. But the minute I'd heard it was for six weeks *and* we'd be out in the fresh air and not stuck inside of some factory, manufacturing license plates or something, I was all on board.

Six firefighters were standing in a half-circle, waiting for us when we finally got to the training site. All of them were dressed in various forms of their turnout gear, with most of them in the typical navy t-shirt and trousers clipped up over their shoulders with suspenders.

I shifted a little in my spot.

Since getting shipped off to prison over two years ago, it'd been a long time since I'd felt any kind of desire. That had been long-since beaten out of me, not just by the harsh prison system but by the person that'd actually gotten me sentenced in the first place.

But damn, did those guys look good in their uniforms. I did have eyes, after all.

"Welcome, gentlemen." A man, tall with broad shoulders, a built chest and an easy smile, nodded to us as a group. "The name's Jackson. I'm going to be your trainer for the next six weeks. We're going to start on the basics for the next few days and see how you all do. Once you've made it past that, then we'll graduate into actual search and rescue drill training. Sound good?"

He didn't wait for the murmur of 'yessir's from our group to begin moving to one of the small training stations. None of us moved, even as he gestured for us all to come closer with a wave of his hand.

We knew better than that. One step out of line and it was back to SAC.

It seemed to have amused our trainer however, because he soon let out a soft chuckle before turning to Barlow. "You mind?"

Barlow quickly cleared his throat and waved his hand at us. "You heard the man. Go."

Tyson nudged my shoulder, "Come on, roomie," and nodded his head to me as he brushed his way to the front of the pack.

I wasn't so much of a fan of being front and center in a crowd, especially since this jumpsuit already made us all stick out like sore thumbs. But I was also not about to be abandoned by Tyson's overeagerness to get his front row tickets to whatever demonstration we were about to watch.

He was kind of the only friend I had at the moment.

"Like I said…" Jackson squatted down, his long legs spreading apart to accommodate the thick tree stump in front of him. On top of it were a few tools, a frayed rope, some kind of rock-looking thing, and a dozen smooth pebbles. "We'll be starting with the basics: how to make a fire. To understand how to fight forest fires, you're going to need to know *how* they get started and how easy it is for them to spread."

Up close like this, I could see the salt and pepper strands in Jackson's dark hair, with patches of grey accumulated at both temples, along with the slight lines in his face that expressed his age. He was probably twice my age, which historically speaking had always been my type, and was handsome enough to be distracting.

While talking, he rested both of his forearms on top of his thick thighs, which immediately had my gaze darting away from him. Of all times to be attracted to a man the second I laid eyes on them, it just had to be *now* while I was trying to not fuck this up.

Sometimes life felt like one cruel and twisted joke.

I barely recalled any of the information as Jackson ran through the basics on using a flint (the rock-looking thing) on a dried out fiber (the rope) and then stopping the spread of it with an immovable and inflammable object (the pebbles). It wasn't until I was being tugged away by Tyson over to another station close-by that I realized I'd kind of fucking screwed myself over by letting my mind get distracted.

"Can't believe they're letting us play with fire on the first day. They're nuts," Tyson was saying while grabbing at the flint.

I shook my head. "We're low-risk. That's why."

"So says you," he shot back at me.

"I'll just let you take the reins on this one," I said, glancing back over my shoulder to the rest of our sixteen-person brigade.

Most of them were already getting busy with trying to start and stoke their fires, while the other firefighters were walking about and observing. Our

COs hung back but had watchful eyes for any of us screwing around.

Belatedly, I caught sight of Jackson turning toward Tyson and I, and slowly rising to his feet, an interested arch to his brow.

I quickly turned back around again, my cheeks burning. I really hoped he wasn't coming over here to observe us.

That's the last thing I needed—an up close and personal distraction.

"Okay, so he said to strike this on this thing…" Tyson had the flint pressing up against the starter, flicking it a few times. "And then to put it on the rope."

Sparks flew as he struck the starter, but nothing caught. Leaning over the stump, I squinted at what we had on it. "I think you have to press it against the rope while you're striking it."

"Yeah, but that guy didn't do that."

I tried to think back to the display Jackson had out for us and to no one's surprise, my mind was completely blank. All I could remember was how the veins in his arms had flexed when he'd been moving his hands together to strike the flint and catch the rope on fire.

Fuck me… we're so going to fail.

"Maybe use the ends of the rope?" I suggested. Logically, it made sense… right? Less densely packed material for the fire to burn through.

"Oh, you're a fucking genius, pumpkins."

I rolled my eyes at the nickname.

"How we doing over here?" I tensed up at the familiar voice. "Get your flint working yet?"

Jackson hovered behind me, his large body not only imposing but hard to miss.

"Yeah, look at this." Tyson struck the flint once more over the frayed edges of the rope, immediately lighting it on fire. However, it died just as quickly as it'd started, leaving the edges of the rope singed and slightly smoking. "Aw, what the fuck?"

Jackson moved around me and lowered himself to get closer to the stump; one of his knees dug down into the dirt while the other leg was propped up to allow his elbow to rest on it.

"Try again, but this time, make sure you cup your hand around the flame until you can get it to catch properly. The wind out here will blow a flame out quicker than it can catch it. You've got to let yours get enough oxygen first before it can spread up the rope."

As fascinating as the information was, all I could focus on was how deeply *blue* his eyes were. They lingered on me for a moment before quickly darting over to my companion as he struck the flint once more.

Tyson quickly let go of it in order to cup both of his hands around the small embers forming on the rope. He blew on it softly, letting it smolder just as we'd been instructed, and soon, the rope had a healthy flame eating away at it.

"Very nice," Jackson praised. He leaned forward and quickly huffed the flame out, grabbing the flint and starter. "Why don't we have your partner try it this time."

"Oh…" I held my hands up, shaking them. "No, I'm good. I got the gist of it."

"It helps doing it yourself. Practicing the motions is a lot different than watching."

The way he said that last sentence, for some reason, immediately shot straight down to my groin. I cleared my throat, needing to rid myself of the weirdly dirty thoughts. "Yeah, I'm good."

Ignoring me, he set both of the tools in my hand. "Go on. I'll be right here."

The sub in me wanted to desperately let out a whimper.

I'd clearly been celibate for way too long. Maybe it was biting me in the ass not to have taken Tyson up on his numerous offers of getting off with him after lights out. But the potential for a ticket had never seemed worth it, especially since I'd been determined to have a clean wrap sheet for when I finally got out of SAC.

The felony on my records was already going to make my life hard the second I stepped outside of those doors three years from now. Adding onto it just seemed stupid.

Until now, apparently.

Slowly lowering myself to my knees, I gripped onto the flint and starter tightly. My hands shook slightly when I held it out toward the rope that was shoved my way by Tyson, whose overly eager smile was more than a little foreboding.

He may have confidence in me but I certainly didn't.

"Remember," Jackson said. "Strike it and then stoke it."

"Right…" I mumbled.

Feeling both sets of eyes on me, I fought the urge to make up another excuse and instead, struck the flint against the starter harder than I meant to. Sparks flew everywhere, causing both men to lean back quickly to avoid getting hit.

"Oh! You got one!" Tyson pointed to the rope.

I dropped the tools in my hand quickly and cupped both of my hands around the ember, watching as it glowed a deep red.

"Now blow on it," Jackson's voice was nearer to me this time, practically in my ear.

A shiver raced up my spin.

I did as I was told, though, leaning over to blow gently on the ember until it grew brighter. It took a few more tries but soon, it was beginning to smoke, catching the frays that Tyson had burned up with it.

"That's it," came Jackson's voice again, lower this time. "You're doing so good."

I took in one last deep inhale and let it out, encouraging the flame to live. It seemed to do the job a little *too* well, because I soon had a healthy flame that hungrily began to eat up the rest of the frayed edges of the rope, expanding out far enough to burn right against my hand.

With a yelp, I jerked myself back from it.

Jackson acted quickly, taking out some kind of thick towel from the back pocket of his trousers and patting it against the flame, snuffing it out almost instantly. He then full-body turned to me, reaching out with both of his hands.

"Let me see."

He pried my hurt palm away from my body, holding it out into the sunlight where he could see a little better.

The skin was bright pink and already starting

to shift into an ugly red where the flame had touched.

It didn't look so bad now, but *fuck* did it hurt.

"We're going to need to patch this up before it gets too deep," he said, his eyes growing serious.

"Um, what—" I didn't even get the chance to finish my sentence before he was tugging me up onto my feet again, still tenderly holding onto my wrist and hand.

With a whistle, he caught the attention of a nearby firefighter, nodding over to Tyson. "Watch him for me? I've got to take this one to medical."

CHAPTER 2

Jackson

It was my fault.

I'd gone too far in my teasing and now I had an injured inmate sitting in the medic station with an icepack strapped to his hand while I was rifling through the unit's first aid kits.

It wasn't every day that we got such a pretty looking inmate moved into the program. More often than not, I was dealing with the kinds of guys that you'd never want to cross paths with on a sidewalk in the middle of the day, let alone take home to your mother.

But this one was different.

With his big brown curious eyes, his soft features, and the unsure way he carried himself, he wasn't the typical kind of felon I worked with.

What could such a pretty young thing like him

have done in his past to end him up here of all places?

Caught up in a gang, maybe?

The innocent ones always did. And then they ended up doing something stupid and landing themselves behind bars.

A. Gonzalez.

That was the name stitched onto the front of his jumpsuit.

A soft whine, along with a single long scratching drag against it, had me turning toward the door. Shaking my head, I leaned far enough over in the small room to catch the door handle and tug it open. Roxy, my golden, trotted in happily, her tail wagging.

"What, you thought we left you out, huh," I said with a chuckle, and closed the door again.

She panted at me and then turned to our newest companion—Gonzalez.

"You afraid of dogs at all?" I asked him, craning my head back around to look at him tucked into the only chair inside of the medic station. He looked so small in his large oversized jumpsuit, only furthering my curiosity on why the hell he was here.

"Um, not usually?" he said, eying Roxy warily.

"Don't worry, she's not trained to take down inmates or anything if they decide to run—unless it's after dark." It was meant as a teasing note, but Gonzalez seemed to take it a little more seriously than I meant for it to land, because he stiffened up immediately. "I'm kidding."

Still, he didn't seem to relax at all. He only stared guardedly at my dog.

I really needed to stop teasing this poor kid.

However, the small squawk he let out when Roxy trotted over to him and sat down in order to rest her head in his lap had me smiling. Her doe-eyes glanced up at Gonzalez curiously, watching him as he leaned fully back in his chair to give himself a bit of distance.

"She's a softie. Especially if you feed her scraps from the mess hall," I said, trying to keep the amusement out of my voice.

What *I* needed to do was to keep my own distance. Getting chummy with an inmate spelled disaster in too many fonts to name.

"Noted," he mumbled.

I didn't have the heart to tell him that Roxy wasn't usually one to hang out around the inmates, choosing to keep a wide berth between herself and them. I wasn't sure when that behavior of hers started, but I didn't really blame her for it.

The guys who came through here weren't the violent type by any means, at least not outwardly, but a criminal always had a certain air about them that was a little off-putting. Despite that, though, Gonzalez didn't seem to possess that trait at all. In fact, it seemed like the complete opposite.

Something that Roxy, along with myself, seemed to have picked up on.

"Here we go," I said, finding the right kit and tugging it off the shelf. "I should've grabbed your hand away from that flame sooner. That's on me."

Truth be told, I'd been distracted—*heavily*—by the enraptured look on Gonzalez's face as he watched his flame turn from small embers into something more tangible. I don't know why, maybe it was because of those doe-eyes or maybe it was that slight smile that he wore. But either way, he'd gotten hurt because of my negligence, and to me, that was just unacceptable.

These guys may have only volunteered to be here in order to win favor with their parole boards, but that didn't mean I was supposed to be lax in my own job at teaching them the proper safety measures when it came to dealing with fire in any capacity.

"It's fine," he mumbled, scooting forward while trying to not disturb my dog.

I grabbed the rolling stool and sat down on it before rolling over to where he was. The small rolling tray next to him was the next thing I grabbed while placing the first aid kit on top of it and popping the top open. It was packed nicely, thanks to Riviera, who'd been in a manic mood all last week while she cleaned the entire station before any of our inmates were dropped off today.

I grabbed the ice pack off his hand and assessed the burn. It wasn't too deep, thankfully caught early, but it definitely was hurting him. The middle was a bright red while the edges were a softer pink. Thankfully, no blisters had formed, though.

"How bad is it?" he asked, looking down at his palm.

"You'll live." I snatched the gauze out of the kit and began to unravel it. "It's a Christmas miracle."

He stared at me curiously in response, which was only encouraging me further to play with him.

I liked a challenge, which in this case, was

going to be my downfall. This inmate didn't need me poking at him with my own brand of weird humor.

He was a felon, in prison for something serious, even if it was non-violent. Getting mixed up with that was both stupid and morally egregious. Not just for me, but for him, too.

But damn, was I forming a soft spot.

His hands flexed slightly when I spread the burn cream over the wound, coating it generously. Even if a burn didn't *look* severe on the outside, it didn't mean it wasn't hurting like one and wasn't worse underneath the first few layers of skin.

That was what sucked about burn wounds. Until they looked like your skin was actually melting off, not many people took the pain seriously.

Gonzalez let out a soft sigh once the cream began to soak into his skin.

"How's that feel?" I asked, already knowing the answer.

"Better. I didn't think I had my hand on it that long for it to hurt this bad."

"Well, we're warm blooded. So, even if you didn't, it doesn't matter. Your body's cooking it from the inside, which is why it hurts."

"Oh." He blinked, finally looking at me again. "Really? That's crazy."

"The body's a weird enigma."

He was quiet as I dressed his burn the rest of the way, making sure to keep the gauze tight enough to not fall off while moving but not so much that it would irritate his healing skin underneath. A fine and delicate line to tread that I was thankfully well versed in.

"There we go. Good as new." I reached over and patted Roxy's head.

Standing up, I collected the kit and stored the unused materials back inside of it before latching it once more.

I probably should've taken more of my time dressing his hand, using it to talk with him as much as I could. Having sixteen other inmates in the program, I wasn't going to get any specific one-on-one time with any of them while they were here.

Not like this, anyway.

However, I had a feeling if I did that, it was going to lead me into not wanting to give him back at all. And that was just something I was going to have to suck up.

He'd be out of here in six weeks and never to be seen again.

"Thanks, nurse," he mumbled.

His words had me whipping around again, my eyes going wide.

Was that a joke back?

His cheeks were tinged a darker hue that looked pretty on his tanned complexion, eyes averted so as to not catch mine.

A grin split across my face. All right, maybe I *would* make up some excuse to keep him here for just a little bit longer—

Just then, the door to the medic station was thrown open and an angry CO was storming inside the tiny room. "What the fuck did you do, Gonzalez?"

Roxy began to bark instantly, clearly uncomfortable with the sudden burst of aggression.

I stepped in front of them both, blocking the CO—Browne, according to his nametag—from advancing any more. "We had a burn situation. I'm cleaning him up now."

Roxy quieted instantly with a small huff.

The CO eyed me. "He was supposed to be escorted by one of us before you took him anywhere. You know that, right?"

That was the problem with COs coming onto my property. They always seemed to want to have a big-dick complex with me and show off in front of the inmates that they were the big bosses in charge and that everyone else around them was to fall in line.

In the real world, outside of the prison system, life just didn't work that way. I, along with the rest of my staff, deserved and would demand respect. It didn't matter that we were dealing with criminals of whatever caliber.

SAC had hired *my* force to run this program and having a bunch of their defunct cops coming in here and stomping their feet when they didn't get there was a sure-fire way of getting them kicked out and replaced with someone else on their squad.

However, at the same time, I didn't want to be having *that* conversation in front of Gonzalez who looked two seconds away from pissing himself in fear.

"Look…" I plastered a smile onto my face. "I get that, but this was an emergency."

"Really," the CO drawled. "Doesn't look like anyone's dying in here."

"That's because I know how to do my job." My smile widened, maybe turning a bit sardonic in the process. "Unless you wanted me to call an ambulance and get EMS involved in *that* mess. I figured this was the best way to avoid the paperwork."

At the dreaded *P-word*, the CO faltered.

"Right… well… he needs to get back with the other inmates."

"Absolutely, I'll have him out as soon as I feed him some pain killers."

Browne narrowed his eyes. "What *kind* of pain killers."

Interesting.

So was Gonzalez here for selling dope on the streets?

That would certainly go along with my gang theory. He must be if I was getting that kind of question. Non-violent was usually like that—drug trafficking or something else that was equally lower on the felony totem.

"Tylenol. Two hundred milligrams," I answered.

The CO slowly nodded, shifting until he could see Gonzalez over my shoulder. "The second he's done with you, you're going back to your cabin. There's uniforms there waiting for you and we'll be doing a head count after a strip search. So don't think about doing anything stupid."

"O-Okay." His small voice answering back had me wanting to crack my knuckles and shove Browne back out into the hallway.

Back down. It's not your place.

Curbing the urge, I folded my arms over my chest instead. "We all good here?"

"Yeah, but I'm standing right out here. He needs an escort," Browne said.

Right, whatever.

"Sure thing." I had the urge to slam the door in his face when he finally stepped back out into the hall, but stopped myself at the last minute.

If anyone were to suspect I was giving any of the inmates special treatment, that would be a one-way ticket back on a bus to SAC. As much as I wanted to spend more time with Gonzalez for god knows what reason, I wasn't willing to risk his small sabbatical of freedom to do so.

I was a selfish bastard, no doubt, but not at the expense of someone else.

He'd clearly worked hard in getting SAC to see him as a non-threat—this program was only available to those kinds of inmates who showed exemplary attitudes while incarcerated.

Hopefully, sometime soon, I'd get to see him again. Though, maybe next time it wouldn't be over an injury.

"Thank you." His voice was quiet as I slipped two Tylenol into his hand, and faced the front of the bottle toward Browne to show him the brand.

"Yeah, no problem." Once the CO nodded to me, I set it down and fished a cold water bottle out of the mini fridge on top of the counter, handing it over. "Just let me know if the pain gets worse and we'll reapply that burn cream again."

He nodded before tossing both pills back and taking a generous swing from the water bottle.

"I appreciate it, thank you." He flashed a little, cautious smile at me.

My heart clenched tight in my chest. Jesus, he really was beautiful. Such a shame he decided to waste his life on doing something stupid and getting himself locked up.

He held his hand out with the water bottle in it, handing it back to me. I shook my head, waving my hand at him to keep it. It was the least I could do for causing him to get burned in the first place, even if it was an accident.

"Let's go, Gonzalez," Browne's gruff voice cut through the room again.

Roxy whimpered softly at him moving, standing up slowly from his chair.

Gonzalez hesitated and then reached down to pat Roxy's head gently.

Her mouth opened, her long tongue lolling out and to the side while she panted at him. His smile widened slightly, clearly amused by my dog and her rather insatiable nature when it came to pats and attention.

"Bye… um…" He glanced over at me briefly.

"Roxy," I said, knowing that's what he was searching for.

"Roxy." He patted her head one last time before stepping around us both and heading out the door to follow his CO.

Roxy turned and whined at me again.

"I know, girl." I squatted, pulling her into a hug while rubbing at her sides. "We'll see him again soon."

Hopefully.

CHAPTER 3

Ayen

My hand felt like it burned for the rest of the night.

I tried to not take it as a sign of the days to come—ones where I'd be left coming back to my cabin with more bruises and burns than I'd left with that morning. Sometimes, it felt like a penance; usually during my darker moments while I laid away in bed, staring up at Tyson's bunk as he tossed and turned above me while the distant sounds of the jail settling down for the night echoed around me.

That sort of thing happened a lot when I'd first gotten sentenced. The adjustment had been hard and not just because I wasn't used to having my every move watched or to follow a strict schedule that deviating from got me thrown in the hole for a few days.

I'd never felt such profound loneliness as I did those first couple of weeks. I no longer had my beautiful house, or my annoyingly noisy neighbors, or the garden I'd worked so goddamn hard to tend to while I'd been left for weeks on end playing my dutiful house-husband role.

That small slice of utopia that I'd created for myself had been the only thing that I felt was really *mine.* And yet, I'd flushed it all away in a matter of thirteen minutes.

Some would say it was justified, but the courts had thought differently.

Self-defense only counted if the person who was trying to hurt you was a stranger breaking into your house and not the man you vowed to stick with through thick and thin.

At least I had Tyson to keep me company here, too, or rather, to help with keeping my busy mind occupied and not stuck on a certain hand-some fireman and his sweet-as-pie dog.

"How's your hand?" Tyson nodded to my bandages as we sat down at one of the tables inside of the mess hall. He already was digging into his plate of food by the time we both got comfortable.

"It's fine. Still kind of hurts but I'll manage."

He nodded again, shoving another fork-load of eggs into his mouth. Honestly, I couldn't really blame him. We got shit for food back at SAC, so freshly cooked eggs and bacon felt like we'd somehow reached heaven without even realizing it.

I sliced a bite onto my own fork and ate slowly.

While it was true my burn hurt less than it did

yesterday, it was still all I could focus on during the night along with watching my back.

The cabin Tyson and I were staying in was also occupied by two other guys, Alvin Richards and Lucas McMurphy. They had been fine enough last night after lights out but I knew better than to trust anyone with my eyes closed and my back facing away from the door.

If there was a bigger lesson in prison than not letting your guard down when you least expected it, I didn't know what was.

Sure, we were all considered non-violent, but desperation made you do crazy things. This was the first time any of us were actually all out on a program like this. Outside of the cabin was a long stretch of forest that was acres deep that, given the right circumstances, anyone could get lost in before our COs were any the wiser.

All of that was purely speculation on my part, of course. But it didn't hurt me to consider all of the possibilities. I was not strong, nor was I adept in any kind of physical combat, so if some kind of fight broke out, I'd be a sitting duck waiting for someone to punch me stupid.

Suddenly, I felt something wet against my ankle.

Jumping away from it, I clutched the side of the table and looked over to see what it was. I spotting a familiar dog wagging her tail as she watched me curiously.

"Yo, what the fuck?" Tyson said.

Relaxing back into my seat, I brushed a hand over Roxy's head a few times, smiling when her tongue began to loll to the side of her mouth.

"Sorry about that," said a voice from behind me. "She doesn't usually run off like that."

My entire body stiffened, but not uncomfortably. No, this was much different as I felt an electric pulse race up my spine.

I felt him before I managed to look up, Jackson's looming presence hovering over me.

"How's your hand?" He nodded down at it.

"Fine," came my automatic response.

I could feel Tyson giving me a weird look, but he kept his comments to himself while shoveling the rest of his food on his plate into his mouth. He was smart to do so or else he'd soon find my shoe kicking him in the shin.

"You sure?" To my surprise, Jackson swung around to my left side—opposite of Roxy—and sat on the stool. "Let me take a look at it."

I didn't fight him when he grabbed my wrist in a firm hold, flipping my hand over until it was facing palm up. My cheeks suddenly felt flushed as my fingers twitched, trying to suppress them from shaking at the contact.

How sad was it that the mere touch of an attractive man was practically making me melt in my seat?

Carefully, Jackson peeled the bandages off of my hand and tossed them onto the table. Roxy's face dug into my lap until her head was comfortably resting nuzzled against my stomach, much like the last time we'd met. I grazed my free hand over her soft fur, letting it distract my mind while Jackson continued to poke and prod at me.

"This doesn't hurt?" he asked, pressing along

the outside of the burn where it was still bright pink. "At all?"

I never was any good at lying, especially when it came to pain. And I was sure my wince told him as much. But the alternative was to admit that I'd been up with it all night, and that was a little *too* embarrassing to own up to by now.

He chuckled at me and shifted his body to the side to pull something out of the pouch at his hip. "Good thing I brought this with me this morning."

Jesus, am I that transparent?

He took out the tube of burn cream that he'd used a day earlier and uncapped it with a quick flick of his thumb. The dollop he squirted onto my hand was generous, much more than the one he'd given me yesterday.

Did it really look that bad?

Sure, it hurt like a bitch, but I'd had broken bones that felt worse.

It then occurred to me that he probably wasn't up for dealing with any of the paperwork that would follow me complaining to the work program board if I let it go untreated. I wasn't too aware of what the long-term effects of an untreated burn were, but I doubted he'd want to get questioned by the board about it. Not like they'd ever do anything for *me* but it could cause Jackson and the rest of his crew a headache of paperwork.

Unfortunately, as government property went, we were expendable to only a certain extent. When it came to 'damaging' said property, the kind that could result in some kind of lawsuit, that's when things down the pipeline moved rather quickly in our favor.

It wasn't ever much, but prison healthcare beat the unforgiving nature of being out on the streets without it.

After capping the tube and setting it down onto the table, Jackson shifted my hand between both of his. His thumbs rolled gentle swirls around my skin, massaging the cream into it thoroughly.

It felt nice as I watched his fingers work, enraptured by them gliding over my skin again and again.

Physical touch was always my weakness, even with my ex. I loved to be touched and not just sexually. To have fingers coarse through my hair, to have a pair of arms wrapped tightly around me, to have a body fit perfectly against the curve of my back.

I missed a lot of it, now that I wasn't allowed to have anything in prison. Tyson had offered a few times to relieve the tension that every man in that facility felt at some point, but I never liked the idea. Sneaking around behind the guards watching in order to get in a quickie felt dirty to me. At least in the way that being used purely for sexual gratification did.

My ex had been my first lover and had spoiled me rotten when we first met. There was a time in my life where I wanted for nothing and those had been the best, most blissful years of my life.

Until he somehow got it into his head that I owed him. That's when the real downfall began.

Jackson worked his fingers up slowly from the tips of mine and down to where the burn in the center of my palm was, coating all of it in a nice thin layer of the cream that began to slowly soak into my skin.

His touch was gentle as he worked, taking the kind of care that I wasn't used to receiving.

"Wow, didn't know this place came with VIP service," Tyson teased.

I shot a glare at him, praying that it would be enough to shut him up. One of these days, Tyson was going to get us both into trouble for spouting off nonsense to the wrong person. If he so much as insinuated anything to the COs about Jackson and I, we'd be pulled from the program faster than either of us could blink.

"How's that feeling? Better?" Jackson fanned out my fingers, completely ignoring Tyson's remarks.

Truth be told, it actually did feel a lot better. There was no more of that uncomfortable pinch that lingered every time I moved it or that dull ache of pain that seemed to flare up right when I finally stopped thinking about it.

I forced myself not to pull my fingers together, wary of spreading the cream too much or getting it caked onto other parts of my skin where it didn't need to be.

"Thank you," I mumbled, avoiding eye contact.

For some reason this entire act, while ultimately innocent on the surface, felt so much more than that. It felt intimate in a way I hadn't been with anyone else since my ex. My touch-starved nature was rearing its ugly head and making me feel things that I really didn't need to be feeling at all.

Let alone toward the head of the damn Cal Fire Inmate Program.

I wasn't sure what Jackson's deal was with seeking me out personally like this—he could've just as well had someone else, a CO most likely, come and get me to bring me to the infirmary to make sure my hand wasn't getting infected.

Instead, he'd gone out of his way to come all the way over to the mess hall and check on me.

At least, that's what it was feeling like. Although, who knew. Maybe he was just there to grab breakfast before training began. My over thinking this entire situation was probably just me blowing out a kind gesture way out of proportion.

The guy was just trying to be nice, probably even pitied me.

I was sure all he saw was some kid who had gotten himself involved in something stupid and wound up behind bars. That's what I would've thought looking at me. I wasn't the typical run-of-the-mill criminal with a hardened past and the faint wrinkles embedded into my face to prove it.

I looked like the kind of person that would have a simple 9-to-5 at a local convenience store and occasionally have trouble reaching the top shelf to stock products. Not have a rap sheet that was fifteen charges long.

Not to mention this guy was most likely married with a gaggle of kids at home. That's what hot guys like him always had waiting for them.

Me lusting after someone like him because I'd

been starved of any form of human contact that wasn't in exchange for commissary wasn't his problem. It was mine to deal with and get under control before I did something stupid—like flirt back.

Jackson let go of my hand finally, grabbing the scraps of gauze he'd used on me yesterday.

"You shouldn't need to get that wrapped again. We won't be doing anything strenuous today, just a few demonstrations and then some prep work. But if you feel like you need it to be wrapped for that, stop by with your CO to the medic station and someone will patch you up again."

I nodded, my lips pressed together tightly.

"Just let that cream soak in before touching anything, though," he went on. "It's best to let your body do what it naturally does."

"Thank you," I mumbled again, not knowing what else to say.

Roxy huffed against my stomach when her owner rose from his seat. Her big brown eyes flitted between us both while she continued to stay comfortably stuck on my lap.

Jackson let out an amused chuckle before recalling her back to his side. "You boys have a good breakfast."

My gaze locked onto his back as he left, heading over to the buffet where the spread of food was still laid out and one of the prep workers was standing behind the plate display.

Without realizing it, I let out a slow breath.

"Next time, let me get burned," Tyson said. "I want a hot daddy to rub cream all over *my* hand."

I wrinkled my nose. "You're disgusting."

He laughed loudly.

It had me thinking, though—just who *was* Jackson and why did it feel like every time he came around me, there was this weird tension there?

It had to be in my head.

There was no other explanation to it. This guy was nice and was trying to be a good host while we were on his turf.

What else would he want from me, anyway?

Right?

CHAPTER 4

JACKSON

TRAINING WENT AS SMOOTHLY as it could go considering the fact that none of these inmates had any sort of exposure to firefighter procedures before in the past.

I had to say, out of any of the groups we'd had come through here over the last few years, none of them had ever been as proactive as these guys were.

Sure, there was plenty of bumbling and knocking things over but aside from that, we had a good group this time around. It was rare to see so much cooperation among a bunch of criminals who were used to doing things in their own way, on their own time—which was most likely part of the reason they were even here in the first place.

But still, it was a nice change of pace for once.

I'd been careful to mind myself when walking

around the groups as they'd broken up to practice what they'd learned, keeping a careful distance between me and Gonzalez for the time being.

Whatever had possessed me to walk up to him during breakfast and slather a bunch of burn cream all over him like I was trying to perform some type of fucked up version of a Thai hand massage had me frustrated.

And not just mentally.

Not just for my lack of boundaries that I'd been forcing myself to abide by since he got here, but because seeing his eyes widen at the sight of my fingers carefully moving along the ridges of his hand and working between the tendons had turned me on more than I'd expected it to.

What I wouldn't give to see that same expression while I ran my hands along his body, feeling out which parts of him were oversensitive and watching him squirm when I finally found them.

It was fucked up—all of it. Yet my mind had completely attached itself to the idea and no matter what I did, it continued to play over and over again. A non-stop loop that was driving me fucking mad. I kept rolling the fantasy over and over in my head as I made my rounds and steered clear of him and his friend.

What I actually needed to do was head to the bar after this and go get laid.

Clearly, I was pent up for whatever reason and needed to clear my head. Once I was done, I could come back to the station clear-headed and focused and not continue to obsess over a pretty little inmate that I was growing suspicious of being a sub.

Because what else would he be with how obediently he'd let me touch him and seemed to lean into the heat of my body so close to mine?

Ugh.

Fuck…

When the sun finally set, we called it enough for the night.

Inmates filed into the mess hall to grab dinner and settle down for the rest of the evening while I headed to the staff cabins to grab my things. During these programs, I tended to opt for staying on property. More as an ease of convenience than anything else. My house was more in the city and battling traffic everyday just to arrive at the ass crack of dawn was bad for my blood pressure.

Tonight, though, I'd stay in the city and deal with fighting my way back to the sticks in the morning. It was worth it in the end if it got me to stop focusing so heavily on Gonzalez and take my desires elsewhere.

A casual hookup hadn't ever failed me from working out my frustrations in the past.

"Going somewhere, Hall?"

I looked over to my colleague, Ryan, as we entered the staff section of the training grounds. "Yeah, into the city."

He raised a brow at me. "You're going back home for the night? That's rare."

"No, just the bar. You want to hitch a ride?"

He laughed and slapped me on the back on our way in through the doors of the main pavilion. "Not a chance. Last time I went with you, I could barely function the next day. You drink like a fucking ox and my liver can't handle that right now."

"Least I got you laid," I quipped back and headed into the locker room. Mine was toward the back of the row with a beat up looking door and a lock that liked to jam on me sometimes. I found mine and quickly rotated the dial for my combo.

"Yeah, as well as a concussion from falling face first on the pavement the next morning from my hangover."

"Hey, that was *after* your hookup," I pointed out. "So, I'm still taking credit for a job well done."

My locker creaked as I opened it. Stripping out of my gear and hanging it up, my shoulders began to relax instantly. Rolling them back a few times felt nice, along with my neck cracking on each side as I rotated it.

Next to me, Ryan pulled open his own locker. The bright fluorescent lights above us bounced off his bald head, still slightly slick from sweat from being under his helmet all day in the hot California sun.

Even though up here in the more forested parts of Sacramento was a lot cooler than in the city, we still got those massive heat waves that were brutal under all of our gear. These past few days we could get away with the bare minimum coverage but starting next week, some of us were going to need to gear up completely when the real training began.

"Have fun on your escapade," Ryan shot back. "Just make sure you're still functionally drunk when you come back tomorrow. Wouldn't want you to get burned like that inmate."

His chuckle had my hand clenching around the side of my locker door tight enough to hurt.

A harmless joke, that's all it was. There was no need for the sudden anger that flared through my chest. I probably still had some residual guilt left over from the incident brewing in me that was causing me to have such a knee-jerk reaction.

Gonzalez was fine.

Honestly, his hand looked almost healed aside from the still pinkened skin when I last saw it.

During training today, he hadn't made a peep at all.

Not that I was really paying attention to him to notice.

Still, he was an adult. If he really needed medical attention, he knew how to get it.

I ignored the small voice in the back of my head that whispered doubt about that—given his shy and passive nature. I had to trust that if there was something going on with him, either someone else would notice or he'd actually pull on his big boy pants and deal with it.

Chewing at the inside of my cheek, I slammed my locker shut a little harder than necessary.

"You good there, Hall?" Ryan raised a brow at me again.

"Yeah. I'll see you tomorrow," I said as I waved and headed back to my cabin to change into something more fresh and say goodbye to Roxy for the night.

I hadn't felt this kind of protective instinct over

a man like Gonzalez in a long ass time and it was really beginning to throw me for a loop.

He reminded me so much of my cute little submissives that I loved to take back home with me from the clubs I frequented all throughout my twenties. Back then, I had a lot of misplaced emotions over what had been going on at home.

Being a young, gay college kid who'd been essentially disowned by his only parent had rocked my world more than I really ever realized until later in life.

I'd wanted to save the subs I took home. Do the one thing for them that I'd wished someone had done for me.

Learning the hard truth that not everyone wanted that had been a long and grueling lesson. In the end, I'd turned my passion toward firefighting, teaching new recruits, and rehabbing criminals through work placement programs.

It was better this way. It kept me busy and I got to see people strive to meet their goals and push them until they were across the finish line instead of trying to placate myself in another relationship with a doomed timeline.

Roxy growled happily at me as I entered my cabin, a toy stuffed in her mouth while her feet tapped against the hardwood floor. I swept my hand over her head a few times before shedding my sweaty clothes for something fresher.

Tonight was all about getting my head back on straight. No more of this obsessing over an inmate business.

CHAPTER 5

The bar wasn't as nearly packed as I wanted it to be, but I supposed that's what I got for coming in on a Wednesday night.

Thankfully, by the time I was served my second beer, I spotted a cute blond over in the corner of the bar hanging out by the pool table. He had on a pair of short-shorts that were frayed at the ends and a cropped top that didn't quite show off his full mid-drift but did tease a little bit of skin. His hair was messy, tossed on top of his head, giving him that 'barely put together' look that was so in right now.

Tossing back the rest of my drink, I left the glass on the bar and slid off of my stool to head over to him.

He was on his phone, scrolling for something, his bottom lip pinched between his teeth.

"You up for a round?" I asked, grabbing one of the cue sticks off of the rack.

He looked up, his eyes widening briefly before he grinned. "Oh. Yeah, sure. But you're going to have to teach me."

"My pleasure." I flashed him a smile.

After handing him one of the sticks, I moved closer to the table and snatched the blue chalk cube up to rub on the tip to freshen it up a bit. With a wink, I tossed it lightly at him and said, "I'll take stripes."

Lining up my cue, I pinned it back twice before striking the rack, sinking two of the stripes balls into the left-most pocket.

He let out a gasp and clapped. "Wow! Impressive. I didn't know I was in the presence of a seasoned expert."

The way he said it had me snorting softly to myself.

Sometimes the younger ones liked to put me in a box. I think it was my refusal at dyeing my hair and letting my grays grow out instead of trying to pretend like I wasn't forty-five. I wasn't so much attached to ages as long as whomever I was with was at least in their mid-twenties.

Anything below that and I ran the risk of a clinger.

"Mind showing me?" he said, coming closer to me with a sway of his hips.

He was hot, I'd give him that.

He pressed himself against the lip of the table and bent over, sticking his ass out, and very poorly secured his cue on top of one of his hands.

I chuckled, getting up in his space in order to

correct his posture using my hands on his hips as a guide.

"Try that instead. And hit the solid colored ones, or else I'll win," I said.

He grinned at me over his shoulder. "And what happens if you do?"

"How about I take you home?" I moved his hips again, fixing the way his body was tilted before I let him go again.

"I like the sound of that," he said before whacking his cue against one of the balls closest to him.

While I meant what I said, there just wasn't any heat behind my promise. Sure, the kid was hot and would most likely be a fun time, but for some reason I wasn't feeling it.

Maybe I needed another drink in me. Or maybe I'd been spending way too much time in the sun.

"*Oh*, did you see that? I hit one," he said, standing back up.

As he turned, he pressed his entire body against mine. His cute little cock was already hard and rubbing against mine. "How about we skip to the part where you win and take me home."

Man, how easy would it be to take him up on his offer?

I cupped his face, squeezing slightly as I looked down at his round features.

The only problem was that this kid's eyes were a soft blue and not the deep rich brown that I was hoping they'd be. There was a dusting of pinkish makeup around his eyes, bringing out the blue even more. His skin was pale, not the tan that I'd been fantasizing about running my tongue over to taste how salty it'd be after along day of working under the scorching sun.

Fuck.

What a damn bust.

"Sorry," I said, letting him go. "I just remembered I've got a thing in the morning."

He pouted. "Seriously?"

"Rain check?" I asked, even though both of us knew this would be the last time we'd see each other.

"Yeah," he waved his hand, rolling his eyes and pulling out his phone again. "Sure. Whatever."

I pecked him on the forehead as an apology. "Hope you find someone to take you up on that offer."

He smiled a little, waving me off again. "Go away before I make you take me home."

I had to laugh at that.

Setting my cue stick back on the rack, I headed out and climbed into my truck.

Well, so much for trying to fuck my energy out with a stranger. I didn't typically like to resort to using my hand but apparently, that's where this was headed tonight. At least with masterbating, I wouldn't have to pretend to replace the features of one man for another.

Getting back on property was easy with the late-night traffic. Soon enough, the familiar wooden sign stating 'CAL FIRE INMATE WORK PROGRAM' greeted me.

I parked my truck and killed the ignition just as something flashing caught my eye.

Two COs were running together with their flashlights bobbing on the ground, followed closely by two of my guys who were sprinting after them.

My heart hammered in my chest as I kicked my door open.

Fuck, were they heading for the inmate cabins?

I slammed my door shut and ran after them, hoping like hell I was wrong.

CHAPTER 6

Ayen

I winced as cards were tossed onto the floor.

"You motherfucker!" McMurphy shouted, standing up to hover over the other man. "I saw you sneak in another card! You think this is fucking funny, don't you?"

"Fuck off," Richards snapped back, shoving McMurphy away as he stood. "I didn't sneak fucking shit! You're just shit at the game."

I shuffled back from where they were, slowly inching myself toward the corner of the room that was as far away from them as possible.

The night had started off simple enough—a card game to pass the time after lights out. Richards had apparently snuck in a deck from SAC and stashed it under his bunk mattress until the COs had retired for the night.

We—Tyson and I—had figured, what was the harm in a few rounds of cards?

It wasn't like there was anything to bet that would get anyone heated.

Apparently, that had been dead wrong because halfway through the second game, McMurphy had tossed a few cigarette butts down in the center of our card game while saying he'd swiped them up from the ground after one of the COs, Matthers, had been busy chain smoking behind the mess hall.

To me, it seemed rather nasty to suck on the remnants of a used butt just in the hope that there'd be some nicotine left, but apparently I was in the minority with that opinion.

"Calm down, both of you," Tyson hissed, quickly kicking the butts under one of the bunks before standing, too. "You're going to get us kicked out."

"Fuck you, Asper! You want to fucking fight about it?" McMurphy suddenly turned his rage away from Richards and onto Tyson.

"What the fuck is your problem, man?"

"I don't have a fucking problem." He shoved my cellmate back hard, causing him to stumble.

"Oh, no you fucking didn't," was all Tyson said before he swung.

I scrambled up from the floor right as both Tyson and McMurphy slammed down onto it. My heart pounded hard in my chest as I froze, not knowing what I could do to even help Tyson. I wasn't good at fighting, or hurting anyone for that matter.

They both rolled around on the floor, trading

blows with each other hard enough for thuds to be heard as fists smacked against skin and bone. I winced at every single one of them, trying desperately to look for a way to break them up without jumping headfirst into the fray.

Tyson's fist shot up to grab at the sheets on the lower bunk next to me, trying to pull himself up off the floor. Both the top blanket and sheet ripped away from where it had been tucked against the wall and shifted across the bed messily as he tried to stand up.

The give in it wasn't enough, though, and soon sent Tyson flying back down onto McMurphy's chest.

Richards lifted his foot to slam it down onto my cellmate, and instantly, I had my hand wrapped around my pillow and tossed it at him.

It barely had any effect aside from getting him to look up at me when it hit him and turn that scowl into a downright snarl.

"You have something you wanna say, Gonzalez?" he spat out.

My arms flew over my head instinctively, years of this same situation suddenly flashing through my mind, mirrored by what was going on. Soon, I'd be hit in the back or on the arm hard enough to break the protective hold I had over my face. The force of it would stun me enough to pry my arms apart and next a fist would come flying at my face, upper cutting me hard enough to rattle my teeth.

That's how it always went. I'd be back in the damn house with no one but my oblivious neighbors to hear my screaming.

My breaths hitched in and out of my chest hard as I waited for the familiar blows. My entire body shook as I hunched in on myself, praying that it would be over soon.

A crash coming from the front of the cabin had me sinking to my knees instantly, practically curling up in a ball on the floor as panic began to take over.

"What the fuck is going on in here!" someone shouted. "Get the fuck up off each other!"

There was some more arguing and what sounded like a couple of our COs breaking up the fight. I didn't dare to peek, though, afraid that I'd be met with a fist to my eye and a concussion to follow.

"Jesus," someone said over me, a familiar voice, laced with worry.

Worry?

"Gonzalez?"

My entire body was most definitely shaking visibly.

Oh god, was I going to get shipped back to SAC?

Only two days into the goddamn program?

I was never going to get another work program like this if I got sent back. No board was going to look at my record and cut me some slack if they thought I was involved in some fight.

Hands came around to grab at my wrists in a gentle hold, pulling at them. "Hey, come here."

I was frozen solid, stuck in the protective position while I rode through my panic attack. That was the shitty thing about having PTSD, it came at the worst fucking times.

The hands let go of me and instead, I felt a pair of arms wrapping around my body and quickly plucking me up from the floor. Instinctively, my fingers latched onto the hard muscles of the shoulder I was thrown up onto, holding me tight to the person that was carrying me.

"Hey, it's okay," he said, patting my back. "You're all right."

A soft noise escaped my lips.

I was carried through the cabin and out into the cool night air. Breathing in deeply, I caught a familiar spicy scent that had me relaxing almost instantly. Back inside the cabin, I could hear the COs yelling, something about illegal gambling.

"Gonzalez." I was carefully swung back down onto my feet and Jackson's face suddenly appeared in front of me. "What happened?"

"I... um..." I tucked my arms tight around my body, holding myself while I shook.

He shrugged off his jacket and draped it over my shoulders. The inside of it was warm and had his scent practically melted into the seams. I nuzzled my face against the collar, letting the spicy smell of him soak into my bones and bring me back down.

"Were you guys gambling or something?" he asked.

I shook my head.

He didn't seem like he was judging me, at least from the tone of his question.

Well, I guessed that was kind of a lie, though. Just because I wasn't directly involved in the gambling didn't mean it wasn't going on and that I wasn't exactly participating in it. I wasn't after the prize but I was still slapping down my cards in order to up the pot's stakes. I personally wasn't playing to bet on a couple of used up cigarettes, but that didn't mean the other three weren't.

By association, I was guilty, too.

The one thing about prison life was that we were an all-for-one society, even if none of us believed in it. Privileges were either given or revoked due to other inmates behavior and when one of us fucked up, the rest suffered.

That was why the violence rates could get pretty bad. If there was one bad apple that was making life unbearable for everyone else, he needed to be taken care of.

By all intents and purposes, whatever happened to McMurphy, Richards, and Tyson in there was going to become my fate, too.

"Gonzalez?" Jackson asked again."

"Ayen," I said quietly, mumbling it into the fabric of his jacket.

"What?"

"*Ayen.* My name."

His eyes widened briefly.

After tonight, I would never see this man again. Might as well leave him with a little piece of me. Not that he'd really care. All I was to him was a number and a vaguely familiar face.

Before he could say anything back, one of the COs, Stinner, came stomping out the front door of the cabin. "Gonzalez!"

I winced and quickly hid behind Jackson.

To my surprise, the man shifted just enough to block me entirely from the COs view.

"He wasn't doing anything," Jackson said. "You know that, right?"

"He was fucking gambling! That's against the rules."

"He was cowering in the corner trying not to get hit. My bet is that he was probably asleep when all of that went down."

My gaze shot up to stare at the back of Jackson's head.

Why was he defending me?

To a CO no less?

What could he possibly be getting out of it?

"Go look at how messy the bed he was next to was," Jackson went on. "The sheets were pulled back and everything."

Stinner let out a loud scoff but didn't argue. "Whatever. We need to separate all of these guys for the night. The bus won't be able to get out to us until morning."

"I've got a spare staff cabin. One of them can bunk with me, there's an extra bed. I'll take Gonzalez since he had nothing to do with this."

My jaw dropped open.

Wait, was he serious?

"We're going to have to discuss that with the other COs," Stinner was saying, but Jackson was already reaching back to grab my arm.

"That's fine. I need to go open up the medic station so we can get those other two checked out. Unless you want to call an ambulance?"

I bit the inside of my cheek to keep from grinning.

The dreaded 'A'-word. Every CO's worst nightmare.

Not only would the prison be held responsible for the inmates' care while there, they'd also have to ship out a few COs in order to guard the doors to make sure no one got the bright idea of slipping out of their room and getting out onto the streets.

And literally *no one* wanted guard duty in a hospital. Not only was it boring as all hell to wait outside of a patient's room twiddling your thumbs, but I doubted any of them would be getting overtime.

Not with the way our Warden worked.

"Yeah. Sure. We'll meet you over at the station with them," Stinner said. "He needs to be hand-cuffed, though."

Jackson sighed, dropping my hand. "All right."

I held out my still shaking hands to Stinner, who slapped a pair of cuffs on them, wrenching them tight enough to hurt when I moved my arms around. He was one of the COs that was known to be in a pissy mood if things like inmate fighting cut into his 'me time' away from all of us.

Jackson finally took me by the wrist again and led me away from the cabins.

The lights coming off of the buildings we passed by gave us just enough illumination to see where we were going but not enough to look like we'd stepped out onto the center of the sun.

As we grew farther and farther away from the cabins, my heart began to slow and I could breathe again.

Jesus, I hadn't been that up close and personal to a fight since I first came to SAC. My first week there had been quite the initiation into prison life, with a guy in my unit being stabbed and another one being dragged out and beaten up in the yard during our rec period while I'd been standing close by.

After everything that had happened leading up to me being arrested and going to jail, I'd never had a good track record with being met face-to-face with aggression or imminent threat.

The one time I'd defended myself had landed me in prison. So...

"You okay?" Jackson turned back to look at me right as we reached the medic station.

I swallowed thickly. "Yeah. I, uh... I hope you don't think I was involved in any of that."

Why did I say it like that?

And why would Jackson even care?

Did I *want* him to care?

It wasn't like his opinion of me should matter. If it did… well, it'd just complicate things.

Right?

"Oh…" He lifted a hand and very gently dragged his fingers through my hair, brushing it back away from my face. "No, not at all. You're far too sweet to be involved in any of that."

My entire body flushed with heat as the air in my lungs caught in my throat. I was so glad it was dark out there because I was sure my face was bright red with how hard I was blushing.

What the hell did that even mean?

His thumb traced along my forehead before dropping back down to his side. "Let's get you cleaned up."

CHAPTER 7

JACKSON

AYEN.

What a pretty name. It was fitting for someone who looked and acted like him.

I ran my gaze over him, taking in his curious expression as he wandered around my cabin. One of his hands gripped at his wrist, rubbing over the red ring that had been left from the too-tight cuffs.

I'd somehow managed to convince his CO to take them off before bringing him to my cabin after I'd gotten the medic station opened up—another thing that I was surprised they went along with. I had a good track record with them, though, and technically, this was *my* program. So my rules typically superseded whatever they had bickered about amongst themselves.

SAC got a good tax write off by working with my program—inmate rehabilitation was all the rage and made for good bragging rights when it came time for the Warden to be schmoozing it up with the governor about how well their programs were running and raking in the grant money when the fiscal new year rolled around.

Mine had one of the better success rates, so pissing me off and cutting SAC loose would be detrimental.

Which was probably why I got my way tonight.

"You can take the bed." I nodded to the door that was closed just down the hallway. "I'm fine with the couch."

Ayen whipped around with wide eyes. "I can't *take your bed*. I thought you had a spare?"

"I lied." I grinned. "I promise, I don't have cooties."

His cheeks visibly flushed a cute light pink in the soft lighting of my cabin.

It was a nice place, with a full sized bedroom, kitchen, living room, and small dining room. There was a reason I didn't mind staying here during the entire program. Compared to pretty much everyone else on the property, I was living it large.

"I—that's..." he stuttered. "That's not what I meant."

I walked over to him slowly, my dick stirring as I watched him track my movements. I hated seeing him so afraid back in his cabin while that fight was happening. Thankfully, by the time we'd come gotten here, he'd perked up a bit. I never wanted to see him like that again; not on my watch at least.

How bad had prison been for him to have that kind of reaction?

I didn't want to think about it—if I did, it was only going to make me mad.

Instead, I grabbed his wrist and pulled it from where he'd been stroking it with his hand. I ran my thumb lightly over the irritated skin, the ridges of where the cuff had been digging into him instantly annoying me.

The COs that came in here with their aggression barely in check were always the ones that pissed me off the most. Not because they were particularly more of an asshole than the rest, but because they took all those pent-up feelings out on the inmates who were only trying to learn, and hopefully, make something of themselves when they finally got out.

"I think I'm going to have to wrap you up in bubble wrap from now on," I murmured.

He huffed out a laugh. "I don't think that's the take-away from all of this."

"Let me at least put some ointment on this. Should heal you right up." I couldn't help the need to care for him. It was a burning desire that was blooming in my chest and only seemed to get worse the longer I stayed in his presence.

Touching him in any capacity was beginning to become addicting—so much so that I was trying to make up any little excuse to justify myself.

"No, it's okay." He stayed rooted to his spot, even as I tugged at him to follow me to the bathroom. "You've done enough as it is."

"Are you sure?" I didn't want him to say yes. I wanted him to let me take care of him.

But, of course, he merely shook his head and slipped his wrist out of my grip.

I wanted to argue but he'd already been involved in enough tonight. My pressing him to do what I wanted him to do was only going to create a weird dynamic between us that I didn't want to happen. I already had him out of his element and in *my* space. There was no sense in pushing his boundaries while I was trying to make him feel more comfortable.

"You want water or anything?" I stepped away from him and headed into the kitchen. I flexed my fingers together at my sides while I mourned the loss of having them wrapped around him in some capacity.

Right now, I was really starting to regret not taking that cute blond home and fucking his brains out because this was getting to be ridiculous.

How was it that an inmate that I hardly knew could render me into such a goddamn needy mess?

I heard him follow me by the sound of the old and worn floorboards creaking slightly under his feet. "I'm okay."

Even with his refusal, he still was seeking out my company. That had me smiling a little bit to myself.

Jesus, I needed to get it together.

Turning back around, I fixed him with a look over my fridge door as I pulled it open. "Not even if it's ice cold?"

He let out another soft laugh—a delightful sound. "Is this you not taking *no* for an answer?"

Yes.

"Well, only when it comes to hydration." I slipped a bottle out from the top shelf and handed it to him. "I never play about that."

He uncapped it and took a generous swig. My coat looked massive still hanging off his shoulders and dwarfing his already petite frame. But somehow, it looked good on him.

Really good.

Right, even.

It had me thinking about putting him to bed in one of my t-shirts next.

My stomach clenched at the thought, possessiveness rearing its ugly head once more.

I wanted to keep him here permanently but there was no way the COs were going to allow that. Chances were that as soon as the sun was up, a bus would be rolling by to pick all four of them up and ship them back off to SAC for poor conduct.

It hurt my heart to think that Ayen would be caught up in all of that when it was obvious to anyone with two fucking eyes that the poor kid was way too scared to even be involved in any of that drama. Maybe he had been fucking with the cards initially, but I highly doubted he instigated that fight or was ever involved in it in any capacity.

I couldn't see him as the type.

Especially with how I'd found him curled up in himself while he shook through his panic attack.

Fuck, seeing him like that had really upset me. More than I cared to admit. He wasn't supposed to be scared here, none of the inmates were. So walking into *that* and seeing him shielding himself like he was ready for someone to start wailing on him had me tearing through that damn cabin in order to get to him.

Getting him out of there had been my only priority. Getting him to safety—to *me*—was the single thought that had been rattling through my brain.

Ayen capped the half finished bottle again and stared at it for a long moment while I leaned against the door of my fridge, watching him. The cool air from it felt nice against my skin even though it wasn't that humid out tonight.

"Why... are you doing all of this?" He glanced up at me. "I... You defended me to Stinner..."

I shrugged. "He was being an ass."

Which was true, in a sense. That CO coming out of the cabin hot and ready to pick a fight had my protective instincts flaring instantly. There was no way I was going to let Ayen go with him when he was already scared. Turning him over to a CO like that would keep me up all fucking night worrying about him.

Ayen frowned at me. "But he's the CO... it doesn't really matter what his attitude is like. Aren't you supposed to... Uh—" He cut himself off, his lips pressing together tightly.

"'Listen to him?" I guessed. "Not at all. He's in my neck of the woods."

"You own this place?" His eyes widened in curiosity.

Damn was he cute.

I fisted my hands together, pretending they were holding onto him.

"Kind of. I run the program and have been for

a decade." I lifted away from the fridge door and let it swing shut.

His eyes widened more. "Wow, that's amazing."

"Thanks. It's been quite the wild ride."

"I bet tonight has added to that list..."

I shrugged. "They weren't the first to fight on the property and they won't be the last. Sometimes it happens when you give someone a little too much freedom too soon."

He nodded slowly, looking back down at his water bottle with a concentrated look on his face. I wondered what my words meant to him.

Did he relate?

Was he the type of person to not know what to do with the freedom given to him?

Clearly his trouble with the law had been something like that—as all criminals were.

Freedom was what you made of it. It could give you everything and it could take away everything. It all depended on your choice with what to do with it.

To be honest, since meeting him, I'd been insanely curious as to what his charges were. As a non-violent offender, they weren't anything heinous like sex crimes or murder. But I couldn't see Ayen being a drug runner or something like that—he was too sweet, too soft around the edges that people in the drug business didn't have.

Whatever it was, I wanted to know. Not even just for my own curiosity's sake but to better understand him, too.

What had caused him to lose his freedom in

the first place and what was he willing to do to get it back?

This program was the first step.

What would be his next?

Ayen's voice was quiet as he said, "Thank you."

I smiled. "You're welcome."

"You never answered my question, though." His eyes met mine again. "Why are you doing all of this?"

"Why can't I?" I challenged.

His brows pulled together. "What do you get out of it? I can't really give you anything."

A dark part of me whispered that there were *plenty* of things he could give me but I quickly clamped that down.

I wasn't interested in coercing him into bending over and letting me touch every inch of him. He was my unattainable grail.

"Look, I may not know you or anything, Ayen, but I can tell the type of person you are. My gut says you would never intentionally hurt someone."

For some reason, a sad look passed over his face and his gaze dropped down to the floor where he stared at his feet. The silence between us was both startling and strange, and had me wanting to ask him what happened before I bit my tongue and stopped myself from doing so.

Whatever it was, it was probably none of my business. He didn't owe me anything, even if I had gone out of my way tonight to protect him. If he wanted to tell me in his own time, then he was free to do so. I'd never push anything.

I'd done that out of my own selfish need to keep him safe and nothing more.

"Why don't you go rest up for the night," I said to break up the tension. "Seems like tonight's already been long enough."

"But, the bed..."

I cut him off by grabbing him by the shoulders and spinning him around. He didn't fight me at all when I led him through my cabin and down the hallway to my bedroom.

"I'll survive for one night," I said, and opened the door for him. "Get some sleep."

He looked like he wanted to argue with me but soon thought better of it at the last moment. A small sigh escaped him when he finally relented.

"All right... Thank you, I appreciate it."

"Of course." I smiled and stepped back.

I itched to touch him again—to run my fingers through his hair or cup his face and press a good-night kiss to his forehead before he headed off to bed. Anything that would bring him closer to me so that I could feel his body heat soaking through my thin t-shirt.

I forced myself to hold my smile. "I'm going to have to keep the door open, though. Just in case one of your COs decides to pop in and do a check."

"Oh. Yeah, of course."

"All right..." I backed away slowly down the hall. "Holler if you need anything."

"I will. Thank you."

I flopped down on my couch and let my elbows rest on my knees as I watched the shadows of his figure dance in the light spilling out into the hallway from my overhead light. I laced my fingers together in a tight hold, squeezing them together while I kept my inappropriate thoughts to myself.

What I wouldn't give to join Ayen in that bed right about now. Cuddle up behind him and pull him against my chest and see how well his body fit against mine.

Would we be tangled up awkwardly or would he scoot back enough to let me perfectly curl around him?

Ah, fuck.

I need to stop this train of thought before it got out of hand. Or rather, before I needed to put my dick *in* my hand. Because masturbating while in full sight of Ayen if he glanced out the bedroom door was not going to happen.

I sighed. For now, I'd just have to settle myself with the fact that he'd be tucked between my sheets and hopefully, getting his scent all over them —mixing with mine.

Tomorrow, I'd let my fantasies run wild.

Tonight, I'd get some shuteye and deal with what judgment came in the morning.

CHAPTER 8

Ayen

I SLEPT WELL THAT NIGHT, surrounded by a comfortable bed and pillows that felt like heaven against my face.

It'd been two long years since I'd slept on a proper mattress with actual back support and not the flimsy material of my foam mattress back in my cell with a steel bed frame underneath it. Two long ass years since I'd actually felt well rested by the time I finally blinked my eyes open in the morning.

I stretched my arms over my head and sank further into the covers surrounding me. Jackson's scent was all over them, enveloping me in him just like his jacket had. I savored it all, memorizing it for when I was back in my cellblock at SAC later on today when the bus finally came to pick us all up and bring us back.

As sad as it was to be leaving this place after only a few days, I couldn't say I regretted any of it.

Especially meeting Jackson.

I was never going to see the man again after this, and while that kind of choked me up inside, at least I was able to see him one last time before leaving. It seemed so silly to be lusting after a man I barely knew in the grand scheme of things—but even if it was just the idea of him that I had been enamored with, that was something that I would cherish for the rest of my time while I was locked up.

The entire time he'd been nothing but kind to me, going out of his way to help me when he was never asked to. He was a good man, one that anyone would be lucky enough to know, let alone be with.

Sitting up, I peeled back the covers and climbed to my feet. My entire body cracked, easing the tension in my bones almost immediately.

Damn, I was going to miss this bed.

There was a delicious smell wafting from down the hallway that I found myself following. I spotted Jackson in the kitchen cooking something over the stovetop. His shirt was off and he was in just a pair of sweats that did everything to highlight the kind of assets he had.

Jesus, as if my lusting for him wasn't bad already.

Most likely feeling me staring, he glanced over his shoulder at me and flashed me a smile. "Morning."

I blinked a few times, trying to clear the image

of his body now ingrained into my brain. Roxy lifted herself up from where she'd been laying down on the floor over by the dining table and trotted over to me, her tongue hanging out of her mouth as she panted happily.

I bent down to pet her before turning back to Jackson. "What time is it?"

He glanced over at the clock before answering. "Just after eight."

My eyes widened. "I need to get over to the bus."

"Woah, woah, woah." He grabbed my arm just as I was starting to head for the door. "It already left."

"*What?*"

Oh fuck, fuck, fuck.

I was in such deep shit.

"Yeah, about two hours ago."

If there wasn't solid ground under my feet, I had no doubt I would've melted into the damn Earth.

Fuck, I was in *so* much trouble.

Why the hell didn't the COs come looking for me when the bus had come?

Could they not find me?

It wasn't like they had a giant headcount to keep track of. There were only four of us! As soon as SAC found out I was still here, I was going to be thrown in the hole the second I got back.

Anxiety spiked inside of my chest at the thought.

I'd only been there once and it had been the worst three days of my life. I never knew that I was the kind of person who needed human interaction in order to survive but I sure learned that weekend.

"Ayen…" Jackson's voice jerked me out of my thoughts. "You're all right. The bus already left."

"That's the *problem*." I could hear the shaking in my voice. "I was supposed to be on it."

He shook his head. "No you weren't, honey. You're staying here at the program."

Wait, what?

I stared at him, trying to find the hidden joke that he was trying to tell.

Was this some kind of prank?

A test?

To see if I'd go along with it and not correct him, therefore making it seem like I was taking his word over my COs?

They'd be the type to do that fucked up shit.

Especially Stinner.

Oh fuck.

Roxy whined at me, her nails tippy-tapping against the hardwood floor as she shifted foot-to-foot.

Jackson set down the wooden spoon he'd been using to move around whatever was in the pan and then turned the burner off. When he faced me, he cupped his hand around my face, tilting it up to look at him.

"You didn't get left behind by accident, if that's what you're thinking."

I blinked at him again.

Wait, what?

He smiled a little. "I talked with the Warden this morning when he called and explained what I saw last night. He agreed that it wouldn't be in the program's best interest to punish you when you had nothing to do with the fight."

My mouth fell open.

What?

He went out of his way to talk to the *Warden*?

His thumb trailed along my cheek gently, sending a shiver up my spine. His touch was so gentle that it made me want to lean into it more. "You wanted to stay here, right?"

I nodded, completely shell-shocked.

He'd defended me to the Warden?

But why?

What did he even get out of that?

I was one less number to worry about if I was gone.

Holy shit, I owed this man my damn life.

Or at the very least, some kind of favor.

Was that why he'd done it?

To get something out of me?

I couldn't imagine what the fuck he'd want from an inmate who had nothing to give. I didn't have any money and I certainly didn't have any pull with any of the local gangs.

I was essentially useless to him.

So then, why?

"I want you to finish out this program," Jackson went on. "I think it'll be good for you. Maybe you don't agree with me but that's the way I see it. This program isn't about toughening people up or teaching them to learn a bunch of useless facts about fire fighting. It's about finding the piece inside of you that is dedicated to helping people. I may not know you, Ayen, but I can tell that you can understand that."

I swallowed thickly.

Even though Jackson would never know it, his words meant a lot to me.

Up until the day I'd gotten arrested, I'd been considered a wallflower, a shy and naive boy who never knew what he wanted out of life. There wasn't a day that passed by where I didn't feel like I was in the way or that I was a burden to someone.

Especially my ex.

Even now, two years later, it hurt to think about.

All those nights I'd spent trying to convince him that I wasn't meant to be some house husband who stayed in line and did whatever he wanted—I had dreams and passions, too, and just because I didn't know what they were or where I wanted to go with them, didn't mean that they weren't *real*.

Hearing Jackson talk about something like that had the memories of my past flooding back into my mind, reminding me of the person I'd always been dying to be but never got a chance to because the justice system was fucking rigged. No one cared about a kid who was barely legal at the time being manipulated for years on end to the point of snapping and doing something that could never be taken back.

All anyone saw of me now was a cold-blooded murderer. Not the abused husband who'd been trying to run away only to get caught in the end.

But not Jackson.

He saw the *real* me.

Or at least until he found out about what I'd

been sent to prison for. I was sure after that, he'd change his tune real fast.

Most people did, but then again, could I really blame them?

Until then though, I'd bask in his confidence in me.

"Thank you," I said quietly.

He smiled and slowly let go of me. "Did you want something to eat? I made pancakes. They're probably not as good as the ones down at the mess hall, but they do the job."

My skin burned where he'd touched. The remnants of the heat of his hand on me felt like a brand that I never wanted to fade. I liked how it felt, him touching me so casually and like we'd been doing this for a while.

I swallowed again and nodded, taking a seat in one of the chairs at his small dining table, Roxy following me over to join me.

I watched the muscles in his back move as he grabbed the pan and jiggled the pancakes out onto a plate, giving me a nice show on how strong he really was underneath all of that firefighting gear. Even without him being shirtless like that, I knew he was built. But seeing him without anything covering the stark contrasts of his muscles had me wanting to reach out and touch them.

He was certainly strong enough to throw me, all one hundred and thirty pounds, over his shoulder like I was nothing.

"Syrup?" he asked, while opening the fridge.

"Sure, thank you."

He hip-checked it shut before walking over to

me with the plates, the bottle of thick syrup tucked under his arm.

The smell was divine as the plate was set down in front of me. He drizzled a nice helping of syrup over my pancakes before moving it over to his and doing the same. A set of silverware was already laid out nicely on a cloth napkin next to me.

"Thank you... for everything, Mr. Hall." I spoke quietly, not at all surprised when Roxy nuzzled her face onto my thigh.

He chuckled. "Please, call me Jax."

CHAPTER 9

By the time I made it back to my cabin, it was well after roll call and the beginning of the third day of our training.

Jackson, or rather *Jax*, had left soon after breakfast and walked me back to my cabin where one of my COs, Barlow, was waiting for me.

"You've got this cabin to yourself for the time being, Gonzalez. *Don't* make me regret that decision."

I nodded to him before ducking inside to change into my uniform for the day.

I hated that Tyson had been sent back to SAC and I hadn't. He'd only acted out of self-defense and yet, he had been punished just the same as the two who'd started the altercation.

He was the one who had been looking forward to this work program since signups were posted.

He'd talked *me* into coming along and yet here I was, the one who got to stay while he was shipped back.

It didn't seem fair. Not when Tyson was a good guy who only wanted to do the right thing at the end of the day. He had a hot temper but only when it was triggered. I'd never quite asked him what he'd been sentenced for, but from the stories he'd told me, it had something to do with drug peddling for one of the local cartels.

Petty shit that a kid his age, sixteen at the time of his sentencing, didn't need to be caught up in, let alone serve a ridiculously long sentence for.

As sad as my sentencing had been, my five years was nothing in comparison to his eighteen. By the time he'd get back out onto the streets, he'd be well into his thirties. I had no doubt that he'd make something of himself, but waiting until that could happen had to be torture.

Thankfully, it was never too late to turn your life around with a drug charge on your record. People dealt with that kind of shit all the time.

Mine was a different story, but that was something future me would get to deal with. For now, I simply needed to keep my head down and continue surviving. Three more years and I would be up for parole.

By the time I got changed and out the door again, Barlow already had an impatient frown etched into his face.

Wordlessly, he led me back to the training grounds where there was a demonstration already going on. I sat on one of the stumps in the back, keeping to myself while I tried to concentrate on what was going on.

I hated that feeling of being alone. Without Tyson around to buffer my social awkwardness, I was going to be doing a lot of shit by myself for the next six weeks. And while in hindsight it wasn't as bad as being thrown in the hole for misbehaving when I got back to the prison, I was also going to heavily miss the companionship.

I knew most of the others in this program but we weren't friendly. Not like Tyson and I were.

Whatever. I was a grown ass adult. I needed to get my act together and stop being upset that I no longer had a friend to hang out with. This program was meant to look good on my record and hopefully, get the parole board to give me a lighter parole sentence once I got out.

I was already looking at a minimum of a year being monitored.

Hopefully, that would be it, though.

A shadow suddenly loomed over me, causing my entire body to tense. I waited, feeling the person behind me hovering closely and hoping they'd pass by soon. When nothing moved, I forced myself to look up.

Jackson was standing right by my stump with Roxy lying down at his feet, her head resting on top of one of his shoes. His arms were crossed over his large chest while he watched the demo ahead of us, a blank expression on his face.

I forced myself not to grin at him and instead, turned back to the demo just as one of my fellow inmates was called up as a volunteer to shoot off a fire extinguisher at one of the blazing fire pits.

For some reason, having Jackson at my back felt comfortable.

Safe even.

Such a difference in how it'd been with my ex. I'd lived in constant fear of that man and what he would do to me if I so much as sneezed wrong. For our entire almost ten year relationship, I'd walked on eggshells. I never knew what would make him flip and go nasty. I often felt like his moods were on a light switch and with one quick flick he'd go from loving and nice to mean and abusive. It was emotionally and mentally draining, that's for sure, but that was no real excuse for what I'd done.

In a way, I was sad for what had transpired between us in the end. No one deserved to be left in the state the bullet had left him in after it'd lodged itself into the left side of his temporal lobe, effectively robbing him of everything but the shell of his former self.

But as fucked up and selfish as it was to think about, I wouldn't take it back. Because in that moment, at the very end of it all, my survival instincts finally kicked in and it was either him or me.

And I chose me.

Probably for the first time in my life.

Jackson unfolded his arms and began to clap, pulling me out of my thoughts while the rest of our group erupted into a smattering of claps to mimic his. One of the volunteer firemen took back the extinguisher once more and thanked his participant before dismissing him back to his stump.

"You want to go up there next?" Jackson whispered at me, his face suddenly twisting into an amused smile.

"You'd have to drag me up there by my hair," I quipped back, not thinking twice.

He only chuckled but didn't push any further. "I'll keep that in mind for next time."

A shiver rolled up my spine.

His words almost sounded like a promise.

A promise I almost wanted him to follow through with.

CHAPTER 10

AYEN

THE BAG that was strapped to my back was heavy, weighing me down as we trekked through the forest. The vegetation wasn't particularly dense but with all of us in heavy protective gear and lugging the bags around, it made for a difficult walk.

After the demonstration of putting out a fire with hand-held intervention, gear had been distributed amongst all of us for a day-long hike into the woods where we'd be shown different burn sites and how to go about spotting the signs of what would constitute a controlled burn and what wouldn't.

I had to say, I was actually pretty interested in learning all of this. Never in my life did I think I'd ever care about forest fires or helping to control or stop them, but with Jackson's words still ringing in my ear from this morning, it had me feeling inspired.

Maybe that was the point of his speech to me —to get me thinking about doing something with my life after I got out, something important that would give back to my community in some way. Maybe he was just being nice and wanted to help a kid like me out because that was kind of his job and there was nothing deeper to it.

Regardless of what his motives were for reassuring me this morning, I still wanted to make him proud.

I sucked the fresh mountain air into my lungs, breathing deeply; it felt nice to be out here in the open again.

Having been locked up for so long and only getting an hour of rec time every day was demoralizing and always had me feeling restless like I was in some kind of perpetual hamster cage.

I understood that going to prison was punishment and that punishment wasn't supposed to be comfortable. Doing penance for my sins wasn't supposed to be some walk in the park where I got to just hang around for five years in some cushy cell while my ex's family had to take care of what was, essentially, a thirty-nine-year-old adult baby for the rest of their lives.

But damn did it feel nice to finally be free for a little while.

I felt something brush against my leg and turned to look down at it, spotting Roxy happily trotting along next to me. I smiled and looked toward the back of the group where Jackson was taking up the rear.

He was engaged in a deep conversation with Barlow, who was visibly sweating from our hike. My CO was nodding along to whatever Jackson was saying while he was fixing his eyes down at the ground with a strained frown.

Clearly this hike wasn't on his list of things he wanted to be forced into doing—especially with his heavy uniform on.

I turned back ahead to face the rest of the group, ignoring the subtle feeling of eyes on the back of my head.

I was probably blowing it out of proportion, but would it be wrong of me to assume Jackson sent Roxy up here with me to keep me company?

I was the only one out of the group not walking next to someone, after all.

I brushed my hand against her head as we walked, petting her every so often as I whispered how much of a good girl she was. She seemed happy to accompany me, her tail swaying behind her while she navigated the slightly rocky terrain with ease.

Eventually, we reached a large set of stones that looked to be carved down intentionally, giving most of us a spot to rest while we took a water break. I claimed one of the smaller rocks toward the far right side and set my bag between my legs. The zipper parted easily as I peeled it open, trail rations and my thermos of water were right on top. I tossed some of my jerky to Roxy after ripping open the bag, belatedly realizing that I probably should've asked Jackson first before doing that. I winced.

With my luck, his dog was on some super

fancy diet that only contained fresh cooked ingredients from a local butcher shop.

"How we doing over here?"

I looked up mid-chew to Jackson coming over to us. Roxy let out a few barks and circled around her owner's legs, before coming back over to me.

"Good. Hey, listen... your dog isn't on a special diet or anything right?"

He laughed. "Uh oh. Did she manage to weasel something out of you?"

I looked down guiltily at my pack of jerky. "Uh..."

"I swear it's the eyes," he said, flashing me a smile and bending down to grab his dog and ruffle her fur. "She'll get you to give her anything with the right look."

I smiled a little and shoved another slice into my mouth. He wasn't mad, that was a good sign. I hadn't realized how much my heart rate had spiked when he'd come over until I was starting to feel my body relax again.

Jesus, who knew PTSD was such a bitch?

"You got enough water?" He nodded to my bag.

"Yeah. I'm all good. Did *you* drink anything yet?"

"Hey now, I'm the one that's supposed to be taking care of you. Not the other way around."

You, he said.

Not *you guys,* as in the whole group of us.

Why did that small, subtle word feel like it had something else behind it—like it was charged with more than just him looking out for me because I was technically under the program's care?

Jackson had a way of saying things rather flippantly, even with the underlying message sounding so much more than what was being said on the surface level. I was the king of over-thinking everything, too, that much I was conscious of.

But then, why was I getting the feeling that he was purposefully not looking at me now?

Instead, he was focused on rubbing Roxy's belly as she rolled around on the ground, getting her golden fur dirty with bits of dead leaves and dirt.

"Well, you've done a good job so far," I said, shoving another piece of jerky into my mouth.

His head snapped up to look at me, freezing me in my place.

Something passed through his eyes, causing my stomach to clench with excitement. I doubted he was trying to give me what I could only describe as bedroom eyes, yet the intense focus was making me squirm.

Shit, I really did over-think all of this, didn't I?

Jackson rose to his feet and stepped around his dog, coming closer to me.

My gaze tracked his every movement, my heart picking up its thrumming beat again as he slowly squatted down in front of me and, without warning, gently cupped one of my legs.

His fingers worked quickly at the laces of my boot, gently pulling it off of my foot and setting it down next to the rock I was sitting on. He rested my heel against his thigh and pushed the cuff of my pant leg up just enough to expose my ankle to him.

I swallowed, his fingers brushing over the skin

right above where my sock was and trailing down to my ankle bone. He eased pressure into the tendon, running his fingers up and around a few times while tingles spread throughout my entire leg.

I let out a little groan of pleasure and tightened both of my hands around the pack of jerky as I stayed very still, not wanting to break the moment—wherever the hell it was leading to.

Around us, our group was already beginning to pack up, our break over with.

"Hey, what's going on with him?" The crunch of Barlow's boots were making their way over here.

"Looks like he twisted his ankle," came Jackson's easy reply.

Glee shot through me almost instantly.

Jackson's eyes flitted up to find mine again, searching me for any kind of objection while he continued to massage my lower calf and ankle. He wouldn't find one, though, because there was no way in hell I was breaking up this moment.

"Jesus fuck, Gonzalez," Barlow grumbled. "Are you the clumsiest motherfucker on this planet, or what?"

"Guess so, sir," I said, ripping my gaze away from the man in front of me to focus on my CO instead.

He sighed. "You need to go back to medical?"

"I think he'll be all right with a little more rest," Jackson said, leaning back to show Barlow my ankle. "The swelling's already coming down. Elevating it for another forty-five minutes should do the trick."

Barlow grunted. "We don't have forty-five fucking minutes, Hall."

Jackson made a show of glancing back toward the rest of the group, a frown on his face. My leg involuntarily twitched in Jackson's hold, causing him to tighten his hands around it to secure me.

Thank fuck that I decided to put my rations pack on my lap or else I'd blow my cover with how turned on this entire interaction was making me.

"Why don't you all go on ahead? We should be able to catch up by the time you reach the first site." Jackson's head swiveled back around to Barlow again.

"He can't walk on it at all?"

"Not if you want this sprain to turn into a strain."

Barlow grunted.

"It's that or I carry him back to medical," Jackson went on. "Either way, he can't be on it right now."

"Shit..." Barlow mumbled.

The man dragged a tired hand over his jaw, scratching at the stubble forming there. He looked back out across the group to where the three other firefighters and several convicts were standing together in a small group, their packs already on.

There were no other COs that decided to come on our hike together, choosing to voluntarily stay behind once they were told how far we'd be going today. I had a feeling that Barlow drew up short in their lotto and hadn't actually wanted to come with us, but rather *had to* and he was now regretting that choice.

"You think he'll only need forty-five minutes?"

Jackson nodded. "Should be about that. I've got an ice pack in my bag I'll slap on and see how we do with that."

Barlow nodded, dropping his hand from his face. "All right. I'll radio you when we get to the site to see where you're at. If you do have to head back, you need to let me know."

Jackson's thumb stroked along the edge of my sock, sending small pulses of pleasure right to my groin. "Of course."

As my CO stepped away and headed back to the group, I let myself relax again.

Trying not to read into Jackson keeping me back just yet, I slowly sealed my rations back up and stuffed everything into my pack again but kept it on my lap. Roxy perked up once the group started to file out of our resting area and head down the path again, leaving Jackson and I behind.

"Forty-five minutes, huh," I said as soon as we were completely alone.

He turned back to smile at me, a rather smug look on his face. "Technically, the protocol is half an hour, but what's an extra fifteen?"

My stomach clenched with excitement. Both of us knew that this bogus excuse was, well, bogus.

So why was Jackson leaning into it?

I wasn't going to complain about spending more time with him, though, and maybe our situation from last night and into this morning had left more of a lasting impression on him than I thought.

All of this was fun and games, though. It

wasn't serious—it couldn't be. Not with me being actual government property.

"How's it looking, Doc?" I rolled my foot in his hold. "You think I need to take it easy for the rest of the day?"

He chuckled and patted my leg before pulling the cuff of my pant leg down again. "I think you'll live. Just barely, though."

After getting my shoe back on and laced up, he grabbed me by the arm and hoisted me up off the rock. Without even having to ask, he slipped my bag over his shoulder and nodded for me to follow him.

Thankfully, by now, my body had calmed down somewhat, though I was still buzzing from our close proximity.

We walked at a slow pace; much slower than what we had been when we were with the rest of the group. I didn't mind, though. Not if it meant stealing a little time with Jackson without the watchful eyes of my COs around.

Roxy fell in line next to me, keeping up pace with me easily.

"I'm surprised she likes you so much," Jackson said after minute

"Does she usually get scared of inmates?"

He hummed thoughtfully before answering. "Not exactly. She typically keeps her distance but that's not due to any kind of past experiences or anything."

"Oh."

For some reason, that made me feel special. Like I'd been chosen out of the however many dozens of inmates who had come through this program before me.

None had been trusted before this, so what made me so different?

Almost as if reading my mind, Jackson spoke again. "I think it's your soft nature."

My face flushed.

Soft.

If only he knew what I'd been sentenced for— I doubt he'd think of me as 'soft' then.

Holding that gun in my hand, though, the one my ex-husband had bought only a few months prior as a tool to intimidate me with, and pointing it at him, had felt powerful then—holding a tool that could take a life with the simple pull of a trigger was both exhilarating as it was terrifying.

I knew it made me a fucked up monster to think that way, but it was the truth.

That had been the only time in my life that I had ever felt in control of anything.

In prison, I'd been mandated to take a bunch of psych evals and see a counselor regularly to work through and process what had happened. And while I'd told them over and over again that I was sorry and that I regretted my choices, deep down I wasn't.

I never would be.

Perhaps that feeling would go away in time when I got out and started to live my life the way *I* wanted to, but who knew.

Not many people could come back from attempting to kill someone. It fundamentally changes you as a person, no matter what the intentions were behind the action. Deciding to take a life was a crossroads that very few chose to take, and the suffering that followed, those haunting dreams that still kept me up sometimes, were my cross to bear.

"Hey…" A hand on my arm stopped me from walking. "Where did you go?"

"Huh?" I glanced up at Jackson, confused.

He was frowning down at me. "You disappeared… You did that yesterday, too."

Disappeared?

"I did?"

Looking around the trail, I didn't see any footprints from my boots that told me I'd wandered off the path. We were still on the same trail and walking at the same casual pace we had been.

"Yeah…" Jackson turned to face me fully, his hand coming up to cup my jaw. Using his other hand, he tapped lightly on my forehead. "Up here. You went somewhere."

My eyes widened.

Oh.

How the hell could he tell that?

I wasn't saying anything out loud, nor was I distracted in my thoughts for that long. Either he'd been watching me the whole time, or I'd somehow made it obvious my mind had drifted away from our conversation.

"Oh. Sorry."

"What were you thinking about?"

Being there in the middle of the woods alone with him was doing some fucked up things to me. I wanted to stay like this, with him touching me and keeping me close like I was something precious to him. But at the same time, I was petrified that we were going to get caught.

How would this look to anyone, especially a CO, passing by?

I'd be dragged back to SAC faster than I could blink and probably thrown in the hole until my parole hearing.

Hell, Jackson would definitely lose his job, too, if people thought he was fraternizing with the inmates.

"Nothing," I said quickly. "Just about what you said this morning."

His brows pulled together for a moment as he tried to recall our conversation. Whatever he remembered had his expression softening, though, and he reached out, moving his thumb over my cheek like it had this morning.

I wanted to lean into it so bad, nuzzle my face into his hand while he continued to touch me.

"It's the truth, Ayen. You deserve to find yourself while you're here, or whatever truth you're searching for at least."

My lips parted, though I had nothing to really say to that.

His belief in me to change, or rather, become a different person than the one who was caught and thrown into prison, was touching. Back home, I didn't have anyone. Not a mom or dad or any siblings who were eagerly waiting for me to get released.

That was what had made me so susceptible to my ex's attention. I basked in it, reveled in it, even, because it was the first time in my life that I truly felt wanted.

Hearing all of this was addictive.

Could I believe Jackson?

Did I want to?

I'd trusted my ex in much the same way and look where that had gotten me.

But this man was so much different than Alex. He was compassionate and dedicated with his work and with the inmates that were here, and he took the time to check in on me, even without me asking for it.

"I want to trust you," I whispered.

His lip quirked up into a smile. "You can."

My breath hitched as he leaned forward, his gaze darting down to focus on my lips.

CHAPTER 11

Jackson

Ayen was still as I leaned forward to kiss him, his cheeks pink with a light flush while my impulsive desires took over and drove me into pulling him closer to me.

His lashes fluttered down over those beautiful brown eyes of his, hiding them from me. I longed to stare into them again and watch his pupils dilate like they had right before he'd closed them on me but held off on asking him to open them again.

Instead, I tilted my head and brushed my lips over his.

They were just as soft as I thought they'd be, pursed enough for me to deepen my peck into an actual kiss.

He let out a small, barely audible noise from

his throat that had me wanting to back him up into the nearest tree immediately.

Fuck, I wanted him.

I'd never wanted someone this badly in my life. We had a good twenty-five minutes until I needed to check back in with the group. That was plenty of time to get Ayen undressed enough to touch him and to feel the rest of him to see if his body matched these perfect lips of his.

The radio at my hip screeched loudly, jerking us both apart.

"*Fuck.*" I ripped it off of my belt and flipped to the channel it was signaling me to go to. "What?"

"Mr. Hall," CO Barlow's voice crackled over the frequency. "How's Gonzalez's ankle doing?"

I held back rolling my eyes.

Barlow struck me as an overbearing watchdog that didn't know when to trust the authority of those around him. He was constantly double-checking my and my team's work, even with our track record being as stellar as it was.

It had me wondering what the hell he was like back in the prison and in his element—I'm sure he was known for running a tight ship but translating that into the outside world with a work program was never a good fit.

To do this kind of job, flexibility to the unplannable was your best bet.

"He's doing fine." Ayen quickly averted his eyes while I spoke, clearly flustered with what just happened. But he didn't step away from me or put any distance between us. In fact, he'd practically tucked himself against me. "We'll be meeting up with you all in a bit."

"Make it quick. We're almost at the site."

"Sure. Will do." As I flipped back to the main channel, I sighed.

The atmosphere was awkward now and still filled with that unresolved tension that had been brewing between us since this morning. I'd been trying to convince myself that I was reading into it, seeing signs that weren't really there when it came to Ayen and his sweet attitude.

But he continued to play with me—bantering back and forth—and had not at all leaned away from me as I pressed at those boundaries that separated inmate from volunteer.

He'd whole-heartedly leaned into them with me.

"I, uh..." Ayen cleared his throat. "I guess we should get going then."

I frowned.

Fuck, maybe I really *was* reading way too much into all of this. He could just be placating me because I was the only familiar face around now that his friend was gone.

Guilt curled in my stomach. "Yeah, of course."

I waved him on and began walking, silence falling over us the entire way there.

CHAPTER 12

WE AVOIDED each other for the rest of the day—or rather, I kept my distance.

I couldn't bear to look at Ayen if it turned out I really had misstepped and crossed over a major boundary and he now hated me for it. I wouldn't blame him, as I would obviously feel the same in his shoes. To have someone you trusted pressure you into something...

Fuck.

My head was an entire mess, toggling between replaying exactly what happened and filling in the blanks of what 'could've been'.

The noise he'd made had been enticing, but it wasn't like I could judge anything off of just that.

He hadn't leaned away from me or fought me off, but what if he'd simply been scared?

I had no idea what his past was like, and aside

from that small glimpse the night I'd pulled him out of his cabin after that fight, I couldn't exactly claim to know anything.

The more time I spent with Ayen, the more I wanted to get to know him. He had a deep inner world that I was desperate to learn about, especially when he got caught up in whatever memory or thoughts that took him out of our conversation for a time.

In all my years of doing this program, not once did I ever think about looking into an inmate's rap sheet. Yet, as soon as we'd all gotten back from our hike and the inmates had been sent to the mess hall for dinner, I was pulling up a chair at the COs table.

"You look like shit," one of the other COs said to Barlow once he slid into a chair at the table with a tray full of food.

"You try walking in eighty degree fucking heat with this fucking uniform," the man grumbled back, digging his fork through a scoop of corn.

"How's Gonzalez's foot, Hall?" one of the COs, Stinner, I think his name was, asked. "Heard he was hobbling around all afternoon."

I paused with my fork at my mouth as I tried to think of some excuse.

"He's probably faking it," Browne chimed in. "Remember what he was like when he first got put onto the unit?"

The entire table erupted into laughter, which made my blood boil.

But I could either sit there and be mad at them for talking shit, or I could use this to my advantage and dig up some info out of them on the man who was beginning to haunt my every thought.

"Why? What was he like?" I asked.

Browne scoffed. "He acted like this scared little puppy. Always trying to get sent to the infirmary for... what the fuck was his excuse?"

"Panic attacks," Stinner volunteered.

Browne jabbed his fork in the direction of his coworker, nodding. "Yeah. That shit. Funny considering he's a *hot one*. So I don't know why the fuck he was trying to play the baby bird card."

My brows shot up practically into my hairline. "Pardon?"

Stinner leaned over toward me. "He's got a body on his rap."

"Stop talking, both of you," Barlow snapped. "Hall, you keep that shit to yourself or we're all fucked up the ass by the state."

I ripped my gaze away from the group in order to scan through the entire mess hall, searching for him—my so-called baby bird. It took me a minute to find him tucked into the corner away from everyone else, where he ate quietly by himself.

Was that why everyone stayed away from him?

Because they were scared?

But they're all non-violent.

For some reason, remembering that eased me.

Ayen wasn't violent, of course he wasn't. He was the furthest thing from it. Murdering someone was serious, but to be in this program, it had to be either a complete accident or for a good reason. He wouldn't have been let out of SAC otherwise.

How long was his sentence, anyway?

That'd give me a good indication on what kind of charge it was.

Underneath the table, my leg began to bounce.

"Hall, you hear me?" Barlow said.

"Yeah, no worries. I'm not all that interested in his background," I lied. "I'm here to make sure they all walk out of this program still alive."

Stinner laughed. "Close call the other night with that fight?"

"Where the fuck did they swipe the cards from, anyway?" Browne asked.

"Who knows and who fucking cares."

My mind wandered as their conversation deviated from Ayen. My heart squeezed; watching him eating alone by himself as he hunched over his food had me fighting the urge to go over there and claim a spot at his table. His gaze was moving slowly around the hall, taking in the other inmates around him, until he caught sight of me watching him.

A small, quick, smile was flashed my way before he looked back down at his food again.

My entire body relaxed at the sight of it.

Was I forgiven for earlier?

Without any hesitation, my mind was made up. I had to know.

Later tonight, after lights out, I'd sneak over to his cabin to talk to him about what happened during our hike.

I had to make sure we were still good or else it was going to kill me.

CHAPTER 13

JACKSON

IT WASN'T hard to sneak out from my cabin and over to the inmates' after lights out.

Not many firefighters were eager to be moving around the dark property this late at night unless they were coming back from the city, and as far as I knew, no one had taken off for a night at the bars.

With only one CO on watch for the night, the rest were asleep in their cabins, making it easy for me to avoid the view of the cameras as I reached Ayen's cabin.

The door was unlocked, unsurprisingly, and opened with barely a creak as I slipped inside. Outside, the world was silent, only broken up by the occasional chirping of a cricket nearby.

Fishing my phone out of my pocket, I unlocked it and shined the light down at the floor.

"Ayen," I whispered into the dark.

A figure shot up from the bottom right bunk immediately, kicking back until he was pressed flat against the wall. The sound of panicked breathing broke up the silence in the cabin, filling it with an anxious tension.

I kept the light tilted down so that it didn't flash in the window and catch the attention of whoever was manning cameras as I walked over to the bed. "It's just me."

"Jax?" He sounded terrified.

Poor baby.

"Yeah."

There was the slow sound of him letting out a long and barely controlled breath, the gasp and hitch in his throat at the tail end of it, had my heart sinking in my chest.

A sigh left him as his silhouette finally relaxed. "What are you doing here?"

I wanted to pull him up from his bed and hold him against my chest until he finally relaxed again. The urge burned as I ignored it. "I wanted to talk to you without all the COs around."

He was quiet when I sat down at the end of his bed. His legs were drawn up to his chest protectively, his arms wrapped around them in a tight hold.

I wanted to reach out and touch him, pull him away from the corner he'd squished himself into. This was the second time I'd seen him have this kind of reaction—to immediately shrink away from whatever perceived danger he thought he was in and try to hide.

My hand tightened around my phone.

I wanted to find the motherfucker who had hurt him enough to illicit that kind of response and show them what *real* fear was like.

"Everything okay?" he asked.

His eyes reflected in my phone's light as I slid it face down toward the wall so that the light bounced off the bottom of the top bunk and cocooned us in the soft glow. He was watching me curiously, no hint of being scared or upset at all reflected back at me.

"I think so." I hooked my leg up over my knee. "I hope so."

"Is Roxy okay?"

I smiled. "Yeah, she's all good."

Ayen slowly stretched his legs out in front of him. He scooted across the small twin mattress in order to come closer to me, swinging his legs over the side of the bed. We were only a few inches apart now, enough where I could feel the heat of his body refracting off of him.

"Is this about earlier?" His eyes were drawn to the floor.

Shit.

"Yes." My throat was tight as I said the word.

Don't get me wrong, I'd been rejected plenty of times in my forty-five years on this Earth. I'd always taken it in stride and never once thought badly of the other person who was doing the rejecting. That was simply a fact of life and one that I accepted wholeheartedly.

This felt worse for some reason, though. Like I was suddenly back in high school and getting turned down by my first crush.

"I'm sorry," he mumbled.

Incredulously, I asked, "What are *you* sorry for?"

"I..." His shoulders sagged inward, practically pinching up against his ears. "I got you in trouble, didn't I?"

"Why would you think that?"

He glanced at me. "Isn't that why you were sitting with the COs?"

I couldn't help it, I burst out laughing. "No, of course not."

Was it better if I was honest with him about what my intentions were with sitting with the COs?

Or did I hold off on that for now and steer our conversation elsewhere?

It might freak him out if he thought I was fishing for more info on his background, especially with a murder charge tacked onto him.

"I wanted to talk about earlier, too." I moved again, hooking my right leg up onto the mattress in order to face him fully. Not being able to help myself and because I was clearly half a masochist, I reached out and grabbed at the hands resting in his lap. "How did you feel about what happened earlier?"

"I liked it," he whispered.

My heart raced in my chest. "Do you want to do it again?"

My voice had dropped low, thick with want for him. I could already feel my cock growing hard in my pants and had to force myself to remain still until Ayen answered me. I *needed* his truth—to know I wasn't the only one feeling this insane spark between us.

"Yes." He swallowed hard enough that his Adam's apple bobbed. "D... Do you?"

"Absolutely." I let go of one of his hands and cupped his face, pulling him closer to me. "Tell me to stop if you need me to."

He shook his head in my hand, his tongue darting out to wet his bottom lip.

I yanked him in for another kiss, this time not holding back like I had in the forest. Here, no one was around to interrupt us, or catch us in the act. I could savor the taste of him, memorize every part of him as much as he let me.

Ayen exhaled out a small noise when I swiped my tongue against the seam of his mouth, beckoning him to open it for me and let me in. He only hesitated for a second before he was parting his lips, allowing me to deepen our kiss.

He was shy when his tongue met mine, gently pressing it along the side while I rolled mine around, tasting every inch of him like I'd been dying to for the past few days. He moaned again and leaned his body toward mine, one of his hands coming up to grasp at the front of my shirt.

My cock strained at the front of my pants, begging to be let out. From just a kiss, I was already getting this turned on.

What the hell was this man doing to me?

Without breaking our mouths apart, I snaked a hand around Ayen's back and hooked it low enough to bend him backward and lay him down onto the bed. He let out a small gasp when our bodies pressed up against each other.

His cock was hard against my hip, small and cute, just like he was. I was dying to see and touch it, to feel how lost it would get in my large hand while I let him fuck himself inside my fist.

How much cum would he spill as he reached his climax?

What kind of expression would his face twist into right before he came?

"I want to touch you," I told him, breaking our kiss while a thin trail of spit kept us linked for a second longer. "Will you let me?"

He nodded quickly, already lost in what we were doing.

I loved how riled up he could get so easily.

Normally, in situations like this, I wanted to take my time. I liked to savor the moments before the actual act, watching my sub squirm and beg while I teased them until they cried. I wouldn't be able to get that far with Ayen, not with him looking already fucked out of his mind with just a simple kiss.

He was wearing a pair of cotton pants that were doing nothing to hide his arousal. I tugged at the drawstring until it came loose, and then hooked both sets of my fingers under the band and scooted the material down his hips. He popped free of the garment easily, his cute little pink cock already wet at the tip as it rested against his stomach.

"Um, Jax..." His expression suddenly grew worried, his gaze darting over to the door to the cabin.

"Don't worry, baby. I got you." I rubbed a hand up and down his side a few times. "We'll be quiet."

He trusted me; he said so himself that morning. I wouldn't let him down with that. As much as I wanted to get lost in him and let us both drown in this pleasure, I wasn't going to let him get caught and punished. His outcome would be far worse than mine, anyway.

The most that would happen to me was I'd get let go with the heavy disappointment from my chief following me.

Ayen would fare far worse, which I simply couldn't let happen.

Pushing his t-shirt up to his chest, I pressed a few soft kisses along his sternum and down to his stomach.

That seemed to relax him as he sighed softly and sunk deeper into his mattress. "Okay."

My lips soon found the tip of his cock, my tongue darting out to lap up the pearl of precum that had already leaked out of him. His body jerked at the contact, another gasp leaving his lips.

"Shhh," I rubbed his side again. "Be good for me and cover your mouth, okay?"

He nodded quickly and slapped a hand over his mouth, moaning into it.

So obedient.

I absolutely *loved* that.

Lying down on my stomach with his thighs parted on either side of me, I held his hips down in a tight hold and licked up the length of him. His cock twitched from the contact while his balls drew up toward his shaft, more precum leaking out of him.

Shit, if he was already reacting this much to a

few swipes of my tongue, how was he going to handle being in my mouth completely?

"When's the last time someone had you in their mouth, baby?"

He shook his head quickly, the muscles in his stomach flexing.

"*Never?*"

He shook his head again.

I let out a soft 'tsk'. "Well, that's changing tonight."

Honestly, what kind of guys did he date before this for them to deny him like that?

Some Doms were too selfish and didn't deserve to have a beautiful and perfectly little obedient sub like Ayen under them.

If there was no give and take to a relationship then what was the point?

Grabbing his free hand, I brought it up to tangle in my hair. "You tell me if it gets to be too much, okay?"

He nodded once more.

"Good boy," I praised, because he really was.

He groaned against his hand again, clearly liking hearing that.

Without another moment of hesitation, I licked up the length of him again and then slipped his cock head into my mouth. His body jerked instantly, his chest expanding with how quickly he sucked in a breath.

I held him still while I rolled my tongue around his tip, tasting the saltiness of him and teasing that slit that kept insisting on squeezing as much precum out of him as possible.

He moaned against his hand loudly this time,

his fingers tightening their hold in my hair, and it drove me absolutely fucking insane.

It was like he couldn't decide on whether he wanted to thrust up into my mouth or just lay back and let me do whatever I wanted to him. Either one I would be fine with in any other normal circumstances, but tonight I wanted to spoil him. He wasn't going to have to work for anything if he wanted it.

I curled my tongue around the underside of him while I slid my mouth down on him more, bobbing up and down a few times to wet the skin as I went. He was a little heavier on my tongue than I expected, but I could wrap my lips around him perfectly.

I wondered how many people had had the pleasure before me to see him like this, naked and begging to be tasted, and never took the opportunity to do so.

What a damn shame.

However, at the same time, I was thankful that I'd be the first one to do this to him.

The memory would be ingrained into his brain for the rest of his life.

As I moved my mouth down until my lips were pressed into the soft curls at his base, he didn't even tickle against the back of my throat, just barely reaching my uvula. I stayed there for a long moment, letting my mouth tighten around him as I swiped my tongue around him a few times.

This felt good—this felt *right*. He was meant to be here, laying on this bed while he had his cock stuffed into my mouth.

My cock hurt with how hard I was, causing me

to grind my hips down into his mattress, aching for some kind of relief. I wanted to bury myself inside of his tight little hole and feel him squeeze around me until he had me coming.

"Jax..." His voice sounded so broken through his fingers.

I pulled off of him immediately and wrapped a hand around him instead. "Does this feel good, Ayen?"

He choked out another quiet moan. "I'm... I'm gonna..."

I grinned, stroking my hand up and down him slowly. "I want you to. I want you to come right in my mouth so I can taste you, honey. You'll do that for me, right? You'll let me have it?"

"Fuck." Ayen's hips rolled forward, practically trying to grind himself up into my hand. He was so pretty like this; the image of him was going to be burned into my mind after this for the rest of the night.

Maybe forever.

I wrapped my lips around his cock head again, massaging my tongue around and under the sensitive tip while my hand did the work in stroking him in a smooth rhythm. His body arched up under me, one of his legs coming around to hook around my back to hold me against him. I let spit dribble down from my mouth to my hand, slicking it up while I continued to stroke up to where my chin was.

"J-Jax—"

He didn't get to finish whatever it was he was trying to say to me, his orgasm taking over and spilling his cum into my mouth. His strangled gasp had me deep-throating him again, getting him all the way back toward my throat so he could empty himself right into my throat. Just as I'd wanted him to.

His hand tightened in my hair hard enough to hurt my scalp, but damn, the pain was worth it to see his twisted up face fall into bliss. He let out a silent scream, his mouth dropping open while his eyes screwed tightly shut.

His body jerked with each spurt of cum he shot down my throat, thick and warm while it slid down into my belly. He held onto me for dear life, letting me help him through until he was finally done and lying completely spent on the mattress.

Beautiful...

So, so beautiful.

The hand in my hair fell down onto the bed next to him uselessly as he panted, his eyes finally opening again while he blinked wordlessly at the bunk above him.

The look on his face had me chuckling as I slowly slid my mouth off of him to sit up, licking my lips to swipe up whatever remnants were left behind.

Delicious.

His cock lay wet on his stomach, a thin sheen of sweat starting to gleam on his skin. Jesus, I wanted to lick at every inch of him, lap at him like a damn cat.

"Jax," he mumbled.

Leaning over, I pressed a soft kiss to his lips.

I wanted to stay, so goddamn badly. But I'd

already been here long enough to press my luck. We'd have to continue another day. Now that I had a taste for him, I wasn't going to give him up. I had him in my veins, my addiction already manifesting.

"Be good and get some rest, okay?" I spoke softly. "I'll see you tomorrow."

He nodded at me wordlessly, pursing his lips again for another kiss.

Smiling, I pressed my lips to his once more before climbing off of him and grabbing his pants from where I'd tossed them. They slipped on easily and I was sad to cover up that beautiful little cock of his once more from my view.

He sighed softly when I tucked him in, snuggling down into the thin sheets like they were made of the finest silk.

My feet felt glued to the floor, and I was unable to move as I watched him drift off to sleep.

How bad would it be if I stayed just until the sun came up?

I could sneak out then… run back to my cabin and shower before morning roll call.

Maybe I could even wake up earlier than that and roll Ayen over onto his side and see just how far I could coax my cock inside of him before he woke up.

I gripped myself through my pants.

Shit, I really needed to go *before I actually gave in to my desires*.

It was a chore to force myself to take my phone and leave.

By the time I got back to my cabin, I was already missing him. Roxy whined at me when I finally shut the door behind me, clearly smelling Ayen's scent on me. She obviously missed him just as much as I did.

I crouched beside her to run my hands over her soft coat. "I know, girl. Me too."

CHAPTER 14

AYEN

My eyes shot open the moment the sun peered in through the window.

Blearily, I looked around for any signs that last night had happened and it wasn't just some wild dream my brain cooked up because I was horny beyond belief for a man twice my age and who should be staying far, far away from me.

Nothing seemed out of place. The door was still closed and none of my belongings had been moved around at all.

Grabbing at my sheets, I lifted them to my nose and inhaled deeply. I could smell Jackson but it was barely there, only a faint whiff that could've been left over from spending time with him on our hike.

But it was still there, even if barely.

That spicy scent that I wanted to bury my face in and drown was still embedded in the sheets.

Keeping the sheets pressed up against my nose, I slipped my hand under my pajama pants and fisted my half hard cock. A moan left me instantly as I felt the slight stickiness left over from my cum and his mouth that had been slicked all along my skin.

I stroked myself slowly, remembering every single detail of him going down on me.

I wasn't lying when I said that had been my first time doing something like that. Alex had always been grossed out with giving blowjobs and had only ever wanted to stick his dick into something hot and tight like my ass.

There had been the occasional holiday blowjob that he'd *allowed* me to give him, but it never lasted long until he was pulling me up from my knees and bending me over to stick his dick inside me.

I shuddered at the memories.

To my surprise, though, Jackson had been almost enamored with having his mouth wrapped around me. I didn't have much experience in the sex department but it almost felt like he'd *enjoyed* giving me a blowjob, perhaps even more so than getting off himself.

In fact, I didn't remember him touching himself at all that entire time.

I wondered what his cock looked like. Judging from how far out it'd tented his pants, it was probably huge.

I whined softly, my hand speeding up as my hips rolled to fuck up into it. I wished he didn't have to leave last night, but I understood why he did. I really wished I could've at least reciprocated something and not left him high and dry while I fell asleep content as a damn pillow prince.

Would there be a next time?

I sure as fuck hoped so.

I wasn't going to be satisfied with us only having that one encounter. I needed more of him. Whatever he was willing to give me, I'd take it. I craved it like I craved breathing.

My orgasm spilled out of me, thick cum coating my hand and sticking to my sheet as I glided my cock against it, pretending that it was Jackson's mouth instead.

God, it felt so fucking good coming down his throat.

Collapsing back onto my mattress, I blinked my eyes open again and stared at the bunk above me. Since I was alone in the cabin for the time being, I could probably sneak him back in there tonight.

As long as he was up for it, at least.

Fear curled in my stomach right then, my nature at second-guessing myself rearing its ugly head.

I needed to stop before I talked myself out of it again.

That was what had happened yesterday back on the hike when I'd tried to pretend like Jackson kissing me was nothing. Because it was anything *but* nothing and yet, I'd gotten too self conscious that he'd feel like he made a huge mistake and regretted it so I'd covered the awkward tension for him by pretending like nothing happened and plowing right on to our task.

I'd been feeling sick to my stomach by the time we'd caught up with the rest of the group and could barely function when he started to completely avoid me. And that was when I'd figured that he really had regretted the kiss.

But last night had proved otherwise.

Smiling to myself, I kicked off my sheets and wandered to the small bathroom to clean myself up.

I didn't know what I was going to do to get him alone in order to invite him back here tonight, but there had to be some way to slip him a private contact.

A note maybe?

That might be found though and used as evidence against us.

Today, we were going on another hike to more burn sights, one that had already had a controlled burn and they were now reinvigorating the soil nutrients. Maybe after our hike I could catch up with him and talk to him.

Hopefully, we would still be on the same page by then.

CHAPTER 15

AYEN

"ALL RIGHT, split up into groups of two," one of the volunteer firefighters, Mac, as I remembered from our first day, called out to us. "We're going to be doing some surveying while we're out here and gathering test samples for the quality of the soil to send back to one of the labs we work with. We want to make sure that the soil has been properly enriched after our burn and it's reading in the reports."

Our group began to separate themselves into teams, dividing amongst themselves with little hassle. I stood still, rubbing my fingers together at my sides while people moved around me, easily finding their partner and heading over to the tool kits with sample vials in them.

Fuck, this was like getting picked last for teams in high school gym class all over again.

With only twenty-one of us left, I'd be the odd man out and would need to add myself as a third to someone's group.

But who?

A hand at my back pressed against me, gently motioning me forward.

Looking over my shoulder, I spotted Jackson, who nodded toward the tool kits.

"Go on, grab one."

That was the first time I was seeing him since last night. His expression didn't betray anything but his hand sure did, gently tracing along my lower back in small circles where no one could see.

My stomach flipped at the contact while I tried to fight the smile that was trying to work its way onto my face.

I dragged my feet over to the tool kits. There was only one of them left after each of the groups had grabbed theirs. Inside of it were small glass vials, a set of strangely colored liquids, field sheets, and a set of small tools used for digging up dirt.

I hooked it around my waist and tightened the belt until it was snug against me.

Sure, I wasn't exactly thrilled that Jackson was forcing me to be social, but hopefully, it was only for one day. If I played my cards right, I could potentially mess up one of these tests on purpose and get him to come over to show me, giving me ample opportunity to ask him to stop by later.

"Uh oh."

A hand slapped down on my shoulder. I looked up to see Mac staring down at me.

"No partner, huh?"

"Uh..."

"I'll take him." Roxy trotted over while Jackson followed close behind. "He's still got that ankle thing going on."

"Oh, right. I forgot about that." Mac patted my shoulder. "Keep to the flatter terrain while you're out there, okay? There are a lot of exposed roots since all the undergrowth was burned. We don't need you tripping over something and breaking anything."

I gave him a firm nod. "Of course."

Roxy pressed her wet nose against my palm.

"I'm going to take him down by the river bed," Jackson said. "Less roots down there."

"Good idea." Mac stepped away to attend to another group who was struggling to get their belts on, leaving Jackson and I alone again.

"River bed, huh," I mumbled, making a show at fixing my belt while I could feel my entire face heat up.

"Well, the river's loud this time of year. It will help cover up any screaming."

I choked out a surprised noise and snapped my head up to look at him again. "*Screaming...*"

He grinned, shrugging. "I like that you're loud."

Oh. My. God. This man.

"You're a bit full of yourself thinking I'll be screaming your name." My voice was quiet as I spoke. Even as I said the words, though, I knew they were lies. I could barely contain myself last night and it was just a blowjob.

What was going to happen if this progressed into *more*?

I probably *would* be screaming Jackson's name.

He chuckled softly. "Who knows, maybe I'll be screaming yours."

The inside of my cheek hurt from how hard I had to bite it to keep myself from grinning back. Jackson's acceptance of my verbal need was so different than my past with my ex, to the point where it was kind of startling. Alex had hated how noisy I got when I was turned on and always had me pressed down face first into the mattress while he fucked me so it would drown out my moaning.

I'd learned to like it like that, or so I let him believe seeing as how it was the only intimate contact I'd had my entire adult life. If I didn't enjoy it somehow, then it'd feel like a total chore and would be another thing I added to my ever-growing list of things I hated about marriage.

Jackson winked at me before stepping away, heading over to one of the other firefighters to speak with him for a moment. Roxy stayed by my side, sitting down next to me and leaning her body against my thigh to rest.

I stroked her golden fur, luxuriating in the feel of it under my palm, anticipation racing through me.

A short whistle had both Roxy and I looking over to where Jackson was gesturing. She lifted herself up off the ground and trotted over to him, her tail swishing as she went. Jackson shook the other firefighter's hand before squatting and brushing his hands all over Roxy's face.

She yipped at him as he stood, sticking by the other firefighter's side while Jackson headed back over to me.

"I'm going to have her go with the rest of the

group. I don't need her jumping in the water the second we get down there."

"Does she like the water that much?"

He rolled his eyes affectionately. "Oh, you have no idea."

CHAPTER 16

THE RIVER WAS ABOUT HALF a mile from where the group had set up their temporary test site.

While Jackson and I headed down that way, the rest of the groups fanned out east of us, all of them following the trail of where the controlled burn had begun while we were at the end of it.

The trek down to the edge of the river was easy, thanks to all of the underbrush having been cleared out and burned back into the soil. The vials inside of my kit clinked softly on my hip as we walked. Jackson and I were close enough that our hands kept brushing together every so often, causing shocks of adrenaline to spike through me.

I was dying to take his hand, but figured crossing that kind of line with him would turn him off. There was a difference between just wanting to fuck someone and doing the lovey-dovey shit.

Jeopardizing whatever this was by getting too ahead of myself would be my biggest regret. So, in order to behave myself, I slipped my hands into my pockets.

"So, where do the samples get sent after we take them?" I asked, the sound of the river growing stronger the farther we walked.

"A lab out in Riverside. They test to see if there's any toxic waste in the soil that'll prevent new growth. We haven't had that happen out here in decades, but we always test just to be safe."

I nodded, interested at the information. "What made you want to do all of this? The wild fire stuff."

"Hmmm." He thought for a moment before answering. "Aside from helping people, I find the taking care of nature part fascinating. There's a lot that goes into it, aside from just the controlled burns and making sure nothing gets out of hand while they're going on. We have to account for burn sites with highly dense populations of certain animal species and taking into account how many deaths will occur and if it's worth the temporary displacement."

"Were you always interested in this sort of thing?"

He laughed. "Actually, no. I was working at a dog rescue before I got involved in any of this with my older brother. That was a long time ago, though."

I smiled. "That's right up your alley."

"You think so?" Jackson brushed his shoulder with mine. "I got tired of it, though. There are so many people that don't know how to properly take care of their dogs. We'd get these poor rescues in that were just a mess. Lot of humane euthanasia. Eventually, it wears on you."

I nodded slowly. "I can see that."

"What about you?" he asked. "What were you doing before the jumpsuit?"

I kind of appreciated that he was being a little more cavalier about my situation—it made me feel less like a pariah. Maybe it wasn't his intention, but it made me feel better nonetheless.

"I, uh... actually didn't have a career."

"No?" His brows pulled together in surprise.

"Yeah... I was actually a stay-at-home husband."

Jackson immediately halted in his tracks, stopping so short that his boots made a divot in the soft soil. "You're married."

Even though whatever we had going on could be seen as highly unethical, I was happy to see he had some morals. Sleeping with a married man was apparently on his list of no-nos, which was partly funny and yet also comforting to me. There were too many people in this world who didn't take their wedding vows seriously enough.

Turning to him, I let out a soft sigh. "I used to be."

"'Used to be'." He shook his head. "What does that mean?"

"Um..."

Jesus, how did I even get into this?

My relationship with Alex was so complicated by the end. I could barely wrap my mind around what happened in order to talk to a therapist about it, let alone right here and now with Jackson.

He waited patiently, though, for me to speak, rubbing his fingers together at his sides in an anxious sort of way.

I wondered if he was seeing me differently. Someone who was once married and now a felon in a program and fucking around with one of the firefighters. See, those things didn't tend to look as bad when you were just dealing with surface level shit. Once people got to know each other, that's when the real mess began to manifest.

I couldn't look him in the eyes as I talked and instead, crossed my arms over my chest while I stared down at the ground. "I, uh… served my ex divorce papers on my twenty-first birthday. I wasn't planning on it being that day but it was the only day I knew he'd be gone for the majority of it so I could pack a bag and leave before he got home and discovered the papers." I huffed out a laugh. "Clearly, that didn't go over very well."

"Why do you say that?"

"Well, he's kind of the reason I got sentenced. So..."

"*Fuck*, Ayen," Jackson murmured.

He cupped his hands around my face, tilting it back to force me to look up at him. He was shaking his head, a pinched expression on his face. "He hurt you, didn't he?"

Over the years, that question had been asked so many times that I'd lost count. Even before my divorce, or my attempt at it, anyway, I'd had friends who would notice my bruises or the bite marks on my skin and ask me if they were from Alex.

And over and over again I'd promised them that it wasn't him, even when it was obvious and no one believed me, yet they still did nothing to protect me. To help me get out when I needed to.

During my trial, I'd been asked repeatedly if Alex's stalking had been the cause of me pulling the trigger, or if he'd hurt me the night he came to my apartment, that I thought I'd be safe from him.

I'd been forced to re-live the grim truth, to describe in excruciating detail what transpired on that night.

The fear that choked me as I watched him break down the door to my bathroom, with my phone pressed to my ear and emergency services rattling in my ear about how they were only a few minutes away. The cool steel of Alex's gun that I'd stolen a week earlier resting heavily in my lap, the muzzle of it blurring as I raised it with my shaking hand at the man I once thought I'd loved and pulled the trigger, effectively ending both of our lives in a single split second.

Even after all of that, answering that question never got any easier. No matter how many times how many people asked or how many times I recounted that night.

"Yes," I said, tears burning behind my eyes.

"Oh, honey." Jackson shook his head again, pulling me against him. "He never deserved you."

Shock hit me instantly.

No one had ever said that to me before, let alone meant it.

I was just a runaway kid at sixteen, living off

the streets until one day, a man in a suit had found me rifling through his garbage and had invited me to come stay with him for a few days until I could find a shelter that would take me in. Those few days had turned into weeks and then into months, and then soon I was walking down the aisle to marry him.

Alex had made me feel like the luckiest son of a bitch for pulling me off the street like a stray cat and giving me a home like he had. The abuse was simply my burden to bear in order to keep living the life he provided. It was a small price to pay, until it became bad enough where it wasn't so small anymore.

But even then, I thought my karma had earned me that little spot of hell that I called a jail cell.

Yet here Jackson was, telling me the complete opposite with such sincerity that it was hard to peg him as a liar.

I began to shake my head, a knee jerk reaction to the comforting words.

He tightened his hold on my jaw, preventing me from continuing. "Ayen, you listen to me. He. Didn't. Deserve. You. What you did to him… he fucking deserved that."

"I'm…" My words were failing me. My thoughts were getting all jumbled up in my head as my emotions were beginning to get the better of me. I wasn't expecting to come out here and cry about my past with a man I wanted to rail me into the goddamn dirt like an animal. But here we fucking were. "You don't know…"

"I don't have to know the details, baby. He

hurt you. If he hurt you, then he deserved whatever he got in the end." I felt his lips press against the top of my head, peppering kisses into my hair as he spoke.

I sucked in a sharp breath while a sob choked me.

The validation I needed over two years ago had finally been delivered.

It felt as amazing even as it hurt.

I believed wholeheartedly that I would've died that night if I didn't do what I did, but did that justify me taking matters into my own hands?

I still didn't know. But it was too late now to dwell on the 'what if's now.

Jackson pressed his lips to my forehead, trailing soft kisses down to the bridge of my nose. "He can't get you anymore."

My body sagged into his, almost completely boneless.

The truth rattled me to my damn core.

But he was right.

Alex would never hurt or touch me ever again.

CHAPTER 17

Jackson

I LOWERED Ayen to the soft mossy ground slowly, hooking my arm around his waist from behind to keep him from moving too far away from me. My lips found his easily, molding against those soft, plush cushions that he opened for me immediately, sucking me in with the kind of desperation I felt down to my bones.

His cheeks were still wet from his tears, brushing up against mine when he tilted his head to the side to deepen our kiss.

I wanted to kill that son of a bitch he called a husband. If the man wasn't already fucking dead, I'd leave this property tonight and go find him to finish the fucking job.

How dare he put his hands on Ayen?

My sweet baby bird who couldn't even hurt a fly but had apparently been forced to do the worst thing a human could ever possibly do. And the justice system punishing him by forcing him into prison with other offenders who'd knowingly broken the law because they thought they were above it was just the cherry on top of an already fucked up cake.

What kind of 'justice' was that?

And after he got out, he'd have to deal with that on his record for the rest of his life. That sounded like no justice to me.

It infuriated me. I hope that man rotted in fucking hell for the rest of eternity.

Grabbing at the front of Ayen's waistband, I unbuckled the tool kit from around him. The vials inside of it clinked softly as I pushed them away from us so that they wouldn't get damaged. I at least still had some sense about me, even though my mind was filled with *Ayen, Ayen, Ayen.*

I'd show him how to be properly treated— what being with a *real* man felt like. Not some spineless coward who beat their partner because deep down they knew they weren't good enough.

My father was like that. Growing up, he'd been the stereotypical jock that had wanted his sons to follow in his footsteps and join the military and make something of themselves.

Carter had done that, acted as the proper son that my father should've been proud of. But nothing had ever been good enough for that man. And eventually, it'd weighed on my brother too much for him to bear it any longer.

My brother, and Ayen both, deserved so much better in the end but still had shit to show for it.

When Ayen's legs came up to wrap around my

waist, I scooped him up again into my lap and worked the zipped on the front of his jumper down until he could slip both of his arms out of the sleeves. He wrapped his bare arms around my neck while I rolled my tongue along his. The tent in his pants was pressed up against my waist, teasing me.

Fuck, I needed to get him naked *pronto.*

Keeping him against me with one arm, I used the other to shed my jacket and toss it onto the ground behind him. I laid him back down, keeping him half in my lap with his legs still wrapped around me.

I stroked my hands along his bare skin, touching him and teasing him as I went. Using both of my fingers, I pinched at his nipples, driving a small, surprised squeak out of him that had me chuckling against his mouth.

"Sensitive little thing, aren't you," I said, my voice low and husky. I trailed my lips along his jaw, tracing up to where the shell of his ear was. He shivered again when I nipped at it, taking the lobe into my mouth and flicking it a few times with my tongue.

"Jax," he moaned.

God, I loved the sound of him saying my name like that.

"Want do you want, baby?" I asked, letting go and nuzzling my nose against the side of his face, inhaling his unique scent. I couldn't fucking get enough of him. I need to touch and taste him as much as I needed water to live. "You tell me."

"You." His thighs squeezed around me. "I want you."

That cute little cock of his jerked against my waist, still covered by the bottom half of his jumpsuit. Mine was also dying to get out of my thick trousers and find that soft heat of his that I knew would feel like fucking heaven once I pressed up against it.

"You want all of me?" I asked. I had a feeling, but I needed to be sure. I wasn't going to press him if all he wanted was another blowjob or something low-key, which I'd be more than satisfied to give him.

He nodded, rolling his hips against me. "You have anything on you?"

"Condoms? No. Some kind of lube? I can get creative."

He huffed out a laugh. "I know that wasn't meant to be sexy, but…"

I grinned and lifted myself up from where I'd buried my face in his neck. His smile was a dream, a beautiful change from the absolutely heart-shattered despair that had been on it a few minutes ago. I hated that look on him; it felt too much like angels crying or something equally as biblical.

"Are you okay with that?" I reached over to grab the pack I'd thrown onto the ground the second I'd taken him into my arms. "No protection?"

I slid it back over to me and parted the zipper with one of my hands, my other finding the spot right where Ayen's jumpsuit was still partially zipped and his skin was showing at his hip. He was warm under my hand, solid. I squeezed him, making sure all of this was still real and not some fantasy my mind had cooked up in a dream.

"He was my first," Ayen said, his fingers flexing around my arm. "My only."

I'll be your last, is almost what came spilling out of my mouth in response. Fuck, I really had it bad for him. Not even inside of him yet and I was already hearing the damn wedding bells.

Though, I doubted Ayen would ever want to get married again. Not after what happened with his first husband.

I was getting ahead of myself.

Grabbing the travel-sized bottle of aloe I kept, I shoved my pack away again and set the bottle down next to us. "I'm clean."

He nodded, not even needing me to elaborate further as he said, "I trust you."

My heart thundered in my chest.

The fact that some other man had taken advantage of him killed me. He was so trusting, maybe a little too much so for his own good. And for someone to have taken that and used it to their advantage truly sickened me.

That stopped here. I don't know how I was going to accomplish it but starting now, I wouldn't allow anyone to take him for granted again.

Ayen unhooked his legs from around me, pulling them back just enough to help me lift him and slip the bottom half of his jumpsuit and boots off of his body. He was as beautiful as I remembered him from last night, now fully revealed to me through the breaks of sunlight through the thick canopy over us.

His tanned skin was flawless and smooth, a dusting of hair trailing down to his hard cock that rested against his lower belly, straining to be touched. I fisted my hand around it immediately, not being able to help myself.

Ayen groaned, his back arching. "Ohhhh…"

I stroked my hand down him slowly, lovingly. Beads of precum leaked out from the engorged tip and down to my hand where I spread it along his shaft as I continued to move my hand, working him.

"Jax," his voice was strained. He reached out to grab at the moss-covered ground, fingers clenching tightly around it. "Please…"

My own cock jerked in my pants, completely on board with the begging.

I'd had subs before beg for me to fill them, on their hands and knees as they presented them-selves to me like cats in heat. None of them had ever come close to turning me on quite like this. Ayen's unabashed *want* for me was so intoxicating that I was willing to drown on it.

"Hold still," I told him and let go of him.

Standing, I quickly kicked my boots off and yanked my undershirt off, tossing them both toward my pack with little care.

Ayen sat up on his elbows to watch me, his eyes practically bulging out of his head when I shrugged my pants down and stepped out of them.

"Like what you see?" I teased.

His mouth dropped open, his eyes directly narrowing in on my cock.

Its heavy weight bounced while I moved, sinking back down to my knees on the soft moss in front of him and scooting closer so that he could wrap his legs around me again if he wanted to.

"Fuck," he mumbled. "You're fucking huge…"

I chuckled, scooping the bottle of aloe off of the ground. "Oh, he flatters me."

"Um…"

I glanced at him, uncapping the bottle as he spoke.

"So, the last time I did this was three years ago."

"You'll be okay, Ayen. I won't hurt you." Probably. Good thing I had a ton of aloe in this bottle.

He didn't look convinced in the slightest, and instead of leaning back and parting his legs for me, he shot forward and wrapped a hand around my shaft. A small gasp left my lips. Not only were his beautiful, long fingers practically dwarfed when wrapped around me like that, but he squeezed me perfectly while stroking up and down a few times.

"I knew you would be," he mumbled, more to himself than to me. "I could tell."

I lowered my lids halfway over my eyes. A deep heat settled into my gut. "Did you?"

Grabbing his wrist, I held him still and rolled my hips back, rearing them forward in a slow motion. He kept his hand firm around me as I fucked myself into his fist, a small and strangled moan leaving him.

"I'm gonna bury myself so damn deep in you, Ayen," I breathed out. I wasn't even pressed against his pretty hole yet and I was already getting lost in the blissful lust. "You want that, don't you?"

He nodded with his lips parted, wet from obsessively licking them. If we had more time, I'd let him take a taste of me. But even now, we were working on borrowed time. Soon, I'd need to radio in to the group and check in so that a search party wasn't sent after us.

While I continued to move my hips, I let go of his wrist in order to drizzle a generous amount of aloe on my fingers, rubbing them together a few times to coat the digits thoroughly.

"Lean back, honey," I said.

Obedient as ever, he let go of my cock and lay back down onto my jacket. He lifted his legs up from the ground automatically, tilting his hips back just enough to reveal himself to me.

I groaned and traced my thumb along his rim, circling around it a few times while his body clenched and unclenched to try and tease one of my fingers inside of him. His balls were drawn up tight, swollen from how much he needed to come.

What a pretty picture he made.

"Fuck, you are gorgeous," I told him, meaning it.

I slipped my thumb inside of him slowly, the heat of his body engulfing me immediately.

"Oh," Ayen mumbled, fanning his legs out more for me.

I pulled out the digit and smeared more aloe over him, coating him generously before working my finger back inside. His head fell back to rest against my jacket.

When I slowly added another finger, he let out a high-pitched whine, his body jolted when I curled them inside to search around for the sweet spot.

"Mmm, right…" He gasped. "There."

I smiled, stroking along the gland a few times until his body was rocking itself to work my fingers deeper as I added a third. He was a damn natural, taking in the intrusion and bearing down just enough to get his body used to it again.

I couldn't wait to sink inside of him, let him ride me until he came all over the both of us.

"Jax," he murmured.

I slipped my fingers out of his hole, and he clenched around the emptiness a few times with a whine. I grabbed one of his legs and hooked it around me, pulling him closer toward my lap. Slathering more aloe over my cock, I fisted my hand around the head and gave myself a quick few strokes to coat myself.

The head of my cock pressed against his entrance, rubbing along that tight rim until he opened up to me again, begging me to slide in again.

"Ready?"

He nodded wordlessly.

Grabbing onto his other leg, I pushed it down against his chest and held it there while I breached him. He squirmed under me, his nails digging into my arm to hold on while I slowly worked myself into his tight little hole.

Fuck, it was like a damn vice grip, trying to milk me of my cum before I could even get halfway inside of him. I could see how he'd make the perfect little sex doll, being so good for me and letting me do whatever I wanted to him.

Ayen's body jolted again when I rolled my hips, nailing him right in that sweet spot of his that had him choking out a soft 'please' to me.

Jesus, he was going to actually be the death of me.

I started us slow, moving in shallow thrusts until I felt his body open up to me. It didn't take long, his hole greedy and needing to be pounded into like the good little sub he was meant to be.

I kept my hold on his hip firm as I began to pull almost all the way out of him and then slam back inside until my hips were pressed flush against his ass. The soft clapping sounds of our skin making contact with each other was drowned out by the creek next to us, barely heard even as Ayen's body rippled from how hard I was slamming into him.

His moans were loud and so slutty sounding that I had to reach over and grab his chin to force him to look at me as he continued. I needed those sounds directed completely at me. His pupils were blown out, completely lost in the lust of our bodies finally coming together after beating around the bush for so long.

"Fuck," I gritted through my teeth. I wasn't going to last long, not at this rate. He was too much of a turn-on for me to hold back.

Ayen's mouth dropped open while he rapidly pulled in lungfuls of air. I adjusted my hips just enough inside of him to nail his sweet spot with each pass of my cock head.

A few tears leaked from his eyes as he stared at me, so damn gone and lost to the pleasure that was no doubt racking his body.

He painted me the pretty goddamn picture of himself that I was going to burn into my memories for as long as I walked this Earth.

He bared down on me, clenching tight. "J… Jax…"

"Come, baby," I demanded. "You be a good boy and come so that I can fill you up."

His eyes squeezed shut while his body tensed. Without even having to reach down between us and touch him, his cock began to pump out thick squirts of cum, coating his stomach entirely with it.

I held him down when he began to squirm again, overwhelmed with the pleasure, keeping him pinned while I worked my cock in him as deeply as I could. The caveman part of my brain was taking over, driving me into fucking him hard and fast.

He cried out, his nails digging into my skin again, causing my hips to stutter. My entire body tensed up as I exploded inside of him. Cum poured out of me in what felt like wave after wave, coating him from the inside out as I continued to try and thrust myself inside of him.

Some of my spend leaked out between us, dripping down onto my jacket and causing a sticky mess when I finally slowed and fit my hips against his ass, grinding down to get myself nice and seated.

Ayen collapsed back against the ground, blinking a few times with a dazed look on his face. He was still panting, his skin slicked in a fine layer of sweat that I gave in to my desires and licked a trail up from his stomach to his cheek. He tasted fantastic—just as I thought he would.

A small smile played on his lips, despite his tired and worn out expression.

I kissed along his jaw and up to his mouth, brushing back some sweat-slicked hair from his face.

"Mmm..." He turned to press his cheek against my hand, his words slurred as he said, "That was good..."

Pride swelled in my chest. "Good."

CHAPTER 18

HONESTLY, I couldn't even remember getting back to my cabin after our trip in the woods.

I think the sex had been so good that it'd melted my brain somehow, completely washing away any other memories outside of Jackson's touch.

How bad was it that I was already craving him again, a few hours after parting for dinner and now alone back in my cabin?

My body was sore, my hole even more so. But it was the good kind of sore; the kind you felt after a really good workout and that the resulting burn afterward felt satisfying instead of punishing.

I wondered how much trouble I'd get into if I snuck out of my cabin tonight and went over to his. With my luck, chances were it'd be a night of random check-ins and I'd get caught trying to sneak back over after Jackson and I had our fill again.

My stupid, addicted brain was already trying to reason with me that it was worth it.

What was a little danger in the face of getting off like that again?

He'd been so gentle afterward. Taking care to clean me up and kiss me every so often. He'd even dressed me and got me looking somewhat decent before quickly half-assing my kit and walking me back to where the rest of the group, and Roxy, were waiting for us.

She'd come trotting over happily when she'd spotted us, her nose zeroing in on me the second I got within range where she'd sniffed at me for a suspiciously long time.

How embarrassing was it to have a dog sniff out the cum still leaking out of your ass by said dog's owner?

Good thing no one else was paying attention or else Jackson and I would've been screwed.

We'd had to pretend to ignore each other while all of us inmates were dismissed for the evening. And even now, looking back on it, I could feel the heat of his stare following after me as I headed to the mess hall to try and force myself to eat something while my head was still up in the clouds.

And now here I was after lights out, laying alone in my bed and debating with myself on whether or not I should try and chance it.

Whining at my own indecision, I buried my face into my pillow which no longer had the faint scent of Jackson embedded into it. I missed him so fucking much that it was physically hurting me.

I needed him.

Reaching under my covers and back behind me, I snuck a hand under the waistband of my pants and traced my fingers along my sore hole. I couldn't believe he'd been able to fit himself inside of me with that monster cock.

It'd stretched me to the point where I thought I was going to black out, but the pleasure had been too incredible to let go of. He'd known exactly how to work me to get me falling over the edge.

Now I just felt empty, though.

I dipped my fingers into my hole, pretending for a second that they were much thicker and a little more calloused. This wasn't the same, fucking myself with my own fingers, but at least it was better than having nothing at all.

One time being under the man and I was apparently addicted.

Eventually though, my hole grew too sore to continue moving my fingers inside of it, forcing me to slip my hand out of my pants and clench around nothing. Life was unfair. I'd finally gotten to meet a man that I clicked with, both physically and mentally, and yet I couldn't have him.

At least, not in the way that I wanted.

We'd have to resort to sneaking around and hoping like hell we wouldn't get caught.

There was a soft scraping sound coming from over by the cabin door that pulled me out of my wallowing.

Sitting up slightly, I blinked a few times to adjust my eyes to the darkened room.

A figure slipped in through the door, tall and familiar, before closing the door and latching it softly behind him.

My heart leapt into my chest.

"Baby?" came a faint whisper.

My heart clenched at the nickname.

I kicked my sheets off of me and slid over across the bed, making room for him as he slowly shuffled over to me. "Come lay with me."

He let out a soft chuckle and made his way over slowly, patting along the bunks until he found mine and lowered himself slowly down onto the mattress.

I backed my body up into his the moment his arms came around me, pulling me back against his chest while he buried his face into my neck. I felt him breathe in deeply, his body slowly relaxing.

"I missed you," I whispered in the dark.

Jackson squeezed me. "I missed you more. You feeling okay?"

I nodded. "Better than okay."

He chuckled again and kissed a line from my neck up to my jaw. "I love the sound of that."

I traced my fingers along his hand tucked against my chest, feeling the way the tendons flexed under his skin and the pronounced veins that soon disappeared at his forearm. I had half a mind to tell him to pull down my pants but I knew I was still way too sore for that. After going years without sex, my pent up frustrations weren't letting me off that easily.

Jackson moved his hand from my waist to slip under the band of my pants, almost as if reading my mind. He fisted it around my half-hard cock and stroked lazily, breathing out slowly as he buried his face into my neck again.

"I can't get enough of you," he mumbled.

I swallowed, his words, coupled with the sparks of pleasure from his hand moving on me, created a pit of heat that settled low in my gut.

"Jax?"

He hummed softly.

"Do you care? About what I did?"

I hadn't meant for that to be the question that I wanted to ask him—in actuality, I'd wanted to ask him about his life, to get to know him better, but instead, my stupid mouth had let *that one* slip out instead.

His hand didn't pause at all in its movements. His lazy stroking continued as he said, "No."

My gut clenched. "Why not?"

Instead of answering me, he shifted us backward, pulling me along with him as he leaned until he was flat on his back. Tightening his hold around my waist, he scooted me closer, enough until I could comfortably rest the back of my head against his chest. This position gave me room to let my legs fall apart, the motion of his hands tenting my pants more prominent.

I groaned at the feeling of his hand moving on my cock, letting my eyes fall closed.

God*damn,* he know how to work his hand. It was hard to concentrate on anything outside of the rolling pleasure boiling inside of my veins.

"If he wasn't already dead, Ayen, I would've left tonight to go find him," came Jackson's easy response.

My eyes snapped open. "What?"

"You already took care of that though, so."

"No, I didn't."

His hand slowed until it stopped. "What do you mean?"

I shifted my head to the other side in order to glance up at him. "He's not dead. I was charged with attempted murder in the second degree."

"Second de—? It was self defense?"

I sighed and sat up, grabbing his arm and yanking it out of my pants. So much for just spending the night with him and relaxing. Of course I had to be the dumbass that brought this subject up.

Twisting around, I moved until I was hovering over him, surprised when he pulled me back down to lay on his chest while his arms came to wrap tightly around me again. His hand found its way into my hair, gently moving through the tangled strands.

"Tell me," he said.

"It's a long story."

"I want to hear it anyway."

"No…" I sighed again. "You really don't."

He grew quiet, his hand idly carding through my hair at slow enough pace that it had begun to make me feel drowsy. I blinked a few times, forcing myself to stay awake—*needing to*—while he was still here.

We had such precious little time together. I

didn't want to miss any of it because my stupid body was running on fumes.

"My father," Jackson murmured. "He was a lot like your ex-husband. From the sounds of it, anyway."

His tone was even, but being so close to him like this, I could feel the sudden hitch in his voice as he said the words. I hadn't been expecting him to open up to me at all, not like this, anyway. I wanted him to keep talking but I didn't know how to ask.

"We always walked around on eggshells around him," he said after a while. "After my mom died, he changed into a different person. Things got worse."

"I'm sorry." My heart hurt for him. I'd never been close to my parents, but I knew the lost feeling as a child with having no one you could trust in the world. The love of a parent was something that could never be replaced.

"My brother and I were always trying to get him to be proud of us. We were military brats, so you can only imagine the kind of disciplinarian he was."

I winced.

While Alex had never been in the military himself, he'd run our household like the fucking barracks. Back when I was a teenager, if even a single thing was out of place or not to his liking, I got punished. I'd learned his habits quickly, making sure to keep from angering him or else I was sure he'd throw me out onto the streets to fend for myself.

It wasn't much different after we'd gotten married, but at least I had a little say in what went on under that roof. His expectations of me had been astronomical, though, which counteracted most of the privileges I'd been granted once I became his legal spouse.

"Alex was like that," I said softly. "He wasn't military, but…"

Jackson's thumb moved across my cheek. "I'm sorry he treated you that way, Ayen."

"I didn't know any better. He took me in off the streets when I was sixteen. I was a runaway so I thought he was this… I don't know. Messiah figure. I think that got to his head."

"That seems to be a running theme with abusers." He had a slightly ironic tone that was tinged with sadness. "They get a savior complex after a while."

I sighed. "Yeah. And then blame you for it when reality comes crashing down and they realize they're not shit."

He chuckled softly.

I tilted my head to the side and pressed my ear over his heart. It beat steadily under me, the thrumming sound of it comforting. I raised my hand to grip his bicep.

If anything were to happen to me, I knew Jackson would protect me. He'd done it plenty of times so far and that wasn't even life and death shit.

He was a noble man with a good moral compass. He saw injustice and he fought against it. That was the kind of man that deserved the world.

"At least you had your brother. I'm glad you were there for each other."

Jackson grew quiet again, his fingers pausing in my hair. My body tensed, realizing I'd said something I shouldn't have, though I didn't know what. I waited, with baited breath, for him to speak again.

I needed to stop assuming things like I knew what I was talking about. I was so desperate in wanting to know Jackson that it'd led me to putting my foot in my mouth. Despite us being this close physically, that wasn't my green light to believe I knew anything about him personally.

When he finally spoke, he said, "Used to. He's gone now."

Shit…

"I'm—"

"It's okay," he cut me off. "He was sad for a long, long time."

I squeezed my eyes shut. I could fill in the blanks there to know what had happened. What a damn shame. If he was even half the man that Jackson was, then the world had lost a light when he passed. I ached for Jackson and his loss. It was never fair to lose a loved one far sooner than you expected to.

That was the kind of shit you couldn't prepare for and the blow was always massive.

Thankfully, Jackson began to speak again. "I don't talk to my father anymore. He doesn't deserve to know what's going on in my life after the bullshit he pulled. I doubt he misses me, anyway. He was always disappointed in me."

That had me shaking my head.

Sitting up, I lifted myself just enough to press my lips against Jackson's. It was hard to see in the dim lighting of the cabin, but I felt him smile, though, and tilted his head to the side, catching my lips fully with his.

"He didn't deserve you," I said when he pulled away, repeating his own words back to him.

"Oh, my sweet, Ayen." He sighed. "Tell me your ex's last name. Was it Gonzalez?"

Oh lord.

"No."

"Tell me."

"Absolutely not."

He brushed the backs of his fingers along my jawline. "Why?"

"Because I'm not letting you go to jail, too."

His smile was practically shit-eating as he said, "What, you don't want to be bunk mates?"

I rolled my eyes and buried my face into his chest before he could see me smiling. I didn't need to be encouraging him into going out and finding my ex-husband and smothering him with a damn pillow while he stared blankly at the ceiling.

Would it be the hottest thing anyone had ever done for me?

Sure, absolutely. But I wasn't going to let this saint-of-a-man wind up behind bars because of me. I wasn't *that* good of a lay.

"Ayen."

I shook my head. "There's no point. He's in a vegetative state."

He huffed out a surprised laugh. "What?"

"That's why I was sentenced. The court felt that I'd purposefully aimed poorly. So, instead of me getting off with self defense, I'd gotten charged with attempted second degree."

"What kind of bullshit is that? Where would they have preferred you to aim?"

"The prosecutor argued that I had plenty of time to hit him in the chest. But I'd aimed for the head instead, resulting in the bullet getting lodged and rendering him pretty much brain dead. The evidence for my defense of him stalking me for four months beforehand was thrown out due to a technicality. So to the jury, it looked like he'd come over to sign the divorce papers and I'd shot him instead."

"*Jesus,*" he choked out.

Weirdly enough, it actually felt good to get all of this off my chest.

In prison, I couldn't exactly talk about what had happened leading up to my crime. Not because I wasn't allowed to or anything, but just because most inmates really didn't give a fuck. There was always someone worse off than you, so trying to gain any kind of sympathy was met with a fist to the face and someone stealing all your commissary.

"Yeah, so." I shrugged. "I got five years."

"You shouldn't have gotten any," he argued.

"Not according to the court."

"I swear to god." Jackson's hand grabbed at my pant leg and lifted my leg to swing over his hips. He then moved down to grab at my ass, lifting me up until I was practically lying completely on top of him. "Who was your lawyer?"

"A court appointed one."

I could tell he was just barely containing his rage. And while a man getting upset or aggravated around me normally had me wanting to run for the hills, with Jackson it was the complete opposite.

I felt safe. His anger was directed toward those who had hurt me, those he'd protect me against if it came down to it. He let his anger be the fuel that kept me shielded from the danger.

"It's okay," I said, nuzzling my cheek against his chest. "I only have another three years."

"That's three years too long, Ayen. You shouldn't have any at all."

While I agreed, the state had its own opinions. Once I was up in front of a parole board, I'd lament about how sorry I was until they agreed to let me go. I would say just about anything to them if they wanted me to, as long as it got me the fuck out of SAC.

"Have you tried appealing?" His fingers worked their way back through my hair.

"No. My lawyer didn't feel like there was a point with my sentence being less than a decade."

"I'm getting someone to see you. I know a lawyer."

"It's okay, Jax. I'm all right." Well, as good as I could get, I guess. I was on a unit with non-violent offenders, so most of the time, the worst things that were fought about were people being too noisy or inconsiderate while others were trying to sleep.

"I don't want you going back there, Ayen."

Unfortunately, I would have to.

Eventually, this program would end and I

would be shipped on a bus back behind the tall, barbed wire walls of SAC until the rest of my three years were finally up.

Did I want that to happen?

Absolutely not, but that was the reality I was facing. Getting worked up about things I couldn't change would only waste precious energy I didn't have.

"I know it sucks."

He let out a slow breath, his chest deflating with the motion.

Guilt began to brew in me, fear that he was mad at me starting to take root. There was a point in time where I didn't want to care about other people's opinion of me, and had been determined to come here with that same mindset to practice.

How funny that I'd failed so spectacularly at it.

He didn't need to feel sorry for me, or like he had to do something in order to prove to me that he cared. Him simply being here and not treating me like I was a psychopath was enough of a heroic act for me. I didn't need him going out and avenging my honor or something equally as stupid that would land him in serious trouble.

"Jax?"

"Yes, sweetheart."

Ugh, I'd never get enough of the pet names and endearments. They sounded perfect falling from his mouth.

"Stay with me tonight? I usually wake up before the sun comes up. I'll help you leave before headcount starts."

"I'll do you one better." He lifted his hips up off the bed, just enough to retrieve his phone from his pocket. He quickly unlocked it and set an alarm, tossing it onto the bed near the wall. "Now, we can both sleep."

I smiled and relaxed into him, letting my eyes fall closed while the sound of his heart beating under my ear lulled me to sleep.

CHAPTER 19

Jackson

Leaving Ayen to head to my own cabin after spending the night sleeping with him was its own special brand of torture.

I'd woken up before my alarm had gone off, just for the specific purpose of being able to watch him sleep. He was so peaceful with his head lying on my chest and the gentle noises of him breathing deeply cutting into the silence inside of the cabin.

I'd gotten hardly any sleep myself at all last night. Instead, I spent most of the night lying awake thinking about Ayen's ex, his disaster of a trial, the way he'd been treated before he'd ever been arrested, all of it. I couldn't stand the injustice that my baby bird had faced in his only two decades on this god-forsaken planet.

Where had the people who were supposed to be fighting for him gone?

His parents were out of the picture, but what about his ex's parents?

Where the fuck were they in all of it?

Every new piece of information that he told me had solidified my hatred for the man who'd done this—who'd started it all. Ayen had pulled the trigger, but that man had been the one to place the gun in his hand, even if he hadn't done so physically.

And the fact that the courts completely dismissed that was beyond me.

By the time I got back to my cabin, Roxy was already up and whining for food. After quickly feeding her, I popped into the shower to wash away the residual anger that I still felt. I wasn't even sure if that would ever go away—not when at the end of this program, I'd be forced to let Ayen go back to the one place he absolutely did not belong.

How he'd managed this far to still stay so soft and sweet was beyond me, but I'd be damned if I wasn't going to protect him in the future from further misery.

Once clean and dressed again, I grabbed my phone and scrolled through my contacts, hitting the 'call' option once I reached the one I'd been looking for. I pressed the receiver to my ear while I headed back into the kitchen, my body restless and needing something to do.

"'lo?" A groggy voice on the other end answered me.

"Nina? It's Jax."

She groaned loud enough to be insulting. "What the fuck, why are you calling me at… six-fucking-thirty. Are you serious, Jackson?"

"I need a favor."

"Fuck you," she grumbled.

"It's serious, Nina. I wouldn't be calling you like this out of the blue if it wasn't."

There was a long sigh on the other end, followed by some rustling around as she most likely was sitting herself up and getting out of bed. While I waited, I grabbed the box of instant pancake mix and set it down on the counter.

Roxy trotted over to me, curiously poking her nose at my thigh while I grabbed a mixing bowl from the cupboard.

"Okay," Nina finally said, sounding much more alert. "What is it?"

"Can I meet with you? It's probably better if we talk in person."

"Geezus, Jax. You wake me up at six in the fucking morning… to ask me to meet with you later? This couldn't have been a text because…?"

Despite her surly attitude, I knew Nina would go to the ends of the Earth to help me. It was just in her nature, too. She was a bleeding heart like me; the constant desire to help the unhelpable was like a sickness that could only be cured through situations like this.

I'd known Nina for close to my entire life and not once had I ever seen her *not* rip the shirt off her own back to give it to someone else that needed it more.

"I had to make sure you actually looked at it

instead of ignoring it like the other ten messages I've sent you."

There was a pause on the other end before she mumbled, "Touché."

Pouring some mix into the bowl, I measured out the wet ingredients with one hand before tossing my measuring cup into the sink next to me. "It's about an inmate in my rehabbing program. I want to help him and I think you can help me with that."

"Oh, Jackson." She sighed. "If they're already sentenced, there's not much I can do."

"I think his can easily be overturned if we got the paperwork to the right judge."

At least, that was what I was hoping for. I had no fucking clue how the justice system worked outside of what a normal person walking down the street knew. I'd worked with inmates for a long time, sure, but them talking about their charges or what went into them receiving them in the first place was never discussed.

Me getting privy info from the COs had been a miracle and one that I knew would never happen again.

Everything that I learned after this was either going to be through Ayen, or hopefully, Nina.

"You say that like I have a magic wand. I'm not superwoman, you know that, right?"

"Yeah, but you're also the best damn lawyer that I know," I argued, setting my skillet down onto my stove and turning up the heat.

"I'm the *only* damn lawyer you know."

"I have other friends!"

"Name two. And don't say Mac, you fucking loser."

I rolled my eyes practically to the back of my head. "What's wrong with being friends with my coworkers?"

"Well, for one, what else do you guys talk about besides work?"

"Look, not everyone can dish like we do."

"We're gay, Jackson. No one can."

I huffed out a laugh. "All right, fine. Whatever. Can you please meet me in town later today? He's only got five more weeks here, so I need you to look at his case file, pronto."

"I'll look at it but I can't promise you anything."

"That's fine. I just need another set of eyes on it because it's driving me insane."

"Why?" she asked.

"You'll see." Roxy whined at me again, her big doe eyes reminding me instantly of the man I'd had to leave behind an hour prior. "Text me when you want to meet. I'll take the day off today and meet you whenever."

"Fine. But you're paying for our food."

"Deal."

When the other end of the line dropped, I pulled my phone away from my ear and set it down onto the counter next to me. While I believed in Nina and her skills as a defense lawyer, she had a point. She wasn't a miracle worker and simply thinking that Ayen's case could easily be overturned given the right circumstances didn't mean that those would ever be presented in the first place.

The justice system was already fucked as it was for innocent people. It was downright rigged if you were ever convicted of anything, even if it was false or not. The odds were stacked against you the moment a pair of cuffs was slapped onto your wrists.

Though even with all of that, I still couldn't let Ayen go back without a fight. It'd eat me alive if I did. If there was even a shred of a chance in getting him out of prison and giving him the freedom he so truly deserved, then I'd do whatever I could to see it through.

Even if by the end of it all he chose to stop seeing me.

All I cared about was getting him out of a place where he never should've been. Anyone with half a brain would think the same if they knew the facts. And I was sure once I got a hold of his case file, and saw the dark and horrible truth, that feeling inside of me would only grow.

There was no doubt in my mind that he was wrongfully convicted.

Probation for ten years, sure.

But prison?

No. It was too far for my baby bird.

Roxy whined again, pulling me out of my thoughts.

I reached over and placed a hand on her head, rubbing along her temple toward the back of her skull.

"I know, girl. I miss him, too. But we'll see him soon."

Her big brown eyes didn't look all too convinced.

Actually… since I was going to be taking the day off from here in order to meet up with Nina, I'd need someone to watch Roxy in the meantime.

Who better than the inmate she was whining to see?

"You want to go see Ayen?" I asked her.

Her tail began to wag.

At least while I was gone she could keep him company.

Not to mention it would give me an excuse when coming back here to meet up with him again without the COs catching wind of what was going on between us.

It was the perfect plan.

Roxy let out a soft 'woof' in what I imagined as stark approval.

"All right, girl. Give me a second and then we'll go see him."

CHAPTER 20

JACKSON

"Thanks for meeting me."

Nina lowered herself into the seat across from me, her wide-rimmed sunglasses still perched on her nose. The bag she'd brought with her, a large leather satchel that I recognized from her court hearings, was set down onto the chair next to her.

"Did I have a choice?" she asked, though there was no real bite behind her words.

"Funny."

Her sharply cut hair, angled down toward her chin, was slicked back with the arms of her sunglasses as she slid them onto the top of her head. Her beautifully done eye makeup had a dark and smoky look to it, bringing out the clear blues of her eyes, and was angled in a way that complimented her angular features.

Under the table, I was bouncing my leg like

crazy. My pent up nerves from coming back from the courthouse early this morning with the thick folder sitting next to me on the table felt like it was burning a hole in me. I'd chanced a look through it while I'd been waiting for her, only getting to the fifth page before a sick twisting in my gut had forced me to stop.

There weren't any evidence pictures attached to the documents, but the descriptions alone had made me nauseous. How Ayen went through any of that and still got convicted was beyond me when there were so many more violent offenders out there still walking the streets.

I'd managed to cash in a favor at the county court's office from an officer friend of mine—who had not so subtly given me a sideways look when I'd told him what I needed to get passed along to me—but had, thankfully, been able to pull some strings and get me the papers without much fuss from the county clerk.

Now, I didn't know what to do with them. How we would get any of this in front of a judge was beyond me, but that's where Nina came in.

Hopefully.

"So," Nina's voice brought me out of my thoughts. "What's made you about this inmate so much? Aside from your ridiculously sensitive moral compass."

I slid the file over to her. "Just take a look—"

Her hand slapped down on top of it, preventing me from moving it any further. "Jax, be honest with me."

Tension burned inside me.

My and Nina's relationship dated way back,

far enough that we'd both consider each other childhood friends even if we didn't exactly meet as 'kids'. She was essentially a part of my life, despite us hardly seeing each other these days.

With her firm taking off the moment she'd made partner, and me running the work program for inmates, we were lucky if we got to texting each other for more than an hour or two every few weeks.

Still, regardless of all of that, I knew I could trust her. At least with helping me figure out if Ayen had a real shot in getting this entire case thrown out or not.

Her knowing about me being intimately involved with him, though?

That was the more dicey question.

"I feel bad for him." Not exactly the entire truth, but true nonetheless.

She raised a brow. "That's it?"

"What more do you want from me?"

"I just didn't think you were spending enough time with any of them that would get you close enough to get their side of the story."

"When you work with people long enough, you start to see their humanity," I said.

Her sigh was long, but she didn't argue with me. Lifting her hand away from the file, she let me slide it closer to her, flipping open the front flap to look over the cover page detailing the highlights of Ayen's case.

While she read silently, I ordered us a light lunch and two coffees, needing the caffeine myself from barely sleeping last night. No matter what I did, I replayed Ayen's words in my head so many times that I had them memorized by now.

The hitch in his voice when he spoke, the dead tone of him telling me it was pointless to even try to get his sentence overturned, all of it. And while he lay sleeping peacefully on my chest, I'd promised myself that I wouldn't let this go no matter how hard he fought me on it.

That son-of-a-bitch husband wasn't going to win and taint Ayen's life for the rest of eternity. I wouldn't let him.

Halfway through finishing my plate of food, Nina finally pulled her head out of the documents. "Jesus, this kid has had it rough."

I nodded and chewed slowly.

If she saw half of what I did just from that file alone, I knew Ayen had a real chance. Nina was a viper in the courtroom. A lawyer not to go toe-to-toe with if you knew what was good for you. She'd gotten that reputation from college and had allowed it to be carried with her all the way to the firm she worked at now, not letting the 'boy's club' stop her from doing some great things for people.

I admired her every damn day for not giving up and making something of herself that my late brother would be proud of.

She sighed. "I'll be honest, this is going to be a tough one."

Lowering my fork, I said, "You don't think he can be proven innocent?"

"It's not that. The problem is that a lot of his evidence proving spousal abuse wasn't put in front of a jury. So all it seems like from that perspective is spousal estrangement gone wrong."

"We can't get all of that in front of another jury?"

She shook her head. "He wouldn't be going for a re-trial since he was already convicted. I could see about getting a judge to look at it, but you know those asswipes. They protect each other and if one degenerate decided on something, there's not typically any other judge who will actually go against the original judgment. Especially, if they're in the same county circuit."

Leaning back in my seat, I let myself sit with the information.

Ayen's original lawyer had told him that going up in front of a judge for a dismissal was pointless, and while at the time I'd thought that was complete bullshit—and still do—maybe it was because of the abhorrent politics within the justice system.

Forcing my baby bird to relive any of that shit in order to have the slim chance of a possible overturned conviction was a big ask, and understandably, not something he should be put through again.

But on the other end of the tossed coin, what *if* it was the thing that got him out of prison?

What *if* putting this file in front of a judge— the right one this time—got him set free and his record wiped in exchange for parole and time served?

I doubted he'd even care about the parole part, anyway.

"I need him out of there, Nina." My voice was soft as I spoke.

Her eyes widened briefly, caught off guard by

my sudden confession. It wasn't every day that I opened up and bared my soul like this, especially about a taboo subject involving an inmate that I absolutely had no business getting entangled with.

This was the real deal, though. My feelings for Ayen were all encompassing, to the point where the four weeks I had left with him were feeling like hours now. Our time together was slowly dwindling away by the ticking of a grandfather clock, ominously waiting to chime at midnight.

I couldn't let him slip through my fingers and be lost to the system for another three years.

What happened if someone were to hurt him while he was there?

There was no guarantee that he'd be safe, regardless of what part of the prison he was in. Anyone at any time could deem him as a threat and take him out.

I could never forgive myself if that happened. Not when I could do something to try and prevent it altogether.

Whatever Nina saw in my eyes had her slowly nodding her head at me, a thoughtful look crossing over her face while she placed her hand over the stack of papers.

"If you're actually serious about this, if *he* is, then I need to talk to him," she said.

"I can set that up."

She nodded again. "Let me know when. I'm going to take this with me and head back to the firm. I'm going to have some of my colleagues look it over. If there's a possibility that we can get this overturned for wrongful conviction, then we're going to need all the damn help we can get."

I breathed out a slow breath, relief washing over me. "Thank you, Nina."

"Don't thank me just yet. Get your boy on board and then we'll talk."

Warmth curled in my belly.

My boy.

I loved the sound of that.

CHAPTER 21

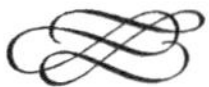

After parting ways with Nina, I climbed back into my truck and hit the road.

Being that it was only a little past one, the inmates and my coworkers would still be out on the trails training, it gave me very little to do back at the property without even my dog to keep me company.

I supposed I could pass the time going to the gym or even heading back to my cabin to get it cleaned and ready to sneak Ayen over later tonight. Hell, there was also probably a mound of paperwork that needed to be tackled back at the property office for the next batch of recruits coming in less than four weeks.

Plenty to do while I waited for the sun to set and the program to get back from their day adventure.

Something burned in my mind, though.

An address to a care facility only a few miles away from here.

Drumming my fingers along the steering wheel, I glanced back in my rearview to the traffic idling behind me. All I had to do was turn at this next light and I'd be on my way to CWI Generations. I could see for myself the one man who had gotten my baby bird thrown in prison.

The light shifted up ahead, the two cars in front of me slowly letting off the brakes and moving forward. I ghosted my finger over my turn signal, indecision freezing me.

Ayen didn't want me to get involved, explicitly told me not to, in fact.

I wanted to behave, especially for him. Even though it was killing me not to know. Not to face his ex and look him in his dead eyes and curse him for what he'd done.

Behind me, a horn blared.

Fuck it.

I pushed down onto the turn signal.

CHAPTER 22

Ayen

"Does anyone have any questions before we wrap up for the night?" The firefighter's voice boomed over the group. When no one answered, he waved his hand. "Return your gear and head to the mess hall. Good work today, gentlemen."

Shrugging off my heavy coat and letting it drop onto the ground behind me felt amazing, especially when a soft breeze trickled in through the trees and washed over my sweaty body.

Roxy let out a bark when I bent to pick up the coat again, her tail wagging happily. I brushed my hand over her head a few times, smoothing back her soft coat.

"Did you have fun today as my partner?" I smiled when she barked at me again. "Yeah, me too."

Talking to a dog like she was human no doubt

had me looking a little insane. But with no partner to keep me company all day, I found myself replacing my human interaction with Jackson's dog instead. To no surprise, she was incredibly well trained and took commands like a champ.

He'd given me a crash course of it this morning before jetting off into the city for whatever reason. All day, my thoughts had been tripping up on him, wondering what in the world he'd skip out on training for when he was the one who was supposed to be running the program.

Of course, my mind had immediately gone into full disaster-mode and convinced myself for half of the fucking day that he was out meeting with someone else.

Could I even call that cheating when we weren't exactly in a stable relationship?

It sure felt like a fucking stab to the chest every time my mind got itself worked up. Thankfully, Roxy was my rock and had worked me down from going actually insane to only slightly fucked up.

After handing in my gear, I led Roxy through the property, following after the other inmates heading to the mess hall. While passing by, I took a glance over to the staff parking lot; Jackson's truck was still missing from the lot.

It was hard to not let that bother me. I missed him horribly, more than I wanted to admit to myself. The longer I dwelled on his absence, the more it was making it all the more difficult in ignoring my very obviously budding feelings.

"Hey, Gonzalez," someone called out to me. Turning, I spotted one of the firefighters, Mac.

"I'm going to walk the dog back to the staff cabins. Thanks for looking after her today."

My heart squeezed. "Oh. Uh, sure."

Roxy's doe-eyes turned to me, a whine leaving her when Mac tapped on her collar and whistled at her to follow after him. I stayed rooted to my spot while they walked away. If I knew I was going to be giving her back so soon before seeing Jackson, I would've at least savored the remaining time we had together.

Now I really was all alone.

I dragged my feet as I headed into the mess hall. The food tasted like ash while I ate, tucked away in the back away from everyone.

While in prison, I'd gotten used to being alone. I'd spent most of my formative years surrounded by someone all-encompassing, his presence bleeding into every aspect of my life until I reached a point of not even being able to breathe without him there.

Prison had given me a harsh reality check into my co-dependence issues. Slapping me in the face with how much of my life I had relied on someone loving me. The past two years, I'd kept everyone at a distance, even Tyson. We were friends, of course, but the kind that you left at work when you went home for the day.

Jackson had been my first taste of the forbidden fruit after having gone sober for so long. He'd sunk down deep into my bones and made a home there, rooted indefinitely.

How could I start to pluck the blossoms that grew from it so soon after they'd begun to bloom?

I couldn't be that cruel to myself, even with my

subconscious screaming at me to stop before he got hurt. My lingering need for him was an unrelenting beast that I'd need to put down eventually. For the sake of both of us.

Regardless of how much it killed me to think about.

By the time I finished up and made my way to the communal showers, I was starting to feel the fatigue from the day settle over me. We hadn't done a lot of hiking today but the gear we'd put on had been heavy and hot under the sun.

Learning how to move in gear like that gave me an even more impressive outlook on Jackson's job. Without adding the actual firefighter or search and rescue parts to the mix, the guy had a lot of guts getting into situations like that. It took a special breed of person to brave a natural disaster and keep a level head.

The hot water sluicing over my skin melted all of my stress away, leaving me feeling boneless and ready for an early bedtime. I disregarded the other inmates tossing their towels around and snapping them against each other's asses while getting dressed, and quickly hustled out before I became an unwilling participant.

Getting back to my cabin, I was surprised to see the inside door slightly ajar but didn't think much of it, until I stepped inside and caught sight of the figure sitting on my bed.

"Woah, woah," Jackson said, quickly getting up and putting his hands out toward me when I jumped hard enough to knock into the front door. "It's okay. It's just me."

I slapped a hand to my chest, exhaling shakily. "What... the hell..."

He chuckled, though his eyes were sympathetic. "I'm sorry. I didn't mean to scare you. You okay?"

Lifting myself away from the door, I peeked out the window to where the dying sun was still coloring the horizon.

Why was Jackson here so early?

Wasn't he afraid of getting caught when it was still light out?

"Ayen?"

My head snapped over to look at him. "Oh, sorry."

He gestured for me to come closer to him, holding out his arms to me. I practically leaped into them, letting him sweep me up off of my feet and cradle me to his chest while he settled back down on my bunk. I instinctually buried my face into the crook of his neck, pulling in a lungful of his musky scent.

Fuck, I missed him.

As sad as it was to actually feel my entire body begin to relax, I was grateful that he hadn't waited until late tonight to come see me.

He brushed his hand along the back of my hair, threading his fingers through the wet lengths while he placed soft kisses against my temple. "You do okay today? Roxy treat you well?"

I nodded, letting my eyes drift closed. Honestly, I could fall asleep right here and not even care.

"Good," he said.

"You?" I mumbled.

"My day was okay. For the most part."

Pulling away from him, my brows knit together and I stared at his face, taking in the tired expression. "What were you up to today?"

His arms were still locked tightly around me, only shifting slightly down toward my hips when he ducked under the lip of the bunk above us and pulled me with him as he leaned back against the wall. We were kind of crunched in under there but it felt safe like that. Like we were in our own little pillow fort.

"I met with a friend today," he said, his hands squeezing my hips. "A lawyer friend."

My stomach dropped. "Jax..."

"I told her about your case. She's interested in it."

I sighed. "Well, she's going to get real uninterested pretty soon. There's nothing that can be done when I only have a few more years left."

Jackson brushed his hand along my jaw, a slight frown tugging down on his lips. "I know you think that, but three years is still a long time. Especially, when you shouldn't be serving any time at all."

I shrugged. I'd come to terms with my situation long ago. Wasting time lamenting about it would do nothing for either of us. "I get that, but that's how it works in the States. You get fucked and then you have to deal with it."

Jackson shook his head. "No. Not this time. We're going to do something about it."

"I appreciate your confidence, but——"

"Baby, I looked through your file. You have a very strong case."

I froze in place.

My file?

He saw...

His hands tightened around me when I tried to lift myself off of him. "I'm not scared of it, Ayen. You did what you had to do. Reading over your case only solidified my opinion of that fact."

My eyes began to burn.

He was never supposed to see that.

My shame, my guilt.

The horrible things I'd had to talk about in court, only for them to get thrown out in the end for bullshit reasons that I still couldn't grapple with.

Jackson was supposed to remain ignorant to all of that. I'd given him the cliff notes version, the important highlights that were heavily filtered so that I could spare him the fucking gory details about what went on between Alex and I and the fallout afterward.

I knew, eventually, that my public record would be the fucking death of me, but I thought that would come three years from now when I was applying for a job as a busser at a seedy restaurant.

"Hey…" He cupped my face. "None of that."

His lips were soft against my cheek, kissing my tear away as it slipped from my eye.

"Why did you look," I choked out.

"Because I wanted to understand you and prove to you that what I said was real. I haven't changed my mind at all about you, baby."

"But——"

He made a negative sound in his throat, tightening the arm around my waist in order to crush me against his chest. He was gentle as he ran his fingers through my hair again, not at all caring when my tears made the front of his shirt wet.

"My friend said that she's bringing your case to her partners at the firm she works at. She's a fucking shark, so I know what she's going to do everything possible to get your case at least put in front of a new judge." His voice was soft as he spoke. "I'm getting you out of there, Ayen. I swear I will."

"What if you can't?" I had to force the words out of my mouth. "What... if nothing changes?"

He was quiet for a long time but his heartbeat remained steady under my ear.

"Then I'll wait."

So simple.

Just like that.

Like it was an easy decision to make.

Maybe it was.

Maybe this was what I was... what *we* were meant to be doing. For some reason, maybe a sign from the damn universe itself, this program had come to me at a time when I needed it most. I'd been brought here to meet this man who was now promising me a future, something that I never thought I'd have again.

He was showing me that there was more to life than letting my past ruin me.

I lifted my head and leaned forward to kiss him. "Stay with me tonight?"

He smiled against my lips. "I'd love to."

CHAPTER 23

JACKSON

I SLEPT WELL with Ayen cradled against me, his warm body acting like my own personal space heater and keeping me toasty all night long while our bodies were entangled with each other.

He fit perfectly, practically molded against my body like a second skin that was always meant to be there. I loved it. I loved everything about the situation and only regretted having to wake us both up once the sun was beginning to lighten the sky outside of the cabin's window.

I brushed my lips along the column of his neck, sucking just hard enough to wake him but not enough to leave marks behind like I was dying to. When I got him out of this mess, and I could finally take him home back to my place in the city, I'd make sure that every inch of his perfect tan skin was flushed red from my teeth.

I rolled my hips against his, both of us already half hard.

A soft moan escaped him, breathy and still half asleep. He craned his neck back, giving me more access to run my tongue up to the shell of his ear.

I wanted to take my time with him, savor all of this. He was meant to be taken slowly, lovingly, with the time and care and dedication of a seasoned lover who knew how to worship him the way I'd been dying to since I first laid eyes on him.

He moaned again when I moved my hand under his shirt, caressing his stomach and the faint happy trail leading down to the waistband of his pants. He ground his hips up against mine, teasing me with his eagerness.

I rolled him over onto his back and moved on top of him, pining him down against the mattress with my hips against his. His lashes fluttered open, showing me those pretty doe-eyes of his that were still hazy from sleep.

God, he was so fucking gorgeous it was honestly unfair.

Bending down, I caught his lips with mine, loving how easily he parted them for me to slip my tongue between. I dipped my hand under his waistband while I shifted my hips up just enough to wrap my hand around his pretty little cock.

It stiffened instantly with a few long pumps, drawing another groan out of him.

That sound was music to my damn ears.

He brushed his hands over my pecs with his gentle touches all the way down to where my jeans were belted. He rubbed me over top of the material, making my cock jerk against my leg where it was pinned inside of my pants.

I pulled away from our kiss, nipping him until I reached his ear again. "Tease."

He chuckled softly.

Letting go of his cock, I pulled my hand out from his pants and moved it around to the small of his back, getting ready to lift him up and pull him into my lap.

Before I could though, Ayen's shifted his hand from where he had been rubbing me through my jeans and slipped it into my pocket in order to tease me some more. I groaned when he brushed the fabric of my pocket against the sensitive tip of my cock while retrieving something from it.

I was barely paying attention to anything other than getting him flustered and naked under me and it wasn't until his body stiffened under me that I was broken out of my own haze.

Ayen shoved an elbow at my chest, practically knocking me right off of the bed from the force of it. At the last second, I grabbed onto the lip of the top bunk to catch myself. "Baby—"

"W-What the *hell is this?*"

As soon as I turned to look at him again, my entire body froze. Pinched between his fingers was the folded over sticker of the visitor pass I'd been given yesterday by CWI.

His hand was shaking, eyes wide in disbelief as he stared at it.

Fuuuck!

"Ayen, listen. I can explain." A stabbing pain shot through my chest when he skittered away from my outstretched hand, lunging off of the bed in order to press himself against the wall farthest away from me.

"Why do you have this?"

"Baby…" I lifted off of the bunk.

"Why do you have this!" His eyes were filling with tears again, although this time it wasn't out of pleasure.

I wasn't sure what to say.

How could I explain any of that to him?

My heart knocked against my ribcage. "Ayen…"

He took in two shuddering breaths before he said, "Did you visit him?"

I nodded. There was no point in lying when he was holding the evidence right in his hand. I didn't want to, anyway, although I would've rather he found out about this much differently.

Going to visit his ex-husband had been eye opening, more so than I could've ever imagined before stepping into that situation.

Ayen was shaking his head, mumbling 'no' over and over again.

"It's okay." My voice was soft as I spoke. "Nothing's changed."

"Did you see him?"

I hesitated before nodding again, imploring him with my gaze, begging him to try to understand.

He let out a pitiful sob and slowly slid down the wall until he collapsed onto the ground. My instincts were screaming to go to him, to pull him up into my arms and rock him until his grief passed.

What I saw in that care facility had been shocking, but not because it had been caused at the hands of Ayen. True disgust had filled me when I saw the man who had abused my baby bird for so long was being well taken care of by the staff there with, presumably, his parents' money lining their pockets.

The anger I felt, the unadulterated rage, was a feeling I'd only ever felt one other time in my life before, and that had been at Carter's funeral where I'd witnessed my dad shedding a single tear over his casket while it was being lowered into the dirt.

Ayen's ex didn't deserve to have a healthy amount of weight on him, or to be clean and smelling fresh when I'd approached him in his wheelchair, or the privilege of being able to stare out the window where a bird feeder was hanging to entertain what little was left of his mind.

What that scum of the earth had earned was a one-way ticket to hell, and nothing less.

Instead, he got to spend the rest of his life being taken care of like a baby while my *own* was stuck behind bars.

Not wanting to scare him, I lowered myself down onto the floor as close as I could get. "Honey..."

His legs were drawn up to his chest, arms curled tightly around his knees, while his shoulders shook from his sobs. It was brutal to watch, and even worse to think that he believed I saw him any differently than before because of it.

I would never. I *could* never.

"Go..." he finally choked out.

I shook my head, reaching over to breech the distance between us. "Ayen—"

He slapped my hand away the second it touched him. "Go!"

Stunned, I stared at him.

"Leave," he swallowed. "Or I'll scream."

That aching sharp pain stabbed me in the chest again. Robotically, I climbed to my feet, still staring down at him. Hoping that he'd change his mind. But all he did was simply bury his face back into his knees and hold himself tighter.

The air in my lungs was sucked out breath by breath as I crossed the distance between him and the front door.

Regret was a knife that carved my heart out of my chest when I opened the door and snuck out into the morning sun, leaving it behind.

CHAPTER 24

AYEN

I HAD no idea how long I stayed curled up on the floor for.

Minutes?

Hours?

It was hard to tell. I'd eventually exhausted myself to the point of lying down on the dusty and worn hardwood floor, with my cheek pressed against it. My body had shut down the second I closed my eyes, wanting to forget any of this ever happened.

A loud call was what brought me back, the sound of Barlow roll calling everyone.

I contemplated staying there curled up in a ball and getting written up for it.

How bad would my punishment be compared to the deep betrayal I felt?

In the grand scheme of things, everything else simply paled in comparison.

Eventually, though, I forced myself up and wandered outside to the line-up, barely functioning.

"Gonzalez, why the fuck're you still in your pjs?" Stinner said.

My gaze drifted up to where he loomed over me, his shadow temporarily blocking out the sun burning my eyes. No words came out of my mouth—not even a single thought. My mind was blank, my body running on simply muscle memory alone.

"Get the fuck back inside and get dressed. Jesus Christ," he spat.

Turning back around, I headed into my cabin again without any kind of arguing. Getting myself together was a blur, as was the rest of our head count and heading into the mess hall for breakfast before we got started for the day.

That sticker was branded into my skin—Jackson's handsome face grainy and barely decipherable on the horrible laser scanner that had been used to print up a visitor pass for him.

The worst part was that if I'd never found it, he never would've told me.

How long would he have gone carrying on the ignorance?

For the rest of our weeks together?

After that, too?

I'd told him—*begged him*—not to go find Alex. But he'd done so, anyway.

To what, prove to himself that it 'wasn't that bad'?

That I wasn't the type of person who was capable of such a violent act?

Whatever he'd told himself in order to convince himself that he was fine with seeing Alex like that was a complete lie. *No one* could handle something like that; no matter how prepared you were going into it.

A bright and charismatic man being reduced down to someone who pissed and shit in a diaper all day wasn't the kind of thing you simply witnessed and got over while convincing yourself that he deserved it.

The reality was that, eventually, Jackson was going to come to his senses and see just what kind of monster I was to leave someone in that state, regardless on whether or not it was accidental. Soon, he'd see the real reason I was meant to be behind bars and our little fantasy together would come crashing down.

I was sick to my stomach when he'd asked the first time for Alex's info, knowing that by walking down that road I was essentially letting what we had slip right through my fingers. That's why I'd begged him to let it go, to just forget it.

But of course, Jackson being Jackson could never do that. He had to see the disgusting mess for himself and try to prove that he wasn't like everyone else who saw me for the murderer I was.

"All right, everyone!" Mac's voice snapped me back into reality. "Partner up!"

Blinking a few times to clear my head, I realized that I'd somehow transported myself from the mess hall to a designated training area where there were work stations set out for us to gather around.

Across the way, I caught eyes with Jackson who was watching me with a pinched expression on his face. Roxy stood at his side, wagging her tail while she pranced in place from where Jackson was holding onto her work vest.

Immediately turning away from them, I gathered around the closest workstation where another inmate, James Barker, was already standing.

He glanced over at me when I stood next to him, his arms crossing over his chest.

"You're my partner for this," I forced myself to say.

He gave me a weird look before shrugging. "Whatever."

CHAPTER 25

For the next week, everything went the same way—me avoiding Jackson like the plague and him keeping his distance from me.

There were no more midnight rendezvous, no more quiet meetings when no one else was looking, no more subtle brushes of our hands together as we walked back from the training area and parted ways at the mess hall.

I felt the void of him in everything that I did. From sunrise to sunset, my body hurt from how hard I was punishing it in order to keep my feelings tamped down far enough to numb me from the inside.

I kept a rotation of partners during our training, keeping myself preoccupied and not giving it up to fate or chance that I'd be randomly placed with Jackson and Roxy.

Nothing felt right.

My soul ached.

And there was fuck all I could do about it.

"Can you get your fucking head on straight, Gonzalez?" Barker hissed while tossing a large pack at me.

I stumbled back, catching it in the chest.

"You know, when you said you wanted to be my partner, I didn't know you were going to be fucking useless."

The words barely stung. He was all bark, anyway.

Quietly, I set the pack down and looked through the contents, ignoring Barker's huffing as he repacked his own the way he wanted it. Judging by the contents, we were most likely heading out to the fire that was burning a few miles east from here.

The call had come in late last night, all of the firefighter's radios blaring with the emergency signal. So far, the fire hadn't spread rapidly, but it was burning enough to keep the property's fire-fighters set up as reinforcements.

Mac had suggested for us to head over there this morning and using it as a learning opportunity for a once-in-a-lifetime deal at seeing how a real forest fire was dealt with. The excitement had been palpable among the rest of the inmates, excluding me, who were more than ready to actually put some of this training into action.

Now that we were all here and successfully piled off of the bus that'd brought us, Mac was explaining something that I tuned out completely. Even with us being a mile out from the fire, the air was hazy with smoke and the smell of burning wood.

"You coming or what, Gonzalez?" Barker said, throwing his pack over his shoulder. His fire-resistant coveralls bunched up at his shoulders, making it difficult for him to straighten out the straps of his bag.

"Make sure you keep within the radius of the firefighters," Mac called out. "If any of you stray off the path, use your whistle to call out and one of us will come find you. If you start to feel intense heat or thick smoke, fall back immediately and use your whistle!"

I sighed and zipped my bag up before tossing it over my shoulder and working my arms through the straps. It was heavy on my back but not to the point where it would slow me down. Luckily, we were only going to be getting close enough to observe from a distance and take some pictures that we would later observe back at the property.

There would be no heroics going on today, thankfully.

Just as I was about to follow Barker over to where our group was gathering, something grabbed my bag from behind me and made me halt in place. Without me even getting a chance to look behind me, something tugged at one of the loops at my waist, hooking something on it.

I darted my gaze down, spotting a familiar radio now clipped there.

My heart stuttered when I looked up again just as Jackson was moving around me and heading back toward the rest of the group, Roxy following closely behind.

What?

Ghosting my fingers over the radio and ignoring the way my chest suddenly tightened, I quickly followed after Barker who had our camera looped around his neck. In a wide formation, we started in through the tree lines at a slow pace.

I wasn't sure what the hell we were supposed to be taking pictures of, having completely checked out by the time we'd climbed onto the bus, but now I was regretting not paying attention. Especially, when Barker started to hiss at me once more.

"Can you keep up? I want to get good photos."

"Why?"

Honestly, what was the point?

It wasn't like we were receiving extra credit for any of this.

"Does it fucking matter?" he snapped back and kicked his way through a tall bush.

We were moving a bit of a distance away from the rest of the group, though I could still see them through the haze. The reflectors on their jackets helped with their visibility to me, becoming even more pronounced when I pulled my goggles down over my eyes to keep them from watering.

"I was just wondering," I said.

"Well, if you have to know, I want to get as close a picture as possible. I overheard Browne talking about bringing some of our accomplishments to the Warden and getting us special privileges when we get back. We're apparently the best group they've had so far."

Somehow, I doubted that, but hey, if living in a

little fantasy world kept Barker happy, then who was I to spoil it?

All I wanted to do was keep my mind off the very obvious thing plaguing it.

I brushed my hand over the radio again in disbelief.

Why had he gone out of his way to give it to me?

Setting me up to be caught with it was a possibility, but even Jackson couldn't be that cruel. There would be no reason for him to do that when we were already actively avoiding each other.

He hadn't even looked at me, either. Just gave it to me and dipped.

I hated how much that man haunted me.

"Woah, Gonzalez, look!"

Breaking out of my thoughts, I stumbled and ran right into Barker's back, causing us both to fall into the dirt.

"Jesus, fuck! Watch it," he spat out.

I grunted and slowly pushed myself up onto my hands and knees, watching him do the same out of the corner of my eye. The haze had grown thicker in the time we'd spent walking this way. Even through my coveralls, I could feel the telltale signs of heat.

I grabbed at the scarf hanging around my neck and pulled it up over my nose.

"What I was trying to fucking say before you fucking shoved me," Barker went on, getting to his feet again. "Was that I think I see fire."

"Fire?" I lifted my head. "We should head back then."

"No way. Shots this close up are gold. I'm not passing that up."

Getting to my feet, I brushed the dirt off of myself. "We're not getting caught up in a damn forest fire, you idiot."

"We'll be fine." He waved his hand. "We're too high up for it to get us."

"What?"

What the hell did that even mean?

"Did you not pay attention to any of the demonstrations? The air is thick up here because of the smoke rising. That means the fire is down farther. I bet there's a hill we can stand on to see it."

"We're not getting that close." Turning to glance over my shoulder, I realized I couldn't see jack shit. Not even the subtle reflections from the other inmates and firefighters' coveralls.

Shit, we'd gone too far away from the group.

"Barker, come on. Let's just go back. You'll get your shots when we're back with the group."

My anxiety was already rising from potentially being this close to a wild fire. That shit was unpredictable and I wasn't about to get caught in something I had no idea how to get out of.

He ignored me completely and set off in the direction of the thick smoke, the reflectors on the back of his coveralls slowly disappearing from view. Panic flooded me, my mind being torn in two different directions of wanting to go back to try and find our group or follow after Barker to make sure nothing bad happened to him.

The guilt would eat at me if I went back to the group and left Barker behind to potentially run into trouble without any help. He was being an idiot, true, but no one deserved to go out like that.

Quickly darting through the trees, I caught up with him just as he was coming up to a small overhang. The heat was intense the closer we got to it, and soon, flames were dancing wildly among the dry brush.

My hand shot out to instinctively grab at the back of his coveralls. "We need to go back."

He raised the camera up to his goggle-covered eyes and snapped a few pictures. "Damn, this is *so* cool. You ever see anything like this?"

"No," I admitted. "And I don't really want to. Come on, let's go."

I tugged at him and tried to force him to come back with me, but all it really did was get him to tell me to 'fuck off' while he snapped more photos. My skin felt like it was melting inside of my suit, the heat intense enough for sweat to trickle down my back.

Barker pulled himself out of my grasp in order to move along the overhang, bypassing a tree that was half-rooted out of the soil and hanging over the empty air of where the fire was. He grabbed a hold of one of the branches down close enough for him to reach, using it as a way to swing up onto the bend in the tree's trunk.

"What the hell are you doing?"

"Shut up," he said, lifting the camera again. "You'll thank me when we get extra time out in the yard—"

Beneath him, the tree gave way from the overhang and crumbled to the ground.

CHAPTER 26

"BARKER!" I screamed out just as the ground beneath me crumbled, too.

I plunged down to the ground, the six feet completely knocking the air out of my lungs when I landed onto the hard dirt. A groan escaped me while I rolled onto my side, prevented from moving any further from the pack on my back.

I'm so going to fucking kill him.

"Barker!" I called out, the haze so thick down there that it was hard to see anything. Whatever he'd said about smoke being more intense at the top of that overhang was fucking wrong, that was for sure.

I didn't hear anything from him, just the fire crackling way to close for comfort.

I hauled myself up, my shoulder nagging at me from where I'd fallen on it. Quickly checking to make sure that it was still in place, I stumbled forward while patting the ground in search of my partner.

He was lying prone on his side, with part of the tree pinning him into the dirt and no other movement visible. My heart leaped into my throat at the sight, fully convinced I'd just witnessed a man dying in front of me.

Crawling over to him, I shook him a few times, relieved to see that his mouth was open and he was pulling in a few labored breaths.

"Shit, come on." I patted my hands against his chest and face. "Wake up!"

Sweat was pouring down my face and causing my goggles to fog up from both the heat of the fire and my own body's rising temperature.

Barker let out a soft groan but otherwise didn't move.

The fire was probably about fifty feet away from us, and gaining fast. If we didn't get out of here now, we were fucking cooked.

Craning my neck up to where the overhang loomed, I noted it was a steep climb and wouldn't be easy at all to make. The dirt was rich and not packed enough to help us climb it. The second our hands dug into it, it was going to crumble away just like the tree had.

The air was too hard to see down further but maybe the incline tapered off enough for us to climb up it again.

"Okay," I said to myself, and threw my bag off of my shoulders to give me more room to work. I tucked both of my arms under Barker's armpits in order to heave him out from under the branch that was pining him. "Come on!"

My boots dug down into the dirt as I pulled, leaving deep tread marks that helped with me pushing back and counterweighing the branch.

Finally, when I was able to tug him free, he collapsed into my lap like dead weight. I panted and swiped a hand over my brow.

"Barker, you gotta get up." Slapping his cheek a few times did absolutely nothing. Not even earning me a groan.

He wasn't much bigger than me, but I had barely any muscle on me to begin with.

How the fuck was I going to carry him to safety?

Suddenly, my memory from earlier snapped into me.

I put my hand to my hip where the radio was still attached. Relief washed over me strong enough to bring tears to my eyes. I owed that man a fucking kiss, despite whatever the fuck was going on between us.

Tugging the communication device off my belt loop, I pressed the side button and said, "Help! We need help! We're near the fire!"

There was a pause of silence on the other end that felt like an eternity, but finally, a crackling response came back that I could barely make out.

Fuck, I needed better signal.

Clipping the radio back at my waist, I grabbed Barker again and pulled him up with me as I stood. Adrenaline was pounding through my veins, allowing me to drag him slowly as I followed the incline.

The popping sound of wood and embers exploding nearby had me jumping and stumbling as I tried to pick up the pace. This was not where I was going to die. Not after all the shit I'd been through in my life.

Getting taken out by the stupidity of someone else was not only ridiculous, but downright unacceptable as a way to die. If I was going to kick the bucket, it was going to be on my own terms. Not from some dumbass trying to one up the rest of us while endangering himself and dragging me along with him.

About fifty feet from where we'd first landed, I grabbed at the radio again and screamed into it. "Help! Near the fire!"

Finally, a clearer response came. *"Who is this? What direction?"*

"Gonzalez and Barker! I think we went west!"

I fucking hoped we did. If I was sending them in the wrong goddamn direction, I was going to be so pissed at myself.

"West?" The voice repeated.

Stopping under another overhang, I slowly lowered Barker down to the ground and ripped the pack off of his back. I had the contents of it emptied out all over in record time and dug through them to find one of those forest ranger compasses that Mac had sent us off with.

Finding it, I held it up toward the canopy of trees, trying to pinpoint the sun through the dense smoke overhead.

"Hello?" The voice called again.

I put the speaker up to my mouth. "I can't find the sun." My voice cracked.

It was getting harder to breathe in the smoke billowing from the burning foliage around us. I coughed into my scarf a few times, trying to clear my lungs in order to talk again.

There was a brief pause on the other end to the radio, and then a familiar voice was talking to me.

"Ayen, what way are you facing the fire?"

Fuck, I wanted to cry.

I pointed the compass toward it. "North. Barker's passed out."

"Use your whistle."

"Hurry," I begged.

"Whistle, Ayen."

With a shaky hand, I pulled it out from where I'd tucked it under my coveralls and brought it up to my mouth. Then, with the biggest lungful of air I could manage, I blew like my life depended on it. At this point, it did.

CHAPTER 27

Jackson

"Over there!" Mac called out, but I was already running for it.

The radio was clutched so tight in my hand that I knew once I let go of it, there would be a permanent impression left behind.

The whistle was faint, followed up with Ayen's soft voice saying, *"Did you hear it?"*

I lifted the radio up to my mouth. "I'm coming."

I crashed through overgrown brush and tangled saplings that left scratches sliced into my cheeks and hands. Behind me, I could hear Roxy and Mac and whoever else had heard the distress call following closely behind.

Giving that radio to Ayen had been an impulsive move, but one that had ultimately given me peace since I wasn't going to be able to watch over him while we split off. Now, I was regretting not simply forcing him to partner up with me and dealing with his attitude later.

Another whistle sounded off, this time much closer than the last one. I pivoted and headed for it, the smoke becoming much denser as the heat from the fire was growing more intense.

"Ayen," I called into my radio again.

He was coughing as he said, *"Are you almost here?"*

Fuck, I was never letting him out of my damn sight again. I didn't care how much of a temper tantrum he threw. He was going to be stuck to my side like a fucking glue trap until this god forsake program was over with.

"Jax!" Mac called. "I think I see them!"

Roxy's bark had me completely turning away from the direction I'd been heading in and moving deeper into the thick smoke.

She led us to a steep incline just as Ayen blew on his whistle once more from right down below us. He was coughing loudly by the time I leaned over to see him kneeling down in the dirt with the contents of his pack scattered around him and another inmate passed out next to him.

"Ayen!"

His head snapped up, his body wracking with more coughs.

I swung my pack from my shoulder and threw it down onto the ground. Ripping through it, I tossed a long tether rope to Mac and twisted around to find the grappling clips to go with it.

Roxy barked again and danced between us

both as we worked, clearly anxious that she couldn't get down there and rescue Ayen herself.

"We're going to have you tie this around him, Ayen," I called down to him. "You're going to need to lift him up from there to help us pull him up over this incline."

"Okay..." His cracked voice was fucking killing me.

Focus, Jackson.

He needs you fully functional.

Mac tossed one end of the rope down to him with a large slipknot already tied into it. With the other end, he walked backward around a large tree trunk and wound it around, coming back over to me to collect two clips that he attached to his belt. I handed him a set of gloves and shoved my own hands into a pair.

"Tell us when you get that around his waist," I called down to him again.

"Do I just..." He began to choke again.

Fuck—with the way the incline was curved over them, it was creating a sort of vacuum seal for all of the smoke to collect under and not rise to dissipate into the sky like it should have already.

"Just put it around his waist for me." I held back from ending that with 'baby' by the skin of my teeth.

If I wasn't so good at catching myself before it was too late, I realized that breaking the news to Mac that I was sleeping with one of our inmates at a time like this would go down as one of the dumbest possible decisions I could ever make while staging a rescue operation.

"Okay..." he said.

"You do it?" I asked.

"Yes."

I stood and grabbed onto the rope, pulling the tension until it was taunt. Leaning back over to look down at him, I discovered Ayen was already trying to lift the other inmate up from the ground. His body was shaking, the other man's dead weight clearly tough to bear.

"That's it, just a little bit more," I encouraged.

Mac and I strained as we pulled on the support line. The angle was awkward and not at all ideal for a proper load haul operation but we were working on borrowed time and trying to find a better solution was a risk I wasn't willing to take with Ayen involved.

Mac took the brunt of the weight while I brought up the slack, keeping the tension around the trunk as tight as possible while we hand-over-handed it.

Finally, when the inmate's head popped up over the side of the incline, Mac leaned backward in order to allow me to let go of the rope.

Dropping to my knees, I fisted my hands tightly in the inmate's coveralls while hauling him up the rest of the way over. He was still passed out cold, but with a few quick taps of his cheek, his eyes fluttered under his lids.

Still alive.

Good.

With quick movements, I slipped the rope off of the inmate and loosened it up enough to toss back over the side to Ayen.

"Tie that around your waist. We're going to help you walk up the side——"

I was cut off by him dissolving into a deep coughing fit, choking on the smoke surrounding us to the point where he collapsed back onto the ground. He was bent over on his hands and knees, trying to pull in as much air as possible.

"*Fuck,*" I dug through my bag again.

"Jax, stop. We just need to get him over here." Mac grabbed my shoulder, trying to pull me back up. "Put on the rope, Ayen!"

"He can't *breathe,*" I snapped, jerking away from him.

"If we spend time looking for a breathing apparatus then he's as good as dead. We need to get him up here *now* before he passes out."

I was inches away from tearing my fucking hair out. Both sides of my brain were screaming for two different things: jump down there and rescue him by hand or try to find him something to use to breathe into. Neither side was interested in following Mac's orders, no matter how much sense they made.

My fear was making me act irrationally, to the detriment of Ayen.

"Ayen," Mac called again. "Get the rope around you and we'll pull you up."

I crawled over to where the incline dropped off. "Ayen, just put it around your waist, sweetheart, and we'll pull you up."

His hand fisted in the dirt, slowly inching forward to where the rope was. Tears and sweat were pouring down his face to the point where he was having a hard time seeing where he was going. He patted around on the dirt, feeling for the rope.

"To your left... yes, right there," I said. "Now, put it around you... that's it."

I stood quickly, grabbing at the slack and waiting until he finally was able to get it around him. Once he tugged it twice to get it snug around his waist, Mac and I yanked on the other end hard enough that I felt my shoulders strain.

If Mac couldn't tell how desperate I was to get him up before, he certainly did now with how quickly he was having to change his hand-over-hand and toss the extra rope back away from his feet while I used both of my hands together for longer strokes to choke up on.

Ayen grabbed at the side of the incline, his hands digging down into the dead grass and dirt to help us haul him over the side. He collapsed instantly the second he was over, his legs still dangling off precariously.

I tossed the rope and dropped to my knees to grab him, scooping him up into my arms to drag him the rest of the way onto safer ground. He fell into me, becoming dead weight the moment I had my arms tightly secured around him.

I brushed my hands over his face, the grime from the smoke and dirt leaving streaks across his beautiful face. The relief at seeing him still alive and breathing was unmatched, overtaking me so hard and fast that it practically knocked the wind out of me.

When I'd first heard that distress call, my entire world felt like it'd suddenly caved inward. I hadn't wanted to believe it, having only given him my radio as an overprotective safety precaution that my stupid possessive self needed to fulfill in order to actually walk away.

I never thought he'd need to use it.

Never in a million years.

If I had, he would've never left my side today.

The fear that had completely stolen all other sense of rational thoughts from my mind was nothing like I'd ever experienced in my life. Not even when my father's alcoholic rages resulted in Carter and I walking away with black eyes and bruised bodies.

I never *ever* wanted to feel like that again. My heart was already outside of my body and being carried around by a man that I'd only know for a short time. And coming face to face with the reality of that fact was both startling and mind-boggling.

When Ayen's eyes blinked open, they were unfocused. His mouth dropped open to try and suck in as much clean air as he could.

Finally, he mumbled, "Jax..."

"You're okay." Tears leaked from my eyes as I brushed more grime from his face. "You're okay. I got you."

And I'm never ever letting you go again.

CHAPTER 28

Ayen

A SOFT BEEPING hummed in the distance, just out of reach.

The dark, inky black of forever stared back at me—a void so cold and desolate that it made it hard to breathe or move anywhere that wasn't right in front of me. I was bound to this place, unmoving and unfeeling aside from the deep searing pain of loneliness that consumed me from within.

I couldn't remember anything before this.

Who was I?

Where did I come from?

Where had I been going before I reached this place?

The unsettling thought that maybe there *was* nothing and no one that I'd been trying to find— that I *was* no one—hovered in my peripheral, pulling me down further into the darkness. I choked on it, breathed it in and let it take hold of me.

This would be it, then. I would dissolve into oblivion.

How sad.

But then, a single memory, or maybe it was a dream, foggy in recognition at first but becoming clearer with more concentration, suddenly began to flourish in front of me. Faces that I couldn't place but felt like home, voices that I could recognize even in my sleep.

And a touch that I'd become so intimately familiar with that I craved it even now...

The touch of a hand gently running through my hair, soothingly and loving.

I missed it.

I wanted to drown in it. Let it bleed into me. Filling every crevice that the darkness had frozen over and consumed and hoped that it could pull me away from this awful place.

Distant voices were beginning to break apart the silence that cocooned me in a straightjacket. Where were they coming from?

"—maybe. We'd have to wait and see."

"How long will it take?"

"I had to do a lot of sweet talking to get into his chambers, but the judge was interested in looking over the files sometime this week."

Silence.

The air surrounding me suddenly felt charged somehow.

"Will he wake up?"

The hand moving through my hair froze.

I reached out in front of me, heartbroken at the obvious fear in the voice that had stopped it. I didn't want those warm feelings to disappear and leave me trapped here with the cold darkness again. My limbs felt numb, hard to move and sore while I fought against the binds that tethered me to this place.

I wanted out. I wanted to be set free and go to where I was meant to be.

To who I belonged to.

Wading through the never-ending void was a hard fight, the current strong as it tried to drag me under again.

A something soft touched my cheek. A teardrop that wasn't my own.

"*Please…*"

A deep breath.

A sorrowful voice.

"Please, wake up."

Where are you? I wanted to say, but my lips felt sewn shut. *Come find me.*

But there was nothing. No one to reach out to me to lead me like I wanted them to. I would have to make this journey alone, chasing after the one thing I'd been desperate to find all of my life.

I wouldn't let it be just out of reach this time. My regrets weren't going to keep me from having what I wanted. Life was too short to live in fear of the what ifs and I was tired of sabotaging myself from what I really wanted.

Fingers brushed through my hair again, giving me a sense of hope as they traced along my temple. A soft kiss placed there.

Didn't I deserve happiness, too?

Yes, is what the void answered back, the voice sounding suspiciously familiar. *Of course you do.*

Coming back into my body was nothing like the movies. It was not a slow and gradual awakening that felt peaceful or finite. It was a hard slam of my consciousness being forced back into my body that left me gasping for breath and practically rocketing off of the bed that I was lying on.

There were things strapped to my arms and on my chest, wires that got tangled when I tried to lift up my arms and shield my eyes from the blinding light above me. Tears clouded my eyes, keeping me from seeing straight.

"Ayen, *don't.*" A firm hand gripped my wrist, pinning it back by my head.

Panic flooded into my system. I was being restrained just like the void had done to me.

Claustrophobia was closing in on me—

"Baby, stop." He grabbed my other arm. "Just breathe, you're okay."

My body twisted in the bed sheets, battling against the body hovering over me and trying to grab at my other arm that I flailed around wildly. Something was covering my face, tight and uncomfortable, that sent me into a blind fight or flight. The machine next to me was blaring loudly, some kind of code going off that was making me dizzy to listen to.

I want—I want...

"Shhh." Warm lips brushed along my forehead, strong fingers lacing with mine. "I'm right here. You're okay..."

My body heaved a heavy sob with the familiar feeling of safety suddenly surrounding me.

"I know, sweetheart." More kisses along my temple. "You've got to keep everything on, though. You breathed in a lot of smoke. They need to monitor your oxygen levels."

Smoke?

Memories slammed into me.

The fire.

Barker falling down the incline.

Me radioing for help.

Jackson rescuing me—

Jax.

"That's it," he murmured. "Just relax for me. You're okay. I'm right here."

The machine next to me gradually stopped screeching, settling down to a slow and steady beeping that reminded me of my dreams. I let my body relax back into the bed, suddenly feeling how tired I really was from fighting both in and out of my head.

How did I even get here?

The last thing I remembered was Jackson throwing the rope down to me and being pulled up over the overhang. My lungs still burned a bit from the memory of choking on all of that smoke. Overwhelming darkness had hit me so suddenly that I could barely piece together what happened after that.

Jackson slowly lightened up on his hold on me, his fingers coming up to brush under my eyes where tears had collected, wiping my skin clean of them. Having him here with me made it easier to be at ease again—I didn't have to worry about being claimed by that awful darkness again.

Not when I knew Jackson would be here to pull me back out of it.

When my eyes finally focused on him again, he smiled lightly at me. The bags under his eyes were prominent, as was the shadow of his facial hair coming in. He looked tired, like he hadn't slept in days.

How long had we been here for?

My arm was heavy when I lifted it, like it weighed a hundred pounds more than I remember it being before all of this. There was one of those heart rate monitor clips attached on my pointer finger, the wire falling down somewhere off my bed to the right of my hip. An IV line stuck out from the hollow of my elbow, prickling me slightly when I tried to bend my arm up to grab at Jackson.

I wanted to touch him—needed to. I had to make sure all of this was real and not a trick of my mind.

He caught my wrist easily, gently kissing each of my knuckles before placing my hand back down onto the bed next to me.

"Jax," I mumbled, feeling miserable all over again.

He planted himself down onto the bed by my hip, the mattress slightly dipping while he was being careful to keep from sitting on any of the wires that were hooked up to the other sets of machines on my other side. Those monitors displayed all sorts of confusing looking graphs, too intense for my muddled mind to make any sense of.

"I'm right here, Ayen. I'm not going anywhere."

"Promise..." More tears were collecting along my lash line.

"Oh, honey. Of course I do." He dragged the pad of his thumb under my eyes again. "I think the drugs are making you a little weepy."

Probably.

Or the fact that I almost died trying to save an idiot.

What would've happened if Jackson never gave me that radio?

Or if he never heard my whistle?

I'm certain that I'd be a piece of fried chicken by now, never having gotten to tell him that I regretted ever pushing him away, or that I—

My heart thumped.

That I loved him.

"The doctors should be in soon to check on you," he was saying, completely oblivious to my world-shattering realization. "Once they give you the all clear, then we can sit you up and get some food in you. It's been a few days, so I'm sure you're starving."

A few days?

Jesus, now I really felt bad for dragging him into my mess. Getting involved with me like this was probably never on Jackson's agenda. We'd started out by giving in to our mutually shared spark of passion, and now he was stuck tending to me at my bedside in a damn hospital.

Why wasn't he back at the program?

Why was he torturing himself by sitting with me?

Was it because I had no one else to stay with me?

"Ayen, stop."

My gaze snapped to him, catching him shaking his head at me.

"Whatever you're thinking. Stop it. I'm here because I want to be. You have no idea how worried I was about you."

How did he...?

I couldn't be *that* transparent, right?

"Seeing you down there like that." His Adam's apple bobbed visibly. "I thought I was going to lose you."

My chest tightened when his voice cracked and a thin, wet sheen grew over his eyes.

How could he cry for me when I absolutely didn't deserve it?

Him being upset over my well-being was the last thing he needed to be dealing with. Getting hurt while in his program was probably going to cost him so much more than just me lying in this damn hospital bed. I wouldn't be able to live with myself if it resulted in the program getting shut down because of my stupidity in not dragging Barker back to the group when I should've.

"You must hate me," I mumbled.

"No, I don't."

I reached up again toward his face, desperate to wipe his tears away like he had mine. He tangled our hands together instead, twining our fingers in a tight hold that he pressed against his chest.

"I will never *ever* hate you, Ayen."

"Why?"

How could he not?

I could've cost him everything. Maybe that was why he was sitting here with me in the hospital—he had no job to go back to.

His mouth opened to answer me, but was soon cut off by the door to my room sliding open. Lifting my head up slightly, I was surprised to see a tall woman walking in with a cardboard tray with two coffees in her hand.

She stopped short at seeing us, her eyes bouncing between me and Jackson before she slowly lifted a brow. She was striking to look at, her features reminding me of those high-end fashion models that would be plastered all over NYC billboards promoting some kind of luxury perfume.

"Am I... interrupting something?"

Jackson sighed, letting go of my hand and devastating me even more when he slid off the bed to walk over toward her. "No."

She offered him one of the cups and then worked her own out of the holder that she then tossed into the small trashcan by the door. My gaze was glued to Jackson as he popped the small lip of the cup up and took a generous swig of it, clearly needing the caffeine.

He needed to go home. Now that he knew I was fine and wasn't going to die and cause him a mound of paperwork, there was no more obligation to stick around.

"Ayen, it's nice to meet you," the woman said. "I'm Nina. I'm going to be handling your case."

Oh, his lawyer friend.

In response to that, I forced myself to sit up.

"Shit—" Jackson darted back over to my side of the bed. "Ayen."

His arm quickly hooked around my midsection, holding me up when I began to sag forward. Clearly, my body was still exhausted with what it had gone through during the fire, enough that I was barely able to sit up on my own. Or maybe that was from whatever drugs they'd been giving me to keep me sedated while I recovered.

Either way, it fucking sucked.

Jackson leaned away briefly to set his coffee down on the little lip of the monitor next to me, and then wrapped both of his arms around me and very carefully readjusted me back against the mattress once more.

Nina appeared at my other side, her perfectly manicured hand reaching over to press on a button on the side of my bed that slowly raised it up into a soft incline, allowing me to sit up and still lean back into it.

"There we go," she said, before stepping back.

Jackson sighed, running a hand through my hair in an absentminded way to brush back the pieces that fell across my forehead, sending a shock of pleasure racing up my spine. Him being bold like this in front of his friend was thrilling as well as a little scary. If she reported us to the Warden, we were done for.

Surprisingly, though, she didn't seem at all fazed by it and simply walked across the room to retrieve something out of her bag that was sitting in one of the reclining chairs. A file that was probably two to three inches thick was carefully held in her hand with the pages bending from how heavy it was.

She held it up toward me. "I went through all of your documents with a few colleagues of mine. They all agree that you got pretty shafted."

My cheeks suddenly felt hot. Honestly, I never thought I'd hear a lawyer say it so bluntly. Sure, I knew it just from being in this predicament and while at the time, my court appointed lawyer had been sympathetic to a point, to hear that said from someone else other than Jackson felt... well, validating.

Of course, Jackson's opinion was important to me, but sleeping with someone tended to muddle up the brain from thinking clearly.

"Nina's planning on meeting with Judge Callahan to discuss what can be done." Jackson squeezed my hand gently. "You could have a real shot in getting out of this."

Behind him, Nina nodded. "This will all be pro bono, of course, so don't worry about any of that. But going through your case file, there's some solid evidence that your defense attorney purposefully withheld that could've swung the jury in a different direction, as well as the prosecution trying to bury witness testimony in order to win their case. That's enough to get a judge's eyes on it, at least."

This was all beginning to sound too surreal to hear.

Sure, I'd imagined this exact scenario plenty of times late at night in my cell when I let those dark thoughts get the better of me, but my fantasy rapidly turning reality was seeming to be too good to be true.

The other shoe had to drop eventually.

Right?

It had to. That was how much my luck worked.

"There is one thing," Nina went on. "About the program."

Here it comes...

God, if the program actually got shut down because of me and Barker, I was never going to forgive myself. A decade's worth of work to be put into it, only for a couple of dumbasses to fuck up and get the whole thing completely disbanded. I had no doubts that Jackson would find another path to help people as he always had, but being the cause of collapsing something that he'd taken pride in for so long would fucking kill me.

Nina's gaze darted over to Jackson expectantly.

It dawned on me then, though, that if the program *had* been shut down because of us, then why was Jackson here in the first place?

I would've assumed he'd be too angry at me to want to wait around in a hospital room for me to wake up.

There could be an argument made that he was simply waiting for me to wake up in order to yell at me, but then again, why go through the trouble in soothing me?

If he was angry at me, he wouldn't have bothered. Jackson was a good man, a compassionate one. But he wasn't *that* nice.

He slowly turned to me and sat down on the bed again, hiking up his leg so that it was resting against my side. There was no hesitation in him when he reached out toward me and dragged his hand along my forehead and into my hair once more. Clearly, he wasn't worried about Nina tattling or about her caring in general.

Though, I was kind of curious on how that conversation even went.

"Yeah, I'm sleeping with one of the inmates in my program."

"Oh wow, really?"

"Yeah, can you take a look at his case file and get the charges dismissed?"

"Yeah, sure, no problem."

How was she not freaking out?

Jackson pulled in a slow and deep breath before he spoke. "They're sending you back, Ayen."

My brows furrowed.

Sending me back where?

"To SAC," he clarified after a moment.

Oh.

And there was the other shoe.

"We're going to get you out of there, though." He blinked hard a few times, his voice growing gruff from emotion. "I swear it. You just need to hold on over there a little longer."

I had half a mind to ask him to come visit me. I'd only ever had one visitor come and see me, and that had been Alex's mom. The entire hour had been spent in silence while she cried silently to herself, her eyes fixated on my uniform and the SAC logo stitched at the breast.

Finally, when time was called and the hour was up, she'd gotten up from her seat and left without a single word said. For some reason, that had hit harder than if she'd come to scream at me for ruining her son's life. Just watching the pain and devastation on her face as she wept was enough of a message to get across that I'd irrevocably ruined their family more than any kind of speech ever could.

Better to keep Jackson away from any of that, though. Not to mention if any of the COs that attended the program with us caught wind of it, it'd rouse suspicion.

Because why in the world would he randomly be visiting an inmate from his program in prison?

Actually.

How the hell was he visiting me now?

Where the fuck were the guards?

A light kiss was pressed to my forehead before Jackson stood. "Hang tight, okay?"

All I could do was nod and wonder.

CHAPTER 29

Ayen

Falling back into the rhythm of being at SAC was, sadly, too easy.

I'd hoped that with spending a total of just over three weeks outside of these walls that I'd somehow lost my paranoia of looking over my shoulder every five minutes to make sure I wasn't about to get jumped.

But apparently, things like that were a hard habit to break. Maybe I never would quite get rid of that paranoia that came over me every time I felt someone brush past me while walking by, waiting for the inevitable toss up or the press of a shiv against my kidney and the whispered threat to give them all my commissary or for an elbow to be shoved in my ribs and told to fuck off.

Life outside had felt peaceful. Life with *Jackson* had felt peaceful.

Now, all I had was my tiny cell with my cellmate again. No more sunsets to watch, or clean mountain air to breathe in, or cute golden retrievers to bury their cool noses in my side. I guess the only silver lining to all of that was that we *all* got sent back to SAC, including Barker, in order to 'reevaluate' those eligible for the program.

Luckily, no one seemed inclined to blame me or bother me much, and they were more focused on being pissed off at the Warden for punishing us all collectively for the decision. Even our COs were a bit baffled by having us *all* be sent back.

And at least I had Tyson back, too.

"Sooo, what's the letter say this week?" He swung down into my bunk where I'd squished myself against the wall.

Before he could take a peek at it, I folded the few pages up carefully and smoothed them out on my lap. "Just some updates on my court case."

Which wasn't a total lie.

Since coming back here some five weeks ago, Jackson had been regularly sending me letters with updates from Nina about her meeting with the judge and whatever else was going on in the outside world. I lived for hearing from him. I was thankful that he'd even wanted to remain in contact at all.

Receiving every letter was like getting a piece of my soul to finally come alive again. I missed him deeply and often found myself daydreaming about what we could be up to if I'd just bitten the bullet and let myself be partnered with him the day of the fire.

I'd long since forgiven him for visiting Alex and kicked myself often for not talking it out with him before everything had happened. By now, the program would've been done and over with, anyway, and I'd be back at SAC, but at least I would've gotten a few more weeks with him in person.

I missed him.

Tyson nudged my shoulder. "Hey, what's—?"

"*Gonzalez!*"

My body jolted at the sound of Barlow yelling for me.

I scrambled off of my bunk and tucked my letter under my pillow. Tyson followed me as we headed out onto the platform overlooking the common area. There was a folded up piece of paper in Barlow's hand that he waved at me once he spotted me.

"Let's go. Lawyer's here."

"Knock 'em dead." Tyson slapped my ass.

Flashing him a look, I quickly jogged down the steps to the common area and followed after Barlow as he walked to the door. Once it was buzzed open, Browne appeared on the other side with a set of handcuffs ready to go. Automatically, I held up my arms and let him cuff me, waiting patiently while he attached the short bar in between my wrists to keep me from reaching out and grabbing anything on the way down.

My stomach twisted uncomfortably. Either Nina was visiting me to tell me the bad news that there was nothing she could do for me, or this was her telling me that she's actually performed a fucking miracle and gotten us a court date.

I didn't want to get my hopes up over it, but with each letter that came in with Jackson pleading with me to hang on just for a little longer, it had me wanting to.

Hope was a dangerous thing when you were in prison. It let you paint a false reality that could quickly come crashing down once the pieces of the puzzle all finally found their homes. I'd give anything to see Jackson again, even if it meant having to stay locked up for the rest of my three years left.

Barlow and Browne escorted me down to the visitor center and into a small, private room where Nina was already sitting at the table, a thick folder in front of her. She smiled at me and stood once I was brought over to her, her eyes growing a little sad when I raised my arms up to carefully squeeze into the stationary seat attached to the table.

Once the COs had the door shut, she sat back down again. "How are you?"

"I'm okay." My palms were clammy when I wiped them against my thighs. "What about you?"

She snorted. "Busy. You've got me running around quite a bit."

Instantly, I felt bad. "I'm sor—"

"Oh stop," she chastised. "I've been dying for a good case."

See, the funny thing about Nina was that she reminded me a lot of Jackson. Both of them were the kind of workers to love running themselves into the ground and did it with a smile on their faces. Sitting around and doing nothing was like a death sentence to them and the more work piled onto their plate, the better off their mental health was.

"Well, you're welcome then," I joked.

She smiled at me. "That's the spirit."

Opening up the folder, she spread out a few pages and spun them around to face me. "I've already submitted your appeal. We've got a court date on Friday. What I need from you is to go through these and read them, and then, if you agree to what's written, I need you to sign and date them."

A court date.

She really is a fucking miracle worker.

Looking back up at her, I asked, "You actually did it."

"Hey, don't give me credit yet. We've still got to meet with the judge. I'm trying to get you time served. Callahan's not one to overturn a conviction even with substantially more evidence submitted. But as long as I can get the evidence that was previously thrown out about your past history with the victim, then we have a shot at getting you out of here."

My heart thudded. "How soon?"

"As soon as fucking Friday, kid."

Holy shit.

"Like I said, though…" she went on. "We've got to meet with the judge first and see what he says. He could order a retrial with new circumstances with the new evidence submitted or he could throw out what was used previously and have us start over with what's left. It's all up to him what will happen."

Honestly, she could be talking gibberish and

it'd still sound the same to me. All I was hearing was that *yes* there was a real shot that I could be getting out of here soon.

As soon as fucking Friday, like she said.

I could see *Jackson* as soon as Friday.

Blowing out a breath, I nodded at her and set my hands down on top of the table. "Okay, tell me where to sign."

CHAPTER 30

JACKSON

"YOUR HONOR, given that the evidence presented here was not allowed or presented at the first trial, our appeal is for a resubmission of said evidence. We find that at the time of the trial, since the evidence of the defendant's past abuse with the victim was not taken into account, nor were the circumstances surrounding the inciting incident given proper context and presented to the jury, it directly affected my client's current conviction."

Hearing Nina speaking so eloquently to the judge, and the entire courtroom, gave me the peace of mind that she was going to try her damned hardest to get the case turned over in our favor. She'd been working tirelessly on it while I'd been running around as her errand-boy, gathering whatever evidence I could while she put together a new case file to present to Judge Callahan.

The old one had been a fucking mess and tracking down Ayen's old lawyer even more so. How the hell that man was able to still practice up until last year was beyond me.

Seeing Ayen in his SAC uniform was jarring, to say the least.

My heart had sunk when he'd been walked into the court room, his head tilted down, while two COs were on either side of him, holding onto his arms like he'd bolt at any second if given the chance. The chains between his cuffs had rattled like bells and caused a chill to run down my spine —a sound I'd probably never forget.

But once he'd lifted his head up enough to allow for one of the CO's to unlock his ankle chains in order to allow him to sit properly, his gaze had scanned over the gallery and landed directly on me. Seeing his eyes light up like that had made it all worth it—the running around, the sleepless nights worrying about him, taking a leave from the program in order to help Nina pull all of this together. Every. Single. Minute.

My hands itched to hold him again. My dreams had been filled with his warm body tucked against mine, and waking up to a cold and empty bed every morning was devastating.

I didn't believe in any form of a higher power, but today I was fucking praying as if I regularly dropped to my knees every goddamn Sunday.

"Ms. Cabone, I'm inclined to agree with you." Judge Callahan's arm swept over his desk at the stacks of paperwork from Ayen's case file. "I've been going over the evidence that was previously labeled inadmissible and while I agree that adding it back in would've changed the outcome of the jury's decision to convict Mr. Gonzalez, I'm not sure I agree with a re-trial. I feel it'd just be dragging out the inevitable."

My head was growing fuzzy from not breathing. The entirety of my body was frozen, unable to move to even begin to force myself to pull in some much-needed air.

How could I when in a single second, everything could change?

This was a moment in time that I'd never forget, no matter what the outcome was at the end of it.

My gaze was glued to the back of Ayen's head, his hair shaggy and longer since that last time I'd seen him. I longed to run my fingers through it, to tangle them in the soft lengths and watch his body relax and him begin to fall asleep from the attention.

I was grateful that other than that, he didn't look any worse off than when I'd seen him in person last. Fighting with myself constantly to not show up at SAC's doors and visit him had been the biggest struggle of my life. Letters were getting me through the weeks only so much, and if he was going back to prison again today, I might just jump over the bench and fight one of the officers myself to get thrown in there with him.

"Your Honor," Nina said. "My client's been serving for two and a half years and has been a model inmate. He recently rescued a fellow inmate during a work program incident that saved both of their lives."

Judge Callahan nodded slowly. "Mr. Gonzalez."

Ayen's shoulders visibly tensed. "Yes, Your Honor."

"Reviewing your case file, I found that a lot of the testimonies that you gave were compelling. I'm not sure what caused you to get involved with a man who was almost twice your age, but upon reviewing what you said about your relationship with him, I'm really struggling to make sense of what compelled the previous court's decision with not including that background."

Ayen's head bobbed as he nodded.

"Given that it was pretty clear that you were not in a safe spot at the time of the crime, I'm compelled to dismiss you with time served and a sentencing of probation instead, which I think is what should've happened in the first place." Judge Callahan sat back in his chair. "A minimum of five years probation and a ban on owning and operating firearms. I also want you to undergo a psychiatric eval upon release and have that submitted to the courts as well."

"Thank you, Your Honor," Nina said as the gavel was slammed down on the sound block.

Ayen's head snapped to the side to look at her, clearly just as shocked as I felt.

Holy fuck, she did it.

He's fucking free.

My legs were numb when I finally pushed myself up from the hard wooden bench. Nina reached out to steady Ayen as he climbed to his feet, one of the bailiffs coming around with a key to unlock his cuffs from him.

My baby bird was coming home.

The rest of the courtroom seemed completely unfazed while the next case number was called forward, and Nina and Ayen were quickly ushered out through the same side door Ayen had come through when he'd first been called in.

I followed after them from the public side of the court, pushing through the double doors to the main entryway into the courthouse. The marbled floors echoed softly from jogging in the leather loafers that I'd stuffed myself in to blend in with the rest of the gallery.

I didn't often find myself in a suit and tie, however I wanted to make today special. I'd *hoped* today would be special.

Fuck, I can't believe he's free.

Coming around to the backside of the private rooms, I stopped short at seeing two officers caging Ayen in while they spoke to him. One of them was giving him a small box of things while the other had the cuffs he'd previously been chained in swinging from his hands.

Nina was nowhere in sight, but that meant she was probably off signing paperwork or something to make it all official or however it worked on cases like this.

Ayen clutched the box in his arms tightly to his chest, turning at the sound of me making my way down the hallway. His eyes went wide again in the same way they had when he'd spotted me in the gallery.

Forcing myself to slow into a casual walk, I raised my hand to both officers as I approached them. "Afternoon, gentlemen."

"He here to pick you up?" one of them asked Ayen.

"That's right," I answered for him.

Smoothing my tie against my chest, I brushed my arm with Ayen's when I stopped just next to him. He vibrated against me, the shaking in his body barely detectable if I wasn't standing so close to him. Thankfully, I was within arm's length if he dropped from the sudden adrenaline crash.

"Is... is that all?" Ayen asked.

One of the officers shrugged. "Just make sure you get your paperwork before leaving."

Subtly, I put a hand on the small of his back, coaxing him to lean into my side just in case he began to waver on his feet. He wasn't worrying me just yet, but as soon as the officers turned around, I was going to sweep him up into my arms so he could fully relax.

The stress of being in court, the anxiety of waiting for a decision. It was a lot to handle even if the outcome was exactly what we'd hoped for.

The box in his hands wasn't filled with much. Just a change of clothes and some personal items, most likely from when he'd first gone into jail over two years ago. Luckily, I'd done up a whole closet for him back at my place that was filled with new clothes and shoes. Some sizes I'd guessed on, but as long as he was comfortable, it didn't matter.

"Have a good day, gentlemen." I forced a warm smile on my face.

As soon as they stepped away, so did Ayen, surprising me. He bent and set his box down carefully by my feet, his SAC uniform bunching around his midsection from how oversized it was.

When he straightened up, his eyes were filled with tears. "You came…"

Oh, my baby bird.

Cupping his face with both of my hands, I brought him back in again. "Of course I did."

"You wore a suit…"

"Had to give us some good luck."

He let out a watery laugh. "A suit is good luck?"

"My tie is. But it felt a little weird wearing one over a plain t-shirt."

Ayen buried his face in my chest, wrapping his arms around my waist to squeeze me tight enough to crack my back.

"Come here," I said, and lifted him clean off his feet.

He laughed in delight, clinging to me while I spun us around a few times. We probably looked absolutely ridiculous celebrating in the middle of a courthouse like that, but I couldn't bring myself to really care.

It wasn't every day that a damn murder charge was appealed to time served and a few years of probation.

What was that in the face of spending another three years behind bars when now, Ayen could *actually* begin his life over again?

Fucking priceless, in my opinion.

I owed Nina the most luxurious vacation known to man. Hell, I owed her a brand new Mercedes and a newly built house on top of that, too.

"Guys," came Nina's very unimpressed voice.

"Seriously. We're in a courthouse. Have some fucking decorum."

Ayen breathed out another laugh when I finally set him down again and he wrapped a hand around my tie to tug me down into a chaste kiss. I wanted to fucking melt against those plush lips of his.

Unfortunately, she was right, though. As usual.

"Sorry," I said, and instead, put a hand on Ayen's back again. "We all set?"

She waved a giant stack of papers at us. "Yup. You're a free man, kid."

"I can't believe it." Ayen rubbed his hands over his face a few times. "You actually did it..."

"*We* did." Nina nodded to me. "He's been my errand bitch for the past few weeks."

Honestly, I'd do it all again in a heartbeat. Even if the outcome was different than this, he would always be worth it to me. Doing *anything* for Ayen would be worth it, no matter what I got in return.

Ayen breathed out slowly, leaning back into my side once more. "I owe you guys so much."

"Just stay out of trouble, that's all I'm asking," she said.

I pressed my lips softly against Ayen's forehead. "I think we can manage that."

CHAPTER 31

JACKSON'S HOUSE in the city was as nice as I'd been expecting it to be.

A raised ranch on a quiet cul-de-sac that was painted a light shade of yellow to compliment the ridiculously blue California sky behind it. The rest of the neighborhood was quite the same, giving that picturesque feel to it that I'd only ever seen in magazines before while waiting in line at the grocery store.

This was the kind of neighborhood that a golden retriever and a family of four made sense in, and it felt wildly disproportionate to be bringing someone like *me* into it, given my history.

But none of that seemed to matter to Jackson at all, or faze him when I practically fainted at him offering me a room at his place.

How the hell did I deserve any of this?

This morning, I'd woken up in a damn jail cell and now, I was walking up the perfectly groomed lawn of a man who had fought to free me. All of it felt too surreal to even fathom, let alone believe that it would be my life for the next however-long Jackson decided to keep me around.

Carrying my little box of worldly possessions with me up to the red front door, I felt a rush of relief roll through me when he unlocked it and ushered me inside.

I loved this man. So much that it was actually ready to burst out of me.

"Want a tour?" he offered.

I dropped the box by the door and grabbed onto his tie again, wrapping it around my hand twice to pull him down. "Maybe later."

His mouth was hot on mine, tilting enough to deepen our kiss and draw a moan out of the both of us. He grabbed onto me, his hands on my hips, and spun me around to press me against the wall right next to the door while his hard body ground into me.

Finding out that he missed me was the best news out of all of it.

Sure, our spark *seemed* like it hadn't died throughout our letters, but that was all subtext in order to get around the COs reading them, anyway. Seeing it—*feeling it*—in person, was a whole different story.

One of his hands smacked the back of his front door closed and then he rapidly stripped me of my uniform and tossed both scrub pieces onto the floor. Then he was sweeping me up and throwing me over his shoulder like a sack of flour.

I laughed and kicked my feet, giddy like a fucking teenager. "I missed you, too."

He slapped my bare ass. "Ayen, you have no idea how much I've missed you."

God, that was music to my fucking ears.

I got a quick sweeping look of his house on the way back to his bedroom. It was well kept and modern looking with plenty of natural light coming in from the large bay windows in the living room. A lot of it was an open concept, aside from the kitchen that was blocked off with a thick wall separating it from the rest of the house.

My gaze trailed along the walls of the hallway when we went down it. Pictures of Jackson with friends and Roxy were all displayed, along with a few of a man I didn't recognize but who looked startlingly like Jackson in an armed forces uniform.

Carter.

I smiled at the picture. He was just as handsome as Jackson was.

The hallway disappeared in place of the walls of Jackson's bedroom where I was tossed unceremoniously down onto the bed.

Another laugh bubbled up from my throat and I clumsily grabbed at Jackson to pull him up onto the bed with me, not caring that he was halfway through trying to get himself out of the *incredibly* well-fitted suit he was wearing.

Damn, I need to find an excuse to get him back in that again.

His lips found mine again while one of his hands grabbed onto my shoulder to press me back down onto the mattress. It was soft under me and felt like a damn cloud with how thick the duvet was.

I parted my lips for him, welcoming him in and tangling our tongues together in a deep kiss. He wrapped his large hand around my cock, stroking it lovingly and like we had all the time in the world.

Which... I guess, we really did now.

There was no rush for us to come together before the inevitable clock rang, signaling time was up. We didn't need to be afraid of getting caught by the COs and dragged apart and convicted of something as stupid as giving in to our own emotions.

We had all the time in the damn world to have each other and there would be no one in our way that could stop us.

Jackson trailed his warm lips down my body until he parted my legs and dragged his tongue over my fluttering hole.

Threading my fingers through his hair, I arched my back with each thrust of his tongue inside me, wetting me all around, softening my hole, and lapping at the underside of my balls when he came up for air.

"Missed you." He nuzzled his nose against my inner thigh, inhaling deeply and squeezing the backside of my knee.

"Please," was all I could manage to say between my garbled thoughts and the pleasure that was racing through my veins.

I was being overtaken by all of the intense emotions—my want for him, the desire to keep him close to me and never ever let him go, and the love that I was drowning in that was dying to be let out.

He seemed to know exactly what I meant because before long, he was leaning back from me and shedding the rest of his clothes off and tossing them somewhere onto the floor at the foot of the bed.

He wrapped his hand around one of my ankles, holding onto it while he leaned across the bed to grab something out of the drawer and toss it onto the bed next to me. Snatching it, I lifted it and smiled at seeing the fresh and unopened bottle of lube.

"Just for me, huh?"

He grinned, running his hand up and down my leg a few times. "To be fair, I figured you'd want to nap first."

"Not after seeing you in that suit."

He laughed. "I'll keep that in mind the next time I wear it."

"Just make sure you bring this with you, too," I said, tossing the small bottle back at him.

He brought my foot up to his lips and pressed his mouth along my sole in tiny kisses, following it until he reached my ankle. Him worshiping me like that was melting me down to my bones. The devotion this man showed to the smallest things when it came to me gave me a sense of pride in myself that I'd long since thought was dead.

How in the world I'd been lucky enough to meet him, let alone entangle myself with him like this, I'll never know. But there wasn't a goddamn thing in this world that I was going to do that would mess this up again.

I was tired of pushing him away when all he'd ever done was take care of me and treat me the way I'd always been desperate for. Jackson was a good man, one that I absolutely didn't deserve in the slightest.

From here on out, though, I was going to do everything in my power to earn him.

I loved him too much to let him get away.

He gently set my leg back down and flipped open the cap on the lube, slathering a generous amount onto his fingers and circling them around my hole a few times. A deep groan bubbled up from my chest when he slid two fingers inside me, easily finding the spot that drove me fucking wild.

He stroked his digits back and forth a few times, opening me up just enough to add in a third.

I squirmed on his fingers, wanting more than just the few fingers moving inside of me. I needed *all* of him.

"Jax," I pleaded.

"Fuck, look at you," he murmured. "Just as pretty as ever."

The praise had my gut twisting pleasantly. Enough to make my toes curl.

He pulled his fingers out of me with a soft 'pop' that had me clenching around air instantly. I missed the feeling of being filled, and my patience grew thinner by the second. I'd waited so damn long to have him again that now that we were finally here and just at the precipice of finally being together again, it was driving me insane.

Thankfully, he didn't keep me waiting long and was soon dragging the head of his cock along my hole to get himself nice and lubed up while he stroked the rest of it along his base. The head of his cock slipped in easily, opening me up once more while I bore down.

He grabbed at the back of my thighs with both of his hands, holding them apart while he thrust into me a few times, getting deeper and deeper with each pull of his hips.

I was dizzy with pleasure, the feelings overwhelming my body in a way that being wasted and high at the same time was.

I loved it.

I was addicted to it.

"You always take me so good, Ayen."

He let go of my legs to lean back over me, curling his arms around me in a protective cocoon and encasing me with his body.

I dug my nails into the muscles of his shoulder blades, holding him tight against me while he sunk deep enough that his hips were flush with my ass.

He took his time with me, working himself in and out of my ass with the kind of care that a long time lover would take with their beloved. He kissed me like one, too, like fucking me wasn't enough. He had to brand me with his very essence and seep himself down deep into the core of my bones so that he could never leave.

I wanted to wear him like a tattoo imprinted into my skin that it would eventually scar over. That way, I'd never forget him or us and what we shared together.

Because we truly did have all the time in the world to be together like this. Not even an act of God could pull us apart at this point.

I came with his name on my lips, feeling the full body rush of my orgasm stealing the air out of my lungs and replacing it with his as he breathed into me.

"Fuck, baby," he whispered, his hips clapping against me until he shuddered and warmth filled me.

Jackson peppered my face with soft presses of his lips, covering every inch until I was sure that my face was covered in them.

"I love you." The words came tumbling out of me before I could stop them, my mind and emotions too caught up in all of this.

"Oh, Ayen." His forehead rested against mine. A soft smile crossed over his face. "*I* love *you*. Stay with me?"

My eyes prickled with tears. "Of course I will. As long as you'll have me."

He grinned. "Guess you're stuck with me indefinitely, then."

I'd take it.

Not a bad deal at all.

EPILOGUE

Jackson

Readjusting the comfortable weight of my gear once more, I looped my bag up over my shoulder and secured the straps across my chest.

A hand slapped against my shoulder twice, hard enough to make an audible sound. "Looks like it's going to be a long one, today."

I glanced out at the group of new inmates that had come in just last week and were already moving into their next phase of training.

I nodded and nudged my fellow coworker, Mac, with my elbow. "You make it sound like you're going to be slacking off today."

"Can you blame me? Your boy's got everyone running on a tight leash these days."

Amusement trickled through me. "Scared he's going to make me scold you?"

"Wouldn't be the first time."

I slapped him with one of my gloves. "Get to work, then."

With a huff, Mac sauntered off to go join the rest of the firefighters gearing up. Roxy's barking had me craning my neck to look across the crowd of inmates, following her bouncing form in between the gap in the inmates' groups.

She was following along diligently as Ayen's keen eyes roved over the inmates, checking everyone's gear and adjusting some as he passed on through. His dark t-shirt clung to his slender frame, filled out nicely with a delicious layer of new muscles from lifting heavy things all day. His jumper pants, held up at his shoulders by thick suspenders, hugged his bottom half in such a good way, one that made me drool.

My baby bird wasn't such a baby anymore.

Pride swelled in my chest, not for the first time today. He'd been taking over our program days more often lately, and seeing him flourish like this was incredible to watch. He was a natural leader, even if he second-guessed himself sometimes. He led with a compassionate hand, a rare thing in this field nowadays but so much more needed.

Once he cleared the last of the inmate checks, he made his way over to me, Roxy merrily bounding after him, her tongue hanging from her mouth happily. He patted her head lightly, a small smile playing on his lips.

"Hey you," I greeted, bending down to grab Roxy when she got close enough and rub her sides, cooing words of praise and love over her smiling snout.

"Everyone's all set."

"Good." The gold ring on my left hand shone in the sun when it caught the light just right as I passed a hand over my dog's head. I smiled at it, the new addition feeling right at home.

Glancing over, I caught the sight of Ayen's matching one just as he pulled a glove over his hand. "We all set?"

"Yup." I stood up straight again, casting a glance over his shoulder to make sure everyone was preoccupied before I leaned in and pecked his lips. "Are you?"

He breathed out a laugh, cheeks suddenly dusted with a soft rosy tint. "Yeah. You sure you want me leading this one today?"

"I think you're more of an expert on the 'getting lost in a forest and finding your way out of it' than I am at this point."

He grinned, shoving me lightly. "He has jokes today."

"What can I say, I love your smile."

Ayen let out a soft sigh. "You need to stop or I'm going to drag you back to our cabin."

Like that was even a threat. I'd toss the rest of the day's itinerary out the window to throw him over my shoulder and head back to our cabin for the rest of the day. Getting married a few weeks ago had done nothing to slow down our libidos.

In fact, it had made them worse in my opinion.

"Behave," Ayen mumbled, most likely sensing my fast growing dirty thoughts. Or simply seeing the way my pupils were already dilating.

"Since you asked so nicely," I said, quickly pressing my mouth to his lips again.

Honestly, at this point, we couldn't be blamed for being all over each other. We'd just come back from our honeymoon, so we could blame it on that at least.

Someone clearing their throat nearby had us breaking apart quickly. Looking over, I spotted Mac giving us both a look, his brow arched, that suggested we'd better get going.

I patted Ayen's hip lightly, nodding forward at the inmates.

"Lead the way, Boss."

He laughed. "Oh, I could get used to that."

As he sauntered off with Roxy in tow, I took up the rear, and shouldered up with Mac who was busy running through a checklist that Ayen had assigned to him earlier that morning. His hand quickly flicked over the paper with his pen, checking things off as we leisurely followed behind the group slowly moving toward the edge of the trail.

"All right!" Ayen called out. "Stick with your partners and make sure neither of you get left behind. If you get lost, use the radio or your whistles to signal to us where you are. Keep track of landmarks so we can locate you quicker!"

Pride swelled in me when the group of inmates murmured their acknowledgement and then marched forward together in a tight group. On either side of them were their COs, keeping a close eye on all of them just in case they decided to lash out or do anything ridiculous. It rarely happened but once in a while one of the inmates got uppity and it was a real threat to those determined to make good on their time here. Mostly, we'd had a stunning success in this program and we'd like to keep it that way for years to come.

"He's doing good up there," Mac said, lifting his head up from the clipboard finally.

Yes, he really, really was.

I was so proud of my little-but-not-so-little birdy.

Our future together was bright and I couldn't wait to see what came next.

Thank you for reading Jackson and Ayen's story.

Oh, and if you enjoyed this book, maybe you'll do me a huge favor and leave a review. Even a few words would mean the world to me, and it also helps other readers find the stories you love.

For more in the Smokejumpers series of sizzling firefighters, watch for <u>Xavier</u>, a continuation of Gage and Xavier's story, coming soon!

In the meantime, why not check out some of the other books in my backlist. A handy list is on the very next page!

Love,
~Eve Riley

XAVIER

Dear Reader,

When I left off with Gage and Xavier's story, I had originally intended to leave it as it was, BUT so many of you had questions. Now, usually I would have made you wait and I would have answered those questions—mostly about Dexter and the twins, Greyson and Asher, in their own books in due time. Simply because that's typically how things play out in my head and the kids in Gage's book weren't ready for their full on detailed stories yet. I'm a chronological writer, I guess.

Anyway, then I saw that a few of you felt Gage was more of a happy for now kind of ending rather than a happily forever after, and well, I had the idea that I needed to fix that.

So I started working on Xavier, a continuation from where Gage left off, mostly. I did answer some things about the three young men, but not enough to detract me from writing their books later. Yep, more breadcrumbs. Lol

I do so hope you enjoy!

Love,

~Evie Riley

XAVIER

**A long-distance relationship. A lonely home.
The flames burn fiercely when they are together.**

Xavier Cruz has just celebrated his one-year sobriety, and he and Dexter are slowly mending their father/son relationship. Will Dex finally reveal his big secret?

Gage Torres is troubled that this may be his first Christmas without his younger brothers. Will the trickster twins have something up their sleeves for Gage again this year?

Living with the love of your life hundreds of miles away is a lonely way to be. Despite all the jet-setting and red-eye flights, it's no longer enough for either man. Something has to give, and soon.

Will the two men survive the long-distance relationship, or will the New Year bring about shocking changes they never could have imagined?

Xavier is a continuation from Gage. Please read Gage first.

CHAPTER 1

Xavier

"I want to congratulate you all on your success today. This marks the beginning of a new life. A life clean and sober and filled with the many wonderful things that comes with living free and independent of that which used to rule you."

Clapping erupted around the small room, our entire group having been crammed in the small auditorium of the local high school for this ceremony. Our chairman, Robert, smiled at us from the stage while he gripped either side of the podium.

When the clapping finally died down, Robert began to speak again. "Today marks one year. I hope to see you all for our next ceremony to celebrate two years and thereafter. Congratulations, all."

All of this felt so surreal. Even the gold chip in my hand, no matter how many times I turned it over onto its opposite side, still didn't feel real. The ridges carved into the face of it, stating that I was one year sober, were smooth to the touch as I grazed my thumb over it.

Pride filled my chest—at least, that's what I hoped it was. Getting back in touch with my emotions through therapy over the last nine months had been intense, to say the least. I never really had that healthy of a relationship with the deeper parts of myself, and that had become rather apparent and a huge slap in the face when I'd begun to really focus inwardly.

On the one hand, I was glad to have finally started to heal myself. As scary as it was to stop drinking and really focus on getting my mental health back in order, just as Robert had said in his speech, it had been freeing.

On the other hand, my future was uncertain. Sure, I had a great job and a boyfriend that I loved dearly, but there were still things that I was struggling with that felt like once I got a few steps put in front of me, something would come along to send me five steps back from where I started.

Namely my son, Dexter.

"Hey." Someone clapped me on the shoulder, bringing me out of my funk. "They're serving pizza and wings, you want me to bring you a plate?"

Danny, my one friend from AA, was giving me a toothy grin while waiting for my answer. He was a bit younger than me, had lost his way after his wife and daughter had died in a horrific car accident that had left him severely scarred on the right half of his body.

Pain killers to numb his injuries had soon turned into a full blown addiction that he'd eventually swapped for alcohol because it was cheaper and easier to get. Unfortunately, it was a tale as old as time and one I knew all too well how it went.

I was glad that someone like Danny, who radiated practical sunshine out of his ass, had found his own light in coming to AA and getting himself clean. That was a man that I could admire.

"Nah, I'm good." Standing, I tucked my chip into my pocket. "I've actually got to head to the station. To save lives and whatnot." That last part was partially a joke, but one Danny found absolutely hilarious nonetheless.

He clapped me again on the shoulder. "All right, then I'm taking your portion of the wings."

"Go for it. But don't call me at ten o'clock tonight complaining of heartburn."

He let out a gasp. "I'd rather down an entire bottle of pepto than call your cranky ass."

That brought a smirk to my face.

At least my reputation preceded me, even here.

Waving at him, I headed out before anyone else could trap me in a long and drawn out conversation about our hopes and dreams now that we all had our one year chips. I had set goals for myself long before this, and while they were all still a work in progress, I was managing.

Once I shoved the door to the outside world

open and stepped out into the fading sunlight, I let myself finally breathe. It wasn't that being in there with a bunch of other recovering addicts made me anxious or anything—quite the opposite, in fact.

But too much of being crammed inside of a tiny room with only one way out had me wanting to crawl right out of my damn skin.

I supposed it was a part of my military training not to want to be trapped in an environment like that. Too many factors played into getting fucked if an enemy were to attack and block off the only line of exit. Or, if for some tragic reason, a fire or something similar were to break out and panic ensued—not much could be done fighting against twenty other people scrambling to get away.

Even now that I was out and a civilian like the rest of society, it was hard to shut that part of my brain off. No matter what I did, my therapist had reassured me—or rather, doomed me?—that I'd always have that gut instinct to survive and get out.

That intuition was what had saved me while in the military, after all.

Shaking my head to rid myself of the thoughts before I delved too far down *that* rabbit hole, I pulled out my cell and scrolled through my text threads, coming upon Gage's. Opening up my camera, I snapped a quick photo of my chip and sent it over to him.

Despite the time difference, he responded almost immediately.

Congratulations, Baby! I'm so proud of you!

There was a smattering of emojis after that, ranging from confetti cannons to hearts.

Damn, I missed him.

Horribly.

Since coming back from Louisiana, I'd had the worst withdrawals from him. Not just because of the lack of sex—which we were more than making up for through texts and phone calls every night—but because I missed *him*. His presence. His energy. His body wrapped up in mine as we fell asleep together.

I'd only had such a short window with him in Louisiana that even now, almost ten months later, it still didn't feel like enough. Our time difference made it complicated to connect with each other at decent times, and our jobs weren't helping that either.

As proud as I was of him for passing his exam and getting into the field of his dreams, I fucking wanted to rip him right out of Louisiana and smuggle him back here to be with me.

Would I ever tell him any of this shit?

Fuck no.

He didn't need to be worrying about my slow spirals into insanity while trying to deal with his own full plate.

Besides, most nights after we said goodnight and hung up, I was good. It was only those few times throughout the month, those one or two nights, that were absolutely fucking diabolical on my mental health. And waking up to an empty bed on top of that when I finally came to was worse than if I just simply jumped off the nearest roof.

While still looking down at my phone, an alert went off that made my heart lurch in my chest.

REMINDER: Dex dinner

Oh, fuck.

Checking the time, I spun on my heel and ran to my truck.

CHAPTER 2

Xavier

"You're late," was all my son said to me the second I sat down in the booth across from him. He had his nose already buried in his menu, a drink half gone with pearls of condensation rolling down the side of the glass and creating a pool on the table.

Wincing, I slipped my jacket off of my shoulders and shoved it into the corner of my side. "Sorry, kid. I got over here as fast as I could."

He wasn't looking up from the menu as I talked. Not even a subtle shift in his brow that indicated he was listening to me. Just his eyes darting over the menu while he scanned it, looking for something to eat.

I loved my kid a lot but sometimes he was difficult to read. Actually, scratch that. He was like a fucking dictionary in a foreign language and I was the idiot trying to translate it.

"Dex?"

He sighed and looked up. "Yeah?"

"I'm sorry."

His face finally faltered, going from that neutral expression to an actual frown. I knew he was upset, even if I was only a couple minutes late. We'd been working on this relationship between us for a couple of months and it seemed that the more I got to know him, the more walls he'd been throwing up lately.

My therapist was adamant that it was Dexter's way of trying to gain control of the situation. I'd been out of his life for a long time, no thanks to his mother. But the logistics of that weren't all that important.

At least not at this stage.

He was a child still, even at the cusp of turning eighteen, and his view of the world was still small. Giving him the space to express himself, no matter if it was happiness or disappointment at me, was what was going to be the thing that would help him in starting to trust me.

I just had to trust the process and not be impatient.

But fuck was it hard not to reach over and pull him into a tight hug and promise him the damn world. He was my pride and joy, my baby, my everything. Losing him had been what hurt the most back then.

The PTSD from the military had only compounded my depression and spiraled me into a person that I barely recognized whenever I got the courage to look in the mirror. A year ago, I'd been a man that was incapable of being there for my son, no matter how much I'd tried to convince myself otherwise.

Here, today, I wanted to prove that old me wrong.

Leaning back in my seat, I slipped my hand into my pocket and pulled out my chip. It made a rough sound as I slid it across the table toward him, the light overhead catching the gold plating that made the thing shine nicely.

He stared down at it, his eyes widening a little bit.

"I was at my meeting to accept my chip," I explained, smiling. "I wanted to get it before our dinner to give it to you."

"Me?" he said, incredulously.

"Yeah, Dex. I want you to know how serious I am about all of this. I know that I wasn't… I haven't been there for you in the past, and trust me, I regret every single second of it, but this is hopefully a small step in proving to you that I'm going to do everything I can to make it up to you. I want to *be* there for you."

He swallowed, his Adam's apple bobbing while he carefully picked up the chip. He rotated it in his hand a few times, much like I had back at the meeting. "One year, huh…"

"Yup."

He was quiet for another moment. "That's pretty impressive."

Grinning, I said, "Just wait until I get my ten year one. I hear that it's *real* gold."

He glanced up at me. "Ten years?"

I could tell by the way that he said that it was laced with hope and mixed with a little bit of skepticism. I could work with that, though. I could prove to him that I was going to keep this thing going. We had the rest of our lives together, and like hell I was going to screw it up any further.

When Dexter slowly set the chip down, he pulled in a deep breath. "Can I talk to you about something?"

My heart stuttered in my chest. "Yeah, of course. Anything."

I hoped it was about whatever had happened to him that he'd been refusing to talk about. While I didn't want my kid to have to relive any kind of trauma that he might have endured, I knew from experience that getting it out was the first step in recovering from it.

Talking about horrible experiences, even through therapy, had taken a lot out of me. But now with nine months under my belt, that weight that had been settled on my shoulders for so long was slowly beginning to get lighter and lighter as the days passed.

I wanted that for Dexter, too. He deserved that. Suffering with whatever he was keeping locked inside himself would eventually eat away at him like it had me. We Cruz boys had been cursed with that prideful sense of self that made it almost impossible to open up about our deepest darkest secrets.

Even to our own family.

"So, I've been applying to colleges," he said, focusing his gaze back down at the chip on the table.

Okay, not exactly what I was expecting. But hey, at least he was opening up to me about something.

"And," he went on. "I got accepted into one for an early admissions."

My jaw dropped. "Dex, that's amazing! Congratulations!"

His smile was a little worn when he finally looked at me again. "The problem is that it's kind of far away."

Oh fuck.

"How far away are we talking?"

Please don't say on the other side of the damn world.

I'd only just gotten him back. Having to say goodbye after only a year would fucking wreck me.

"Louisiana," he said slowly.

My body all but collapsed back into my booth, relief practically jello-ifying my damn bones. Oh thank fuck. I could handle Louisiana. "Where abouts?"

"Baton Rouge."

That's near Gage.

"Mom know yet?"

Dexter shook his head.

Interesting.

I wondered why he wasn't telling Kate. Maybe he was afraid she wasn't going to let him go, or try to talk him into going to a local school here. Having a mom like her, one that was steadfast in her beliefs and convictions, could be both a blessing and a curse.

She'd kept him safe all these years, but she'd also kept him away from many things—namely me—by doing so. It wasn't healthy to raise a child, let alone a boy, locked in a bubble. It created too much confusion once they were thrust into the real world. And while I had no doubts my son was a smart boy, he was also naive to a fault.

"I actually have a friend out that way," I said.

Calling Gage a 'friend' put a sour taste in my mouth. I'd been careful in tiptoeing around the 'boyfriend' talk with Dex, not wanting to freak him out too much by shoving all of my personal affairs down his throat.

It had been hard not to talk about my personal life with him, especially since hiding things from him felt wrong, especially about a relationship.

That wasn't something I was sure about, though. With Kate raising him in the church, I wasn't sure how deeply ingrained her beliefs—and his—were. So pushing the subject didn't seem fair game at this point.

In the future, definitely. But for now, I wanted to focus on our dynamic.

Dexter nodded slowly, tapping his fingers absently on the table. "I wanted to go on a campus tour before I accepted."

He was obviously telling me all of this for a reason. With his mother not involved in any of this, that meant that I had fair dibs. "You want to take a trip out there? I'm sure we could crash at my friend's place."

His eyes lit up. "Really?"

God, he reminds me of when he was a baby.

Blinking back the sudden tears that prickled at the corners of my eyes, I said, "Yeah, of course. Why don't I talk to him and figure out a good time to fly us out. We'll tour the campus and make a weekend of it."

For once, Dexter actually looked excited. "I'd love that."

Pride bloomed in my chest for the second time today. I really hoped this was the beginning to us finally bridging the gap between us.

GAGE

"YOU'VE BEEN STARING at your phone like you're waiting for a dick pic," came a familiar voice from behind me.

Turning to look over my shoulder, I threw Quinn a glare. "Funny. Can't I be happy that my boyfriend's texting me?"

He smirked while ripping the door to his locker open and shoving his dirty shirt inside. "Not much *texting* going on, I see."

He was such a turd, sometimes. Especially since getting together with Jase. Thankfully, that man had softened out more than any of us could've ever imagined. Before they'd gotten together, they were like oil and water.

Though, I guess that came with the territory when one party used to bully the other in high school.

"He got his one year chip," I said, showing off the picture on my phone."

Quinn's eyes softened. "Hey, man. That's great. Sorry, I wasn't trying to be a dick. I was only ragging on you because you've been distracted all day. I don't think I've ever seen you take a boot to the face like that."

I snorted at the memory of Mark slinging his turn-outs at me while climbing out of the fire truck. The damn thing had caught me right on the side of the head, too. Thankfully, the tread was thick enough that it'd bounced right off without leaving much of a dent behind, but damn was it embarrassing.

Quinn was right, though. I'd been distracted since this morning when I'd woken up to Xavier telling me he was on his way to his AA meeting to celebrate his one year. Pride didn't even begin to cover it on how I felt about him accomplishing something so massive. He'd been working so hard on himself over the past year since quitting drinking.

That chip was more than just a small token. It was a symbol that he'd gone and done that damn thing, changing his life for the better. Meeting him and learning about his drinking had been tough. Especially seeing him as the kind of soul that didn't deserve to suffer the way he had in life.

Sure, he'd messed up plenty, but *no one* deserved to go through that shit.

"It's all good," I said, swinging my leg over to the other side of the bench I'd been sitting on for the past twenty minutes. My ass was numb as I stood, making the pins and needles in my leg feel hot. Slapping my ass cheeks a few times did nothing, either.

Guess I just had to ride it out.

Quinn grinned at me. "Hey, you hear about the Christmas party Captain Clarke's making us throw? I totally put Jase on the planning committee."

"You wrote him in?" I tsked and shook my head. "How cruel. You know he can't decorate for shit."

He let out a roarous laugh. "Yeah, that's the point. Come on, I have to pick on him somehow. It's what keeps our sex life alive."

That had me rolling my eyes. Leave it to Quinn to keep up with the light negging. I swear, you could take a man out of high school but you couldn't reform a former bully completely. At least these pranks were much more tame compared to the shit Jase was put through back when he was a kid.

"It's all in good fun, I swear." Quinn lifted his hands up on either side of his head.

"What are you two asswipes talking about?" Jase was walking into the locker room, shedding his shirt that was soaked in sweat. The hair on his chest, normally wiry and curly, was pressed down on his clammy skin.

"Apparently he signed you up for the decoration committee for our Christmas party," I said, smirking when Quinn threw me a glare for ratting him out. I was nothing if not the occasional pot stirrer.

"Really," Jase drawled, looking over at his boyfriend. He grabbed the other man by his waist, slamming him back against the lockers and pinned him there with his body. "Do I have to teach you a lesson in behaving, Sanders?"

Quinn let out a breathy laugh when Jase reached around and slapped his ass cheek, holding it in a firm grip. "I mean… I wouldn't mind."

Rolling my eyes, I slammed my own locker shut. These fucking horn-dogs. "Can you two get a fucking room?"

At this point, they were completely ignoring me in favor of Jase running his tongue up Quinn's neck while the other man let out a slutty moan. It annoyed me more than it should have—okay, maybe I was kind of jealous now that I thought about it.

With my significant other on the other side of the damn country, watching these two assholes get it on was giving me a serious case of blue balls. Don't get me wrong, phone sex with Xavier and sending him sassy pictures throughout the day was all fine and good but it was nothing compared to the real thing.

I craved having him pressed up against me, his dick pounding into me while I begged for mercy. Replicating that with a dildo didn't exactly suffice much anymore, no matter how many sweet words Xavier whispered to me on the other end of the phone.

Bypassing the two lovebirds, I strolled out into the fire station, spotting Ellie over by the bulletin board. "That for the party?"

She flicked her hair over her shoulder, the pen in her hand tapping her clipboard in quick succession. "Yeah. Cap wants us all to pitch in for something. I'm thinking a potluck."

"I'm not much in the ways of the kitchen, so as long as you're good with store-bought, I'm down."

She turned and narrowed her eyes at me. "What *kind* of store bought?"

"Uh… the normal kind?"

Ellie rolled her eyes. "Earth to Gage. You have to at least make to *seem* homemade."

Oh.

"Then from Krista's Scratch Kitchen down the street."

She grinned. "Excellent. I'll put you down for being in charge of the main course."

What the hell?

She trotted off to find her next victim, leaving me standing by the bulletin board like a complete dumbass. Such was the way of Ellie, though. She was always such a little viper that you didn't realize bit you until much too late.

That was also part of her charm, though.

"She get you, too?" Carmen asked, wandering over.

"Yeah. You?"

She laughed. "Oh yeah. By the end of today, she'll have everyone signed up on the damn list."

Just as I was about to hit her back with another comment about Ellie, my pocket buzzed. Digging my phone out, I was expected to see Xavier's name pop up, but to my surprise, it was Asher's.

Excusing myself from our conversation, I ducked out the left door of the firehouse and out the back alley where it was much more quiet.

"Hey, you, long time no talk."

"Yeah, sorry about that," Asher said. "Wanted to call in and check on you."

"Worried I took a nasty fall and couldn't get up?"

I could hear the grin in his voice as he said, "You caught me, old man."

I rolled my eyes.

Little shit.

My brothers *loved* picking on my age despite them being not so far behind me. Now that they were both nineteen, they were going to get a nice little dose of reality once they got up to be my age and *their* bones were beginning to creak every time they rolled out of bed.

"Ha, ha. Very funny."

"I know. Poor, Grey. I got the smarts and the humor."

Smirking, I quipped back. "But not the beauty."

He let out an offended gasp. "Rude. I'm taking you off my Christmas card list."

"Hey, now. Don't be saying that. You're coming home for Christmas, mister."

There was a weird pause on the other end of the line. One that I didn't like at all. "Well…"

Uh-uh, no way. This was *not* happening. My baby brothers were both going to come home to me for the holidays because I wasn't going to be taking any other excuse other than an act of god. They'd been away from home long enough to give me grays every time I looked in the damn mirror by being out in the world without me.

If I was about to spend a holiday by myself—

my first holiday *without* them—I was going to fucking lose it. Xavier was going to have to commit me to the nearest psych ward.

"Ash, don't you dare," I warned.

"It's just… my boss is kind of being a hardass and wants me to stay through the holidays."

I wanted to groan. This fucking boss of his was not only messing with me reuniting with my brother after him being gone for almost an entire fucking year, but was slowly worming his way into Ash's life in more ways than what I was comfortable with.

To me, it was becoming increasingly obvious that my little brother's crush on the man was going from juvenile puppy love to something that was full-blown. How deep it really was, I had no idea. Asher wasn't exactly chatty on the subject. But the unspoken shit said plenty as it was.

"Ash, you're coming home." My tone was firm. There was no option of him telling me 'no'. I'd fly out to Texas and drag his sorry ass back home kicking and screaming if I had to.

"We'll see," was all he said to that.

"I mean it, Ash. You and Grey are coming home for the holidays."

"Do we get to meet this infamous Xavier if we do?"

"Seriously?"

"What?" Asher's voice flipped from challenging to all innocent. "Come on. You talk about him enough whenever we call. Isn't Christmas the perfect time to introduce us?"

I had a funny feeling that was the original reason for my brother calling. If Greyson hadn't put him up to it first, then they definitely conspired together. I'd been slowly working my way into introducing Xavier into their lives with small mentions here and there about him whenever they called me.

It wasn't much, sure, but I wasn't completely leaving them in the dark about it, either. I wanted my brothers to get to know my boyfriend, even if he was across the damn country. At some point, I *would* actually like for us all to meet and hang out, mostly so I could get a read on whether my brothers approved or not.

It sounded silly to want that from two nineteen year olds when I was well into my adulthood and didn't need their approval in the slightest. However, it would also mean a lot to me, too. My history of dating had never been stellar in the past, with me hardly bringing anyone home on top of that.

Certainly not to meet my brothers.

So doing this with Xavier meant a lot. *He* meant a lot to me. I loved that man and hopefully, eventually, my brothers would, too.

"How about I think about it and get back to you," I finally said.

Asher made a small noise. "Fine. I'll get back to you about Christmas, too."

"Tell your boss that if he doesn't give you time off, he's going to find me on his doorstep."

He huffed. "Fine."

"I love you, Ash."

"Yeah, yeah. I love you, too. Greyson should be calling later."

I flipped my wrist up to check my watch; I had

about an hour before that happened. With Greyson already having graduated boot camp and started on his specialized training, that typically ended around five and dinner was at six.

"Got it, thanks."

After ending our call, I pulled my phone away from my ear and stared down at the log. As much as I hassled my brothers, I did mean what I said about seeing them. They could play it off as a joke all they wanted but when push came to shove, they were mine.

We were brothers in name, but honestly, they were practically my kids. I'd raised them proudly, despite my struggles in doing so over the years. Them leaving the nest and becoming successful was a testament to what I'd sacrificed in order to cultivate them into the young men they'd become.

It hurt, of course, them leaving me behind to go spread their wings and fly. But damn if I wasn't proud, too.

Pulling up Xavier's text thread, I shot him a quick message about a phone call later before heading back into the station.

Hopefully, my brothers weren't going to give me any more grief about coming home.

Because if I had one thing going for me, it was following through with my promises.

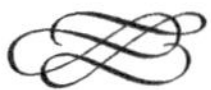

CHAPTER 4

Xavier

Planning a trip to a different state would've looked a lot different if I wasn't also simultaneously trying to do it behind my ex's back.

Was it fucked of me to be doing this without Kate knowing?

Probably. But this was the first time since reconnecting with Dexter that he was allowing me in on something she wasn't a part of. Throwing my precautions to the wind was going to be my only solution to this.

I couldn't let this golden opportunity be flushed down the proverbial toilet the second it'd been presented to me. I had to make this perfect, to show Dexter that he could trust me and that I could handle his shit.

Our conversation about him dealing with whatever demons he had in him still rung through my head to this day. I wondered every night before I went to bed what kind of shit my kid had been put through to create that destroyed look on his face when he'd admitted he couldn't deal with my shit on top of his.

My desperation to know was only in an effort to fix it for him. To create the safe space he needed in order to talk to him about what happened. I wasn't willing to jump to any conclusions just yet, but damn if my mind didn't race every time I thought about it.

Hopefully, this trip would change things.

My phone lit up from where I'd tossed it onto my desk, Gage's name scrolling on it. Smiling, I put him on speaker and continued to click through flights.

"Hey, baby."

He let out that familiar soft chuckle of his. "Hey. Got your message. That's exciting about Dexter."

"You okay with us crashing at your place? I can grab a hotel if not. No worries."

He groaned into the speaker. "I swear to god if one more person ditches me, I'm going to scream. No, you're coming here and staying with me. This house is so fucking empty."

Frowning, I leaned back from my keyboard and swiped the phone off of the desk. "What's going on?"

It wasn't like Gage to sound that torn up about something. He'd been fine texting me throughout the day.

So what changed to put him in such a sour mood?

"The fucking twins aren't *sure* if they want to come home for the holidays." The tone in Gage's voice, while sounding annoyed, was laced with despair.

My man was in the middle of a full-blown meltdown. Or, well, as much of a meltdown as Gage could possibly be spiraling into. That man was the most stable person I'd ever met.

"Hey, I'm sure they didn't mean it like that." Hopefully, my voice was soothing. "They're just being teenagers. Trust me, I have one of my own."

"You know what Asher said to me? That his boss isn't going to give him the vacation days. And then Greyson said that he might be tied up with taking another specialized course to get certified for who fucking knows what."

Not being able to help it, I smiled a little. As sad as it was to hear how cut up about this Gage was, he had a very unique way of ranting about things. He was a charming man who was constantly keeping me on my toes, no matter what we talked about.

Even during sex, I was always tuned in to what that mouth of his was doing.

"Too bad I can't call them to scold them," I teased.

"Would you?"

Rolling my eyes, I said, "No, Gage. They don't even know me."

"So?"

Poor thing. He sounded desperate. I honestly doubted that the boys would actually ditch him for the holidays. More likely than not, they were planning something and trying to throw Gage off their trail. From the stories that I'd heard about them from Gage, that's how they seemed to act.

I could be wrong, obviously, but then again I was more willing to believe that then I would about them being cruel and simply ditching their brother over a holiday meant to bring families together.

Gage had raised those boys better than that, and if the day came that they *weren't* showing up on my boyfriend's door with fucking bows on top of their heads claiming to be Gage's Christmas present, I really would call them up and rip them a new one.

My kid had an excuse to put some distance between us. Gage's did not.

"Baby."

He grunted at me in response.

"It'll work out. I'm going to come keep you company soon."

That seemed to perk him right up. "Oh yeah? What kind of company?"

Oh, that familiar husky tone sent shivers racing up my spine. I loved when he slipped into that.

Leaning back in my chair, the thing creaking under me as I did so, I quickly worked the button above my fly apart and slipped my hand under the waistband. My dick was already half hard, perking right up the moment Gage had called.

My body was so attuned to him that it could predict the man's phone calls. Like a damn satellite radar type shit. I probably needed to be way more concerned about that than I was, but honestly, I couldn't bring myself to care.

"The kind where I wrap my lips around that hard cock of yours," I said.

He groaned instantly. "Oh fuck."

I stroked my cock lazily while I pulled it out of my pants. The tip was already wet with precum, glistening slightly in the dim lighting of my office. Curling a hand over the already swollen knob, I smeared the slick fluid down along my shaft, working myself nice and good while Gage's breathing turned heavy on the other end of the phone.

"Fuck, baby," he said, his voice getting chopped up for a second while he was readjusting himself. "I want you so damn bad."

"Want to know what else I'm going to do to you once I get my hands on you?"

"Yes," he groaned again.

"I'm going to lick the tight little hole of yours until you're screaming at me to let you come. You'll be squirming and begging me while I tease you until you can't take it anymore."

His breathing became labored, the telltale sign of him already touching himself. "Mmmm."

"I'm going to fuck you with my tongue and make you come all over your stomach. Then I'm going to lick you clean until you're hard again." Squeezing my own cock was painful, my own dirty talk and imagining Gage under me was already getting me going.

Spreading my legs more, I gave myself room to reach down into my pants and cup my balls, already swollen and tight with my need to come. I couldn't just yet, not until I had Gage right where I wanted him.

"Baby…" He whimpered.

"My cock is going to fit perfectly in that tight hole of yours, isn't it?"

"Yes," came his quick reply. "Yes. It will."

"I'm going to fuck you so deep that you feel it in your belly. I'll fill you with so much cum that you'll explode once I pull out." My hand moved back up to my shaft, rubbing around the sensitive head again as it leaked more precum. "You'd like that, wouldn't you?"

His only response was to whimper again.

Perfect.

"Once I get you nice and full, I'm going to make you come. Just by telling you to. You'll behave and come for me, won't you, Gage?"

"Ohhh fuck. Yes, I will."

"I want to see it."

The other end of the phone dropped instantly, causing me to blink and pull it back from my ear in disbelief. Before I could even move my thumb over to hit the 'call back' button, a video call appeared on my screen.

Oh, that dirty dog.

Grinning, I answered it. "Show me."

He already had his camera flipped to his crotch where he had his hand gripped tightly around his cock. Fuck, I missed having that thing in my mouth. It was the perfect size and length to suck on. Teasing Gage with it was even more fun.

He'd accused me of having an oral fixation at one point, and honestly, he wasn't wrong.

"Look what you do to me," he growled.

His cock spurted out some precum, drawing a gasp out of him. The camera shook while he tried to keep it steady with the pleasure that was clearly overwhelming his system.

"Keep going, baby. Let me see." My gaze was glued to the screen, my mind no longer focused on getting myself off.

He pumped himself a few times, rolling his palm over his tip with each one and smearing whatever drooled out the tip with each stroke. He was naked on his bed, his legs spread out widely with his feet planted on the mattress while he touched himself.

I wished I was there in the room with him. I'd love to reach out and grab his thigh while he continued to touch himself. Or stroke his hair while watching him come.

My cock ached at the thought.

"Oh, I'm gonna come…" he moaned.

"Come for me, Gage."

His hand sped up, blurring in the camera. His hips bounced while he fucked up into his hand, coming completely undone with just my simple instructions.

"Oh fuck… oh fuck!" He gasped right before cum began spurting out of him like lava, spreading all over his hand and onto his belly. The camera shook along with him.

Setting my phone down for a second while he recovered, I tightened the hold on my own dick and began to move it again. With quick flicks of my wrist, the sounds of Gage's labored breathing sending me right over the edge, I came hard and fast in my own hand, doubling over as the pleasure raced up my spine.

"*Fuck*," I ground out.

"Mmm," Gage let out a slow breath. "Damn, that was good."

I grabbed my phone again just in time to see him lean up and snag a tissue off of the nightstand table next to his bed. While he cleaned himself up, I couldn't help the undying want in my heart that screamed I should be doing that.

I should be the one to clean up my lover after us getting down and dirty. Instead, I was across the damn country with my own rapidly deflating dick in my hand and no one to cuddle up next to and fall asleep with.

Where was the justice in that?

Going into this, I knew long distance wasn't going to be fun. I'd heard horror stories throughout the years of gay guys my own age trying to find love online and the trials and tribulations that went with it.

Did some of those love stories work out in the end?

Of course.

I wanted Gage and I to be a success story, too. But damn if this whole thing wasn't weighing on me.

Our trip out to him was going to be nice, but for the majority of it, I was going to be spending it with my son—rightfully so. Flying us out only for me to get wrapped up in my boyfriend was a ticket to Dexter *never* trusting me again with something that he clearly held so close to his heart.

Something that he'd trusted *me* with and not his mom. That shit mattered.

Regardless of what my own feelings were with

the situation between Gage and I, I wasn't going to fuck this up. For the sake of my son, I couldn't.

"Xavier?"

Snapping out of my thoughts, I righted my phone to see that Gage had flipped his camera around. He was so beautiful, even with him looking like his brains had just been fucked out.

"Yes?"

"You okay?" he asked. "You got kind of quiet."

"Just missing you."

He smiled sweetly. "Awww, he misses me."

"See what you do to *me?*"

"I kind of like that lovesick face you've got on," he teased.

"It's only for you."

"Wow, I'm special, huh."

You sure as fuck are.

"You really okay with me and Dex coming to stay with you?"

"Yes. Please. I need the company. I swear, I'll try and keep my hands to myself when your kid's around."

"I like that you said 'try' and not 'will do'."

"Hey, I'm just being honest!"

Shaking my head, I grabbed my own tissue and cleaned myself up before tossing it in the trash and pushing back from my desk. Today had been a long day, and not just from my conversation with Dexter or my AA meeting.

In general, I was exhausted. And why that was, I still wasn't really sure. At this point, I was chalking it up to getting old, or missing Gage—

both of which were most likely simultaneously true.

He was a beacon of light that I sought after in the darkness. He breathed life into me when I otherwise couldn't possibly go on. There were things that he'd done to me that he'd never know, ways he'd changed me and molded me into a better person that I'd never ever forget.

I was so glad that I didn't recognize the man in the mirror anymore. This version of me was different from my old one. A new shell having been born that I was excited to get to know.

"I love you," I sighed into the phone, flopping down onto my bed as soon as I reached it.

He laughed. "I love you, too, Xavier. You should probably get some sleep. Let me know about those flights and I'll rearrange my schedule."

"Will do."

CHAPTER 5

Xavier

Over the next few days, I'd gotten a solid plan together for traveling to Louisiana. With our housing secured for the weekend, all I needed to do now was somehow get in contact with Kate and get her to agree to let me take him for the weekend.

I had a feeling it was going to be an uphill battle with that one. Knowing my ex-wife, she was going to fight tooth and nail on keeping me from taking him anywhere, especially without her present.

So far, she'd been letting us see each other infrequently. I had a guess that she was only doing it because Dexter was turning eighteen soon and that meant he was going to come and seek me out regardless of her own personal thoughts on the matter.

But whatever her reasoning for her giving up a bit of control was, I wasn't going to question it. I'd take what I could get at this point.

Going the easy route and getting Dexter to talk to her for me *was* an option. However, getting him involved in my and his mom's personal affairs, or what we had left of them, left a sour taste in my mouth. He'd already been honest in telling me that our shit was too much for him to deal with.

Respecting that boundary he'd set up needed to happen for me to stay on his good side.

So, that left me with one other option.

I dialed her number and listened as it rang twice.

"Hello?"

Shit, why was I so nervous?

Speaking to my ex after all these years should not be causing my palms to sweat. We literally shared a kid together—there was no reason for me to feel like hanging up the phone and walking around the block to burn off my sudden excess energy.

"Kate, it's me."

There was a long, drawn out pause on the other end of the phone. One that had me pulling my cell back from my ear to check to make sure the call hadn't disconnected. The numbers were still ticking on by, though.

"Kate?" I said.

"How the hell did you get this number?"

Sighing, I said, "It was in the court documents. I figured you never changed it."

"What the hell could you possibly want, Xavier?"

All right, I really didn't appreciate the hostility. I got that I fucked up in the past and broke her heart, but goddamn. After fifteen years, you'd think she would've let sleeping dogs lie.

"I'm calling about Dex."

There was another drawn out pause that wasn't as significantly long as the last, but still enough that it made me antsy the longer it went on. "And?"

"I want to take him on a trip." Dancing around the subject was hard considering I still wasn't sure if Dexter had told her about him getting accepted into college.

He hadn't said anything to me since our dinner a few days ago, so I was going to act under the assumption that he hadn't. I had a feeling he was waiting to tell her before he toured the campus. There was no sense in getting her wound up if he wasn't even sure he wanted to go to Baton Rouge in the first place.

Kate's influence over Dex, while he probably hated to admit it, was a lot. She was still his mom, after all. No matter how many times he'd told me that her neuroticism had weighed on him over the years, her opinion still mattered.

In the end, Dexter was searching for her approval. That's just how it went with your parents.

"Where?" was all she asked.

"Louisiana."

"What the hell could possibly be in Louisiana that you'd want to take my son there?"

My jaw ached from how hard I clenched my teeth at that.

"*Our* son, Kate."

"Don't start with me."

Jesus, fuck. This is precisely the reason why I was hesitant in calling her. No matter how I approached any of this, she was going to come at me combatively. I could try prancing around and sprinkling fairy dust in her face while trying to ask for her permission and she'd still see the devil in me.

"I'm not starting shit, Kate. I'm being honest and trying to communicate with you. He's my son, too. I want to go on a trip with him before he's off to college and we hardly hear from him."

She scoffs. "You mean *you'll* hardly hear from him."

"I meant what I said. How often did either of us talk to our parents once we graduated high school?" The silence on the other end was all I needed to hear to know I hit the nail right on the head. "He's a teenager, he's going to want to go out and make friends and have fun. He's not going to have time to talk to either of us every day. Let me take him on a vacation for a weekend before he leaves me in the dust."

"I'm not comfortable with that."

"Why not?"

"Because I don't trust you. How do I know you're not going to take him to some… strip club? Or some gay bar and force him to drink?"

The paranoia in her voice was prominent. Normally, I'd be rolling my eyes and telling her to shove it. Realistically, I *did* want to do that. However, the true fear laced in her voice was what held me back from doing so.

Kate's religious upbringing had been a contentious point in our relationship up to a point. I'd let a lot of stuff go, especially with my in-laws, on account that I'd been hiding my true self from everyone and blending in had made it easier to deny myself.

She'd never been pushy with her beliefs back when we were dating and only had been a little more so after we'd had Dexter. There was never a point where I considered her to be a zealot, not in the way that her parents were, at least.

So, it was sad to see her—or rather, hear her—acting like this. What I did to her back then had clearly broken her. I'd never be able to make it up to her, no matter how many times I tried to apologize to her or explain how much it had killed me to hide my true self from the world.

What did it matter in the grand scheme of things, anyway?

She'd walked in on the most devastating situation that could ever be imagined. She'd gone from being in a happy relationship as a wife and mother, to being a divorcee and a single mom.

That shit was fucked on so many levels and my grappling with my newly outed sexuality hadn't helped any.

Now that Dexter was getting to be older, she was slowly losing her grip on him. He was coming to me more and more, no matter what she tried to do to stop it. All she could do was sit back and pray that I didn't 'corrupt' our son like I had been.

I felt bad for her, I really did. Living in her mind must be hell.

"Kate."

"I'm not letting you change him, Xavier." She sounded out of breath. "It's not happening."

"I'm not going to do any of that. First of all, he's still a minor. And second, it's not my prerogative to force him into a lifestyle like that. He's my son, Kate. I love him just as much as you do. I would never ever do anything to jeopardize his autonomy like that."

Her sniffling on the other line broke my heart. As badly as our relationship had ended, I still cared for her. She was still the mother of my child and had been my wife. She hated me but that was all one sided.

I was mad at her for keeping Dexter from me, sure. Anyone would feel the same way. That didn't mean I wanted her to suffer like she clearly was. Whatever conspiracies were running through her mind were obviously ones she'd thought about for a long time.

Fear was her best friend, unfortunately.

"Why don't you think about it," I suggested. "I'm not planning on this trip for another week or two, anyway."

She didn't say anything back, just continued to sniffle on the other end. Just as I was about to end the call, she said, "I'll talk to Dan."

All right, well at least that was one step in the right direction. "Okay. Just let me know. I'm planning the trip from Friday to Sunday. We'd fly back Sunday night."

"Do you have a flight already picked out?"

"Kind of. I have some that are available but I wanted to ask you first before I made anything solid."

"Oh," came her quiet response.

That was how it always went for us back in the day. I made the plans but she was the one with the final say. We worked that way, it gave her a sense of control that her upbringing never had. I'd recognized that early on—seen it in the way her parents treated her when we'd gone over for Sunday dinners.

It always made her happy in the end and was never any skin off my nose. Mostly because she usually agreed with me. Despite our differences, we, at one point, had made a pretty good team.

"All right. I'll let you know," she finally said.

"Thanks. You know how to reach me."

Ending the call, I let out a long sigh before running my hands over my face. I knew going into this it was going to be a monumental task, I just never accounted for how much it would take out of me in the end.

It would be worth it, though.

Dexter was worth it.

So long as Kate agreed to letting me have him for the weekend, we'd finally get that father-son bonding time that I'd been desperate for over the past fifteen years.

Hopefully, luck was on my side this time around.

CHAPTER 6

"You really think she's not going to let you take him?"

"I'm not sure." Xavier sounded exhausted on the other end of the line. "I'm hoping she does. That's all I can really do since she has full custody."

"I thought that shit didn't really matter once they turned sixteen? Can't they choose who to live with?"

Wasn't that how it worked?

Maybe I was being a dumbass in guessing. It wasn't like I ever had any experience with the system aside from CPS coming around that one time after my parents died.

"It's complicated. Dexter doesn't really know me so I don't exactly have a case."

Damn.

"He seems to be warming up to you, though."

"Barely," he mumbled. "But it's better than nothing."

"True."

I felt bad for Xavier. He was clearly trying. To no fault of his own, his son was being rather difficult. To a certain extent, I could understand the situation from both ends. Xavier had always wanted to be a father to Dexter but with his drinking, he'd made that pretty hard on the kid. So it wasn't exactly out of the blue that his kid was giving him the cold shoulder.

The past few months hadn't been as bad with Dexter agreeing to the occasional sit down dinner with Xavier. The sad thing was that it was nowhere near the level of closeness he wanted to have with his son.

On my end, I always felt guilty whenever Greyson and Asher were brought up in conversation. My brothers were close with me, even if sometimes they were little shits about it. When push came to shove, we were a family unit and nothing could break us apart. I'd been a whiny bastard with them leaving, but only out of sheer love for them.

Which is what made me hesitate in bringing anything up to Xavier about them. I didn't want to rub it in my boyfriend's face that I had a relationship with the kids I'd raised while he didn't. Sure, his drinking and his highly erratic job hadn't done him any favors in that department—that didn't mean he had given up because he'd found his relationship with his son to be too hard to deal with.

"I told her to think about it," Xavier said. "So, now I just need to wait for her decision."

I wrinkled my nose at that.

From the stories I'd heard of Kate, I didn't like her. Sure, she'd been blindsided by Xavier's affair and had every right to divorce him and hate him for it. Taking it out on him using Dexter, though, was too low of a blow for me to forgive.

Why involve your child like that?

Why deprive him of a father, just because you didn't approve that he was gay?

That was the part that never made any sense to me, no matter what Xavier did to try and defend her actions. Or rather, seek some understanding with them.

I could get behind her not knowing how to navigate a co-parenting relationship with her ex after splitting with him, or even navigating the unknown about her ex being secretly gay and having to still be attached to him because of your shared kid. But the second she'd completely cut Xavier out of the equation and refused to work with him on visitation, that's where all sympathy for her was lost for me.

Trusting a woman like that who could so easily turn your child against you made a pit form in my stomach. If I were to ever run into her and meet her face to face… I really don't know what I'd do.

I'd be lucky not to spit some nasty shit at her.

"Well, I hope it works out."

"Gage."

Wincing, I realized that my tone had turned rather flippant. Sure, I was being kind of a bitch about the whole situation but fucking sue me. I missed my boyfriend. I wanted him here with me, even if it was only for a weekend and even if I had to keep my hands to myself until his son went to bed.

Having some ex-wife get in the way of all of that was making me fucking cranky.

"Sorry."

He chuckled softly. "I'm eager to see you, too. Don't worry."

"Okay, then hurry up and make her decide…"

"Oh, stop." I could hear the smile in his voice. "If this doesn't work out, that just means you need to come visit me."

"Hey, I can get behind that."

He laughed again. "Then it's settled. Either way, we'll be seeing each other soon."

I wanted to be happy about that… I really did.

These every few months of visiting were slowly starting to become not enough. Don't get me wrong, I loved every second I got to spend with Xavier, there was no doubt about that.

The problem laid in this: I wanted *more*. I was a greedy asshole who was getting tired of only receiving crumbs. When I'd agreed to a long distance relationship, I'd known that it was going to be difficult.

Everyone knew that, even if you weren't in one yourself. Out of hubris, I supposed I never considered how badly I'd be without Xavier. I had lived before him, so I figured I would be *fine* after him.

Clearly, I was dead fucking wrong.

"If the boys ever pity me and come back, I'll drag them along." Though, knowing them, they'd be questioning me the entire time while planning an elaborate prank.

Such is the way of two nineteen year olds.

"Maybe we can get them together with Dex."

"He needs new friends?" I teased.

"He needs friends in general."

Poor kid.

"As long as he can handle psychological warfare, then have at it."

"Think he's gotten enough of that growing up in the church, babe."

"True…" Though hopefully, it wasn't as bad as Xavier was predicting.

Apparently, Dexter had told him bits and pieces about getting dragged to church and put through intense religious indoctrination his entire life. And while I absolutely believed him, I hoped it also had no lasting effects.

Fuck knew that kid had been through enough already.

"I'm excited to see you," Xavier said, breaking me out of my thoughts.

I smiled and pressed the phone tighter to my ear. "I miss you. I hope we can see each other soon. I'm slowly dying over here."

"For my cock?"

Oh, that cheeky bastard. "More for that tongue of yours."

"Shit," he whispered.

"You at work?" I was already reaching for my crotch. My dick was already beginning to stiffen.

"Yes, so don't you dare start anything."

"Hey, I can't promise that I *won't* be sending you a dick pic after we end this phone call."

He swore again under his breath. "Gage. Behave."

"I'd love for you to make me."

"Oh, I will. The next time I get my hands on you."

Fuck, I loved the sound of that. "You got yourself a deal, Cruz."

CHAPTER 7

Gage

Apparently, planning a Christmas party with a fire station full of rowdy adults was like trying to wrangle a bunch of goldfish into a net at the county fair—nearly fucking impossible.

As funny as it was to watch poor Ellie running around while trying to make sure everyone was signed up for at least *one* duty for the party, I also kind of felt bad for her. As our resident mother hen, she was probably the only one keeping us all from showing up with five raw turkeys, two side dishes and a hodge-podge of weirdly cut paper snowflakes tossed around.

"Wait, so who's in charge of the decorations now?" Jase rested his hands on his hips while he squinted at the bulletin board that was freshly tacked with the new list. "It can't just be me.

There's no way I'm putting all that shit up by myself."

With Quinn snickering behind him and catching a stray slug to the arm, Jase turned to look over his shoulder at our party planner extraordinaire with his brow raised high.

"You've got Mark helping you out, too." Ellie had her usual clipboard in her hand, a pen tucked behind her ear to hold back a few stray pieces of hair while another one was in her hand ticking off something on the sheet in front of her. "I can throw Cyrus in there if you really need the extra manpower."

"Woah, woah." Hawke slapped his thighs while hiking himself up to his feet from where he'd been lounging against the steel bumper of one of the fire trucks. "We got dibs on the Scot. McWhiney over there can have someone else."

"You've got plenty of people on set up duty, dude," Jase argued.

"Dibs," Hawke repeated, a sly grin forming on his face.

Oh, if only Xavier were here to see all of this go down.

He'd be doubled over by now, laughing his ass off while ribbing me for having coworkers that loved to argue over a damn Christmas party. Having him here among the chaos would've been a nice change of pace, even if he'd have no fucking clue what was going on half the time.

I'd had plenty of good times with his coworkers off in Cali when I'd gone over for aerial training. Too bad he wouldn't get the same opportunity with mine.

"Station Twenty-One," a voice over the intercom sounded off. *"Engine fifty-seven, respond to a multiple motor vehicle accident on Fifteen and Broad."*

"Let's move!" Captain Clarke's voice boomed. "On-call, gear up! Standby, keep your walkies live!"

As I lifted myself up from where I'd settled down on the floor, the entire fire station came alive all in a flurry of calculated motion. Hustling over to my section to start passing out gear to the ones on duty today, my mind slipped into a straight-lined sense of focus, my hands busying themselves with unstrapping items from the wall in order to pass off to people.

This part of the job, while seemingly inconsequential, was one of the most important that a station had. Getting it wrong—such as gearing up a fellow coworker incorrectly—could be the difference between life and death in a dangerous situation.

Here, we took that shit seriously, no matter how much of a pain prep was at the ass crack of dawn.

Zander was the first one over to me after getting his coveralls on, Cyrus following close behind to the section next to me where Carmen was at. I tossed him a helmet, waiting for him to slip it on over his head and adjust it before handing off the rest of his gear and getting him suited up for the ride over.

He saluted me and jogged over to the fire truck, hopping up onto one of the metal rungs along with the rest of our on-call crew once they were geared up as well. The truck's engine rumbled to life, breathing a sense of excitement back into the otherwise quiet firehouse from just moments ago.

While this job had led to a lot of heartbreak in past times, the adrenaline rush was unmatched.

Things around here could change in an instant. From us arguing about party details, to moving into action, to potentially saving someone's life, all with the quick flip of a switch and our Captain at the helm of our well-oiled machine.

Our crew here were among the best and brightest in our entire state, and every damn time they were out in the field saving the people of our city, they made me fucking proud to be among them.

How could I not be when we were all a tight-knit family that kept each other safe in the face of danger?

Once the doors were lifted from the inside, the truck was navigated carefully out onto the street and soon disappeared, roaring off to whatever was waiting for them out there.

"Nice work, team," Captain Clarke said, the energy around us calming instantly as the garage was slowly pulled back down. "I'll keep an ear on the radio in case they call for backup."

The skeleton crew left behind all murmured our agreements before slowly dispersing back to our usual duties. With dispatch only calling for a single truck, that meant that whatever wreck our station was walking into was more than likely a minor fender-bender.

Per Louisiana law, though, we were required to

be on scene on the off chance that something happened like a gas tank explosion or someone needing the Jaws of Life to get out of their totaled vehicle.

Other than that, hopefully it was going to be an easy day today.

"You still good for the potluck, Gage?" Ellie asked, making her way over to me.

"As long as you're good with me not cooking." The last thing anyone wanted me around was an oven. Or worse, a stove.

She squinted. With no clipboard in hand for her to tap her pen against, she resorted to using her hand for her nervous habit. "As long as it's still from that scratch kitchen you were talking about."

"Yup."

She breathed out a sigh of relief. "Okay, cool. Since you're all set, all I need to worry about is sorting out the knock-down crew."

"Let them fight over it," I suggested. "They'll figure it out."

She smiled in amusement. "I think you have too much faith in them if you believe they'll be able to bicker and come to an agreement."

"Hey, we need to let the kids figure it out for themselves once in a while."

That had her laughing which warmed my heart. I hated seeing Ellie stressed, even if it was for something minor like a Christmas party.

"All right, true. Hey, you know, if you wanted to invite your man to come around for the get together, I'm sure everyone would be good with it."

"Wait, really?" Now, that was a little surprising. "You know he's in a different state, right?" I arched a brow at her.

Not to mention none of my coworkers had ever met the man before. It wasn't like we were going out to the bar and Xavier was tagging along. This would be an intimate get together with all of our families present.

Was that really the kind of thing that I could take a 'date' to?

Every year we did something for the holidays and every year, I went stag. It wasn't ever something that I'd cared about, mostly since for the past few years I'd had at least *someone* single to hang out with who wouldn't be tangled up in the romantic festivities.

Apparently, I'd missed the memo, though, because this year, I'd be the only one left without a date. Besides, Ellie that is. She'd be running around making sure everyone was staying on their best behavior.

Ellie frowned. "You guys aren't going to see each other for Christmas? I know you're long distance, but that kind of sucks, if that's the case. He doesn't want to fly out or anything?"

Holding back from making a face was rather difficult.

We'd actually never had the discussion as of yet. Probably because I'd been avoiding the subject altogether ever since Xavier had brought up coming to see me with Dexter for his college tour soon.

Having him stay with me was already feeling like a 'too good to be true' scenario after our months long dry spell and jeopardizing that by getting down on my hands and knees and begging him to come to a Christmas party with me felt like asking too much of him.

Just because we'd been dating for almost an entire year didn't exactly give me the green light in having him fork over precious time he could be spending with his son before graduation hit. They'd only just started working out their issues with each other.

Guilting Xavier into spending time with me over the holidays because I was missing having my own family around felt kind of… well, wrong.

"Yeah… I'm not too sure about that," I said.

Ellie's frown deepened. "Tell me the boys are at least coming home?"

Ugh, another sore subject.

With still no word from either of them on what their plans were, I was left in total limbo. Hounding them for an answer was only going to make them dig their feet in—something I absolutely did *not* want to encourage.

I felt like we were already at a delicate state in our relationship, and given the fact that I was trying to tread lightly on the whole older brother/guardian thing while giving them the freedom in doing what they wanted now that they were fully grown adults, I already teetered on the 'overbearing' edge of the scale.

There were too many factors that could happen in me pushing them further away from me, even if unintentional. No matter what Xavier said, the multiple times he'd reassured me otherwise and that all of this was me simply getting caught up in my head and causing me to over think my brothers pulling away from me. My gut was telling me—or rather screaming at me—otherwise.

Trusting my instincts on this one was the best thing I could do. I had to be okay with the fact that they'd come back to me eventually, as all good things did once you set them free. A little bit of hands-off parenting wouldn't chase them away, no matter how crazy I felt inside of my own head over it.

At least, I hoped that was the damn case. I was kind of running around blind here.

How the hell did normal parents deal with this kind of shit on a daily basis?

Did it get easier with multiple kids?

It had to, right?

That's why people usually had a whole gaggle of them. By the time you got down to the fourth or fifth one, you were a pro at saying goodbye and the feeling of your heart absolutely being ripped out of your chest.

I felt a hand pat me on the shoulder, bringing me out of my thoughts. "You're doing that thing again."

"Shit, sorry, Ellie. The boys kind of have me wound up recently."

She smiled sympathetically. "My boyfriend has a kid who just turned sixteen and is in that wonderful rebellious phase. He says it gets easier."

"Wait, you've got a new man? Since when?" What the hell have *I* been missing?

She laughed. "It's a relatively recent thing, so

relax. I'm planning on bringing him to the party. He'll need another newbie to bond with, so get your guy to come keep him company."

Sighing, I said, "I'll think about it."

Think being the keyword there.

She nudged an elbow into my ribs gently. "I really hope you do. Every time I see you on your phone, you light up. It'd be nice to finally meet the person keeping our Gage happy."

Damn.

Well, wasn't that the sweetest thing I'd ever heard.

"Thanks, Ellie."

She winked at me before sauntering off to find her next victim, most likely in the form of Hawke, who'd she would hoodwink into letting her take Cyrus away and shoving him over into decorating for the party because of Jase's bitching.

Turning back to the bulletin board where all of our names were up on the duty sheet, I got lost in thinking. Maybe I really should try to invite Xavier to the Christmas party.

He'd probably say no and that was okay. Extending the offer was the least I could do, though. I would hate for him to find out after I let it slip that I had the opportunity to invite him and just didn't. If the situation were reversed, I'd feel hurt, too.

Besides, the worst he could tell me in the end was that he was planning on spending Christmas back home with Dexter.

Pulling my phone out of my vest and flipping it over, I noticed a text message already waiting for me. I'd missed the sound of the notification going off in the midst of the chaos in sending off my coworkers.

Opening it up, I saw Xavier's name at the top and his message directly underneath.

>>*Call me.*

CHAPTER 8

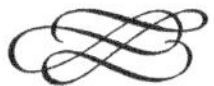

Xavier

The last thing I expected to wake up to that morning was a text from Kate's number telling me to call her with no other context given

While normally at that point I would've been pinching myself to make sure I wasn't in some sort of horrible nightmare where my ex was threatening to take my kid away from me again, my blaring alarm had those thoughts straightening right out and bringing me back down into reality.

Pulling myself out of bed while clutching my phone tight in my hand, I made my way into the kitchen to brew myself a cup of coffee that I'd most definitely need before I had any conversation with Kate.

While her text to me was simple in terms of her request, it also left my mind wandering far too much for my liking.

Obviously, the only reason she'd be contacting me was to discuss my upcoming trip with Dexter. And of course, judging by her text, I had absolutely no idea which way she was swaying toward.

The fact that she was even trying to contact me at all spoke to what little progress we'd made from the last time we'd talked. Sure, it wasn't much, but it was better than what we had before, which was complete stonewalling.

I'd take the stunted communication over that *any* day.

With my coffee finally brewed and a few sips down the hatch, I set my phone down on the counter after putting it on speaker and let the warmth from my mug seep into my hands to keep me steady.

Talking with Kate always set me on edge, no matter what the situation was. I wanted to lie to myself and pretend that I had no lasting effects from our divorce still lingering within me after running myself ragged going through therapy. However, the pounding of my heart told me otherwise.

Thankfully, she didn't keep me waiting too long, answering on the third ring. "Hey."

"Morning," I said, hoping my pleasant tone was at least a little bit of a buffer for the inevitable awkwardness that was about to happen.

She didn't waste time on any of the pleasantries, cutting right to the chase. "I need to lay out some ground rules for this trip."

My heart fluttered in my chest. Jesus, she was actually going to let me take him. No trying to stonewall me into changing my mind or negotiating me down into keeping him here for a local trip. I was *actually* going to get to spend an entire weekend with my son and share an important experience with him—just the two of us.

I didn't know whether to thank Dan for talking some sense into her, or for Kate finally wanting to bury the hatchet for the time being. Either way, I was eternally grateful.

Clearing my throat, I said. "All right. Go ahead."

"He needs to call me every night before bed. I don't want any excuses that you guys got too busy and didn't have time. He's my son, too, Xavier. I want to hear from him. I see and talk to him every single day and this trip isn't going to keep me from that routine."

I could work with that. "Done."

She let out a soft sigh. "I also want updates on what you guys are doing. I… I may have went a little overboard in accusing you of wanting to take him to gay bars and stuff the last time we talked. I know… I know you wouldn't do anything to hurt him. I just—"

My mouth dropped open in disbelief while I stared down at my phone and her number lit up on the screen still.

Not only was that sounding a lot like an apology, but the fact that Kate was *recognizing* she'd fucked up in accusing me of doing something so heinous to our son was the exact last thing I ever expected to hear out of her mouth.

Maybe deep down, Kate really did want to trust me.

Her years of being resentful toward me made

that nearly impossible—a situation of my own making, unfortunately—and while I never blamed her for hating me, I wished things could've been different.

If I was less of a coward in being honest with myself and those around me, if she and her family were less bigoted… So many possibilities of our futures having turned out differently could've happened.

Perhaps with this trip, I could show her that I wasn't out to get her or take our son away like she was so fearful of. All I wanted was to have some kind of relationship with him, much like she had this past decade without me in the picture.

I'd meant what I said when I'd told her about Dexter eventually spreading his wings and flying from the nest, leaving us far behind in his wake. The nature of kids was that was what eventually happened and as parents, we were supposed to come to terms with that on our own time.

Wanting to form some kind of bond with Dexter while he was still around was only natural. Especially, with him getting up there in age. He'd soon be moving from needing protective parents to needing us as guides while he began his own journey through life.

"How about I have him keep you updated every few hours," I suggested. "Sound fair?"

She was quiet for a while, eventually letting out another sigh. "Yes. That's fine."

"All right." This was all going so well that I had half a mind to ask her if I was being pranked. "Anything else?"

"Just… keep him safe. Please."

My heart softened at that. Deep down, Kate was just being a mom. Albeit, an overprotective one. But a mom, nonetheless. In her shoes, I'd be the same way. "Of course I will."

"Thank you." Her voice was quiet as she spoke.

"I'll book us plane tickets and send the itinerary over to you once I've got it all sorted out."

"Okay. I'll be checking my email for it. And… Xavier?"

"Yes?"

"I hope you both have fun."

Smiling, I said, "Thanks, Kate. I hope so, too."

CHAPTER 9

THE FOLLOWING week came and went in the blink of an eye and soon, our trip out to Baton Rouge was upon us.

Since telling Gage the good news right after my call with Kate, he'd been blowing up my phone with all of the local hot spots and attractions to take Dexter to after our tour of the campus. I found it all incredibly endearing how supportive he was about all of this, considering we probably wouldn't be seeing much of each other during most of the day.

I supposed it worked out in the end, considering the trip was a little on the short notice side of things and I hadn't given him enough of a head's up for him to be taking off time from the station. Still, he'd at least be home at a decent hour after work, which would give us plenty of down time to spend with each other after Dexter went to bed.

As much as I hated having to sneak behind my kid's back in order to spend time with my boyfriend, I'd take what I could get.

Waking Dexter up once we landed and were all clear to de-board, I grabbed our things from the carry-on overhead and ushered him down the aisle, sticking close to him as we left the plane.

"You sleep okay?" I asked.

His answering yawn was all the information I needed to know.

Chuckling, I led us down the loading bridge, dragging my suitcase behind me while keeping his duffle slung over my shoulder.

I was glad he'd slept on the plane. Getting to the airport bright and early this morning, while not exactly a struggle, had definitely been quite the trek for my kid. According to Kate, who'd been waiting outside with him when I'd pulled up, she'd caught him up in the middle of the night on his laptop, knee deep in some research that she hadn't been able to weasel out of him.

Fortunately, once we were safely tucked in my car and on the way to the airport, Dexter had shoved a hastily written itinerary at me with all of the sights he'd wanted to see while we were in Baton Rouge after our campus tour.

I'd gone over it on the plane, noting that most of them were ones that Gage had suggested, too. It made me happy that Dexter was looking forward to spending time with me, even if he didn't exactly know how to say it out loud.

These small moments that he was giving me

were showing me that I wasn't the only one wanting to fix this. It was my job to, there was no question about that. Dexter meeting me halfway was nice, though.

Getting through the rest of the airport was easy enough. Since we didn't have any bags to check before leaving on our flight, we breezed through the rest of the terminals and made our way toward the main entrance.

"So…" Dexter said as we stepped onto the escalator that led down to the main part of the airport's lobby. "Your friend from training is picking us up… right?"

Turning to look at my son where he stood two steps above me, I nodded. "Yeah. I haven't gotten a chance to check my phone to let him know we're here. But he said he didn't live too far from here."

"Yeah… I don't know that you're going to need to do that."

Instantly, my brows were furrowing. "Why do you say that?"

If Dexter wasn't comfortable riding in a car with Gage back to his place, then we'd figure something else out. I fucking loathed rideshares with a burning passion, but if it made my kid more comfortable, then whatever.

Looking at him, though, he didn't *seem* put off by the idea. In fact, he was wearing a rather bemused expression, his gaze focused away from me as he looked over my head at something.

"I think he's already here."

Whipping around, my gaze darted to the couple in front of us, and then past them to where the main lobby had travelers coming and going. In the midst of the flurry of people, a lone man stood in the middle with a crudely decorated sign that was being held up, the words, '*Welcome to Baton Rouge!*' in scrolling font.

As soon as he spotted us—or rather *me*—he lifted the sign high above his head and waved it at us, that familiar, blinding grin practically splitting his face in half.

Oh, Gage.

"He always that peppy?" Dexter asked.

Snorting, I nudged my elbow backward into his side. Yep."

I paused at the bottom of the escalator while Dexter stepped off right behind me. He kept himself close to me as we made our way through the bustling crowds and over to where Gage stood.

He lowered his sign just in time to avoid a couple cutting between us, narrowly catching him in the shoulder and checking him backward. As weird as it was to be back in Baton Rouge after so many months of being gone, it was nice to know that the people out here were just as oblivious as they were back in Cali.

"Hey." Gage's arms came up from his sides, the knee-jerk reaction to reach out and hug me short circuiting at the last moment when his gaze darted to the side, catching sight of Dexter coming up next to me. He shifted fluidly into shoving his arm in my son's direction, holding out his hand. "Nice to meet you, Dexter. Your dad's told me a lot about you."

Politely, my son took Gage's hand and shook it, throwing me an eyebrow raise while saying, "Really?"

"Yup." Gage flashed him another blinding smile. "All good things. Don't worry."

Dexter dropped his hand back to his side, narrowing his eyes curiously while his gaze flitted between us.

Fuck, I hoped we weren't being obvious with all of this. The last thing I needed Dexter to pick up on was our god awful budding sexual tension that literally never seemed to go away no matter what we did.

Thankfully, Gage was always the master of distraction and cleared his throat to ask, "Flight go okay?"

"Yeah. No turbulence." Readjusting Dexter's bag on my shoulder, I nodded toward the entrance of the airport. "How is it out there?"

Gage laughed. "Oh, you're going to hate it."

Damn it…

"Why?" Dexter asked. "We're used to the heat in the winter time."

"Humidity's a bitch here, kid," I said, nudging him. "We're in swamp territory."

"Hey! It's not as bad as the summer," Gage argued. "It's only seventy percent right now."

Dexter's mouth dropped open while I let out a soft curse under my breath. See, this was the thing about coming down to the south. While the heat wasn't bad, it was the humidity that made it feel like you were walking through a damn sauna.

I could deal with hundred-degree heat and no humidity. But put me in the mid-seventies with a humidity of eighty percent? I was fucking done for.

"Ew…" Dexter muttered.

"See? I'm not the only one," I said.

Gage folded up his sign and waved it at both of us. "Come on, you two complainers. I've got the AC running in the car. Valet's holding it for me right outside."

Now, that's what I was talking about.

I fought the urge to reach over and slap Gage's ass when he turned and walked in front of us. All right, maybe this whole 'keeping our hands to ourselves' thing was going to be a lot harder than I imagined.

CHAPTER 10

"Make yourselves at home. Whatever you need, let me know," I said, swinging the door closed behind me.

My house wasn't large by any means—comfy enough to house three people and not feel like we were all on top of each other. I'd already made the bed up in Asher's room, leaving the one next to mine, Greyson's, empty. Lord knew if we'd need it once Dexter went to bed and Xavier finally got his hands on me.

He probably thought he was being slick with those subtle looks of his that he'd been throwing my way in the car whenever I glanced over at him at a red light. Or the way his hand twitched on his thigh while he was fighting the urge to grab onto mine whenever I switched the gearshift.

Xavier was funny that way—always trying to

hold himself back on account of trying to maintain that carefully crafted facade of calm he favored around other people. The most ironic part about all of that—or was it the most beautiful?—was how completely undone he became when we got together.

The way his jaw would go slack just as he was about to come, or how tense his body got while driving himself into me, getting those long strokes inside of me as deep as possible. God, everything about us having sex drove me fucking wild and had my toes curling inside of my shoes.

"Earth to Gage." Hearing my name being called broke me out of my dirty thoughts instantly.

Putting on a pleasant smile, I waved my hand toward the living room and showed my guests inside. "Here is the rest of the house. Bedrooms are down on the left with fresh sheets tucked nice and neat. Kitchen's on the right and the fridge *is* freshly stocked. Bathroom is across from the master and has new towels on the sink up for grabs."

Xavier's lip twitched. "You didn't need to do all of that, you know."

Winking, I said, "Let me pamper, okay? This house is in need of guests."

While Xavier breathed out a laugh, Dexter's gaze wandered around the living room. I hoped he'd find himself comfortable here. Seeing as I was kind of dating his dad pretty seriously, and hoped to for a long time, this little trial visit was a bit make or break.

"You like video games?" I offered, nodding for

him to follow me into the living room where I had the entertainment set up.

He was hesitant to follow, but did so after a nod from his dad who soon disappeared down the hall with their bags.

"Uh… yeah. Kind of."

Grinning, I pulled open the door to all of Asher and Greyson's consoles to show him. "My brothers are closet nerds. While they're away, feel free to use whatever. It's all already hooked up to the Smart system."

He blinked in surprise. "Where are your brothers?"

That had me blowing out a breath, more out of frustration than anything. "They're west and east of here, ignoring me. One's in Texas, the other's over in Georgia."

"Oh," was all Dexter said to that.

Quiet kid.

I remembered how Xavier had said he was worried about his kid's social life not too long ago. Maybe sometime in the future, if all went well this weekend and I didn't scare Dexter off completely, he'd warm up to meeting the boys.

Now *that* would be the true testament to how much chaos Dexter could handle.

"You off from school for long?" I asked, swinging the entertainment unit door shut. "I haven't kept up with school schedules in a while since my brothers graduated."

"I've got winter break coming up. I already finished my end of semester tests so my mom let me come on this trip with my dad."

I wondered how true that really was. Not that I

doubted Dexter's sincerity or anything, I just didn't foresee Xavier's ex-wife being so… charitable with letting her son go away with his dad for an entire weekend. I'm obviously biased here, sue me. The stories from Xavier about her, though, still got my blood boiling.

"Well, hopefully you like LSU," I said, plastering on a smile again. "The campus is really nice. I pass it on the way to work every day."

"My dad said you're a firefighter."

"Guilty."

"So… that's how you two met, right?"

For some reason, the way he was asking almost sounded like he was fishing for something. Fuck me, I should've gotten the full story from Xavier on what he'd told his kid regarding us. All I knew was that he was playing our relationship on the down low to keep Dexter from getting uncomfortable.

Which… sucked.

At the same time, it wasn't like either Xavier or I could help that he was raised in a strictly religious household and had no idea what kind of beliefs he had. He knew his dad was out and gay, so at least we weren't going to be running into any problems regarding *that* topic.

Me on the other hand?

I had no idea what the hell I was supposed to be playing this as.

Friend?

Former coworker?

All of them sounded like nails on a chalkboard to me.

Sometimes even *boyfriend* did that, too, but what else was I supposed to call Xavier?

Lover sounded like too much and partner made it confusing when half of us at the station referred to each other that way when working.

"Actually, I went to California to train under him for an aerial program and brought back a lot of what I learned to my station," I said, rubbing my hands together a few times. "I can practically fly fighter jets now." I let out a chuckle and flashed him a grin.

To my utter surprise, Dexter let out a small snort.

All right, progress.

"We doing okay out here?" Xavier poked his head around the corner, both of his brows pulled together in that nervous way of his.

Just as I was about to give him the big old thumbs up, the sound of my radio flagging from where I had it on the charging dock by the door filtered around the room.

Of all fucking times...

"Damn," I mumbled. "Well, duty calls."

"Be safe." Xavier flashed me a smile, his hand flexing into a fist at his side, clearly fighting himself from grabbing at me like he would've any other time.

In response, I clenched my teeth together. Man, I wanted to close the distance between us and peck him on the way out—and judging by his pinched expression, he wanted that, too.

Behave. It's only for a few more hours.

"Have fun today!" I said, and jogged to my bedroom to grab my uniform before heading out.

Never in my life had I ever prayed for some crazy situation to be thrust into when I got to the station, not wanting the bad luck and karma to follow me to my next life.

Today was my exception. Because damn right I was going need all of the distractions in the world that I could possibly get to keep me from jumping Xavier's bones the second I laid my eyes on him again.

That man was temptation on two legs and I was the stupid moth entranced by his flame.

CHAPTER 11

Xavier

"Your friend seems…"

Inwardly, I winced, waiting for Dexter to finish his sentence and tell me he absolutely hated Gage. That would be my luck, honestly, after finally finding a boyfriend I clicked with so damn well that I could've sworn the man was my soul mate.

In an ironic sense, I deserved something like that coming my way for absolutely fucking up Dexter's life with my alcoholism and breaking his mother's heart, among the thousand other things I'd done to hurt others in my past. Those were just my two biggest transgressions at the moment.

I was sure if I thought about it longer than a few seconds, I'd find more I needed to *repent for,* or whatever it was that Kate's parents had spat out at me after finding out I was gay.

"Actually. He kind of surprised me," Dexter finally said.

I glanced over at him as we walked down the street, heading toward a cafe from his itinerary that he was interested in visiting. Apparently, it was one of those fancy cat cafes that allowed you rent a table while cats came and went during your stay.

Funny, I'd never considered my son to be a cat person—seeing as how his mother was deathly allergic—but the more I was getting to know him, the clearer I was beginning to see it. There was so much to Dexter that I just *didn't know* and my desperate need to figure him out was blinding.

"Really?" I asked. "What makes you say that?"

He shrugged at me, shoving both of his hands into his pockets. "I don't know. He's really nice. And accommodating."

"What, you don't think I can be friends with nice people?"

He rolled his eyes at me. Such a teenager. "That's not what I meant."

"Tell me, then." *Because I'm seriously dying to know.*

He shrugged again. "I don't know. I guess… I kind of pictured you being friends with a bunch of meatheads."

Huffing out a laugh, I grabbed onto the door to the cafe when we approached it and nodded for him to duck under my arm and head inside. "The only true meathead I know is currently engaged to an ex-felon."

And what a fucking phone call *that* was to

receive on a Friday night after coming back from one of my AA meetings.

Did I expect anything less from Jackson fucking Hall to have fallen in love with someone with a rap sheet?

Not exactly. Getting it out of him on *how* he met this man was actually the more wild part of the story that I still couldn't exactly wrap my head around.

But whatever.

Love was love, right?

"What?" Dexter gave me a bewildered look.

I shook my head, grabbing him lightly by the shoulder in order to steer him toward the register. "It's a long story. Point is, I've got friends in all sorts of varieties."

"I see that," he mumbled at me.

After paying for drinks and two small pastries, we grabbed a small floor table and settled down comfortably.

The cafe turned out to be really nice and clean considering they had about thirty cats roaming around. Some sat on perches nailed to the walls above our heads, some wandered the floor looking for handouts, and some, like the two that were currently occupying *our* table, were just plain old cuddle bugs looking for attention.

I sipped my coffee silently while watching Dexter's rare smile grace his face, one of his hands buried in the long fur of a pretty white cat and his other stroking over the head of an orange tabby that had completely commandeered his lap the moment we sat down.

Seeing my son happy was a nice change of

pace from our usual standoffs. I liked seeing this side of him, even if it was only for the small window he'd let me in today.

"Too bad we can't take one home," he said after a while.

"I know. You could always come back here and adopt one if you decide to go to LSU."

His mouth thinned into a straight line. "Yeah… maybe."

"You thinking about going somewhere else?"

Dexter sighed. "I don't know. Mom's going to kill me either way, so…"

Setting down my mug slowly gave me the time to reel back my sudden shock of anger and the snap back reaction I would normally have come up with. The protectiveness I felt for him regarding his mother was always going to be there, no matter what I did or how much time passed. My therapist had been pretty straightforward in telling me that it was a trauma response from Dexter being ripped away from me as he had been and my having no say in the matter afterward.

Here was the thing, though—I didn't *want* to still hold onto this resentment. It ate away at me little by little each time it flared up. Just like my PTSD did from my military days. Letting it go was my goal, and damn was it hard to do anytime something like this reared its ugly head.

Whatever Kate's reasons are, they make sense to her.

Even if sometimes I felt like she was being way too fucking paranoid.

"Why do you say that, Dex?"

"Because she's expecting me to go to the local community college. Apparently, Dan's got some in with the Dean or whatever and they can get me in without having me take an admissions test.”

Not to turn my nose up at a community college or anything but that seemed like a rather strange solution, seeing as how Dexter was clearly smart enough—and had the grades—to get into a state school. On top of that, it was a school not even in our home state.

That said a lot about his academic prowess.

“Hm.” Drumming my fingers on the table, I focused my attention on the cat in his lap who was happily licking at his hand. “You tell her about applying elsewhere?”

He shook his head. “Like I said, she’d freak out. She doesn’t even want me staying in a dorm.”

“*Why?*”

Dexter glanced up at me, his lips parting to say something just as one of the bus boys was coming around with a small bucket tucked under his arm to collect the stray dishes left by other customers. When he reached our table, he glanced down at the two cats in Dexter’s lap and grinned widely.

“You got the best ones in the house.” He squatted down to our table so he wasn’t hovering above us. His long wavy hair fell across his shoulder when he reached out to offer his hand to the white cat. “They’re a bonded pair, but you probably guessed that already.”

Dexter stared at him with slightly wide eyes. They were around the same age, if I had to take a stab in the dark. Unlike my son, though, this boy had a lip hoop punched into either side of his mouth and wore a few bangles around his wrist that clanged together when he teased the cat with his fingers.

He was a handsome kid, if not a little gangly for a teenager. A soft laugh escaped him when the white cat turned to rub up against his hand comfortably.

"His name's Fritz," he said, not talking to me at all. "The one in your lap is Steve."

"O-oh," was all Dexter stuttered out.

"They're both up for adoption. But I do have to warn you, they have to go together."

Dexter merely nodded mutely in response, his cheeks slightly colored in a soft shade of red.

Oh.

I think… I was beginning to see why Kate was digging her nails so hard into our kid. Why she was so damn adamant on keeping a watchful eye on both Dexter and I while we were off on this trip. Maybe it wasn't some kind of motherly paranoia after all, but something else entirely.

The bus boy finally lifted himself back up to his feet, bidding us a farewell while throwing a wink at Dexter that had my son quickly averting his eyes and focusing back down at the cat in his lap.

Leaning over slowly, I let both of my arms rest on top of the table while I wrestled with reaching over and grabbing at him to get him to look at me. I settled on giving him space instead because he clearly needed it. "Dex. You… know you can tell me anything, right? I won't ever judge you."

God, I hoped he knew that.

There was nothing in this world that would ever make me love him less. Especially… something like this. Feelings were so damn complicated and as a teenager trying to figure out your place in the world, that made it all the more harder to come to terms with being different than everyone else around you.

Especially, in an evangelical household.

His Adam's apple visibly bobbed as he swallowed. "Yeah. Sure. Whatever. Can we go?"

CHAPTER 12

XAVIER

WE SPENT the rest of the morning into late afternoon in relative silence, wandering the small section of the city Dexter had chosen for the day.

I didn't want to push him into talking to me about anything when he was clearly very uncomfortable in doing so. For whatever reason, he wasn't able to trust me just yet with letting me in. He needed time to figure it out, something I could absolutely sympathize with.

I had no idea if my hypothesis was even correct in assuming he'd found that bus boy attractive. Hell, I could be way off base in assuming that, and for all I knew, he'd just never really met another guy his age with lip piercings, long hair, and a healthy appreciation for cats.

I was sure Kate was keeping his circle small in

order to fit in with her church-going friends and family, and it would be no surprise to me given that, to my knowledge, Dexter didn't have the biggest group of friends at school to begin with.

He was a quiet kid. Kept his head down most of the time and worked his ass off to get where he was with his grades. I mean, clearly, considering LSU wanted to give him a full ride and everything.

My kid was smart enough to go and do whatever he wanted. My only hope was that he wasn't held back by the need to keep his mom happy.

Getting back to Gage's place, we were greeted by the smell of something cooking from the kitchen. After walking for so long under the blazing southern sun, I was ready to chow down on whatever was placed down in front of me.

Leaving Dexter to take off his shoes in peace, I wandered my way into the kitchen, spotting Gage bent over a large boiling pot. He was still in his uniform, though much more wrinkled than how he'd left in it this morning.

Glancing back over my shoulder to make sure I didn't have a straggler following after me, I came up behind him and wrapped my arms around his waist. He sagged into me instantly, tilting his head back to give me access to his neck to leave a trail of kisses up to his ear.

"Missed you," he sighed softly.

I did, too. Badly.

I breathed him in, dreading having to let him go in a few seconds. He felt perfect nestled back against my chest, his body weight a solid form that

I could grab onto versus the figment I'd imagined when we were on the phone every night.

This was what I wanted to come home to every night. Not my empty house with just the sad white walls to keep me company.

"How was your tour around the city?" he asked, looking back at me when I finally forced myself to let go of him.

"Fine. Went to a few places." Nodding to the pot, I asked, "What's all that?"

"No clue. I'll be honest, I totally picked it up from the grocery store on the way home. The package told me to add water and voila."

God, he was so damn charming.

I laughed, swiping the ripped open container off of the counter. "Seafood boil, huh…"

"Southern classic."

My hands itched to grab onto him again and wrap him up into a tight hug while we listened to the sounds of the pot boil in the background. That kind of domestic shit was something I never thought I'd want. I'd been too hardened by my days in the military to settle down into a life of seafood boils and relaxed conversations after a long day at work.

At least, that's what I'd believed. Now I knew deep down, I'd always craved that kind of connection. I'd searched for it for years in between hookups and dating stints that never seemed to work out in my favor.

No one could handle my brand of fucked up, that's what I'd believed. Right up until I met Gage and he'd flipped my world completely upside down.

Leaning over, I stole another kiss before backing off completely. "Work went okay?"

"Yeah, had a small house fire but we got it down before it spread to the neighbors. Not much damage other than the family room in the back."

"Electrical failure?" I guessed.

"Worse. Cat knocked over a candle and set the carpet on fire. The house hadn't had an update since the seventies, so you can only imagine how crispy that carpet was when it went up."

Damn, that sucked. "Least it was only a portion of the house."

"What's what our Captain said. Insurance should pay it out, and hopefully, get them a whole new renovation."

"What happened?" Dexter asked, wandering into the kitchen. His gaze immediately zeroed in on the pot on the stove.

"Oh, just talking shop." Gage waved his wooden spoon in the air. "You like seafood, Dexter?"

"Never really had it."

Gage gasped obnoxiously and then had the audacity to pin a glare in my direction. "What the hell are you feeding this poor boy? Scraps?"

Out of the corner of my eye, I watched the bemused smile cross over my kid's face.

"Funny," I said, bringing my hand up to smack his ass but diverting in time in order to slap his shoulder instead. "Says the man who got it store bought."

"Look, you either want it homemade or edible. You can't have both in this house," he argued.

"Your poor brothers," I teased.

He leveled me with the end of his wooden spoon. "They were fed. That's all that matters."

"According to who?"

He threw a wink at me. "CPS."

Shaking my head and turning back to Dexter, I said, "We can find you something else to eat if you want. I'm sure Gage won't cry himself to sleep for too long tonight."

To my surprise, Dexter's smile widened an inch. "I'll try it. As long as it's edible."

Gage held a hand to his chest in a mock salute. "Scouts honor."

As Gage turned back to the stove to stir his pot, I shuffled both Dexter and I out of the kitchen to give the man some peace and quiet while he finished up. "I don't know about you, but I'm ready to get out of these sticky clothes. Louisiana humidity is no joke."

I didn't know how the hell Gage was able to function in this weather. California residents got a bad wrap for being babies in the wintertime when our temps dipped below sixty-five, but holy hell was the swamp miserable.

Dexter followed me, nodding along. I slipped my shirt off of my body, instantly feeling relief from no longer having the damn material clinging to me.

"Hey, dad?"

I whipped my head around. "Yeah."

Dexter drummed his fingers along the doorframe to his room in a rhythm that sounded familiar but I couldn't quite put my finger on where it was from. He searched my expression for something, finally settling with a nod as he spoke again. "He's a good man."

My eyes widened.

And with that, he disappeared beyond the door to get changed.

CHAPTER 13

He's a good man.

There had only been two other times my heart had ever felt so full—the day Dexter was born and the day we got to bring him home from the hospital.

He's a good man.

God, he really fucking was, wasn't he?

Sticking by me through my journey to sobriety. Helping me into it in the first place. Hell, *pushing* me to be a better man when it came to my kid and repairing the damage from my past with him. Coming to terms with my PTSD and what happened during my military career.

Gage was a one of a kind gem that I honestly never deserved to have, let alone keep all for myself. He deserved someone way less fucked up than me and yet, he'd told me plenty of times that he wouldn't have it any other way.

He got along with my kid, despite his stand-offish nature. Made him *laugh*.

How the hell did I earn a man like Gage?

Rolling out of bed and kicking off my covers, I slapped my hand on the nightstand next to the bed until I felt the familiar shape of my phone. Lifting it up, I sent off a quick text to Gage to see if he was still up.

When the response came a minute later, beckoning me to his room, all I felt was the giddiness of a love sick teenager sneaking out late to meet up with my boyfriend.

Thankfully, the house was quiet when I opened the door to my room.

Across the way, Dexter's door remained closed with him, hopefully, already asleep inside. While we'd turned in a little early after dinner, I figured that given our traveling this morning and our hike around the city, all of it would've tuckered him out in no time.

Gage's door was already cracked from the jam, allowing me to slip inside and close it behind me without making a single sound. He was sitting up in bed waiting for me, his hair still damp from a shower, the lamp on his nightstand dimmed to give the room that perfectly romantic ambiance he was constantly joking with me about over the phone.

I went to him quickly, lifting him up from the bed at the same time as he reached for me to wrap his arms around my waist. Our lips crashed into each other, both of us hungry for a taste of what we'd been dying to have over the past few months.

A small moan rumbled up his throat, quickly cut short when I tilted him backward onto the bed and laid him flat on his back. Our hips ground into each other almost of their own accord once I was on top of him, one of Gage's legs coming up to hook around my left side.

Ripping my lips away from his, I grabbed at his jaw. "I might have to gag you."

I loved how loud Gage got but scarring my poor kid with the sounds of his dad pounding ass was the *last* thing I wanted.

"Fuck," he whimpered.

"Think you can behave for me?" I licked a line down from his lips to his chin where stubble was starting to come in. It prickled my skin, sending a shiver racing down my spine.

"No."

Well, at least he was being honest.

Leaning back, I searched Gage's room for anything that I could use to stuff into his mouth for the time being. There were only a few more precious minutes I had left with all of my brain cells before I devolved into that of a caveman.

Under me, Gage rolled his hips into mine again, causing us both to gasp.

He was such a shit when he was horny.

Before he could utter another sound, my hand quickly slapped over his mouth, muffling it. "You're killing me."

His eyes twinkled in the dim light.

Looking down at him, I noted he was barely wearing anything. Just a simple cotton t-shirt and a pair of loose boxers that were doing absolutely nothing to hide how aroused he was. Honestly, I wasn't much better off in my sleep shorts, the front of which was jutting out from my hips.

Taking my hand off of his mouth and untangling his leg from around me, I slipped myself off of the bed and grabbed a hold of hips, using them to help me flip him over onto his stomach. Gage was already propping his ass up for me by the time I had my t-shirt stripped off and my sleep shorts tossed onto the floor.

"Head in the mattress, baby." Using both of my hands, I grabbed onto the ass that had been teasing me since damn near bright and early this morning, both cheeks fitting in my palms perfectly while I squeezed them a few times.

Perfect.

So goddamn perfect.

Gage's back arched beautifully, leading me to have to bite down on my tongue hard enough to hurt in order to hold back a moan teasing at the back of my throat. Letting go of his ass, I quickly slipped his boxers down his thighs.

He kicked them off one leg at a time, slipping his body forward on the mattress until his upper half was flush with it while he kept his lower half propped up for me. He was such a fucking sight to see, tempting me into wanting to take a picture for my private folder for when I was back home and lonely with only my hand to keep me company.

"Drawer," he said, lifting a finger to point at the one next to his bed.

Leaning over to it, one hand already fisted around the base of my cock, I tugged it open. A single bottle of lube was inside, haphazardly thrown from the last time he'd used it the night before my flight over here when I'd told him to send me a picture of his fingers in his ass for me.

"You're so good at reading me," I said, grabbing the bottle and shoving the drawer closed.

"Xavier, I need you so fucking bad." He whimpered again.

"I know, baby. One more second, I promise."

He was being so patient, letting me get a good look at him before I gave him even a modicum of relief with my touch. Snapping the cap open on the lube, I drizzled a good amount down my cock before tossing it onto the bed.

While working it over myself, I leaned in and planted my mouth right over his hole, delighting in the muffled squeal as Gage buried his head back into the mattress again. I swirled my tongue around his puckered opening, teasing him with the tip before retreating to lap up at his rim again.

His hips gyrated back against my mouth, trying to get as much friction as possible. My hand ached to slap at his ass cheek, to give him a little pain with his pleasure just as he liked. The problem was that my slaps were never quiet and clapping him good and loud on the ass was the only way to do it.

I wasn't into those love taps. A handprint needed to be left behind to appreciate in all its rosy pink glory for it to actually have been worth it.

Before I let myself get too carried away with my thoughts, I popped my mouth off of him and gave him a quick nip, then leaned back. I propped my leg up on the edge of his bed frame, tucking my foot between it and the mattress on top to keep me steady while I caught his hip with my free hand to hold him still.

He groaned at that, already anticipating me sliding into him.

"You've been keeping yourself nice and ready for me, right?" I asked, already knowing the answer but needing to hear it from his mouth anyway.

He tilted his head to the side, mumbling out a tangled 'yes' that was mixed with a quiet moan.

"Good," I praised, sliding the tip of my cock around his hole to coat him generously. His hole was already fluttering, desperately trying to catch my cock with every pass over his pucker.

Finally, I pressed against him, letting myself dip into his hot center slowly. Apparently, Gage was a little less patient than I'd given him credit for and all but slammed himself back against me.

"Fuck..." came my hissed curse, as I nearly erupted right then and there.

This man is truly going to be the death of me.

My balls ached with the need to just let it all go and flood his insides, throwing all of our careful prep right out the window like we were a couple of virgins on our wedding night. My fingers tight on his hip, I held him in place until I could calm down enough not to actually come the second I moved again.

Which I'm sure he'd love to brag about.

Bastard.

Blowing out a long breath, I rolled my hips back until only the head of my cock was seated inside of him. Then, I slammed forward, pulling him back onto me in the same singular motion that had me burying myself as deep as I could go.

His body jolted, both of his hands fisting in the sheets while he kept his face down against the mattress. I rocked my hips again, mimicking the motion from before as his tight heat gripped me perfectly, squeezing when I bottomed out, my hips pressed tightly against the globes of his ass.

This was what was perfect about Gage. His body was so attuned to me that it knew exactly what I needed.

One of his hands untangled from the sheets, coming around to reach between his legs. I slapped his hand away, grabbing onto his cock with my own.

"Mine."

No way was he coming before I told him he could.

He tried to rock back against me, not getting very far when I dug my fingers into his hips again, my nails leaving crescent shaped red marks in his skin. He was trapped in my rhythm game, completely at my mercy just like we'd both been fantasizing about for the past few weeks.

"You missed me filling you like this, baby, didn't you," I whispered, moving my hand down to cup his balls and squeeze them.

He choked out a moan, grabbing onto the sheets again out of desperation.

"That's it." A small grunt worked its way up my throat. "You're... mmmm, so fucking tight."

Fuck, I was *not* going to last.

I'd been without him too long. I wasn't used to

how fucking incredible he felt wrapped around me like this. I could only get myself off so much, my hand paling in comparison to the real deal.

Moving back up to fist Gage's cock once again, I stroked him in time with my thrusts as I pounded my hips against his ass. His body braced against the bed, taking each thrust with his unmoving form.

"Oh fuck," came tumbling out of my mouth, just as the first spurts of cum shot out of him and drizzled all over my fingers.

I followed closely behind, slamming into him one more time before stiffening and letting myself come inside of his tight heat. Both of us collapsed onto the bed, toppled over in a damn tangled pile of limbs that I knew we were going to wake up sore from in the morning.

Neither of us cared, too busy catching our breath and letting the post-orgasm haze settle over us. With my hand still wrapped around his cock, I pressed soft kisses along his shoulder and neck before burying my face there.

He let out a content sigh, relaxing under me.

"Love you," was all I could mumble before letting my eyes slide closed.

CHAPTER 14

XAVIER

LSU's campus was huge.

With a sprawling greenery that was the size of a small town, surrounded by dozens of buildings that made up the rest of the property, it made it easy to get lost once you were past the front entrance gates.

There were a couple of signs here and there pointing toward different directions, but outside of that, you were on your own.

Dexter and I had left early this morning and grabbed a bite to eat before coming over here, giving us the time to wake up and recharge before we took on the massive undertaking of exploring this entire place before we were due back to Gage's house for lunch at one.

With it being winter break, almost the entire campus was deserted aside from us wandering around. Which was kind of nice. Not many people got this kind of an unfettered tour of a potential school without being hassled by a second year tour guide trying to upsell you on the meal package.

As much as it'd kill me to have Dexter living so far away from me, I could see him walking across these soon-to-be-busy sidewalks getting to class with his backpack stuffed to the brim with textbooks and notes. I could see him proudly repping the purple and yellow colors of LSU and excitedly telling anyone who asked him where he was going for his four-year degree.

All of this could be the dad in me being proud of my kid even before he actually agreed on committing to a college before we could even tour one fully. I never had any doubts in me that he'd get into a great school, regardless. He had the drive to go far in life in whatever he wanted to do. Anyone could see that.

"They've got a huge sports program here," Dexter told me while passing by the gates heading toward the stadium. From here, I could spot the familiar yellow goal posts rising up over the buildings blocking the field from view. "They've put a lot of money into their football team."

I raised my brow. "You interested in something like that?"

His head snapped to me while a small snort escaped him. "No offense, dad, but do I look like the type to do a sports program?"

Ironically, he had my build, just without all of the muscle attached to it. He was still a growing kid, though, young enough that his second bout of puberty hadn't yet hit. So, there was still time.

Mentally, though?

No, I couldn't see Dexter running around a football field and getting slammed to the ground while trying to wrestle around for a pigskin.

"Hey, I'm not here to judge your interests," I teased.

If anything, I wanted to encourage whatever it was he typically occupied his time with. Reading, exercising, lounging around playing video games. None of that mattered to me as long as he was happy and still kept up his grades.

Back in the day with my own dad, I'd never had the luxury of sitting around doing nothing. He was of the old school mindset that moving equaled productivity and relaxing was born out of laziness. I'd had a lot of pent up energy when I was younger, which translated to keeping myself busy whenever I had any kind of downtime.

Hence the military.

After a while, though, it weighed on me. I'd had a hard time transitioning into civilian life—my whole adolescence having been molded into creating anxiety anytime I didn't at least keep my hands busy. Sometimes, I wondered if that was the reason I'd ever picked up the bottle in the first place.

Alcohol quieted my racing mind like no other. Once my PTSD took control, abusing it was just another step on my already growing totem pole of vices that would eventually kill me one day.

These days, forcing myself to relax was like learning an entirely new language. I was clunky at it, bad at practicing when I should be, and had a habit of wanting to rely on my old ways in order to make myself feel better.

My therapist had said that, as a form of perfectionism, trying once and failing had resulted in me giving up. Hearing that for the first time spun me around for days. I'd never considered myself to *be* a perfectionist. And yet the more internal work I'd done, and the more I uncovered who I *really* was, the more accurate that damn statement was.

Haunting me, to this day.

I'm proud that I never went back to the bottle. It'd been tempting as all hell, don't get me wrong. Falling back into my old habits, as my therapist had said, would be taking the easy way out. But I'd be damned if I became a quitter.

I hadn't been raised that way and I certainly wasn't going to start.

Dexter nudged me with his elbow, reaching for the door to the main academic building and holding it open for me. "Football's not really my cup of tea."

"So what is?" I asked, stepping inside and waiting for him to follow me before we began strolling leisurely down the long hallway.

The place was three stories, large glass panes stretched up to the ceiling that had round tables on the other side of it, facing out toward the main lobby. The staircase leading up to the first floor was more grand than I'd ever seen a college have.

Twin banners were hanging from the ceiling over the staircase in that familiar purple.

Down on the main floor were a couple of tables with the chairs put up on top of them. A lone janitor was buffing out a part of the floor a few feet away from us with headphones covering his ears. He barely glanced up at us as we walked toward the stairs and took them up to the next level.

"I know it's going to sound lame, but I actually do like to study," he said, clutching the railing as we stepped. "I like learning. A lot of people think that's a nerdy thing to say, but it's genuinely true."

"Nothing wrong with that, kid. We need more booksmart people in this world."

He blew out a breath. "Yeah, I guess. It kind of makes me feel like an outcast, though. People my age care about social media and followers. That sort of thing. There's nothing wrong with that, I just don't... care."

"Can't say I do, either. Gage was trying to get me to join this online platform a few weeks back so that we could share pictures and videos back and forth like our own camera roll. I'm clearly getting old, because I had no idea what the hell I was doing on it."

Dexter was quiet when we reached the top step. I waited for him to pick a direction, but when he didn't, I grew a little worried.

"You okay?"

"You kind of talk about him a lot," he blurted out.

That had me blinking in surprise.

Shit, did I really?

Jesus, this whole time I was trying not to be obvious with my relationship by keeping my hands to myself and this whole time it was my *mouth* that got me in trouble.

"Uh."

What did I even say to him?

Yeah, it's just because we're best friends?

Calling Gage anything like my best friend or whatever felt too small on the scale of what I felt for him. He was *so much* more than that. He was my confidant, my heart, my rock. Our relationship extended past the boundaries of mere labels at this point.

How could I hope to convey that, though, without sounding like an absolutely lunatic?

Especially to my seventeen year old.

"Are... you guys..." Dexter was struggling to get the words out.

A pit in my stomach formed. "We're... uh."

Fuck.

This was like trying to have the damn birds and the bees talk.

Why was this so fucking awkward?

I wanted my son to get to know me, just as I did him. I'd never considered that this would be torturously cringy to speak my true feelings for the man that I was in love with.

He watched me with a pinched expression.

Sighing, I said, "We're dating, Dex."

He nodded slowly. "How long?"

"A year... just about."

He blinked a few times. "Oh."

I slapped my hand to the side of my face to rub at it, scratching a finger through my beard. Hopefully, my cheeks weren't too red. "Yeah."

His expression was morphing into more of a curious one while he watched me carefully. Whatever was going on inside of his head had to be a million questions. He knew I was gay, but he hadn't said what he felt about it outside of him expressing how much it'd hurt Kate, and him by proxy.

Coming face to face with the reality of something like that was different than hearing it and never having to witness it. It wouldn't surprise me if he asked me to get him on a plane tonight and let him go back home to the safety of heteronormativity. That was more comfortable, even if I had my suspicions about him yesterday.

He made a small humming sound before pivoting on his heel and heading down the hallway behind him. I followed after him, my stomach tight with knots. He shoved a hand into his pocket and pulled out a neatly folded up bundle of papers, un-creasing them with his hand a few times.

"Up ahead is the tech wing. It's supposed to be state of the art." He was talking while his head was buried in the papers—maps, I realized when I got close enough.

"Dex..."

He continued to talk like he hadn't even heard me. "I'm not that well-versed in technology. But I'd like to learn a thing or two. They even have a robotics team."

"Dexter."

He stopped short, turning to look at me. "What?"

I sighed. "Talk to me."

Please.

The answering frown was the least of what I

was expecting. "I'm kind of hurt you didn't tell me."

"Hurt?" I repeated.

"Yeah, I—" His gaze darted away from mine, focusing on the hallway we'd stopped right in front of. "I know mom doesn't really care to know... or you didn't want to tell her. I understand that. But..."

My heart softened. "I didn't think you wanted to know, either."

Thankfully, he looked at me again. "I'm not like her, dad."

That hit me hard. I hadn't meant to treat him the same way I did his mom—at arm's length. I wanted our bond to be so much different and here I was, doing what I did to Kate without even trying to meet him halfway and see if he was at all interested.

"Yeah, I go to church. Or, well, I did," he flinched but went on. "But that doesn't mean I hate gay people. I told you I didn't care about it when you told me."

"I know," I said softly. "But hearing about it and seeing it are two different things. I didn't want to freak you out."

Dexter rolled his eyes at me. "You really think you kissing someone is going to freak me out? Trust me, you're not as bad as mom and Dan."

Okay, we'll unpack that later.

"I'm sorry, Dex."

"Were you seriously never going to tell me?" The hurt in his eyes was killing me.

"I was... waiting for the right time." A total lie. Even as I said it, I knew that it was.

Keeping things from my son, even out of paternal instinct, was what got us here in the first place. We'd had a rift between us because I'd kept my distance from him after everything with his mother, believing that I was protecting him while hurting us both in the process.

How was any of that fair?

Yet, I was still doing it.

"Okay, so when was the right time going to be? When we got back on the plane? You know you guys are, like, *really* obvious, right?"

That made me wince. "Sorry..."

He rolled his eyes again. "I'm not trying to be an asshole. I... okay, I know that this is hard to talk to me about. I get that. But aren't we supposed to be trying the honesty thing?"

"Yeah, of course we are."

"So then talk to me? A year is kind of a big deal, dad."

This time I slapped both of my hands over my face and I groaned into them. "I know..."

"That's kind of a marriage time limit."

"What?"

He shrugged at me when I peeked at him through my hands.

"Isn't the saying, if it's been a year, you should know if you want to marry the person you're dating?"

Marriage?

I hadn't thought about that since Kate and I divorced.

Was that true?

Was Gage expecting that?

Neither of us had talked about tying the knot,

mostly due to us being long distance for the time being.

That was currently our biggest hurdle to overcome, which wouldn't be getting resolved until I knew where Dexter was going. If he decided on LSU, great. I'd most likely move down here to be with Gage.

If not?

We'd figure something else out.

We'd come this damn far—even if the distance was killing us both.

"Uh..." I dropped my hands to my side. "We haven't really talked about it."

His lips parted at the same time that his brows pulled together. "Seriously?"

"What?" Now I was feeling a little defensive.

Why the hell was I trying to defend myself to my damn seventeen year old?

"Enough talking about my relationship. Don't we have a school to tour?"

Marching around him, I planted both of my hands on his shoulder blades to guide him down the hallway we were facing. This was a good excuse to get my bearings back, anyway. Coming on this school tour with him hadn't prepared me for the onslaught of fucking questions he'd needle me with about me and Gage.

"Dad." He craned his neck back to look at me.

"How about this," I offered. "I'll tell you about Gage and I while we walk. Sound good?"

For the first time since yesterday, he smiled. "All right, deal."

CHAPTER 15

XAVIER

BY THE TIME we got back to Gage's, I was both mentally and physically exhausted.

"I'm going to take a shower," Dexter said, moving around me as soon as he kicked his shoes off. "I'm sweaty from walking up and down all those stairs."

"Take your time. Whatever Gage is bringing back will probably need time to heat up, anyway."

He nodded and then headed for the hallway. The bathroom door clicked shut a moment later, leaving me to my own thoughts for the time being. Stumbling over to the couch, I threw myself back on it and let my body sink into the soft cushions.

Who fucking knew divulging my relationship to my teenaged son would have me feeling like I'd just walked out of an intense therapy session?

Though, I guess in a way, it kind of was.

Purging myself from all of the secrets I'd been keeping from him about Gage—all PG, of course —had felt nice. Like a weight was slowly being lifted off of me. But now that everything was out in the open, I was having to deal with the aftermath of letting myself be so vulnerable.

Dexter had taken it well, asking me questions practically after every story I'd told him. It surprised me how much of an interest he'd taken in the subject. Then again, that could be him fishing for answers for his own self.

He still hadn't opened up to me about anything, but I felt like, in due time, he would. Coming home today, I felt a lot closer to him, and like he understood me better than he had when we'd first stepped off of that plane.

The front door opened up, coupled with the sound of a key ring full of keys jingling. I slid my eyes closed in time with the door, the familiar sounds of Gage setting his stuff down by the door filling my ears.

I heard him chuckle when he came into the living room, his soft footsteps wandering over to me. A weight was then settled on top of my chest, his warm body laying on me while his leg hooked over mine.

"Long day?" he teased.

I popped my eyes open. "You don't know the half of it."

He kissed me sweetly, his lips lingering on mine for a moment. "You guys didn't get into an argument, did you?"

"No, nothing like that."

He relaxed visibly. "Okay, good."

He's a good man.

Those words were going to haunt me forever in the best of ways. Honestly, I should've picked up on it then what Dexter was trying to tell me. His approval meant a hell of a lot.

"He knows about us," I said.

Gage's eyes widened. "You told him?"

"Nope."

His mouth opened and closed a few times, a wince pinching his face. "Were we... that obvious?"

"According to him we were. I thought we were being good."

"Me too!"

I laughed. "Maybe he's got exceptional gaydar."

Gage groaned, burying his face in my chest. "I swear, I was only making goo-goo eyes at you when he wasn't looking..."

I ran my fingers through his hair, curling them around the soft locks that had grown longer since the last time we'd seen each other. I liked his hair a little on the longer side. It framed his face perfectly and gave him more of a softer side.

"You want to know what he told me?" When Gage nodded, I said, "He told me that he knew the second you met us in the airport. Apparently, he'd had his suspicions before that and confirmed it then."

He groaned again, turning his face to the side. "It was that damn sign, wasn't it? I knew I should've made it smaller."

He preened when I scratched his scalp gently

with my nails. "I think it was more than the sign, babe."

"Was he upset?"

"No, surprisingly. The entire campus tour we talked about it."

"No shit?" When he lifted his head from my chest, he was grinning. "Does that mean we got the gold star of approval?"

"I hope so. He was pretty upset that I didn't tell him about it. He even gave me a lecture about how at the one year mark, I should think about proposing." I laughed.

Thinking that he'd laugh along with me, he surprised me when all he said to that was a soft, "Oh."

That sobered me right up. "Have *you* thought about getting married?"

"To you?"

"Who else?" Trying to tease him again to lighten up the rapidly declining mood, I said, "You got someone else I don't know about?"

"No, no. Nothing like that."

What the hell was going on?

"Gage."

The sound of the bathroom door popping open had him springing off my chest and back onto his feet. His uniform was wrinkled from the way he was laying on me, a deep line formed right across his chest, over his heart.

"I should get lunch started," was all he said, before spinning on his heel and heading into the kitchen.

Sitting up slowly, I stared after him.

What the hell was *that*?

CHAPTER 16

Gage

Stupid fucking idiot.

The mantra I'd been chanting to myself over the past three hours since coming back from lunch.

Seriously, could I ruin a more perfect moment with my dumbass insecurities?

Xavier's wonderful news should've had me jumping over the fucking moon to hear, yet all I'd focused on was the way his face had looked when he'd joked about getting married to me.

That's because he doesn't want *to marry you.*

A groan bubbled up my throat. Picking up the gear bag at my feet, I launched it across the training room, over to where the other ones were stacked.

Why the hell did I care if Xavier didn't want to marry me?

His first marriage had gone to shit, so there were plenty of reasons to not want to do that again.

Sure, it would be different if he was married to someone he was *actually* attracted to, but sometimes people didn't want to chance it. That didn't mean that that person wasn't in love with their partner. It just meant they had reservations about legally binding their life to another's.

"You good in here?" Quinn wandered into the room.

"Yep." I chucked another bag across the room. "What's up?"

"You're making a lot of noise in here. Thought I might have to come rescue you from the pile burying you alive."

I scoffed. "Yeah, if only."

I'd welcome a fucking tower of gear falling on top of me right now and taking me out. It'd save me the damn embarrassment of having to go back home after this and face my boyfriend and his confused expressions while I tried to pretend none of this ever happened.

Why I felt the need to get all up in my feelings about a hypothetical situation was beyond me. We'd never discussed marriage before this—never even had the option on the damn table. The second that door was no longer there, though, I'd gotten butt hurt about it.

And for what?

To torture myself?

Xavier and I were *good*. We were *happy*.

Why couldn't that be enough for my stupid ass brain to comprehend?

"Uh oh." Quinn planted himself right on top of the next bag before I could grab it. "Trouble in paradise?"

Annoyed, I said, "Can you move?"

"Not until you spill the beans, Torres."

"Quinn," I growled.

He simply flashed me a pleasant smile. "Come on, you know you want to tell me."

"Don't you have someone else to pick on?"

"Nah, it's his day off. So I need to fill the void somehow."

This was so fucking typical of him. If he didn't have Jase around to bug, he'd sniff out the weakest link in the chain until he found someone to attach to for the rest of the day. Which just so happened to be me.

Honestly, I didn't have much fight left in me. I was already exhausted from doing mental gymnastics in my head, trying to convince myself that I wasn't crazy in feeling justified over my reaction to Xavier, while at the same time feeling bad about it.

What did that say about me?

About us?

He had enough on his plate to deal with without me adding to it with my stupid lovesick heart bleeding at the mere possibility that marriage wasn't in our future. He hadn't said it out loud but his face had told me plenty.

Wandering over to one of the metal chairs set back against the wall, I flopped down onto it while I leaned forward and rested my head in my hands. Overthinking was my specialty.

And when it came to Xavier?

Forget it. I was cooked.

"Come on, man. Talk to me," Quinn said.

"You can't tell anyone."

"Uh…"

Rolling my eyes, I said. "Besides Jase."

"You got yourself a deal."

I sighed, my gaze directed at the floor. "So, my boyfriend's up from California visiting and earlier when I went home for lunch, he and I got to talking about some things. And… I don't know. I guess I took it a little more personally than he probably meant it to come across."

"I'm loving the cryptic way you're telling me this, Torres."

Ugh.

I let my hands drop from my head when I lifted it up. "We got onto the topic of marriage."

His brows shot up to his hairline. "Wow, congrats. That's pretty serious."

"Yeah, except he laughed in my face about it."

"Yikes."

"I feel like a total idiot. This is the first time it was ever brought up and I froze. He was joking around about it. Meanwhile, I took it seriously and got my own feelings hurt."

"Hmm." Quinn leaned back on the bag, his body shifting slightly. He ran one of his hands over his jaw a few times while he chose his words carefully. "So what exactly did he say to you? I'm just trying to get the full picture here."

"Apparently, his kid was saying that after a year, you should really start thinking about marriage. And I guess Xavier found that kind of funny and joked with me about it."

"Did he *say* he didn't want to get married?"

"Well, he's been married before."

"That's not exactly answering my question," Quinn said.

"His face told me plenty."

"I think I see what's going on." He lifted himself up from the bag and headed over to me, hands on his hips. "You got all up in your head again."

That had me frowning.

He went on. "Gage, you gotta stop doing that. You're getting your own feelings hurt and there's probably no reason for it. What if he *does* want marriage in the future?"

"You should've seen his face, man. It wasn't—he thought it was ridiculous."

"Maybe you just filled in the blanks for him," he suggested.

Frustration was rising in my chest.

It felt like I was talking in circles. I knew what I saw when I was watching Xavier talk to me about it. His tone, the way he phrased things. All of it, coupled with his expression when he'd asked me if *I* thought about marriage was like all one big joke to him.

Why wouldn't it be when the last time he was bound to someone legally, it ended in a flaming pile of shit?

If I were in Xavier's shoes, I'd run for the damn hills anytime someone mentioned the 'M' word to me.

"Yo! Gage!" Zander's face appeared in the doorway. "You got a couple of guests out here waiting for you."

My stomach flipped.

Probably Xavier here with Dexter to tour the place.

Now that his son knew we were dating, he was probably going around on a grand tour of all my usual spots. On any other normal day, I'd be hyped to show them both around the place I spent ninety-nine percent of my time at.

Today, I was tempted to hide in the bathroom and beg Quinn and Zander to make up some excuse as to why I wasn't here.

Dragging myself up from my chair with a sigh, I shuffled out to the hallway and followed Zander back to the main garage. A few of my coworkers were all gathered around one of the front side doors, most likely welcoming Xavier and Dexter in.

Captain Clarke was nowhere to be seen, which was out of the norm for him when it came to new guests at the fire station. Usually, he was first on scene.

Quinn slapped his hands on my shoulders from behind me and steered me toward the group, speeding me up from how I'd been dragging my feet along the concrete floor. As soon as we reached them, the group parted, smiling faces all turning to face me.

In the middle of it all was *not* my boyfriend and his teenaged kid.

But my *own brothers*.

Instantly, my eyes began to water. "What the..."

"Surprise!" Greyson grinned, throwing his arms around me first. Over his shoulder, I could see Asher smiling at us in amusement, holding a medium-sized box in his arms.

I wrapped Greyson up in a tight hug, not believing that he was actually here in the damn flesh. That *either* of them were.

"When the hell did you guys get in?" I said. "When did you get time off?"

And how the hell did they coordinate behind my back?

As Greyson pulled away, he stepped to the side while snagging the box from his brother's hold. Asher came next, hugging me tight enough to practically snap my bones in half.

"We wanted to surprise you," he said in my ear.

Well, they sure as hell succeeded.

Out of any kind of surprise they could've given me, *this* was by far the best one. I'd spent the last two weeks lamenting about spending the holidays by myself and here these two were— conspiring behind my back like the lovable little shits they were.

Asher stepped back from our hug, a wide smile resting on his face. His hair was longer and shaggier than when I last saw him, while his brother's was shaved back to a military cut.

They both looked good.

Happy.

Healthy.

Just how I'd wanted them to be.

"Aw, a happy family reunion!" Ellie clapped. "The Captain's going to be thrilled. You guys are coming to the Christmas party, right?"

The twins exchanged a look.

"Is there free food?" Asher asked. "If so, count me in."

"Ditto," his brother quickly replied.

"Hey, my kinda guys." Quinn offered them both a high five.

"Funny," I said and then nodded to the box. "What's all that?"

Greyson hid behind his twin. "You can't open it until Christmas."

Oh boy... that didn't give off a foreboding feeling or anything. The last time my brothers surprised me with something and refused to let me open it until Christmas morning, I'd gotten a lovely prank spring-loaded whipped pie to the face and two newly turned teenagers cackling endlessly while they recorded the entire thing.

Now that they were actually adults with *real adult money*, I couldn't even imagine what was waiting for me inside of that mystery box.

"We've got our bags outside," Asher said, gesturing to the side door. "We took a rideshare here from the airport."

"I can't believe you two got your flights to come in at the same time and got all the way here without me knowing." As much as I was impressed with their planning, I was damn proud, too. Look how independent I'd taught them to be!

"Asher's plane didn't get in for a few hours, so I was stuck waiting in one of the terminal chairs." Greyson raised his hands above his head, stretching long enough that there was an audible pop that had his body relaxing instantly. "I can't wait to sleep in an actual bed for once."

Oh shit.

"Uh, actually..." Fuck, I totally forgot about my guests. "That might be a problem."

Asher laughed. "I told you he turned your room into an office. You owe me five bucks."

"No way." Greyson's eyes met mine. "You didn't, did you?"

"No!"

"He's definitely lying," Zander said, ever the pot-stirrer.

What the hell.

"I didn't."

"Wait, I thought your boyfriend was up?" Quinn asked, his brows knitting together in confusion, most likely rethinking our entire earlier conversation.

To my left, Ellie gasped. "You got your boyfriend to come visit? He can come to the party!"

Oh. My. God.

"Guys."

"Wait, hold up. Does this mean we actually get to meet him?" Greyson asked.

This was like them teasing me when I'd first told them that I was dating Xavier all over again. "Can you guys be normal about this?"

"No way," Asher said.

Of course.

Why would they be?

They were my baby brothers and under strict sibling obligations to make fun of me until I was dead. Even then, they'd probably be pranking me over my damn casket one last time until I was lowered into the dirt.

"At least try and be on your best behavior," I said. "He's got his son with him. I told them they could stay at the house while they toured LSU this weekend."

"Oh shit, he's a sport's guy?" Greyson asked.

"No? Not exactly."

Asher nodded sagely. "Academics. Respect."

I rolled my eyes. Whatever that meant.

"Anyway, they're there now. I get off here in twenty minutes, so I'll drive us all back. You guys hang here while I go finish what I was doing. Sound good?"

Both of them threw me a thumbs up. "Roger that."

Oh boy, this was going to be interesting.

CHAPTER 17

XAVIER

RECEIVING the frantic text of *'hey my brothers surprised me at the fire station'* was probably the last thing I expected to see when I grabbed my phone to check my notifications on the off chance that Kate had called me.

I was glad that things worked out for Gage and his brothers, and was happy that my intuition about them had been correct. He'd put way too much love and care into them for them to turn around and write him off in order to experience living on their own for a little bit longer.

The holidays were a special time for most families. Coming together in order to celebrate that was more meaningful than a lot of people realized. I'm glad the boys weren't taking that for granted.

Time was so short and life was full of unpredictable ups and downs.

There was no guarantee that there would be another day, so why chance it?

"Hey, Dex?" I called from the living room.

A minute later, he popped his head out from the doorway of his room.

"Gage's brothers surprised him at the station. You mind bunking with me so they can have one of their rooms back?"

He gave me a funny look. "I guess..."

"It's just temporary."

He was quiet for a moment, his expression growing more perplexed. "I'm surprised you're not going to room with Gage? Unless they also don't know..."

"No..." My voice sounded a little strangled while I spoke. "They do."

"Okay, so..."

I rubbed at my cheeks, feeling them grow hot to the touch.

Who would've thought my own kid would be suggesting I bunk with my boyfriend while on a father-son trip?

This entire time, I thought he'd balk at the idea of him finding out I had a boyfriend, let alone bringing him to his house to crash while on our trip.

"I just think it would be easier," Dexter explained.

"No, yeah. You're right. I didn't want you to feel uncomfortable."

He shrugged. "It's not that I don't want to

share a room with you. But I value my privacy to wind down at night."

"No worries." Honestly, I got that more than he knew. Decompressing after a long day of people-ing was the only way I wasn't driven to insanity on a daily basis.

It seemed that Dexter had inherited my introverted nature. Not surprising, considering we were similar in more ways than our looks. He was smart like Kate, driven like me, and intuitive like the both of us.

He was a perfect blend of us both in the best way—the only thing good we'd ever done together.

"We'll work something out," I said.

"Yeah, let me know."

Right then, the front door to Gage's house unlocked and opened, voices filtering in from outside.

"I'm telling you, I'll win in an arm wrestling competition any day of the week. I lift eighty pound bags of feed every day."

"And *I'm* telling *you*, I'm in the goddamn military. I lift that shit for breakfast."

"Hello, you're a medic?"

"Okay, and I still have fitness tests to pass?"

Ah, that must be the twins.

Lifting myself up from the couch, I headed for the front door to greet them. Dexter ducked back into his room to hide, probably overwhelmed by their loud voices. I could sympathize in a sense—it wasn't my forte to entertain a bunch of extroverts, but at least I had Gage as a buffer.

Who did Dexter have?

Me?

I didn't know these two, either, so I'd be just as lost as a buffer, if not worse than not having one to begin with.

Making my way through the living room and into the small foyer, I spotted the twins lingering in the doorway. Both of them had large duffels swung over their shoulders, one of them with a military print.

Behind them, Gage was stepping up into the house, waving his hands for them to clear the doorway while he dragged another bag in through the door. He let out a loud huff of air when letting go of the strap, straightening back up to brush his hands together.

"All right. That's everything," he said.

"Nice," one of the twins said, swinging the door closed behind him.

All at once, the three of them turned to me. A long beat of silence fell over us all as they took me in, their eyes curious while Gage shifted awkwardly on his feet.

One of the twins pointed at me. "Hey, it's you."

"In the flesh," I said, heading over to them to grab the bag Gage had lugged inside.

It was heavy as fuck when I got a hold of it.

What the hell had these two brought home, fucking bricks?

"Wow, you're way taller than I expected," one of them said. "Gage, you got a type."

"Shut up," he gritted through his teeth, face on fire.

"Oh really…" Sue me for being curious, but I had to know. "Do tell."

I was never one to get jealous, but when it came to Gage, all bets were off. I'd never go out of my way to beat someone up if I caught them flirting with him, but that didn't mean I wouldn't be marking my territory with a heated kiss or something similar.

Call me a caveman.

The twin with the shorter hair laughed. "We have stories for days. You want to hear what it was like when he had a crush on the cashier at the mini-mart down the road? Oh, or how about that time he was trying to hit on the guy at the gas station who was buying a bunch of junk food 'cause he had the munchies and could barely understand Gage because he was so high."

"Greyson. Shut up," Gage choked out.

Oh, this was too good. "You guys up for long? I've got all weekend."

They both grinned at me.

"Hey, I like him," the one with the longer hair said, nudging Gage in the ribs.

"Asher," Gage said in a monotone, gesturing to one twin and then the other. "Greyson. This is Xavier. *Behave.*"

"It's nice to meet you two," I said.

"Likewise," they both said at the same time.

"I'm so sorry ahead of time," Gage said to me.

"I think you might be needing that sentiment more than me."

He answered me with a groan.

"Wait, where's your little dude?" Greyson said, glanced around.

"He's taking a breather." Forcing my kid to be social kind of felt wrong, especially after the intense morning we'd had. If he wanted to hide for a bit while these two got settled, I wasn't going to tell him no.

Greyson nodded sagely. "Respect."

Behind him, Gage rolled his eyes. "Okay, you two. Stop interrogating him. You're going to scare him off."

My face twisted into a smile. Not likely, but they could damn well try. I had a feeling we were going to get along fine. I had a few tricksters to deal with back home, so this wasn't much different. As long as they respected Dexter, we'd be all good.

"You guys have a long flight?" I asked, leading them back into the living room.

"Not too bad," Asher answered first. "Grey had to wait for my plane to land while I got to sleep like a baby on my flight over."

"I hate that you can pass out on anything even remotely comfortable," his brother said, tossing his bag down by the hallway leading back to the bedrooms.

"I think the word you're looking for is 'envy'."

I felt an arm snake around my waist from behind, tugging me back while the boys headed for the kitchen together. Gage nuzzled his face into my neck, breathing me in while he had a tight hold of me.

"Quite the surprise," I said once we were alone.

He kissed my neck. "You okay with this?"

"Your house, babe."

He nipped at my skin. "Be serious."

"I am. I'm glad they're here. I had a feeling they'd surprise you, actually."

"Really?" Gage pulled back from me, a bemused expression falling over his face. "What gave it away?"

"You raised them."

His eyes shimmered slightly. "Aw, stop. That's the nicest thing anyone has ever said."

I couldn't help but reach over and cup his face, pulling him into a chaste kiss. "I mean it. Your giant heart reflects in them."

"Ugh." He leaned into me again. "I love you."

Whatever our weirdness from before was about, I was glad that it'd seemingly been forgotten about. I had half a mind to ask him about it while we were alone and in our own little bubble, however, spoiling the mood in order to talk about something that seemed a little more serious felt wrong.

I'd bring it up to him before we left, for sure. For now, though, I wanted us to enjoy the time we had together now that there was going to be a full house.

The soft sound of a throat being cleared had us both untangling ourselves immediately. Dexter was standing just beyond the start of the hallway, his eyes averted while he squinted at the wall.

Jesus, to go from us not touching each other in front of him to getting caught practically making out—how fucking embarrassing. We really needed to get it together.

"Dexter!" Gage clapped his hands together. "How was your campus tour? Did you like it?"

He cleared his throat again. "Good. Fine. Walked a lot."

Gage nodded slowly with a forced smile. "That sounds fun. Er, I'm glad it went well."

The sound of something crashing in the kitchen had us all whipping around toward the noise, a faint 'oops' following right after.

"Oh my god," Gage mumbled, storming into the kitchen.

Maybe Gage would have his hands too full for us to get caught like this again. The thought was a little depressing, considering all I wanted to do was touch and hold him, but if it saved us from an awkward situation like this, then I was all for it.

Turning to my son, he slowly wandered over to me. "They seem... excitable."

"Yeah. Look, Dex, I'm sorry—"

He cut me off. "Can I tell you something?"

I was scared to ask. "Yes?"

Dexter shook his head at me. "You got it bad."

I held back a guilty smile.

I really, really did.

CHAPTER 18

Xavier

To both my and Gage's surprise, the boys got along swimmingly.

Over dinner, there was a bit of a tense debate over who was the first allowed to cut the pre-made turkey Gage had bought and heated up from the store. But once Dexter had won the impromptu rock, paper, scissors battle he'd been roped into, everything settled into a comfortable rhythm, as if we'd been doing this kind of tradition for years.

I enjoyed seeing my son bonding with kids around his age. With both Asher and Greyson out of the house and out living their lives, it gave Dexter a good insight into what was to come once he was officially graduated and old enough to do the same.

Getting ready for that transition in life made me nauseous, despite Gage's numerous hand squeezes under the table every time Dexter talked about going to some far away school that would be at least a plane ride away.

I had to settle with myself that it was okay that my son was going to be spreading his wings and flying from the nest soon. All parents had to deal with it eventually. Hell, Gage was already through the thick of it and barely surviving. If we didn't have each other, we'd be sunk by now.

That part comforted me, at least. We had each other to lean on while our hearts were out traveling the world without us.

"All right, clean up time," Gage sang out as he got up from his chair.

The twins were on their feet instantly, collecting everyone's finished plates and stacking them to take into the kitchen to wash. Dexter and I followed suit, grabbing the leftover food to bring into the kitchen for Gage to wrap up and save for tomorrow.

"Thank you," Gage whispered in my ear as I passed the plate of half-eaten turkey to him. I knew he was thanking me for more than helping him clean up.

My heart squeezed in my chest, the sincerity for whatever he was referring to quite obvious in the way his eyes twinkled as he smiled at me. Too bad we weren't alone or else I'd back him right up into that counter and have my wicked way with him.

"You into video games, Dexter?" Greyson asked, scraping off one of the plates into the garbage next to the sink.

"I play sometimes. I don't have a lot of friends

that are into the kind I like," he said, passing another plate over.

"What are you into?" Asher asked.

"You know those simulator games that are realistic where you do mundane tasks that you'd otherwise hate to do in the real world?"

Greyson kicked his twin in the shin. "Dude, you *have* to show him that farming simulator one you have."

Asher nodded quickly. "You're going to love it. You get to farm crops from a field."

How the hell was that *a fun video game idea?*

Honestly, I'd never understand the younger generation. Half of the shit they found entertaining baffled me.

Dexter turned to me with those big doe-eyes of his, silently pleading for me to let him go hang out with the older boys.

How could I possibly say no to a look like that?

I snagged the stack of plates from him. "Just remember, we've got the rest of your itinerary tomorrow."

"I'll set an alarm," he said, and then followed the twins out of the kitchen, abandoning Gage and I to the rest of clean-up duty.

Gage snorted. "You sucker."

"I know." Setting the plates down on the counter, I brushed my hands on the towel next to the sink before cupping his face with my hands and bringing him in for a kiss. "Would you believe me if I told you I did that for this?"

He smiled. "You *sucker*."

"Only for you." I kissed him again, this time deepening it.

Delightfully dangerous of us to be doing this with our kids mere feet from us in the room next door. At the same time, I had no self-control when Gage was around me. He could simply *breathe* in my direction and I was popping a boner that acted like a fucking compass pointing right at him.

I'm sure there would be a point in time when this enhanced tension between us would die down and we'd eventually fall into a comfortable rhythm of being old and gray together.

Until that time came around, though, I was riding this out for as long as possible. Call me selfish for leaning into my rabid desire for this man. It was more likely that I was on the 'crazy' side of the spectrum than anything else.

Gage moaned softly against my mouth, turning us so that he had his back resting against the counter. His hands came up to rest on my chest, pushing gently until we parted from our kiss. His face was flushed in that beautiful way it always was after a heated kiss, which only made me want to kiss him that much more.

"Xavier…" His pupils were blown as he looked at me. "I have a question for you."

"If it's 'can you fuck me against this counter' the answer is yes."

He laughed, slapping my chest. "Nice try. We'll get caught for sure. I don't know about you, but I really don't want to have to deal with the aftermath of the boys walking in on that."

"True." More than likely they'd avoid the kitchen, and us, like the plague. But his point remained the same. I *also* didn't want to irreversibly scar my kid. "What's up?"

"So… there's this holiday party going on at the station."

I waited for him to finish. When he didn't, I said, "Okay? You have to go help out after this or something?"

"No, no. Nothing like that." He rubbed my chest. "I was thinking that, since you and Dexter are here, you could both come to it? It's not for another week, but I heard Dexter saying he doesn't start school again until after New Years."

"I'd love to…" His eyes lit up instantly, which made me feel bad for immediately saying afterward. "But I have to bring Dex back home to his mom for Christmas."

"Oh…"

I squeezed his sides. "Maybe next year."

"You can't come back or anything? I don't mind paying for a plane ticket for you."

"That's sweet, Gage. But you should be spending the holiday with your family."

He mumbled something under his breath while pulling away from me.

"What was that?"

He shook his head. "Nothing. Never mind. Forget I said anything."

Confusion rattled in my brain, much like it had when he'd pulled away from me earlier when he'd come home for lunch.

What was going on?

I'd never seen him act this way. I'd blame it on his brothers being here, but he hadn't even known they'd been on their way during lunch.

This wasn't like Gage. He was usually the talker and I was the listener. He never shied away from expressing himself or his feelings, but right now this felt like pulling teeth from him.

"Hey…" I grabbed onto his arm. "Talk to me."

"It's fine. I get it."

"Get what?" I asked.

"It's just a stupid party. My coworkers were all bugging me about bringing you."

Shit.

"I'm sorry. I wish I could. Kate's going to want Dex there for Christmas and she'll probably let me have him right after, so I don't want to miss that."

"I get it, Xavier. You don't need to explain things to me like I'm a child."

His arm slipped from my grip.

I silently watched him as he grabbed one of the plates and scraped off the food remnants before dunking it in the pre-filled sink. His movements were methodical and robotic, like he'd put himself on autopilot without even thinking about it.

My stomach hurt with how hard the knot in it was clenching. We'd never really had a situation where we weren't seeing eye-to-eye outside of a work thing. We'd disagreed plenty while he'd been training with me, but outside of that, we were usually on the same page.

Me being sober had made our communications skills even better.

So what the fuck was this, then?

"Gage," I said slowly. "What's happening?"

"I don't know what you mean." He dunked another plate, tossing the fork into the sink with a quick flick of his wrist.

"What did I say?"

He sighed at me. "Nothing, Xavier. Drop it."

How the hell was I supposed to drop it when there was obviously a gigantic cloud of tension looming over us?

We never did this—we weren't like this. Ever since this afternoon, we'd been in this weird spot that I had no fucking clue how we even got into in the first place.

If I did, I would've fixed it by now.

"Baby," I tried again, reaching for him.

He dodged me, moving around to the other side of the trash to toss the last of the plate scrapings into it. "It's fine. Just forget about it."

"I can't when you're upset with me."

"I'm not."

"You are. Unless I'm fucking blind and there's a third person in this kitchen right now." I furrowed my brows, setting my lips into a thin line.

He lifted his gaze up from the trash to give me a look. "Funny."

There had to be more to this than just the party. There was no way he'd be getting this upset that I couldn't come to a work function.

Disappointed?

Sure.

But upset?

No way.

Gage was way more levelheaded than that.

He was the one to get me to actually get in touch with my own emotions and begin to untangle the absolute fucking mess that was my trauma. *He* convinced me to take my sobriety seriously because it was either that or lose my kid.

Gage wasn't the kind of guy to let his emotions run rampant and wild. He was one of the most regulated people I knew.

A little anxious at times?

Who wasn't these days?

We had stressful jobs that were constantly putting us in life or death situations.

Anxiety kind of came with the territory.

This was something way bigger than that. It had to be, or else I was going fucking crazy.

Clearly, he wasn't up to talking about it, no matter how many times I could try weaseling it out of him.

But was this the kind of situation that I let drop and forget about it?

Or did I give him the space he needed to figure out his own emotions before he could actually talk to me about them?

I wasn't sure. Not without asking him, but that was obviously out of the question. Right now, the best that I could offer was a listening ear when he was ready. Until then, I was going to have to suck it up and wait it out until he came to me.

Whenever the fuck that happened.

Bridging the distance between us, I wrapped my arms around him from behind and pressed a soft kiss to his neck. "Come find me later, okay?"

So we can talk.

He nodded silently, working overtime at scrubbing the plate in his hands.

With a sigh, I dropped my arms and stepped away, giving him the space he clearly needed to decompress from this. My heart was heavy as I left the kitchen, and him, behind.

In the living room, the boys were crowded around the giant TV, all of them sitting on the floor and craning their necks up while some kind of video game was playing. I stood behind the couch and watched for a second, trying to distract myself from going back in and begging Gage to talk to me.

"Nice. See that pasture where all the wheat is? Mow over it so you can start making barrels to sell at the market," Asher was saying, pointing to the screen.

"Got it," Dexter replied. The tractor on the screen slowly puttered over to a different colored field with a very realistic sounding engine.

"Nice. It's double drops," Greyson said. "That'll be perfect when you sell your first few barrels. You can buy a longer attachment so you can farm larger areas."

Shaking my head, I stepped away from the living room and headed down the hall to my bedroom, or rather, one of the twin's. Packing all my things up and zipping my bag, I carried it into Gage's room to set it down on his bed.

Following Dexter's suggestion of bunking with Gage was a smarter idea than forcing him to share a bed with me. After all, I'd be sneaking off to see him anyway after what just happened. Might as well kill two birds with one stone.

Heading back to the other room, I quickly changed the sheets on the bed and fluffed up the pillows nice and neat until I was satisfied with what I was leaving behind.

I swung the door shut behind me before making my way back to Gage's room. I had a hunch that he was going to avoid me for as long as possible. Which meant that I was either going to have to drag him to bed, or he was going to pretend like everything was fine and try to go to sleep in order to avoid this conversation.

Both options had me feeling nauseous.

Lifting my bag up from the bed, I let it fall to the floor at my feet and kicked it to press flush against the wall out of the way of the main walkway. I grabbed my phone out of my pocket, and Kate's name flashed across my screen.

Have Dexter call me, please, was all her text said.

Groaning, I let my body fall back onto the bed, bouncing slightly from the sudden weight fluctuation. If Kate was going to demand Dexter to come home a day early, I was going to actually lose it.

No, scratch that.

The more likely scenario was that I would be calling her up and demanding to know why the hell she was cutting our three-day weekend short when I'd been asking for very little from her from the beginning.

Lifting my phone up closer to my face, I typed out a quick *'sure'* and sent it on its way.

I let myself wallow for a total of five entire minutes before forcing myself up from the bed and heading out of the bedroom to go find Dexter.

CHAPTER 19

GAGE

"ANOTHER WEEK?" I overheard Xavier saying from the living room right as I shut the water off for the sink. "That's what she said?"

"You want to call her back and talk to her?" came Dexter's reply.

Snagging the towel off of the rack to dry my now thoroughly pruned hands, I slapped it down onto the counter once I was done with it and headed into the living room. The game on the TV was paused while both the twins were patiently sitting on the floor in front of the couch while Xavier and Dexter were talking.

Xavier had his phone in his hands that he tossed between them every few seconds, a pensive look etched onto his face. "It's just a little surprising, is all..."

Dexter offered his own phone over, waving it

slightly in the space between them. "That's all she said to me, but if you want to ask—"

His father was shaking his head, putting both of his hands up in mock surrender. "As long as she's not expecting us back on a flight Monday afternoon."

"What's going on?" I asked.

Xavier let out a soft sigh and then turned my way. "Kate called." Holding back a grimace should've earned me some kind of award. "And said that we can stay the week if we want."

There's no way I heard that right. "The *whole* week?"

He glanced back at Dexter who merely shrugged. "That's what she told me."

A whole week?!

I'd get Xavier for longer than just these measly three days that could barely even count as an extended weekend since he'd be traveling back home on the third day of it.

Could Kate really be so generous?

Did she have any of those bones left in her body?

I couldn't imagine her calling Dexter up to tell him that she'd done some soul searching and realized that keeping a son from his father was wrong and for them to take their time in getting back to California.

All of it was too good to be true.

Where was the catch?

"If that's okay with you," Xavier was saying, his gaze darting from me, over to the twins. "All of you. I don't want us imposing on anything."

The urge to tell him to shut up and kiss him

stupid was itching me right on the back of the neck, hard to ignore while my mind raced with the possibility that my wish of bringing him to the Christmas party would be coming true after all if I could convince Ellie to move the date up.

Sure, they'd be leaving *right* before Christmas day, but I was still getting them for the week leading up to it. That was counting as a win in my book. Even if I couldn't have Xavier for the entire holiday stretch like I selfishly wanted to.

Oh shit, I needed to go out and buy them both gifts.

What was Dexter into?

I could probably get the boys to weasel some info out of him in order to give me an idea on what to go off of. Xavier was easy—my issue was blowing him out of the water with what I got him, and not just buying him something that he'd tot on for a few days before forgetting altogether in a few months.

A strong hand gripped my shoulder, ripping me out of my thoughts. "Are you okay with this, Gage?"

My gaze snapped to Xavier's, the wariness in them not lost on me.

Our earlier tiff was still hanging in the air between us and not as easily forgotten as I would've liked for it to be. While I wasn't exactly sure why getting so triggered lately by our relationship had been happening, there was still that nagging feeling in me that was telling me something needed to be done.

What that was, I had no fucking clue.

If I dug down deep enough, I was positive that the answer would most likely have something to do with this long distance. Having him so far away from me the vast majority of the time was beginning to wear on me more than I initially suspected, causing these weird rifts that I couldn't seem to stop myself from falling into, and taking him down with me.

Beating out my frustrations on Xavier wasn't fair, especially since he had very limited time with me left—even with the extended few days Kate had apparently granted us with. He was, unfortunately, the closest punching bag that I had and all my brain wanted to do was scream 'fire!' and swing wildly.

The hand tightened on my shoulder once more.

Shaking my head, I said, "Yeah, sorry. It's all good with me."

"You sure?" he asked.

He seemed to be fishing for something—some kind of reassurance that I wasn't simply giving in by being put on the spot. Even with my mood still in a weird place, that was very much appreciated. Getting pressured into doing things for the sake of keeping the peace annoyed me to no end.

"I'm sure. We can work on getting your return tickets sorted out tonight."

Thankfully, he seemed to pick up on the hidden meaning underneath my nicely dressed words. "Why don't we go to that now? Don't need the seats to fill up on us."

"Laptop's in my room." I nodded toward the hallway.

While I dreaded having any kind of conversation that would bring us right back to where we were at in the kitchen, there was also a part of me that needed to purge this toxic shit from my system. Getting it all out in the open—whatever it really was—would get us back on the same page again.

Hopefully.

Xavier smiled at me slightly, his hand dropping back down to his side. "Guess we won't be needing to cram our entire itinerary into tomorrow after all."

At that, Dexter turned to the twins and said, "That means I get to stay up until the sun rises."

"Nice try," Xavier drawled. "You're still going to bed at a reasonable time."

"What's reasonable to you, Xavier?" Greyson asked. "Four am? Five?"

Asher gave him a hard shove on the back. "Yeah, like you'll be able to stay up that long. The military's got you guys in bed as soon as the sun goes down and getting up while it's still dark out."

"Okay. Pot, kettle?" Greyson shot back. "Weren't you the one complaining in the group chat how your boss is constantly waking you up at the ass crack of dawn?"

"Don't see him anywhere around here, now do we?"

"Boys…" I chided. "How about we're in bed by one."

"Fine," they chimed at the same time.

Xavier nodded to Dexter. "You too."

"Sure. Got it," he answered.

Blowing out a breath, I pivoted my body toward the hallway, feeling the energy in the room shift while Xavier followed me and the sounds of the game on the TV came to life again. The boys were good at distracting themselves, giving Xavier plenty of time to talk. However long they roped Dexter into hanging out with them, it would be at least for a little while.

Heading into my room, the first thing I noticed was Xavier's bag by my bed, leaning up against the wall. My lip quirked up involuntarily as my body relaxed at the sight of it. He didn't seem to be too mad at me if he was willing to share a room with me tonight.

That could all be a massive coincidence that aligned with giving the twins back one of their rooms, but I wanted to look at it as Xavier *actually* wanting to spend time with me despite our weirdness.

He shut the door behind us softly once he was inside, turning to me with a pinched expression. "Gage..."

My heart beat solidly in my chest, choking me from saying anything to him.

Expressing myself had never been a problem before. Even as a kid raising my two baby brothers, I'd always expressed exactly what was on my mind. There was never a point in my life where I subscribed to the idea that I had 'nothing to say' about a situation, even if it was a mundane one.

Yet here and now, I was stumbling to form my words properly to express myself.

How could I when I wasn't able to name what was wrong?

My theory was the distance between us affecting our bond—the issue being that there was no real way to prove that was actually what was going on with me unless he left and I could definitely say that was the real problem and not some bandage over top of the real festering wound.

Not to mention that with Xavier being here now, I should be over the moon wanting to crawl up into his skin while I had him, not picking stupid fights.

Everything was so damn jumbled. Nothing was making sense.

Why did I care if Xavier never married me and chose his family over spending one day out of the year with his family when I had him every other damn time?

Because you want him to be a part of your *family.*

Ugh...

Xavier crept across the room, standing before me with his hands outstretched to cup my face. He stroked his thumbs along my cheeks in a gentle way, soothing me despite my raging whirlwind of thoughts.

I'd always been transparent to him, no matter how well I believed I'd covered up the truth. He saw through me and into my soul like a damn pane of glass.

"Sorry," I whispered.

For everything.

He shook his head and bent forward to press his lips against mine in a chaste kiss. I melted into him instantly, my arms coming up to curl tightly around him as he adjusted his hold on me. He walked me back toward the bed, lowering me down onto it the second the back of my knees brushed up against it.

His body was a solid weight on top of me,

comforting in that weighted blanket kind of way. Our kiss was slow, and we took the time to savor the feeling of each other without the feverish need to strip our clothes off and go at it like a couple of wild animals.

This was what made all of the distance and conflicting schedules worth it—having him here with me in this quiet moment with no outside interruptions to rip us apart and force us back into our roles as parents or first responders.

Stressing about him leaving when I should be savoring what little time left I had was only going to make my moods worse and cause further issues that didn't need to be there in the first place. Quinn was right about it all—I was getting too up in my head about things that shouldn't even matter at this point.

What I really needed to be focusing on was soaking up as much time with my boyfriend as possible until he had to go home.

Xavier drifted back from our kiss, his fingers moving from my cheek to trail down my forehead and over my jaw. His treatment of me, like I was some kind of precious piece of ancient pottery, would never cease to get my heart fluttering.

"Talk to me." His voice was soft.

"I miss you," was all I could think to say back. Because at the end of it all, that was the truth. I missed him even when he was here with me.

His expression softened. "I miss you, too, Gage."

We had a week together.

A whole damn week.

Spending it on dreading the inevitable

goodbye was only going to leave me feeling regretful in the end. Xavier would be back; he wasn't leaving me forever no matter what that traitorous voice inside of my head told me.

Regardless of him not wanting to marry me, or not spending Christmas with me, we still had each other. Our bond had been forged in brotherhood during the chopper crash, long before we were officially dating. That wasn't something that could easily be wiped away no matter the circumstances.

Wrapping my limbs around him, I breathed in his woodsy scent and let my eyes close.

I needed to be grateful for what I had before I ended up chasing it away.

CHAPTER 20

Xavier

Two days after Kate's phone call, Dexter and I found ourselves at LSU's botanical gardens.

The place was absolutely beautiful and only an eight-minute drive from the campus. Arriving at the facility right after lunch, there were already plenty of people milling about in the front area leading into the main entrance.

While waiting in line to get in, we people-watched at the kids with their families running around on the front lawn while parents wrestled bracelet tickets onto their wrists. Simple things like this were the unexpectedly fun parts about coming to a new city.

We'd decided to start off working our way to the back of the property and ending at the front, leaving the flower gardens for last, since that's where most of the tourists that were around for the season were convening.

A good bout of rain had cut the mugginess in the air down by about half, leaving us to walk through the trail in a pleasant sixty-five degrees and sunny. The boardwalk leading back to the wetlands was surrounded by tall trees on either side of it, shading us under a nice canopy from the hot sun above.

Dexter had a map of the entire site in his hands that he stared down at while we walked side-by-side. He'd already marked off a few spots that I took as him wanting to stop by our way down, judging by the stars next to them.

This entire trip, I'd been impressed with his meticulous nature. Not being around for most of his formidable school years had put me at a disadvantage for knowing a key part of my son's life that led him into getting into LSU to begin with.

Seeing him like this was a nice peek into a part of what I'd missed for all of those years he'd moved through school.

"You know, if you end up going to LSU, you'll be able to walk here whenever you want." With this place being as large as it was, I doubted we were going to get the full experience of everything on just today alone.

There was a bit of regret in me for not having researched LSU as soon as Dexter had told me about his offer.

I'd been wary to send him off to a major city in the south to begin with, the reputation of the state clouding my own judgment and keeping me from actually being as supportive as I could've been. Don't get me wrong, I was damn happy he'd gotten accepted to a college early, regardless of where it was located even if being gay in the south had always sounded like a death sentence to me. One that would end in ostracisation or worse.

The more I saw of Baton Rouge, the more I was beginning to understand why Gage wasn't willing to leave it behind and why Dexter was considering coming here in the first place. The culture was rich, the people were hospitable, and there was a ton of stuff to do outside of campus life.

Outside of the same prejudices we'd find in parts of California, Baton Rouge wasn't abnormally terrible on that scale. Not enough for me to spend the rest of this week trying to convince Dexter to look elsewhere for school options.

"Yeah, I was thinking that." He folded up the map into a neat square to stick into his pocket. "I'm not really that informed on agriculture. But if I ever wanted to go into a program like that, LSU obviously has a good one."

"I'll say." If these gardens were anything to go by, my kid would be opening up his own damn farm by the end of his Bachelor's. "How are you liking having the twins around? They're not giving you too much trouble, are they?"

Dexter shook his head. "They're nice. I like them. It's kind of funny watching them and Gage bicker. I get an up close personal look into what it would've been like if I had a sibling."

I held back a snort.

There were times before Kate and I broke up where we'd talked about having another one.

Obviously, that never came into fruition with my cheating and breaking up our marriage, though the idea still entertained itself years after that.

At one point, I'd gotten so desperate after having lost Dexter that I'd walked into a damn donor bank and asked to be matched with someone who was willing to have an open IVF journey that I could step in and help co-parent. I'd been chased off the property soon after, my prayers for another child going unanswered.

During that time, I'd even contemplated calling up Kate and telling her that regardless of how she felt about me, Dexter deserved a sibling. Thankfully, I'd never gotten the courage to do that and had let myself wallow until the pain numbed me.

Those were some of my darker days that I'd take to the grave and tell no one about. Something in the universe had been looking out for me back then, not wanting me to help bring another child into this world when I was already severely fucked up and not dealing with it well.

"Do *you* like them?" he asked.

"Yeah, they're good kids." I used my hand on his back to guide Dexter away from the middle of the boardwalk as a large family moved past us, heading in the opposite direction. "I'm surprised you clicked with them so easily."

"I *am* capable of making friends," he drawled.

Wincing, I said, "That's not what I meant."

Even though that's definitely what I'd been implying.

If Dexter wanted to keep his circle of friends small, then it wasn't really my place to say anything. Despite my initial worries about him when I'd talked to Gage about it, he was clearly capable of befriending whoever he wanted with no signs of the stunted social skills that I'd previously worried about.

"Uh huh," was all he said back, guiding us onto another pathway.

"I'm sorry. I know I'm being overprotective."

Admitting that out loud to anyone other than Gage had me clamming up with self-consciousness. We were supposed to be in the 'mentor/guide' phase of our relationship, according to the parenting books I'd been given by my therapist late last year. Except missing out on all of the milestones with him before this stage had left me trying to overcompensate big time.

Now, I was at that fun stage of uncertainty where every misstep felt astronomical.

"It's fine. You're not half as bad as mom and Dan." He rolled his eyes. "I swear they'd lock me up in a bubble if it was legal."

"That bad, huh?" Not that I couldn't imagine Kate going overboard with her overprotectiveness, either. We were both grabbing at Dexter and yanking him in opposite directions, even with us being newly cordial.

Hearing that his stepfather was similar, though, had me curious. "Do you like him? Dan, I mean."

Dexter shrugged. "He's fine. He can get a bit over the top when he's trying to get his point across. He was pissed when I told mom that I didn't want to go to church anymore two summers ago. He tried taking me to this lecture at another church a few towns over to try and convince me to go again."

"That sounds... a bit much."

"That's how Dan is. He's been that way since I can remember. I think he still sees me as just mom's kid and not his stepson, which is fine, I guess. I'm not really bothered by it. It only gets annoying when he tries to ground me or force me into doing things that I don't want to do like the church thing. The entire time, I felt so weird because he barely pays attention to me otherwise." Dexter shook his head. "I don't do anything bad. So, I don't know what his deal is."

How complicated.

No wonder Dexter was standoffish with me. Aside from the obvious that he hardly knew me, having some man trying to come in and take over the father role he'd been without for so long must've felt like a slap in the face no matter how I framed it at the time.

Why were any of us surprised when he dug his heels in to resist the change?

The only consistency he's ever had was his mother.

I wanted to believe that Kate's choice in a husband after me was carefully considered and not an impulsive move in order to fulfill a role that I was no longer available for. No matter how I felt about her replacing me so easily when I'd begged her to let me in.

In the end, Dexter had turned out to be a very thoughtful, smart, and idealistic person that had a bright future ahead of him. None of which I could chalk up to having been born out of my influence.

Maybe now for the future, I could take some credit, but for now, this was still all Kate.

Throwing my arm around his shoulders, I brought him against my side to squeeze him. "Listen, you're an incredible person, Dex. Don't let anyone tell you or let you think otherwise. I'm so damn proud of you. Anyone would be lucky to call you their son."

He blinked up at me, his lips parting in surprise. "You... really mean that?"

"Of course I do. I wouldn't be saying it if I didn't."

A small smile tugged at his lips. His gaze darted away from me bashfully while his voice was quiet, barely able to be heard over the breeze picking up through the trees. "Thanks, dad."

"Anytime."

I let my arms slip from him and back down to my sides. His shoulder brushed with mine as a couple of joggers came up from behind us and passed us on either side, their faces red and chests heaving heavily from their workout.

Both of us fell into a peaceful lull of silence. I didn't think I'd ever be able to express to him how grateful I was that he'd asked me to take him on this trip. In just the span of a few short days, I felt closer to him than I had this entire past year.

Dexter letting me into his world inch by inch felt just as rewarding as getting my damn one year sober chip.

"You know," when he finally spoke again, I looked at him. "If I end up going to LSU, you could move here, too. Gage seems pretty happy to have you around."

Wryly, I said, "Trying to set me up?"

He shrugged, though there was that same small smile playing on his lips from earlier. "Aren't you tired of long distance?"

"God. Yes." I sighed. I was tired of a lot of things that were getting in the way of Gage and I. For one, his weird hot and cold attitude. But I wasn't sure how much of that was from us being forced into close proximity with a full house or something else going on with him. "I don't know if living together is the right move right now, though."

Dexter frowned. "Why not?"

"It's complicated."

He stared at me.

Jesus, who knew my kid would be this invested in my love life. "I think I upset him, but I'm not sure how. So, he's been a little off with me the past few days."

"Huh." Dexter turned back to face the boardwalk. "So, what do you think happened?"

"Kid, if I knew, I would've solved it by now."

He snorted. "All right. True. You guys aren't... breaking up, right?"

Aw, was he worried?

That warmed my heart if that was the case. Going from being terrified of him knowing I was dating someone, to him finding out and trying to give me relationship advice was a one-eighty flip that I never would've predicted but welcomed wholeheartedly.

"No, no. Nothing like that. Sometimes couples go through weird phases. I'm sure we'll be fine once I get him to actually talk to me."

He fell into another contemplative silence, his teeth gnawing on his bottom lip. Sometimes I wished I could reach in there and take a peek at those thoughts that always seemed to be rattling around inside of his head.

"I can ask Asher and Greyson to take me out tonight somewhere. Maybe a local restaurant or something so that you and Gage can have some privacy to talk," he finally suggested.

I threw my arm back around him again, bringing him in so I could press a quick peck to the side of his head. "Hey, no meddling. You just worry about yourself and enjoying your vacation. I don't want you stressing about this. I appreciate you caring, but I swear we're okay. Couples sometimes go through rough patches, it happens. I'm sure you've seen your mom and Dan go through something similar a couple of times."

He grunted at me. "That doesn't count. They preach at each other until one of them gives up and goes to bed for the night."

I held back making a face. "They still make up in the end, though, right?"

"I guess?"

Oh, boy.

Well, it wasn't exactly my place to speculate on my ex-wife's relationship with her husband. As far as I knew, they weren't splitting up anytime soon. "I appreciate you worrying about me."

"Fine. All right. Message received."

"I love you, Dex."

He smiled again, shrugging my arm off of him. "Love you, too, dad."

We pit-stopped at a small pavilion that had a

couple of restrooms attached to the back of it. I leaned against the side of the building while Dexter headed around to the bathrooms, giving me the chance to pull out my phone and check my messages.

There was only one from Gage that was him replying to my message from earlier telling him that we'd arrived at the botanical gardens safe and sound. While at face value, there was nothing wrong with what he'd said back, I could tell we were still at the same place we were two days ago.

Since then, he'd seemed to be masking whatever it was that he was feeling off about, causing us both to fall into a weird and stilted rhythm that I absolutely hated.

Maybe Dexter was right—maybe we did need to take tonight to work things out and talk. I hadn't wanted to push him on the subject since, believing that giving him space would end with him coming around to talking to me about it.

But maybe that was simply my way of being a coward. I'd left it all on Gage's shoulders to bring to me without providing the proper space for him to do so. Telling him I'd be around for whenever he felt like opening up wasn't the same thing as bringing the problem to the table and asking him to talk to me about it.

I could plead with him all I wanted about talking to me, and unless he was suddenly feeling no longer clammed up about it, we were going nowhere.

Typing up a text to send to him, I read it over a few times before hitting 'send'.

<<What time do you get off tonight? I want to take you out. Just you and me.

His reply was almost instant.

>>Really?? Where? I get off at six :)

There was my eager boyfriend. The man loved to be wined and dined regardless of what was going on between us.

<<I'll look up some local spots. We'll head out around 6:30.

A sudden scream shook me hard enough to push away from the wall and swing around to the back side of the building where I'd heard it coming from. My phone vibrated with Gage's incoming text right as I shoved it into my pocket.

"Get away from me!" someone shouted again, sounding a hell of a lot like my son.

My heart thumped hard in my chest as I ran to the bathrooms.

CHAPTER 21

Xavier

Shoving open the double swinging door into the men's stalls, I found a man standing at the back of the bathroom with his hand holding open one of the stall doors at the end. His head whipped around the second he heard me enter, his hands immediately coming up to either side of his head.

"I didn't do anything," he said to me.

He was around my age, maybe a little older, with a bald head, and wide-framed glasses that made his head look egg-shaped. He was tall and lanky, with a backpack slung over his one shoulder. His zip-up hoodie was parted funny, almost like he'd haphazardly zipped it in a hurry. The rest of him was dirty, stained with dark spots along his knees and pant cuffs.

"You followed me!" Dexter shouted from somewhere behind him.

"Get away from him," I snapped, marching down the aisle.

The man flattened himself against the wall, his hands still raised in the air while he scooted along to inch toward the door.

Ignoring him, I headed over to Dexter's stall that was still halfway open, finding him curled up against the corner of it and tucked practically behind the toilet. He had his arms wrapped tightly around him while his entire body shook violently.

His eyes were wide and dilated when they snapped to me.

"What the hell happened?" I asked.

"H-he…" With a shaky hand, Dexter pointed to the side of his door. "B... busted the lock."

Grabbing the door again, I looked down to where the simple metal bar that was used to hold the door in place was now hanging on by a single screw, facing the floor instead of horizontal to the door. My heart sank in my stomach, the picture suddenly becoming clearer.

Whipping around to where the man had been standing, I spotted no one else inside of the small bathroom other than us.

Fuck.

"H-He..." Dexter choked out. "He just... I was trying to... go to the bathroom and..."

"You're okay, Dex." Shoving myself into the stall with him was difficult, even with the way he was pressed back against the far wall. I reached out to grab at his arm to try and gently coax him out but he refused to move.

Tears spilled down his cheeks, a loud sob following right after. He was shaking so hard that I was afraid he was actually having a seizure. Pivoting my body to the side, I got the door shoved closed behind me and kept it that way with a hand planted on the top of it.

Reaching across the short distance, I took Dexter by the arm again, but instead of trying to pull him toward me, I ushered him down to the floor instead, letting him cram himself back into his tight corner without the risk of him passing out and falling.

He buried his head into his knees and rocked himself, his sobs barely muffled while they reverberated against the tiled walls around us.

"Dex, you're okay, I'm right here. I know that was scary." I cupped the top of his head with my hand to run my fingers through his hair. "I wouldn't let anything bad happen to you."

When I caught that guy—because when I got this all sorted out I would hunt him down until I was able to wrap my hands around that skinny neck—he was going to wish he never stepped foot on this damn property.

My military training would be pinpoint focused on making sure that man never walked, let alone tried to peep on another teenager, again.

"How?" he managed to choke out, lifting his face away from his knees just enough to talk. "You —you didn't... you didn't know..."

This was definitely a panic attack, with how hard his breath was coming in and out of him. I'd had very little experience dealing with something like this for a kid, and had even less training on what to do to break someone out of it.

Dexter's face was red from how hard he was

crying. Tears continued to leak down his cheeks and pool onto the fabric of his jeans. He was heaving air into his lungs, not quite catching enough of it before another sob took over and forced it all back out again.

"You screamed and I came." I swallowed the bile rising in my throat and tried to keep my voice level as I spoke. "That's all I needed."

"Not last time."

What the fuck?

"What do you mean 'last time'?"

He shook his head, burying it against his knees once more.

My throat clogged up, a wave of nausea hitting me. "Dex, what do you mean 'last time'? What happened?"

The memories of Dexter's almost confession to me late last year hit me like a train, slamming into me with enough force that I had to lean back against the door of the stall to steady myself.

The urge to deny the truth laid out in front of me—to beg for it to not be real—was bringing tears to my eyes. The evidence was too clear to deny, Dexter's panic attack too severe for this to have been a first time thing.

This was the stuff of repeated trauma slapping you across the cheek with a swiftness that shocked you down to your core. The kind that I'd lived with for the past two decades that still stole my breath away at times.

"Who the fuck hurt you, Dexter?"

When he finally lifted his head again, he whispered, "Father Thomas."

My heart shattered to pieces.

Does your mother know?

Those words were what almost came out of my mouth next before I bit my tongue hard enough to hurt. Now was not the time to be asking him questions. Right now, I needed to snap him back into reality before he actually passed out and hurt himself.

Pushing away from the stall door again gave me enough room to lift Dexter up from where he was and slide him over to me. He crumbled against my chest the second I wrapped my arms around him, clinging to me in the same way he had when he was a toddler.

He buried his face against my shoulder and continued to tremble. I rocked him with me, keeping my hand steady against his back to try and ground him while I spoke to him softly like I had when he had nightmares after Kate and I put him to bed as a baby.

This horrible secret he'd been carrying with him this whole time, not able to talk about it as it festered away at his soul, was the worst injustice I'd ever seen.

Who in their right mind would hurt someone like Dexter?

Take advantage of him in the most sickest and twisted way possible?

I didn't need to know the details to know how bad they were. Dexter wasn't the kind of person to crack easily, not like this. So whatever this Father Thomas had done to him was horrific enough to break him apart.

"Breathe with me, Dex," I said, pulling in a lungful of air.

It took a few tries, but eventually, he was able to suck in enough oxygen to start calming down his nervous system. After a few more deep breathing exercises, he turned to jello in my arms—utterly exhausted from his adrenaline finally crashing.

I hardly felt his weight while throwing one of his arms over my shoulder and hiking him up enough to get one of my arms tucked around his legs, allowing me to stand and get us both up off the floor.

He hardly moved as I readjusted him and carried him out of the bathroom in a half-fireman hold, half-lifted up onto my shoulder. The man from earlier was still nowhere to be found, probably halfway to the parking lot by now.

How long he'd been following my son, I had no clue. We'd been too focused on our conversation to really pay attention to anyone else around us, outside of the occasional need to move out of the way.

It sickened me to think that my son had been targeted, whether abruptly or through a series of carefully planned moves that I hadn't caught on to at all by the predator lurking right out in broad daylight.

What kind of father was I?

I had the kind of military training that would make more people blanch at, and to have something like this slip past my radar?

Fuck.

I was no better than a random man off the street with no training.

The people passing us by on the trail shot me

strange looks when I passed them, though none of them seemed to be reaching for their phones to call the authorities, thankfully. An attendant called to me on the way off the trail but I ignored them in favor of heading right for the parking lot where our rental car was waiting for us.

I tucked a sleeping Dexter into the backseat and strapped him in, trying my best not to wake him while I shut the door and headed over to the driver's side. My hands shook taking the wheel and pulling the car out of park, even more so when I glanced back in my mirror to see my sleeping son's face.

How did I not know?

How *could* I have known?

Two warring thoughts in my head that wouldn't leave me alone the entire fifteen minutes it took to get back to Gage's house. Forcing back my own panic with practiced ease helped me get my kid out of the car and behind the safety of a locked front door.

Dexter stirred slightly when I laid him down in bed and pulled the covers over him, mumbling something in his sleep that I couldn't quite catch.

I didn't know how long I stayed with him, sitting on the side of his bed while I stroked his hair as he slept. Not until I heard voices coming from the front of the house that sounded like Gage talking to someone on the phone.

Slipping out of Dexter's room and shutting the door behind me, I found Gage tossing his work duffle bag onto the floor by the door while he bent at the waist to wrestle his shoes off. He jumped when he turned and spotted me standing there, the person who he was talking to continued to rattle on about something—a party?

Oh, his work party.

"Hey, baby." He smiled, and then glanced down at his phone. "Ellie, I'll call you back later."

He cut her off mid-sentence to drop the call and shove his phone back into his pocket. I watched in real time as his expression fell from the 'happy to see me' down to deep concern.

"Hey, what happened? You look white as a ghost."

He grabbed both of my arms to guide me into the living room, apparently realizing before I had —most likely from his training—that I was about to drop. Right as he hovered me over the couch, my legs collapsed out from under me, sending me catapulting onto the soft cushion.

"Xavier?"

I bent forward to curl my hands over my face, doubling over while the nausea was strong enough to bring stars into my vision. My whole world— the entire axis of it—was now completely off kilter. I'd left this morning living a completely different life to the one I came home with.

My baby boy had been hurt and I wasn't there to protect him.

God, the way he'd said *you weren't there last time,* was going to fucking haunt me.

Gage ran a hand down my back a few times, patiently waiting for me to talk.

How in the world was I supposed to get any words out when all I could focus on was the utter terror on my son's face?

Was that the expression Father Thomas had seen when he'd hurt my son?

Was that enough to stop him or was it the green light to keep going?

Fuck.

"I'm gonna be sick."

Gage snapped into action immediately. Both of his arms hooked under mine to yank me up from the couch and drag me down the hallway to the bathroom. We both stumbled inside, the brightness from the hallway our only light source. I sank onto the floor just as Gage lifted up the toilet seat and pushed my head forward to hover over the clean porcelain bowl.

I clung to the rim, coughing up my entire lunch and breakfast. The clenching in my stomach was painful, causing tears to prickle at the corners of my eyes while I held on for dear life.

Gage rubbed my back through bouts of nausea, not at all cringing away from my spitting bile out of my mouth.

My breathing echoed against the walls of the small bathroom, reminding me of the way Dexter's had inside of that tiny stall.

"Dexter okay?" Gage asked, once it seemed that there was nothing left in my stomach to throw up.

I shook my head, squeezing my eyes shut. "He told me what happened."

His hand froze on my back.

Both of us had gone back and forth on what Dexter had told me last year, or rather what he *didn't* tell me, on what we thought was possibly going on with him. *Neither* of us had ever guessed anything remotely close to this mess.

"The fucking priest." My voice was gravely and my throat burned as I spoke. "At that fucking church she was taking him to."

"Fuck," Gage breathed out. "Where is he?"

"Sleeping."

Peeling my eyes back open, I reached across the way to snag a few squares of toilet paper to wipe my mouth with before tossing it into the bowl and flushing the whole thing. Pitching backward, I settled myself back against the cool tile of the floor, letting my body relax into it.

I had a sense of déjà vu as Gage hovered over me as I lay there, panting, his silhouette shrouded from the light coming from the hallway.

"Oh, honey..."

He gently swiped his fingers under my eyes and belatedly, I realized I was crying.

"I wasn't there..." I said.

The guilt crushed me—more than it had when he'd told me how I was a stranger to him an entire year ago. This was something entirely different, the kind of guilt that I'd felt being the only survivor among my troop and now had to grapple with living when they didn't.

How could I be there for Dexter when I hadn't been at his most vulnerable moment?

How could I call myself *a father*?

"You didn't know," Gage soothed.

"I should've been there," I whispered back.

He shook his head at me. "You didn't know what you didn't know, baby. It's not your fault or anyone else's other than that bastard who hurt him."

More tears stung my eyes. "I failed him."

"Baby…"

I stared up at the ceiling, tracing the weird shadows with my gaze.

What now?

How did I go from here?

It wasn't like I could go to that church and find the bastard and kill him. Getting myself thrown in jail was the last thing Dexter needed. He needed me to be there to protect him, something that I couldn't do locked behind bars for the next twenty-five years.

What he needed was to be home with familiarity. To have the comforts of what he knew, not out here trying to put on a brave face and forced to be around people he really didn't know while we toured a random city for the next few days before Christmas.

How could I, in good conscience, keep him away from all of that when this was the time he needed it most?

"I think… I going to take him home," I said.

Gage's voice was quiet as he said, "Do what you need to do."

GAGE

My heart hurt for both Xavier and Dexter.

After getting him up off the floor of the bathroom, I'd convinced him to let me cook something for the both of them before they headed off for an early bedtime. Whipping together something both comforting and *good* was tough, but I'd managed to make a homemade classic in the form of goulash.

By the time I'd gotten the food on Xavier's plate, he'd already booked two plane tickets back to California for first thing in the morning. While it wasn't my place to tell him how to handle a situation like this, I was sad to see him and Dexter leaving so abruptly.

I could understand from a parent's perspective on wanting to take your kid back to the familiar comforts that they were used to in order to ground them back down into reality, but at the same time,

I was also of the mindset that sometimes distracting yourself until you were ready to face your demons was the best medicine.

Xavier was always going to be overly protective of Dexter, no matter what his age. I found that admirable, even as sad as I was at the time. Putting his child first above all else was the kind of thing he'd only dreamed of a year ago when he'd still been addicted to the bottle.

Having *anyone* take priority over that was impressive in and of itself, no matter how you looked at it.

So really, who was I to judge in the grand scheme of things?

"Mmm, something smells tasty."

Turning to the sound of the voice, I spotted Asher wandering into the kitchen, his shoes still on from coming in. Normally, I'd yell at him to take them off but at this point, I was feeling exhausted myself.

Watching Xavier go through all of that and feeling the mental toll of him showing me his booked plane tickets had me wanting to crawl into bed for the next few days and only to come out to pee.

The other downside was tonight Xavier was sleeping in Dexter's room just in case he woke up with a night terror.

"Leftovers are in the fridge," I said, setting the pot down into the sink to soak it.

"Red sauce? Wow, someone was feeling fancy." Asher popped open the door to the fridge, fishing out one of the containers I'd used to store his portion. "What's the occasion?"

"Nothing. Just wanted to make something for Xavier and Dexter."

"Oh, they're here? I didn't even see them." He tossed the container into the microwave and jabbed the buttons on the front of it after shutting the door. "They have a long day at the botanical garden?"

Sighing, I said, "Something like that. They're taking an early night since they need to catch a plane in the morning."

Asher turned to me with a frown. "Wait, I thought they were staying the rest of the week?"

Turning back to the sink to occupy myself, I said, "Something came up."

Asher was quiet while his food was cooking, giving me time to turn on the sink and rinse out one of the pans I'd used to cook the ground meat in. Normally, I'd be bragging to the high heavens that I'd successfully cooked a meal without having to rely on a store bought base.

Expressing anything remotely close to joy felt wrong right now, though. My stomach was still churning with what Xavier had told me. He didn't have much info about what exactly the priest had done to poor Dexter, but honestly, there wasn't really a reason to force the kid into spilling more details.

It was pretty obvious what happened—given his reaction and the answers to a few of Xavier's questions.

Not to mention that creep who was trying to peep on him got away with not one repercussion for what he was trying to do. Honestly, I had half a mind to call up some of my buddies in the police force and tell them to check the cameras.

Having a guy like that wandering a public space that usually had a lot of kids running around was dangerous.

"So... what happened?" Asher asked just as the microwave went off.

"It's not really my business to say."

He shut the door after pulling the container out, the entire thing ghosting the air with water vapors. "You guys didn't get into a fight or anything, right?"

I shook my head. "Nothing like that. Something... uh, happened to Dexter."

Asher looked concerned at that. "He okay?"

How was I supposed to answer that?

No, not exactly?

Or, yes, hopefully, he would be eventually?

Ugh, this is why I wished Xavier was at least staying up for a little while with me. My brothers could be such damn nosey twits, which made it hard for me to keep things to myself.

I wasn't about to go around spilling all of the details that Xavier had told me about Dexter's situation—he'd told all of that to me in confidence, and regardless of what tactics my brother used to try and weasel the info out of me, I wasn't cracking.

However, straight up lying to my brother when I knew the truth about Dexter's condition felt wrong. I wasn't one to hide things from them, even if it was the brutal honest truth. The world was never going to sugar coat things for you as soon as you stepped into it as a fresh adult.

So why should I?

That would simply be setting my brothers up for failure in a system that was already wildly unbalanced.

"He's... okay, I think. He had something happen to him at the botanical garden. So, his dad is taking him home tomorrow to be with his family."

"That doesn't sound good." Asher fished a fork out of the drawer next to him to stir his goulash around. "What time are they leaving? I can get Grey up in the morning so we can say goodbye."

I smiled a little. "That's really sweet but I think they're trying to get out of here as fast as possible. I can send them a text from all of us once they're back home."

He continued to stir his food around in the container, both of his brows pulled together. "I'm not really liking the sound of all of this. Are they both really okay?"

"Some guy tried to hurt Dexter today." That was as much info as I was giving him. Even *that* I wasn't sure if it was too much.

"Hurt, as in..." Asher fished.

I shook my head at him, turning back to the dishes in the sink. He sighed at me but didn't push it further, thankfully. Out of the two of them, Asher was always good at knowing when to quit.

"Where's your brother?" I asked.

"Out with someone."

"A date?" I glanced over at him.

"Who knows. He says 'friend', so that could mean anyone."

Too true.

If there was one thing Greyson had going for him, it was his gaggle of 'friends' that were actually people throwing themselves at him. He was a good-looking kid, so I could understand the multiple crushes he had accumulated over the years. Couple that with the whole military thing and… well, no wonder he was out on his third day home.

"None for you?" I asked.

He grunted at me, stabbing down into the pieces of noodle and ground beef like he was trying to thatch a bundle of hay.

"Come on, you can't tell me you haven't had anyone hitting you up after finding out you're home." I chuckled.

"Yeah, well. No, I don't."

Okay, that was a total surprise.

Aside from them both being identical, they were both charming to a fault, which had gotten them in and out of trouble many a times during high school. Having to go down to that damn campus every other week had been a true testament to my patience as a caretaker and one that I'd welcomed in dropping the proverbial hat as soon as they graduated.

If Greyson was getting plenty of action, then by default, Asher would be, too. At least patterns from their past suggested as much.

Unless...

"Someone else entertaining you?" I guessed.

Asher's eyes widened briefly before he focused back on shoving a fork full of food into his mouth.

Bingo.

"Tell me."

So that I can rag on you for it.

As brotherly payback and all, seeing as how when I'd finally told them about Gage, they hadn't dropped teasing me about it for weeks. While endearing that they were all for me finally finding someone I clicked with, after about the fourth week, I'd been over it.

"Tell you what? I've got nothing." His tone was a little more defensive than usual.

"Asher Torres, you tell me who's keeping you preoccupied."

He scoffed. "No one, okay? Maybe I want to be single and focus on my work at the ranch."

The ranch...

Actually, wasn't Greyson saying something about his boss a while back?

Some handsome guy that had Asher dragging himself out of bed *willingly* before the sun rose?

I was positive I wasn't imagining that.

"Not your boss at the ranch?"

He choked on his food hard enough to toss the container onto the counter and pound his fist against his chest a few times. I doubled it up by slapping him on the back, finally getting the noodle loose from his throat so he could breathe again.

"*Fuck*," he muttered.

"Wow, so was that a yes?"

He slammed his elbow into my ribs, causing me to yelp and shuffle away.

"Rude," I said, grabbing my dishtowel to snap it in his direction. "You know, I can't be a supportive brother if you don't tell me things."

"There's nothing to tell, I'm serious. My boss is..."

I waited while he trailed off, sure he was going to finish his thought. All he actually did, though, was to sigh and roll his eyes while giving his goulash a glare that could rival my own.

"He's what, Ash?"

"Just. Ugh, it's hard to explain." Waving a hand in the air, he snatched his food back off the counter and quickly finished it off.

I grabbed the empty container from him to dunk under the water in the sink. Well, if he wasn't going to tell me anything, I was just going to have to bother Greyson about it. *One* of them was going to have to let me in.

Besides, this was all a nice distraction from the shit with Xavier and Dexter. Teasing my brothers over their love lives was a much simpler path than trying to sort through my tangled emotions regarding a teenage boy who was close to my own two brother's ages being assaulted by someone that he was supposed to be able to trust.

That kind of shit sent me down into a spiral that I didn't want to be dealing with. This world was already scary enough with the drugs, gang violence, corrupt government, and shitty health-care. Adding predators on top of that was a layer of 'fucked up' that I really didn't want to be thinking about.

Then again, was that a kind of privilege I was experiencing that Dexter didn't have the luxury of?

My heart broke for him, absolutely. How this world could be so dark, I'd never know.

I held back another sigh, scrubbing at the left-over container with a kind of rigorousness that had my hands hurting. Whatever Xavier, and by default Dexter, needed in the future to help this transition easier on them, I would one hundred percent be there to help provide it.

Forget all of the bullshit surrounding my insecurities. That could all wait until Xavier got settled down into a good place again. And Dexter, too.

If they ever wanted to come back before the school year ended for a do-over of this turned-shitty vacation, my place had an open door and a warm bed waiting for them. No questions asked.

Hell, I'd pay for the goddamn plane tickets the minute Xavier called me to ask if it was all right to crash here again.

Hopefully, I wouldn't be kept waiting for long. Because while I wanted Xavier to spend time with his family during this difficult situation, I also missed him, too. As selfish as that was.

"Gage?" Asher hovered over my shoulder. "I think that thing is clean."

"Oh shit." Pulling it out of the water, the scrapper side of my poor sponge was mangled by how hard I'd been rubbing it against the lip of the container, cutting it up and shredding it into pieces that were now floating on the water's surface.

"You good?" Asher asked.

"Yeah, just got caught up in my thoughts."

Like fucking usual.

He threw an arm around my shoulders, jostling me slightly to pull me close to him. "Hey, I know you're sad about your boytoy leaving before the party, but at least you have me and Grey."

Smiling, I set the container down and tossed the sponge onto the side of the sink. "Of course. I'm not complaining one bit. You two surprising me was the best Christmas gift you could've ever gotten me."

He grinned. "Yeah? Just wait until your *real* gift."

The shimmering mischief in his eyes told me *exactly* what I needed to know about the goddamn mystery box he and his brother had teased me with their first day back in the state. I supposed it would be a tradition to prank me after having been gone for so long.

I only hoped that it wasn't another whipped cream pie this time around.

That shit was surprisingly hard to get out of your clothes.

"Uh huh." Nudging him, I slipped out from under his arm to grab the towel hanging off the stove. "Listen, you two need to behave a little bit at the party. Some of my coworkers are a little on the reserved side."

"What about Quinn? He seemed totally cool with Grey and I."

Ugh, of course you think that.

I'd seldom brought the twins around the station when they were kids—mostly because emergencies could rarely ever be predicted and having them be in the way of some kind of chaotic go-go-go was a scene out of my worst nightmare.

Sure, they'd *probably* be fine, but there was always the possibility that they *wouldn't* be. And I just couldn't be taking that lightly. As they'd gotten older, they'd stopped by a little more frequently, but not enough to really know the newbies we'd gotten in recently.

Which tended to be a good thing sometimes.

"Quinn... will be preoccupied at the party." Hopefully.

Knowing Quinn, though, both he and Jase would be getting roped into Asher and Greyson's schemes in no time. Zander, too, probably.

Hopefully, Ellie didn't put me on extra cleaning duty if the twins made a mess of the place.

"Well, either way, I'm excited to see all your coworkers. Greyson, too."

That really warmed my heart, even if I knew Asher was most likely planning something ridiculous. "I'm glad. Why don't you go change and we can grab a movie on the couch while we wait up for your brother to come back with his tales of his nightly escapades."

Asher flashed me a grin. "Hell yeah, count me in."

CHAPTER 23

Xavier

Pulling into the driveway to Kate's house, I killed the ignition and let the car rattle to a cool with Dexter and me still sitting inside of the cab. Both of us had barely talked the entire trip back to California, outside of the occasional check-ins after getting through TSA and then on and off the plane.

While there was a lot left unsaid between us, I was sure we both agreed that the exhaustion from this impromptu trip had won out over that entirely. Dexter wasn't exactly surprised when I woke him up early this morning with both of our bags packed and an outfit laid out for him.

Nor was he taken aback when Gage met us at the door to bid us a soft, heartfelt goodbye that left tears in my eyes when we climbed into the rental car and jetted off for the airport.

Yesterday seemed like an entire lifetime ago compared to now. Idling in Kate's driveway had somehow taken me off autopilot, slowly pulling me back into my consciousness and reality. The gravity of *'now what'* weighed on me more than I'd really anticipated.

There were no rule books that came with dealing with situations like this one. No proper protocol was discussed in Parenting 101 when you first met your baby in the hospital and all of the nurses and doctors came around to congratulate you on your new bundle of joy.

Why could this world be so dark and cruel and why were those that perpetrated against the laws of nature allowed to still walk freely among us with seemingly no consequences?

I was so lost, so goddamn angry.

"Just tell me one thing, Dex..." My voice was soft as I spoke. "And I won't ask you anything else about this until you're ready to talk."

His face was obscured by his hood pulled up over his head, intentionally left like that throughout our entire journey home save for the one time TSA had asked him to pull it down to confirm his identity.

When he slowly turned away from looking out the windshield, his eyes were glazed over from lack of sleep and the rough ride we'd had coming home from being crammed back in economy.

"Does mom know?" I asked.

His lips thinned into a small frown. My heart sank at the way his gaze moved away from mine, his eyes downcast into his lap where he fiddled with his hands.

"A little."

That's all I needed to know.

I reached over to put a hand on his shoulder, giving him a reassuring squeeze and a silent 'thank you' for being honest with me.

None of this was easy to talk about at all, and what little info he'd given me so far was enough to paint the picture he was trying to tell me without actually having to relive the trauma of recounting the entire situation.

I appreciated anything at this point.

But now I had an even bigger problem—my ex-wife and her not informing me about this. If she found out recently, that was one thing, but there was a deep twisting in my gut telling me otherwise.

Kate wasn't one to bring me in on anything when it came to Dexter without humiliating me first into begging on my hands and knees for the damn crumbs she decided to bless me with whenever she felt like it.

I didn't want to be bitter toward her, not when deep down in my heart, I knew that whatever Kate's choices were, they were made in good faith to keep Dexter safe even when I didn't agree with them.

But this was so much different.

This was not her putting him into a private Catholic school against my wishes, or forcing him into some sports club when he obviously wanted to get onto the debate team. This wasn't her bringing him to church every Sunday to sit in some goddamn pew for two hours while praying to a

God that I was pretty sure our kid didn't even believe in.

The second she found out about any of this, she should've been showing up on my doorstep demanding to talk to me. Because that's sure as fuck what I was about to do right now.

Climbing out of the car, I let the door slam shut behind me and grabbed the handle of the one behind me to fish Dexter's bag out. He got out after me a moment later, slowly sliding off of his seat until his feet finally hit the pavement.

His body was hunched in on itself while he grabbed onto one of the strings coming down from his hoodie. Coming around the other side of my car, I watched him hover next to his door for a long moment, staring at the front door that was still closed and the light above it still on from the night before.

"I'll let them know you're tired so they leave you alone to sleep," I said, trying to offer him what I hoped was a reassuring smile.

His frown only deepened, though, his body still unmoving.

This horrible situation, however long it had been going on for Dexter, only seemed to encourage his reserved nature. Not that I could really blame him for wanting to shut himself off from the rest of the world at this point.

What good was any of it to him when all it seemed to throw at him was fucking nightmares?

"I'm sorry, dad."

Wait, what the fuck?

"Dex, no, you have nothing to be sorry for! None of this is your fault."

"But we cut the trip short because I—"

"Son, no. No."

I waved a hand at him, holding my arm up to beckon him over until he finally peeled himself away from the side of my car to shuffle over to me. His body practically sagged into mine when he reached me, allowing me to wrap a tight arm around him as I guided him up to the front steps leading into the house.

I hadn't bothered to call Kate ahead of time about any of this, mainly out of pure avoidance. There was no doubt in my mind that as soon as I called or even texted her that we were coming home earlier than she'd anticipated, I would've had a slew of calls and texts popping up on my notification bar the second we landed.

Call me selfish but I really wasn't in the mood to be dealing with any of that.

Even now, standing there as I rang the doorbell, I felt a headache coming on.

After a minute of us waiting, the lock on the other side of the door clicked as it was shoved back from the dead bolt, the door opening a moment later. A man, tall, with glasses and a large forehead, stood in front of the glass storm door with a confused expression on his face.

Both of us stepped back so he could push the door open. "Dexter? I thought you were coming home later this week?"

"Dan, right?" I shoved a hand in the gap separating the door from the frame. "I'm Xavier. It's nice to meet you."

He glanced down at my hand with very obvious disdain; the wrinkles forming on his forehead were prominent while his face pinched into a sour look. I held my hand there, plastering a pleasant smile on my face when he finally looked up at me again.

When he slowly took my hand, I squeezed his back, giving it a hard shake. "We had some things come up on the trip. I've got Dex's bag if you want to take it."

Ripping my hand away from his, I used it to push the storm door open further while wiggling the strap of Dexter's bag off my shoulder and passed it between us. Dan's eyes widened and quickly, he took the bag in his arms.

While he was momentarily distracted with that, I nodded to Dexter while continuing to hold the door open. Taking my hint, he ducked under my arm to head inside, disappearing beyond the foyer and hopefully, up to his room where he could lock himself in for the rest of the morning to decompress.

I was damn worried about my kid but I also knew that it was important to give yourself the time to come down from the spike in stress hormones. Fuck, I knew I'd needed plenty of that when I was discharged.

"Is there a reason you brought him back so early?" Dan asked.

While he didn't exactly sound annoyed, he certainly didn't look too happy.

Was that from the lack of planning on our end, not communicating, or something else?

Such as him not wanting my kid around in general.

I wanted to believe the best in this man, having

stepped up where I couldn't, in raising Dexter, no matter what my pride and ego said about some other man raising my son. Yet, I also knew the statistics of men treating their step kids like pariahs due to that very reason.

Would Kate bring a man like that around to help raise Dexter?

I certainly hoped not.

"Kate around?" I asked instead of answering him, leaning around him to look deeper into the house.

He huffed at me, sliding the bag down to the floor while saying, "Look, I don't know what your game is, but—"

"Dan?" Kate called. "Did I just see Dexter going upstairs?"

Before either of us could answer her, she appeared in the doorway looking shocked to see me. Her dirty blonde hair was wrapped up in a tight ponytail, the long lengths hanging down behind her. Even though it was early in the morning, she had her makeup down and a nice outfit on.

The only thing that was out of place was her slightly white-dusted hands. Presumably from some kind of bread dough she was most likely making for church dinner this coming Sunday.

"Xavier..." she breathed out.

I grabbed the door to yank it completely open. "I need to talk to you."

"I think it's best if you leave," Dan said, fixing me with a glare.

I ignored him, staring my ex-wife down. "It's

about Dex. You know I wouldn't be showing up here like this if it wasn't important."

Her expression faltered. Even though she clearly wanted to fight me—most likely to tell me to get the fuck off her property—she knew I was right. I wasn't the kind of jealous ex to show up and demand for her to take me back or something as equally ridiculous.

We took our shit with Dexter seriously. There was no such thing as 'needlessly bothering each other' over trivial matters in order to annoy each other to death. Thankfully, that was the one mature thing we both mutually agreed on long ago.

"Kate," Dan said, a little panicked when she stepped out onto the landing.

"I'll be just a second," she said, swinging the storm door closed behind her.

Dan watched us through the glass, wearing a clearly dissatisfied frown.

Not wanting an audience to this—because who knew if Dan was even aware of this situation—I led Kate down to my car and parked us right around the side of it, facing away from the door. I doubted her new husband could read lips, but on the off chance, I was taking every precaution.

"What happened? Why did you bring him home so early?" She crossed her arms. "Don't tell me you got sick of him over having him for just a weekend."

I ignored the jab. "Dexter told me about Father Thomas."

Instantly, her face went white.

"When were you going to tell me?" I asked. "Better yet. When did you find out?"

Her arms slowly dropped from her chest while she swallowed audibly.

It hurt more to know that she kept this from me than her questioning the integrity of my parenting before allowing me to take my own kid across state lines for a weekend.

"He... he told you..." she whispered.

"Yes, Kate. I know it may blow your mind to realize that my son *actually* tells me things, but yeah, he told me. When the fuck were you going to tell me and when did *you* find out?"

She fumbled over her words. "Last summer... he— I was having a really hard time taking him to church because he was refusing to go. It was out of the blue, and..." To her credit, she looked like she felt incredibly guilty. "I'm sorry."

So, around the time he said he'd stopped going to church with her. "Is that when it happened?"

"I-I think so... He didn't want to talk about it."

Yeah, no shit.

"Did you report it? What the fuck happened with the priest?"

"Of course I did!" she spat out. "What kind of mother do you take me for?"

"One that doesn't tell the father jack-shit." All right, it was a low blow. Sue me. I was too angry with her, with the fucking priest—with the rest of the goddamn world—to care right now.

She flinched. "What, so I was supposed to call you up and say to you, 'hey, long time no talk. Just to let you know, our son was molested today!'. Is that what you wanted, Xavier?"

"Yes!" I exploded. "What the fuck is wrong with you, Kate?"

"I was *protecting him*—"

"You brought him there! To that fucking church! I told you I didn't want him raised in that shit, and you did it anyway. You handed him over to a fucking predator!"

Her eyes grew watery, looking as though I'd just struck her with my own hand across her cheek. I wanted to feel bad at her stumbling back from me, shocked to hear something so hateful spilling out of my mouth.

The truth of the matter was that I really *didn't* care. Not when I'd been lied to and misinformed about a situation that definitely was supposed to involve both parents in making a decision on what was best for our child.

I should've been there when the police report was filed and when my son had to recount the entire goddamn thing to a room full of strangers with badges. Or afterward, when I was sure he was feeling so raw and exposed it was a wonder he didn't walk right out into the middle of traffic.

"If you tell me Dan fucking knew before I did, I'm going to lose it," I gritted through my teeth.

"He's my *husband*, Xavier. I wasn't going to lie to him about what was going on."

"No, just lie to the father of your child, instead." I tightened my hands into fists.

I forced myself to step away from her before I yelled something even worse at her; my adrenaline was spiking so high that my vision was beginning to tunnel. This was the same kind of intense aggression I felt whenever I was thrown into combat.

A kill-or-be-killed type situation that was slowly morphing into murderous intent. Wherever that priest was, he better count his fucking days because I was coming for him. No matter what jail cell he was rotting inside. I'd pay him a little visit.

"Xavier," Kate choked out. "Stop. Okay? It's done and over with."

"Where is he? Which jail?"

When I turned to her, she was shaking her head. "He's not—"

I ripped open the door to my car before she even got the sentence out. My thoughts were thundering around me—repeating what an utter failure the justice system really was. Of course the priest walked. Of course they probably transferred him to another parish. Of course my son would never receive any justice.

At that point, I didn't care if I went to jail. At least my son wouldn't have to constantly be afraid and looking over his shoulder.

Kate raced over to me, grabbing the handle from the outside before I could pull it open. She was screaming something at me while I turned the key that I'd left in the ignition, letting the car roar to life.

"Stop!" She grabbed a hold of the front of my shirt, practically throwing herself over my lap to stop me from grabbing at the gearshift. "He's dead! He died!"

My body froze.

"He's dead, Xavier!" she kept repeating. "He killed himself. Please, get out of the car!"

Her nails dug into my arm, using that infamous mom-strength that all women seemed to possess at the most crucial of times, in order to yank me out of the car. I faltered, pitched sideways and crashed onto the driveway, crushing my shoulder in the process.

The sharp and sudden pain was enough to temporarily break me from whatever tunnel vision and hair-brained plan I'd had in going up to Kate's church in order to bust down the doors and drag whatever white-collared fool I could get my hands on to interrogate.

Kate's sobs were what brought me back to reality, along with her nails biting into my skin still.

"I'm sorry," she kept repeating. "I knew you'd go to jail. I'm sorry."

Behind her, Dan hovered just a few feet from where we were, clearly lost on what to do. He'd probably sprinted out as soon as he'd seen her trying to yank me out of the car. Or who knows, maybe it was when we'd begun yelling at each other about our shared responsibility in failing to protect our only child in all of this.

"When," I croaked.

Reading my cryptic question for what it was, she answered, "Right after he was arrested. He hung himself in his cell."

"Coward," I spat out, while pushing myself up from the driveway.

My shoulder screamed from me rotating it a few times to check to make sure I hadn't blown it out of the socket. Outside of the dizzying pain, it would be fine with an ice pack and a few Tylenol.

"He needed you here." Kate sniffled. "Not in a jail cell."

Much the same mantra I'd told myself yesterday after finding out. How funny the way things changed in the blink of an eye.

"You never told me," I said.

"I was going to. Eventually."

I shook my head.

While I wanted to believe her, I didn't know how true that really was when everything finally boiled down to it. Perhaps Kate had the intention to do so back when it first happened, letting the dust settle long enough with the case before bringing it to me because of her genuine—and now proven—fear that I'd do something irrational.

But there wasn't any excuse now that it was almost an entire year later since the actual incident.

"Don't blame her," Dan was saying. "It's not her fault."

"Shut up, Dan," I snapped. I really wasn't in the mood for the fucking peanut gallery to be weighing in on this. "Your fucking church. I'm blaming whoever the fuck I want."

He had no rebuttal to that. Thankfully.

If he opened his mouth again, I really was going to end up taking out all of my aggression on him. Which wasn't going to fair well with asking Kate to let me see Dexter again. In her eyes, I was already on thin ice from the drinking and being out of Dexter's life.

Which... now I supposed the odds were even.

"You're not bringing him back to that fucking

church," I said, slowly standing. "Or any of them."

She shook her head, looking up at me. "I haven't, I swear."

For the roles to reverse like this so suddenly was jarring. Now *I* was on the side of the disappointed parent looking down at the fuck-up that caused out son harm and pain.

Perfect Kate was no longer so perfect.

Letting out a long sigh, I let my anger fade into numbness. At this point, there was nothing that could be done. No matter how much I yelled and screamed at Kate over it, she couldn't wave a wand and go back in time to fix any of it.

That ship had come and gone along with the priest who was, hopefully, now rotting in a hell I no longer believed in but could for this occasion.

At least Dexter was safe from him.

Dan moved closer to us in order to pick Kate up off the driveway. She was still staring at me with those big doe-eyes of hers that I'd gotten so used to seeing during our first few years of marriage. She'd looked to me to be her leader when I'd had no clue what the hell I was doing. She'd put her trust in me in more ways that I probably deserved at the time.

And now here we were, standing face-to-face while we were both lost.

I didn't want to hate her, or blame her, despite my anger. Eventually, I'd probably forgive her, even though for now, that seemed like a very distant wish.

Whatever happened at this point and moving forward, we needed to do it together. No more of this bullshit with us fighting for control over the other. Clearly that wasn't working for either of us.

"Kate."

Her uncertain stare was all I got in return.

"I need you, going forward, to meet me halfway. We can't keep doing this. I'm tired of being left out of things that are important. I get that I wasn't the best dad around the past decade, but I'm here now. We both fucked up. I need you to stop holding my past over my head, just like I'm choosing not to do so with you right now."

She swallowed visibly.

I held my hand out to her. "We're going to *actually* co-parent from here on out."

Slowly, she placed her hand in mine, shaking it. "Okay. No more hatchet."

"No more hatchet," I agreed, squeezing her hand.

CHAPTER 24

XAVIER

"How're you holding up?" Gage asked.

Shifting the ice pack resting on my forehead toward the crown of my head was the only thing that was relieving the pressure from this god awful migraine that had cropped up the second I'd climbed into my car and left Kate's house.

As soon as I'd gotten home, I crawled into bed with my ice pack and my phone, determined to shut out the rest of the world for the foreseeable future.

While I was glad Kate and I had come to some sort of understanding and agreement between us, I was damn exhausted—both physically and emotionally. Much more so the latter part.

"I'll survive," I finally answered.

Probably not the answer he was looking for,

but that's all I could manage to give for now. My brain was too mushed from everything that had happened within the past twenty-four hours. I desperately wanted to pass out and go to sleep but unfortunately my body seemed determined to keep me awake regardless of how fried I felt.

"Too bad I can't give you one of my sleeping pills," Gage mumbled. "I knew I should've slipped one in your bag before you left."

I smiled a little. "As much as I love that you think of me, I'm glad you didn't. I really wasn't in the mood to spend the entire day in TSA jail trying to explain a mystery pill."

"Okay, you have a point."

As soon as I'd crawled into bed, I'd called Gage, not caring if he was busy with work or still sleeping. I'd needed to hear the sound of my boyfriend's voice, even if it lulled me to sleep. Call me childish or clingy, I didn't care.

He had a knack for calming my nervous system down even without the offer of drugs.

"I miss you," I sighed.

"I miss you, too." His voice sounded somber.

While neither of us could've predicted our planned fun-filled week to come crashing down around us, I was glad that no matter what, Gage always took things in stride. He never once made me feel bad about leaving or whined to try and convince me to not follow my gut in bringing Dexter home.

"You and the twins doing okay?"

"Yeah. Asher finally came home last night around two. He was so vague in what he was doing that I felt like some crazy disgraced detective trying to suss out clues as to where he was and with who all night. Of course, Grey was no help."

I huffed out a laugh. "You're such a helicopter mom."

"Ugh, don't remind me."

Despite my teasing, that was one of the things I loved about him. He showed his care through his overabundance of worry and love—a man with his heart stitched onto his sleeve.

"I love you, Gage."

I could hear the smile in his voice as he said, "I love you, too. Get some sleep, okay? Call me when you get up. I'll have my phone on me."

I breathed out slowly as my body finally started to relax. Almost like it'd been seeking permission to give in and finally rest like I'd be dying to since getting on a plane early this morning.

Listening to the sounds of Gage on the other end of the phone, my body finally fell limp and I slowly drifted off into a dreamless sleep.

CHAPTER 25

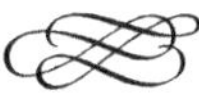

Waking up some hours later, my body felt less like it'd been run over by a truck and more like I had a hangover from a night of partying—way more manageable in my opinion.

Rolling to sit up, my ice pack, now warm to the touch, slid from my forehead and slapped down into my lap. The room was dark, thanks to my blackout curtains that I'd been smart enough to draw over the windows before crawling into bed.

My phone was somewhere buried under my covers and most likely had a message from Gage waiting for me that I'd answer as soon as I had some food in me.

After blinking the sleep from my eyes, I shoved the covers off of me to roll out of bed. The clock on the nightstand read six-thirty on the dot, which meant I slept almost a full ten hours without waking up once.

As impressive as that was, my body was definitely feeling it given the stiffness in my bones from not moving at all while I'd been passed out. Clearly I'd needed it, though.

Despite the still lingering headache, I did feel better. More clear headed. More in control of my emotions. Less likely to snap and go on a murderous rampage.

That last one might still be up for debate.

Heading into my bathroom, I took a quick shower and freshened up before going back into my room to retrieve my phone. Sure enough, there was a message from Gage wishing me a good sleep with a few emojis accompanying it.

To my surprise, directly under that was one from Dexter that simply read: '*Thank you, dad. I love you*'.

"Ugh." I slapped my hand over my heart while my body pitched forward, overwhelmed with both love and guilt that seemed to want to battle in trying to be at the forefront of whatever my emotions were trying to decide on how I felt.

Even though I knew in the back of my mind that Dexter didn't hate me, a message like this was still a nice confirmation.

I hoped he didn't regret telling me anything. I hoped that from now on, we could turn over a new leaf and start fresh—no more skeletons hidden in the closet.

Typing out a heartfelt reply back to him, I sent it on its way before tossing my phone back onto my bed and grabbing a fresh set of clothes to change into for the evening.

I'd give him the rest of the week to be by himself and then invite him over for dinner and a movie or something. With Christmas right around the corner, there was no sense in overwhelming him with a bunch of activities and running around the city trying to fill the awkward void left by him opening up to me.

Starting small after having gone through some major turmoil was probably best, even if he didn't blame me for it. The last thing I wanted was for Dexter to feel like some kind of freak around me now that I knew his secret. That was a common thing for people to feel when opening up about trauma, yet I didn't want that to happen regardless of the circumstances.

I'd been treated like a damn pariah after being forced out of the closet and outed to everyone around me. So, like hell I was going to let my kid have to go through something similar.

Since Kate and I were agreeing to work together now, I'd have to bring up getting Dexter into some form of counseling before he was off to college in a few months. It wasn't good for him to fester on these horrible memories by himself. He needed an expert to help him work through everything to untangle the mess that had been done to him by someone he should've been able to trust.

No wonder he'd kept everyone at arm's length.

Shaking my head, I made my way across my house to the kitchen. I was suddenly starving, having only eaten a small box of raisins on the plane ride over here that had tasted barely edible.

Now that I was back on solid ground, I wanted something that was actually real food.

Passing by the police scanner I kept hooked up to the outlet in my kitchen, I flicked it on to listen to the tones while grabbing a box of pasta out of the pantry. This was the kind of familiarity that grounded me. The only thing missing was my boyfriend crowding up the small space while pretending he knew how to heat a can of red sauce on the stove.

Just as I was setting a pot on the stove to bring it to a boil, the radio went off again with another set of tones, followed by an automated message that said: *"All units and medical personnel, please respond to eight-five-five River Street, Sacramento County."*

I whipped around. That was my street.

Jogging toward my front door, I ripped it open and stepped out onto my porch, facing east to where eight fifty-five was located only five houses down from mine. Black plumes of smoke clouded the sky, billowing up at a fast rate that meant the building that was caught on fire was burning *fast*.

"Fuck."

Of course I didn't have any of my gear with me, but with no sounds of sirens nearby and no flashing lights on the street right outside of the residence, I was going to wager that the next unit on scene wouldn't be there for another two minutes.

Which in the event of a fire, meant life or death.

Sprinting to my closet, I threw on the best thick clothing I had while shoving my feet into a pair of the only thick-soled boots in my closet.

Grabbing another shirt off of a hanger, I used it to wrap around the lower half of my face in a makeshift mask. It'd barely help but until the trucks arrived, there wasn't much else I could do.

Heading back to the front of my house, I found my spare axe sitting against the wall in the hall closet where I'd tucked it into the corner for emergencies.

The weight of it was comfortable in my hand when I gripped it tightly before heading out of the house with the door slamming shut behind me. People were beginning to gather on the sidewalk outside of their homes with the distant sounds of a truck blaring through the streets.

Judging by the way it was echoing against the houses, I'd say it was at least another mile and a half out.

Coming up to the burning house, the heat hit me hard. The fire was contained to the top floor, flames licking out of the open—or rather shattered—window while climbing up to the worn roof. Black smoke had collected on the bottom level, making it impossible to see inside to check if anyone was still in there.

A neighbor sprinted outside from the house next to it, a phone held up to her ear while she chattered on to dispatch.

I grabbed her arm to stop her from heading across the street. "Who's in there?"

Her eyes were frantic. "I don't know! They're an older couple. I have nine-one-one on the phone!"

Older couple. That wasn't good. That meant

there was a potential for either mobility issues or pre-existing health problems. Or both.

"The car is in the driveway!" She pointed to the small car park next to the house. "I think they're still in there!"

Two men from the house across the street were running toward the house—both of them touting leather jackets and bandanas over their mouths. I shoved the woman toward the street again, gesturing for her to wait on the opposite sidewalk while thanking her.

I brandished my axe to the two men, noticing one of them had a pair of heavy duty diving goggles on his head. "Let me borrow those!"

Either I was presenting with a 'don't question me' attitude, or they were glad to have someone leading this thing, because soon I had a pair of goggles shoved into my hands and two guys ready to take orders.

While snapping the lenses over my head, I yelled at them both to get everyone off this side of the street so that when the trucks finally arrived, they weren't trying to crowd manage and get their lines hooked up to the fire hydrant at the same time.

They nodded at me and then sprinted off in opposite directions, corralling people as soon as they got close enough to them. The goggles were tight on my head, but gave enough suction that I wouldn't be tearing up from the smoke burning my eyes.

Getting up to the house, sweat began to pour down my back and arms. Since the top window had already blown out and was creating a vacuum to suck all of the heat out of the top, breaking down this door wouldn't run the risk of causing any kind of backdraft once I got it off its hinges.

My axe cut through the wood solidly, tearing off chunks with each blow. Thankfully, the entire house was old as dirt and gave way easily to a little bit of force from a sharp weapon.

As I pried the door open, smoke began to billow out around me, choking me even through the shirt tied tightly around my nose and mouth.

I stepped back to let the place air out for a few seconds, clearing out as much as possible before moving back toward the opening again.

"Hello!" I called out, carefully stepping inside.

The bottom floor was lit with smoldering embers. Pieces of furniture and all that was left of the carpet were still on fire but had a yellow-y golden hue to them and not the blue-hot like the top floor.

"Hello! Anyone in here!"

Barely above the crackling of the wood around me, I heard a soft cough.

Following it, I almost stepped on him—a man laying face down on the floor.

Tucking the handle of my axe into my belt loop, I bent and scooped my hands under his armpits. He was light compared to what I'd been expecting, clearly much frailer than his height suggested. He coughed again as I dragged him out, kicking back through the chunks of roof that had fallen onto the floor.

Where I found him wasn't that far from the doorway, thankfully, and soon enough, we were back out onto the street.

My lungs burned as I sucked in fresh clean air.

The man in my arms choked and gagged when I set him down. His skin was blackened from the fire and ash that had been coating him by the time I'd found him.

"M... my," the older man let out a deep, chesty cough. "My wife..."

Behind me a truck docked, several firefighters jumping off and running over to me.

"Cruz!" One of them yelled. "What the fuck are you doing here?"

I wiped at my goggles, spotting Eddie, one of my old coworkers at the fire station. "Take care of him, I think there's one more inside!"

"Hey, wait!" he yelled.

Before he could catch me and wrangle me back in, I sprinted for the open doorway once more, ignoring my training in waiting for my geared up coworkers to take it from here. There was something in me that was telling me that any more time wasted out here catching everyone up to speed was time wasted in pulling this man's wife out of the wreckage alive.

Call it my intuition or hubris.

I slipped the axe up into my hands again and carefully ducked back into the house. There was no sign of the man's wife anywhere, even as I traveled to the spot I'd found him at.

"Hello!" Calling out got me nothing, not even when I heard the telltale signs of water beginning to hit the side of the house to put it out.

"Xavier!" someone yelled into the house from the doorway.

Ignoring them, I continued further, choking as

more smoke made it harder to breathe. If there was anyone following after me, I couldn't tell. The sound of the wood paneling was loud as it burned, near ear piercing and making it impossible to think straight.

There was a doorway that led into a small kitchen, almost completely untouched from the rest of the fire by the awkward angle of the house's layout. My heart picked up when I spotted a woman laying face down on the floor, facing away from me.

"Ma'am!" Setting my axe down onto the floor, I rolled her over to pat her face a few times. She didn't flinch at all, not even so much as moved a damn muscle.

I bent down to see if I could hear her breathing, and the sudden cacophony of a ceiling coming down had me jumping back and pressing myself against the cabinets behind me. Debris and smoke suddenly filled the kitchen, making it hard to see where the hell it had fallen.

Waving my arm in front of my face did nothing aside from making me feel lightheaded.

The woman next to me groaned softly.

Oh thank fuck.

I scooped her up, noting she was a little heavier than her husband but not by much. I threw her half over my shoulder in a fireman's hold while reaching for my axe and climbing to my feet. As I finally got closer to where I'd come from, I realized a large partition of debris blocked us in, the ceiling having fallen right outside of the entryway into the kitchen.

Looking around, my heart sunk when I discovered there was no other door leading outside—effectively trapping us like sitting ducks.

Fuck.

The window above the sink was our only escape.

Could we even fit?

We have to. There's no other way.

I wasn't going to die in this damn kitchen—nor was I going to let this woman die with me. As a search and rescue firefighter, I had too much experience under my belt to let something like a fallen ceiling blocking me from the point-of-entry to force me into giving up.

Not when I had a damn kid and boyfriend to get back to.

Shifting the woman's weight on my shoulder, I swung my axe back and shattered the frame and glass all in one go. The glass shards exploded outward, leaving nothing but the remnant pieces still stuck to the frame that I scraped at with the back of my axe head.

It was an awkward angle but I managed to hoist the woman up off of me and out through the window. With a momentary wave of guilt, I shoved her out of the window and winced when I heard her hit the ground outside with a groan.

Well, it was better than burning to death in a fire.

I threw my axe out next hard enough that I knew it would miss her completely and then I catapulted myself up over the sink and onto the ledge of the window. She was on her side, facing away from the house, a pained expression on her face.

Carefully slipping down from the sill, my body pitched forward and I just barely caught myself before I face-planted onto the ground along with her. I was crashing from my adrenaline rush—cut short by the lack of oxygen to my damn brain.

The woman groaned again, clearly feeling how the fire was cooking us by being so close to it. Forcing myself up from the ground, I grabbed her arm and began dragging her around the side of the house, stumbling when above me, another window shattered and rained glass down onto us.

Using my body as a shield to protect her was only so useful when I began to grow dizzy once again.

"Cruz! You fucking idiot!" someone yelled.

My vision blacked out right when a pair of hands grabbed onto me.

"Are you suicidal!" the voice chastised.

Belatedly, I realized it was Eddie.

And then I was gone.

CHAPTER 26

THE LAST PHONE call I ever expected to receive was a number out in California that I didn't recognize.

While I had half a mind to ignore it, something nagged at me to answer it. Almost like I had some guardian angel whispering over my shoulder that it had something to do with Xavier.

Because who the hell else did I know from California that would be calling me this late at night?

"Hello?" I answered.

There was a slight pause on the other end. "Uh, hey, Gage... it's Dexter."

That immediately had me sitting up in my bed. "You okay?"

Alarm bells were going off in my head immediately. There was no reason for Dexter to be calling *me* of all people unless there was some dire emergency going on. Not when Xavier could just do it himself.

I kicked off my covers to roll out of bed and head over to my closet, my heart pounding.

"So... dad was kind of in an accident," Dexter said slowly.

Oh god.

Oh, fuck.

My hands shook while reaching for one of my shirts hanging in the closet. "How bad?"

There was some noise on the other end as the line was muffled. I couldn't tell what it was or if Dexter was talking to someone else to get the information, but either way, I was about ready to throw the fuck up.

Finally when he came back to the phone, he said, "He had a lot of smoke inhalation. They have him on a ventilator."

"Smoke?"

What the fuck was Xavier doing around a goddamn fire the same day he came back from vacation?

What, was his station a bunch of fucking slave drivers?

They couldn't give the man one fucking day to recover?

"Yeah. He wasn't wearing any gear so it was pretty bad. I guess it was his neighbor?"

Leave it to Xavier to play fucking hero.

"I'll be right there. Can you text me which hospital you're at?"

Dexter sputtered on the other end. "You don't have to come all the way out here. I just wanted to call and let you know so you weren't worried that he wasn't answering your calls or texts."

This kid was too sweet for his own good. Despite all of the bad shit that's happening to him and between him and Xavier, he still cared deeply for his loved ones. I could appreciate that whole-heartedly.

"Dexter?"

"Yeah?"

"Just text me the hospital."

He was silent for a moment. "Okay."

"Great," I said, shoving one of my legs through a pant hole. "I'll see you soon."

CHAPTER 27

GAGE

IF CALIFORNIA TRAFFIC had one enemy, it was me. And if California fucking traffic had *no* enemies, then I was fucking dead.

The amount of times Xavier had joked with me that a 'California mile' was actually five disguised with a hat and a trench coat would've given me enough money to buy myself a full week's worth of groceries.

All those times I'd called him out for his over exaggerations and yet here I was, a damn fool for not trusting my very un-sarcastic boyfriend from giving me a harsh reality check in the form of being stuck in jam packed traffic after getting off of a red-eye flight that had me gnawing at the skin around my nails for the entire four and a half hours that it took to get over here.

A damn fool. That's what I was.

By the time my rideshare finally pulled into Mercy General, I was about ready to tear my hair out from all of the stress. Travel had never been my favorite, and doing so when a loved one was laid up in the hospital on a ventilator made all of that ten times fucking worse.

I'd loosely been texting Dexter since he'd called me, thankful for the small updates he'd been giving me so that I wasn't losing my ever loving mind with worry that I was going to arrive to a cadaver already toe-ticketed inside of the morgue downstairs.

Xavier was up on the third floor. There was no actual timeline for him waking up or being taken off of the ventilator but his brain activity was very healthy despite his dangerous dip in oxygen levels.

With my heart in my throat, I took the elevator up while sending Dexter a quick text that I was here. I hated the not knowing everything about all of this. While the good news was good, the bad news is what scared me the most.

Xavier being in any kind of coma freaked me right the hell out. Even if the doctors were hopeful that he would wake up soon.

What if he didn't?

What if I was walking into a situation where I was actually saying goodbye to him?

I was never going to be able to handle something like that. I'd shatter into a million pieces if I didn't go home with Xavier still alive.

To my surprise, when the elevator doors opened up, Dexter was standing there waiting for me. He perked up as soon as he spotted me, lifting himself away from the wall to meet me in the middle of the hallway.

"Hey..." I said, my hands itching to reach out and hug him. Despite us only knowing each other a short while, I still felt a connection to Dexter. My brothers liked him, my boyfriend adored him. Therefore in my mind, he was already family.

"Your flight go okay?" he asked.

I blew out a breath in response.

See, the thing about getting a last minute flight wasn't that the prices were astronomical or that the seat you got assigned to you was of course at the very back of the plane next to the bathrooms. No, the worst part was that taking a red-eye meant you had half the passengers sleeping peacefully and the other half being absolute and downright weirdos.

My luck, I'd been seated between two.

"I made it," was what I finally settled on.

He nodded in response and then pivoted on his heel to lead me back down the hallway. Nurses and doctors moved all about the floor, coming and going in and out of rooms that we passed by. There wasn't so much of a frantic energy to the place as there was a purposeful one.

Which actually made me feel a little bit better. With no codes being called, that meant that everyone here was stable. For now.

Dexter stopped in front of a room that was kitty corner to the nurses' station, the door already propped open.

He led me inside with a wave, stepping back so I could enter before him.

My heart leaped into my chest when I caught

sight of Xavier on the bed. His eyes were closed with a tube shoved down his throat. On either side of him were a bunch of monitors that beeped softly, tracking all sorts of things that I couldn't exactly wrap my head around at this point.

No one else was in the room, thankfully.

"They said he's going good," Dexter said from behind me, his voice soft. "I know it looks bad from here."

Yeah, that was an understatement. But I appreciated the sentiment regardless. Dexter was a pretty aware guy, even for just seventeen. I think he got that from his dad, honestly. That man could read you like a damn first grade level book.

My feet carried me over to his bedside. As long as I ignored the giant tube coming out of his mouth, he looked like he was peacefully sleeping.

"I should've brought flowers or something," I joked, my voice sounding hollow. "This place is so drab."

"I think there are some bouquets down in the gift shop," Dexter supplied.

He really was such a sweet kid.

Nodding, I scooped up Xavier's hand into mine, squeezing it lightly so that I wouldn't disturb the IV-line taped to the top of it. His hand was warmer than I was expecting, relieving the tension that had been building inside of my chest just a little bit more.

Leaving in a flurry earlier had both scared the twins and made them want to come with me. I'd barely gotten them to agree to staying behind and looking after the house while I jetted off to California for the foreseeable future.

I felt guilty leaving them behind, or at all, with them having such limited time to spend with me before they both had to leave for their respective careers again. No matter how many times they'd reassured me while they drove me to the airport, I still felt bad.

This wasn't exactly what either of them signed up for when coming home to visit me right before the holidays.

Leave it to Xavier to play hero and cause us all to be scared to death.

"Dexter," a woman's voice called from the doorway. "We brought you some food from the— who the hell are *you*?"

I dropped Xavier's hand instantly, whipping around to see a blonde haired woman glaring at me as she held a tray of cellophane wrapped food. Behind her, a man with glasses also ducked into the room, stopping short at seeing me just as she had.

Oh fuck.

Why didn't I figure that Dexter hadn't come alone to the hospital?

The kid was seventeen with no driver's license. Obviously, he'd be here with his mother and... stepdad?

"Uh," was all that came out of my mouth.

"This is Gage," Dexter said, waving a hand at me. "Dad's boyfriend."

Instantly, my face heated up.

Oh, man...

I'd never had that whole 'coming out to your parents' experience since by the time I'd figured out that I was down and dirty for the same sex, mine were long gone and buried in the dirt. The closest I'd ever come was bringing a boy home to my brothers and introducing them both to him as my 'special friend' until they were old enough to start calling me out on my bullshit.

But here, with Dexter presenting me to his mother as her ex's significant other, gave me a good slap of reality to what that all might've been like. The embarrassment that no straight kids would ever feel. The anxiety over potentially being rejected. The fear that hatred would follow.

All of this was a mix of emotions that I hadn't been expecting to feel, let alone confront, once I stepped off that plane and into the horrid desert heat.

"O-Oh." His mother cleared her throat. "Um... how did you know he was here?"

"I called and told him," Dexter said.

"*Why* would you do that?" His step-dad frowned.

To his credit, Dexter simply answered him with a very bored, "Because they've been dating for a year and he deserved to know."

When both adults turned to look at me again, all I could think to do was plaster a, hopefully, pleasant looking smile on my face. "It's nice to meet you. Uh, sorry for the conditions."

Dexter's mother, Kate, sighed. She looked worn, like she'd been up all night talking to the doctors and taking care of Xavier. I didn't want to assume much, given that my... *opinion* of Kate wasn't the greatest.

However, she did bring Dexter down here to see him. So...

Maybe she wasn't a total lost cause.

"Gage..." Kate mumbled, not exactly looking at me. "How long are you planning on staying?"

I shrugged.

Not really the most solid of answers but the truth nonetheless. I was determined to stay here until the man lying on that hospital bed—the love of my life—finally opened his eyes. Leaving any sooner would just cause me to have a massive meltdown while I stressed about him never waking up again.

She sighed again. "All right... Well, I'm Kate. This Dan, my husband. You already know my son?"

"Uh..." Glancing over at Dexter was no fucking help as he only gave me a 'you're on your own' kind of shrug. "Yeah... Xavier and I... we introduced our kids to each other when things got serious. So..."

Not a total lie.

Plus, if Xavier, or Dexter, hadn't told her about the college thing yet, I wasn't about to spill the beans in the middle of a hospital room with a man hooked up to a damn ventilator in the background.

"You have kids?" her husband asked, running his gaze up and down me. "How many?"

"Two? Well, okay. They're not *my* kids. They're my younger twin brothers, but we have a pretty big age gap so I consider them mine since I've been raising them by myself for close to a decade."

Both Kate and her husband looked shocked to hear that, along with a little bit impressed. I suppose maybe to a secular couple, hearing something like that was quite admirable. Taking on the task of raising kids that you didn't birth yourself got me all kinds of praise, even if I never asked or wanted it.

Coming from a religious couple, that kind of shit was downright celebrated.

Or at least from what I've heard. I was not exactly a connoisseur of religious upbringings.

"How old are they?" Kate asked.

"Nineteen. One of them enlisted and the other is working on a horse ranch." I grin. "I'm quite proud."

To my surprise, Kate's expression softened.

She didn't say anything to that, just simply nodded before turning to Dexter to offer him one of the sandwiches on the tray and a small bottle of juice she'd grabbed for him. Her husband walked around her to settle into one of the chairs over by the window, unwrapping his own sandwich in his lap.

Ugh, this was so awkward. I kind of wished Dexter had warned me his parents would be here before I'd shown up. Then again, maybe he knew better than to let me get into my head about it and decided that blindsiding me was the better way to go about it.

Or maybe I was reading way too far into this entire situation. Kind of like I usually did with everything else.

"I'll eat in a bit, mom," Dexter said, setting his sandwich down on the windowsill. "Gage wanted to go grab dad some flowers from the gift shop, so I'm going to go show him where it is."

Kate looked like she was ready to argue but then glanced over at me and deflated almost as quickly. "All right... Just be back here in half an hour. Gage, I want your phone number."

"Oh. Yeah, sure." I pulled out my phone to exchange numbers with her, aware that Dexter was hovering close by.

Once we were all set, I flashed her another smile and then headed back out into the hallway with her son tagging next to me. Halfway to the elevator, I looked back to see Kate leaning out the doorway, watching us both like a hawk.

I kind of felt bad that she was so paranoid. Though, I guess knowing what I knew now with what happened to Dexter, I couldn't exactly blame her.

So, instead of feeling the kind of annoyance I usually would whenever Xavier brought Kate up, I waved to her and lifted up my phone, gesturing to it with a thumbs up.

Her shoulders seemed to sag at that, a small nod following before she ducked back into the room.

Dexter pressed the button for the elevator, watching me closely. "She means well... I think."

I glanced over at him. "Tough crowd?"

He rolled his eyes. "You have no idea. This is her being good."

"If it makes you feel any better, I'm ten times worse with the twins."

"Forgive me if I don't actually believe you," he said right as the elevator doors popped open.

Grinning, I waited for him to get in first before following after and letting my body sag against the metal wall. Damn, those airline seats were no joke these days. When the hell did they get so *small*?

"Thanks for calling me, by the way." I said.

"No need to thank me. I do kind of want you to stick around, so I figured letting you into the family drama was a good start."

"Aw, does that mean Dexter approves of me?"

He shot me a look. "Well, if I want to go to LSU, I should probably make friends with the locals."

I laughed. "It's a good school. I'm not going to knock it. Besides, I definitely wouldn't hate if you and your dad moved closer to me. The traffic out here sucks."

Dexter snorted. "Yeah, try living here."

When the doors opened up again, I had to shuffle to the side to make room for the onslaught of people pushing their way into the small, cramped space. Both of us managed to slip out into the lobby, barely missing us being trapped behind the closing doors and being skated up to whatever floor was next on the chopping block.

The front lobby to Mercy General was nice, if not a little boring. Though, I supposed as far as hospitals went, that wasn't exactly a bad thing.

Dexter waved for me to follow him, leading me down the main entryway to a large gift shop that was located right as you walked into the hospital. Thankfully, it was much quieter trapped behind these glass walls.

I spotted the flowers toward the back of the shop—located in a small corner that had a bodega-like set-up with a few buckets of premade bouquets and then a few that had loose stems you could put together yourself.

I opted for the loose ones, grabbing a pre-cut piece of decorative cellophane to wrap the stems in.

Dexter hovered next to me, nodding in approval or shaking his head with each flower I held up. Together, we put together a nice looking bouquet that was both colorful but not too flashy for a 'get well soon' sentiment.

"Nice," I said, holding it up while Dexter tied a piece of twine around it.

He smiled at the flowers, leaning in to breathe in their scent. "I think he'll like them."

"Me too. Would you believe me if I said I never got someone flowers before?"

Dexter snorted. "So dad will be your first? You should tell him when he wakes up. He's a secret sap."

"Secret or covert?"

That had Dexter smiling again.

We headed up to the register, getting in line behind an older woman and her husband who was holding her hand. The sight was sweet, reminding me of all the sappy love stories I couldn't help to daydream about whenever I thought of Xavier.

Which was often to an embarrassing level.

One would think that after a solid year, I would've gotten over the butterflies by now.

"Were you serious about living with dad?" Dexter asked.

Turning to him, I raised a brow. "Only if he wants to."

He stared at me for a long moment. "Why haven't you already?"

"He didn't want to leave you behind and not see you."

"What about after I'm gone?"

I shrugged. "We'll see. I'm trying not to be pushy."

"But you *want* to be," he guessed.

Holding back a groan took monumental effort. See, knowing Xavier, I knew exactly where Dexter got his smarts from, as well as his keen eye. What I *didn't* like was when it was turned on *me*.

"Did he bring up the marriage thing yet?" Dexter asked. "I told him to."

Balking, I said, "Dexter. Leave the match-making up to the adults."

He rolled his eyes at me. "What's four months going to change? I'll still think the same way, you know."

"What, that you want me and your dad to get married?"

"I want him to be *happy*." He sounded annoyed as he spoke. "He needs to stop focusing all his energy on me. What's going to happen when I go to college? I don't want him dropping dead like a fly because he no longer has a purpose anymore."

I loved hearing that Dexter cared about his dad just as much as Xavier cared about him. Not that I had any doubts that deep down inside, their bond had yet to be totally shattered despite Xavier's constant worrying that he'd fucked up beyond repair.

Seeing Dexter just as protective over his dad

was a welcome sight, one that I hoped Xavier got to see one day. It would at least show him that trying to mend this bridge was worth it in the end; that getting sober and taking back his life had gotten him his son back.

And wasn't that a goddamn beautiful thing?

Taking the chance, I reached up to ruffle his hair in the way I always did with my brothers. "Anyone ever tell you that you're a sour patch kid?"

He batted my hand away, though his expression was more bemused than anything. "What's that even mean?"

"First you're sour," I said, reciting the commercial. "Then you're sweet."

"Funny," he said, fighting hard to not crack a smile.

"I really am, aren't I?"

Once we got up to the counter and paid for the bouquet, we wandered around the shop for a few more minutes before braving the crowds and heading back up to Xavier's floor. By the time we arrived, Dexter's stepfather was passed out in his chair while his mother scrolled on her phone, popping her head up as soon as we entered.

She eyed the flowers in my hand warily but said nothing when I placed them down onto the bedside table to Xavier's left hand side. They looked nice against the rather drab colored room, bringing a little bit of life to the place despite the somber mood.

Dexter dragged a chair over for me to sit in, pulling his own right alongside mine.

"And now we wait," he mumbled to me, settling back into his chair.

I sighed in agreement.

Hopefully, not for long.

CHAPTER 28

Faint voices were what broke through the darkness surrounding me. They were hard to make out, the words blurring together with one another while the tones were stilted and disfigured.

I concentrated on them, trying to pull myself up from the void that had swallowed me, figuring that following it would lead me back into the light.

"You should go." One of them was a little more distinct—closer, maybe. *"It's the holidays."*

"But what about you?" Younger sounding.

Where even was I?

Nothing around me looked familiar. Or rather, I couldn't *see* anything that looked familiar.

Had that fire blinded me?

Going in with no gear on had been stupid, I'd give myself that much. The thing about blazes catching so quickly and with civilians inside—elders at that—seconds could mean life or death.

Choosing to go in there with no plan aside from listening to the sheer adrenaline pumping through my veins was what saved those two. At least, that's what I'd like to hope. I'd passed out before I could make sure they were both taken to the ER.

Shit.

Was I *dead?*

"It's okay. I'll be fine. I'll call you guys if anything changes." That voice again. Something else was distorted, hard to piece together while I concentrated on the voices that were drowned out by a subtle beeping sound.

Someone sighed.

"Are you sure?" A woman's voice this time.

Something squeezed my hand. I looked down at it—couldn't see it.

"Yeah, all good. Hope you guys have a good rest of your Christmas."

Christmas?

Oh, fuck.

"You too, Gage."

Gage.

"Bye, dad. See you soon."

Dexter!

I was missing fucking Christmas. I couldn't believe this.

How fucking long had I been out for?

Arriving home with Dexter, there had still been a few days before the holiday. *And* I was making Gage miss it with me.

How the fuck was he even here?

Pieces began to slide together as I traveled further into the darkness, pushing my way through it so I could get back to my kid and boyfriend. Dexter must've called him—probably not wanting him to worry. My kid was always so thoughtful, even if he preferred for people not to see that side of him.

He'd gotten that from his mother. His heart worn on his sleeve, no matter how hard he tried to conceal it from the world.

The beeping was getting louder, more distinct. I followed it. Followed the sounds around me and the hand that squeezed mine in a vice grip. I needed to get back to where I belonged. Back to the people I loved.

CHAPTER 29

XAVIER

WAKING up to a ventilator tube shoved down my throat wasn't as bad as it was getting it forcibly removed by two nurses—one pulling and the other on standby with a bucket under my chin, ready to catch whatever vomit or mucus, or both, that I ended up coughing up as soon as the tube was free from my body.

I choked while gripping the side of the bucket, all but drooling into it as my body fought to pull in oxygen with my own muscles around the heaving coughing fits that wracked my body.

Fuck, was that a bitch and a half.

One of the nurses was slapping me on the back a few times, breaking up whatever had settled in my lungs as I choked it up while the other one was cheerfully giving Gage the rundown on aftercare.

The sad part about all of this wasn't that I could've damaged my lungs permanently by being an idiot and running into a burning building. No, it was that I didn't regret a damn thing. Saving those people had been worth it to me, despite it costing me a few days being unconscious and right now, a bit of my dignity.

Spitting out the last of it, I grabbed the towels that were handed over to me and lifted my hand out to Gage who was hovering nearby, an anxious look etched onto his face.

He took my hand quickly, squeezing it tight just like he had to wake me up. While I felt bad that he'd flown all the way over here in order to be by my side during all of this, I was damn happy that he'd come all this way just for *me*.

Him missing his Christmas with the twins was unfair, yet at the same time I was selfishly glad I had my partner with me, or else I'd probably be losing my damn mind right about now.

"We'll go inform the doctors that you're awake," one of the nurses said, flashing a smile at me. "They'll want to run your levels again, but so far, you're looking really good."

Well, that was a relief at least.

"Thank you," Gage told them on my behalf.

When they left, he blew out a long breath and then collapsed down onto the edge of the bed. I tugged him over toward me using our laced hands, letting him fall into my shoulder and sag against me completely until he was closer to jello than human man.

I brushed my lips over his temple while I

breathed him in. I could actually cry right now, I was so damn happy.

"Merry Christmas," he said, laughing softly.

"I'm sorry," I whispered back.

My throat was still incredibly raw from the tube, making it hard to say anything above a whisper. Gage could hear me all the same though, turning slightly to press his nose against the underside of my jaw.

He breathed out slowly again, his fingers flexing around mine.

I knew this side of him well. His anxiety was finally crashing and now all that was left was relief and exhaustion. If I could offer him more room on this bed to pass out on, I would. Unfortunately, we were both fully grown large men and these beds were only meant to fit medium sized people at best.

"The boys wanted me to wish you a Merry Christmas on their behalf," he mumbled.

I pressed another kiss against his head. Too bad they hadn't come with him. I understood why, of course, especially with how long I was out for.

Still, that didn't make it any less bittersweet.

"Dexter and his mom and stepdad were here this morning," Gage went on. "They didn't want to leave in case you woke up, but I told them they should go celebrate their day together. It's Dexter's last Christmas with them, most likely, so I didn't want them missing that. Sorry for sending them away, I really thought you'd be under still."

I shook my head. "S'okay."

He'd made the right call. Don't get me wrong, I would've loved to wake up with him and Dexter both at my side, however making Dexter sit in a hospital room all day when he should be enjoying the holiday just as Gage had said was a much better option in my opinion.

Was I upset I was also missing the holiday with him?

Absolutely. Gage was, too, so at least we were together on that front.

"The boys..." I mumbled.

"Oh, don't worry. They already ripped through all their gifts and sent me photos and videos." He chuckled. "I swear, I gave them the okay and not even a minute later, I was receiving updates on what they got."

That was good to hear. At least the boys would be at Gage's until New Years Day. Gage would get a little holiday time with them before they were back out in the world.

"You know..." When he lifted himself up, he shifted around until he was facing me, his side resting against the back of the bed. He kept our fingers entangled in a tight grip. "Since we're both missing Christmas, we should do something for New Years."

I raised a brow and mouthed, "Together?"

He nodded. "Yeah, why not? Unless you have some other hot date I don't know about."

Funny, I wanted to say, settling for a look instead. He was lucky I couldn't talk and was too stiff to tug him over to kiss those jealous thoughts right out of him.

Instead, I settled on lifting his hand up to my lips and pressing a kiss against it. His smile was radiant, eyes soft despite the dark circles under them.

When I was finally discharged from this place, we were going to go back to my place and I was going to force this man into my bed to actually sleep, regardless of the inevitable begging to take care of me.

"Is that a yes? The station pushed back the date for the Christmas party. I guess they were too worried about what was going on with you to be in the mood to throw a holiday party. So now it's going to be a joint Christmas/New Years extravaganza."

That was sweet. I knew how much Gage was looking forward to the party. Now, instead of him having to go stag, I'd get to accompany him. Turning him down the first time had killed me, even more so when that hopeful look in his eyes had faded and was replaced by abject sadness.

I nodded firmly, showing him my decision to the question.

When he grinned, I couldn't help mirroring it with my own. "Okay, awesome. I'll let the gang know. They're so excited to meet you. I may have been bragging about how handsome you are, so if you get stared at a lot, that's totally my bad."

I held back a snort, kissing his hand again.

Meeting Gage's crew would certainly be interesting.

He'd talked about them enough over the past year and a half, that at this point, I felt like I practically already knew them, too. I was glad to hear that they were eager to meet me—it made things a lot easier when bringing a newbie into such a tight-knit work environment.

Especially, if one day I did end up moving out there and needed to find a job. I wouldn't mind setting my roots down at Station Twenty-One for as long as they'd have me.

I wouldn't mind setting my roots down in Baton Rouge for as long as *Gage* would have me.

He sunk back into my side, resting his head against my shoulder, his eyes slowly sliding shut. There was a content smile on his lips that I wished I could take a picture of to immortalize forever.

This man had been through hell and back with me so many times since we'd met, all without a single damn complaint. And I'm sure he'd do it a hundred more times if I ever asked.

Glancing down at our laced fingers, I brushed my thumb down along the bridge of his hand, an idea occurring to me.

Before we took off for Baton Rouge, I needed to swing by *Keeton's*.

CHAPTER 30

GAGE

"ARE YOU SERIOUS?"

I swung my bag up onto the bed, and the damn thing's zipper popped open once again. Rolling my eyes, I tossed my phone down next to it in order to grab both sides to force them back together. Wrestling a zipper closed while my bag was overstuffed was the worst fucking task to do by myself.

Xavier had mysteriously left early this morning with hardly any explanation while I'd still been half asleep. By the time I'd realized it, it'd been well past an hour.

I swore that man had no off switch. Two days out of the hospital and he was already trying to run marathons again.

"You don't have to go," I said down to my

phone. "I only wanted to pass along the offer since Grey and Ash were asking me to."

Dexter let out a soft noise on the other end of the line, causing me to smile.

How funny was it that he went from having no friends to two that were up my ass about inviting him to the Christmas/New Years extravaganza?

The second they'd heard about me bringing Xavier home with me, they'd shot me back with a *'well, what about Dexter?'* that I thought was so fucking adorable I could barely contain myself.

Since they were little kids, they'd always talked about having a younger sibling, which, unfortunately, never came to fruition after the death of our parents. Now, with Dexter in the picture, it seemed like they were determined to adopt him under their wings.

"You're actually serious?"

I rolled my eyes again. "I can have them Facetime you and have them ask you themselves."

He grunted at me, no doubt with a finger shoved into his mouth and halfway through chewing apart a cuticle. He'd done that a lot at the hospital, anytime he thought no one was paying attention to him. By Christmas, the poor skin around his nails was ripped to shreds.

Did I blame him at all?

Nope, not one bit. Hell, I'd been bouncing off the walls the entire three days Xavier had been passed out. By that fourth day, just before he finally woke up, even *I* was ready to start taking up a bad habit.

"Come on," I goaded. "You know you want to come."

He sighed softly. "Yeah…"

I grinned, finally getting my zipper closed and grabbed my phone. "Awesome. Pack a bag for a few days. I can have your dad talk your mom into letting you come since you got to spend Christmas with them."

Dexter let out a soft snort. "Was that why you kicked us out on Christmas? So you could have leverage?"

"No."

Maybe.

It wasn't intentional.

At the time, at least.

I'd actually wanted them all to spend the day with each other like families were supposed to. Not be stuck in a hospital room cramped in those god awful chairs while we all stared at Xavier's machines and twiddled our thumbs waiting in silence.

Even now, I kind of felt bad taking Dexter away from his mother for New Years; however, at the same time, Xavier deserved a holiday with him, too. During my time in the hospital and getting to know Kate a little bit better, she'd shown me that she wasn't *as bad* as I'd made her out to be in my head.

There were still some sensible bones left in her body, even if her husband did try to scripture me to death at one point.

Thankfully, I'd perfectly the art of *tuning things out,* thanks to my brothers.

"Uh huh," Dexter drawled. "All right, I'll pack a bag and have it by the door. You and dad got all your stuff ready now?"

"For the most part. Your dad ran off a few hours ago to do god knows what. He's barely answered my texts all day, aside from telling me he was heading downtown somewhere."

Tossing my phone back onto the bed, I looped the handle of my bag over my shoulder to carefully set it down by the door. With my luck, any kind of jostling would pop that damn zipper right back open and then I'd be starting all over again.

"Downtown?" There was a pause. And then, "Oh."

My gaze traveled back to my phone to squint at it.

What did *that* tone mean?

"What?"

"Nothing," he said quickly, flagging my suspicions even further.

Honestly, did I want to know?

No doubt it'd have something to do with the twins and planning some elaborate prank that was either going to embarrass me or piss me off. Such is the way with little brothers and their funny ways with showing that they were going to miss their elder sibling.

Ugh, whatever.

"I'll let your dad know you said yes to coming."

"Thanks," he said. "Text me when you're on your way."

CHAPTER 31

The flight from California to Baton Rouge, while long, hadn't been terrible.

Xavier and I had opted for the 'comfort' seats toward the front of the aircraft instead of suffering with the rest of economy being crammed in the back with little to no leg room and some kid kicking at the back of our seats for the entire damn flight.

Dexter had lucked out and had gotten to have his row, which had been right across from ours, all to himself and used it to his full advantage.

Luckily, I'd gotten a few hours of shuteye while we'd been in the air, only having been shaken awake when the meal service rolled through and Xavier encouraging me to eat something before we landed.

Since getting back from his little impromptu

shopping trip, he'd been acting... off. I couldn't quite put my finger on it, but there was something there that I was picking up on that was definitely fishy.

It was bothering the fuck out of me, but anytime I pointed it out, he'd waved me off and distracted me with some kind of kiss or brush of his hand over my body that had those weird feelings melting away instantly.

I supposed it made more sense for him to be acting this way with the looming issue of him meeting my coworkers in less than a few hours.

No matter how many stories I told about them or tried to prepare him for the absolutely ridiculousness that he was about to be walking into, the full picture wouldn't reveal itself until *after* he got there and saw for himself exactly what I had to deal with day in and day out.

Look, I could only do so much.

At least we had a few hours to ourselves to chill at my place before that.

De-boarding and heading back through security was a breeze. I'd called my brothers ahead of time to meet us at the terminal since I'd left my car with them and like *fuck* I was going to pay for a rideshare that would charge me an arm, a leg, and my left kidney just to be picked up from the airport.

Cramming us all into my little sedan wasn't going to be fun, but it beat paying an entire goddamn paycheck to get home.

"You sleep okay?" Xavier ran a hand through the back of my hair as we stepped onto the escalator heading down to the front lobby.

"Yeah. Wasn't too bad. Did you sleep at all?"

"Wasn't tired."

I narrowed my eyes at him. Wasn't tired, my ass, tell that to the bags under his eyes.

What was going on with him today?

I'd blame it on the jet lag but this had been going on since this morning. There was no way I was reading into things when the red flags were waving themselves right in front of my face.

Just as I was about to point out the hypocrisy in his statement, I caught Dexter on the step above us squinting at something.

"Oh," Dexter said, folding his arms over his chest. "So, it's definitely a Torres thing, then."

My brow popped up at that. "What is?"

By the time I turned around to find whatever he was staring at over my shoulder, there were already people huffing out laughs ahead of us. I scanned the lobby, spotting two familiar teenagers who were holding a comically large sign over their heads.

Their expressions were stone cold while they stared down anyone passing by them and snagging a photo.

The sign read: '*Welcome Home From Prison. Remember to stay away from the goats!*' in big bold-as-fuck letters.

Oh my god.

I'm going to kill them.

"Quite the welcome," Xavier noted, an amused look on his face.

I stomped down the last two steps as the escalator folded together and stormed over to them, aware of more people walking by and laughing.

When they caught sight of me, they quickly turned themselves toward me, the giant sign bending slightly at the top before straightening out once more.

"You two are so ridiculous," I said, quickly grabbing at one of the sides to rip it from them.

Asher cracked first. "Welcome home, big bro. Did you miss us?"

"Hey, Xavier. Dexter," Greyson greeted my travel companions.

"Ugh." I worked quickly to roll the sign into a tight cylinder, and then used it to smack both of them. "I'm returning all of your Christmas gifts."

They both gasped in unison.

"You can't do that," Asher argued.

"Yeah, we're already using them all," Greyson said.

"Get," I said, pointing to the sliding doors with the sign.

Sharing a look with each other that wasn't at *all* remorseful, they quickly jogged for the doors, waving Dexter to follow along with them. Shaking my head, I grabbed Xavier's hand when he brushed it against mine and laced our fingers together.

"They're going to be the death of me, I swear."

He chuckled and pressed a kiss against my forehead. "They'll be keeping you on your toes until you're ninety."

I smacked him next with the sign. "Don't curse me like that."

"Too late."

Despite the weird attitude shift in him today, I

was so damn happy he was going to be coming with me to the holiday party. The second Ellie had heard about me rushing to California after his accident, she'd immediately rallied everyone into sending me their well wishes, along with post-poning the party indefinitely.

Honestly, getting those texts and calls from my work family had me choked up for hours after-ward. Knowing that they cared for me was an everyday thing, but seeing it all in textual proof had been even better.

It reminded me that no matter what I was going through, I could always count on them.

One day, I really hoped that if Xavier moved out here to be with me, he'd find his own place at the station just like I had. We were our own brand of wild, ridiculous, and a little fucked up. Perfect for a newcomer like Xavier to join our ranks.

"Ready for the swamp?" I joked as soon as we reached the doors.

"As long as you're suffering with me," Xavier said, tugging me out into the afternoon sun of Baton Rouge.

CHAPTER 32

XAVIER

BREATHING out slowly for the fifth time since putting on my dress pants and pressed button up, I checked my pocket one last time to keep myself from fidgeting. The party was in full swing, Gage's coworkers meandering around the fire station while classic holiday music blasted from a small boom box over by the refreshments table.

The place was tastefully decorated with both Christmas and New Years in mind. Normally, the mismatching green and red against the gold would come across as tacky, but they'd somehow pulled it off to create a seamless look.

There were two couples dancing in the middle of the station to the music, looking like they were having the time of their lives as they laughed and spun around to pass their partners back and forth. My gaze tracked Dexter, who was deeply engrossed in a game of cards with Gage's captain, one of the paramedics—a feminine-looking young man that kept popping M&Ms in his mouth every few moments and whose name was apparently Newt, and the twins.

I'd been a little nervous taking Dexter to a gathering like this. Mainly, because I'd been afraid of him getting overwhelmed and feeling out of place amongst a bunch of people he'd never met before. The twins had taken him on a tour around the entire station, introducing him to the crew one by one while keeping him squished between the both of them.

I was so damn proud of him for taking Gage up on his offer in spending New Years with us. After what happened at the botanical gardens, I was sure I'd have a shut-in on my hands.

But of course, like always, Dexter surprised the fuck out of me.

"You doing okay over here?"

I looked over to the woman approaching me who had a kind smile on her face; Ellie, if I remembered correctly. She nodded at the untouched drink in my hand. "Don't tell me it's flat. I swear, I had them throw in two entire bottles of soda."

Cracking a smile, I said, "No, it's great. This whole thing is."

"Really? I'm glad. I was worried it was going to be a total disaster."

"Not at all. Couldn't even tell you guys pushed it back. Thanks for doing that, by the way. Gage was really excited that he didn't miss anything."

She laughed. "I don't know about that. I think

he was more excited that he got to bring you along."

I actually didn't know what to say to that. Obviously, Gage had told me his feelings about wanting me to come and the disappointment that followed after I'd turned him down. But hearing it from someone else that he'd wanted to introduce me to everyone here, had me feeling almost honored in a way.

We were obviously serious—at least, I hoped we fucking were or else I was going to be embarrassing the fuck out of myself here in a little bit—and still, having someone else realize it, too, was almost like a confirmation that our relationship was real to not just us, but everyone else as well.

I'd spent a lot of my life denying my true self. Twenty years ago, I never would've imagined that I'd be here, standing in a fire station and talking to a woman—a *stranger*—about the man I was in a relationship with. That I was in love with. All the while I had a hole burning in my pocket.

It was funny how things could change so much in such a short amount of time.

For the better.

"Everything okay over here?"

Both of us looked back to see Gage smiling at us with a slightly wary expression on his face. His preternatural instincts were off the chart sometimes. Especially, when it came to me. He'd been trying to suss me out all day and, thankfully, hadn't done anything that had gotten me to crack.

I'd come close, but hadn't folded completely. Yet.

"All good," I said, looping an arm around his

waist as soon as he got close enough. "Surprised you guys haven't gotten any calls tonight."

Both of them groaned at me.

"Don't jinx us!" Gage huffed.

"Too late. He already said the words." Ellie frowned.

Oops.

Someone clinking a glass with a metal utensil brought all of our attention to the opposite side of the station where two men, Jase and Quinn, from what I remembered of Gage introducing them to me, were grinning with a bunch of streamers and large plastic glasses in the shape of the New Year's date in their hands.

"Mayor just called and said that the fireworks are a go in five."

Captain Clarke shoved himself up from the card table to clap his hands together loudly, gathering everyone's attention quickly. "All right, everyone. Out front on the driveway will be the best spot. Let's get a move on."

My heart began to pound in my chest. I barely felt Gage squeeze me before he parted from me to grab us both a couple of streamers and two plastic glasses to put on. We waited until the boys were heading for the door with their own sets, following closely behind them as we all exited the firehouse and stood out on the triple-wide driveway.

A bunch of people were already waiting on the sidewalk facing the eastern night sky. Some of them were already setting off sparklers and waving them around in the air, while others were lounging in folding chairs.

"Are the fireworks big this time of year?"

Dexter asked while taking a pair of glasses from Asher.

"Oh, the mayor pays for a crazy display," Gage said, sliding his own glasses over his face. "It's going to blow your mind."

Snorting, I settled mine on top of my head, needing the unobstructed view of my surroundings while I got my bearings in gear.

Jesus, I was so fucking nervous it was a wonder I wasn't sweating through this damn button up. Or that Gage hadn't noticed and called me out on how antsy I was. He'd been giving me looks all night but had kept his mouth shut, thankfully.

I really wasn't sure what I would've done if he actually called me out and demanded for me to spill the beans on what the fuck was wrong with me. There was no way I would've kept this secret long enough to lie to him.

I'd barely kept it together on the damn plane.

Dexter waved one of the streamers in the air in front of him, glancing over at me with a knowing look. He'd obviously guessed by now and was doing his best to keep the heat off of me with the twins—something I was eternally grateful for.

"One minute!" someone called out.

Oh, fuck.

"Hey," Gage's arm looped around mine. "You okay? You're sweating."

"Swamp weather, babe," I muttered at him, hoping he'd buy the excuse.

He seemed about to argue with me, but was quickly distracted by someone shouting out a countdown, thankfully. He squeezed my arm in his and lifted his streamer into the air and waved it a few times.

Okay, I could do this.

The worst he'd say was 'no'.

Actually, the worst he could say was *hell no.*

Fuck, now I was getting in my head.

This was such an impulsive decision. Three days ago at the hospital it'd felt right. *This morning* had, too.

Now, I was fucking panicking.

"Five! Four!" People began to chant the countdown.

I'd jumped out of planes, for god's sake. I'd been through active combat.

I'd gotten sober.

How the hell could proposing to my boyfriend terrify me more than any of those things combined?

"Three! Two! One! Happy New Year!"

People began to cheer around me. The first flash from a firework lighting up the night's sky shimmered as it broke over the line of buildings in front of us, raining down over the inky blackness with beautiful flakes of white and gold embers.

One by one, fireworks were shot off from somewhere deeper in the city. From golds, blues, purples, and pinks, they were all mesmerizing to watch explode, illuminating the sky for a brief moment before fading like they were never there to begin with.

I couldn't help but glance over at Gage, enraptured by the way his jaw was slack with awe as he stared at the display. His eyes lit up each time a new one was shot off, the reflection of it mirroring back at me.

"Wow," he breathed out with a soft smile turning up the corners of his lips.

He always found the joy in the little things. I loved that quality about him.

Hell, I loved *everything* about him.

I'd never get enough, no matter how much time passed and how long we spent with each other.

I'd never get tired of any of it.

Before long, fireworks were being shot off in rapid succession, clouding the sky with white smoke as they exploded in unison with each other. People on the sidewalks cheered while the station blew their truck horns and waved their streamers, in anticipation for the final firework.

Unlooping my arm from Gage's caught his attention, causing him to be ripped away from the festivities in order to look over at me.

"Xavier?"

I didn't answer him, and quickly shoved my hand into my pocket to grab at the small box nestled in there. He didn't fight me when I took half a step back from him, his face pinching into one of confusion.

I dropped down to my knee.

The strangled noise spilling out of Gage's mouth was barely audible over the plume of the final firework shooting off into the sky.

I popped the box open, the silver band, hopefully, visible in the dark.

The firework crested high in the sky, the colors of it catching in Gage's eyes when they widened down at me, along with a light shimmering over the ring that he was now staring at incredulously.

"Marry me," I said, just as the explosion from the firework punched through the air and drowned out everything else around us.

The embers rained down in the sky like a gigantic weeping willow, glistening the same way that stars did in the distant galaxy and keeping both of us illuminated just long enough.

"Holy shit," he choked out, pulling in a sharp breath. His hand shot out toward me, splaying his fingers at me. I saw him, rather than heard him, mouth the word 'yes' while the crowd around us cheered loudly at the finale.

His hand was shaking as I took it in mine, popping the band out of the case and carefully sliding it on his finger—a damn perfect fit.

I had to catch him as he fell into me, collapsing with a soft sob. He wrapped his arms tightly around me, burying his face in my shoulder.

With a laugh, I lifted us both back onto our feet, planting my weight back to keep him from toppling us both over.

The lights overhead on the fire station flickered on, announcing the end of the night's festivities and the official beginning of the New Year.

Gage pulled away from me in order to gaze down at the band encircling his finger. He lifted it up to the light to get a better look at it, sniffling. "It's so pretty."

I lifted his hand by the wrist and brought it to my cheek, turning my face to press my lips into his palm. "It has our initials engraved on the inside."

He melted into more tears. "You fucking sap."

That had me laughing and pulling him into a tight hug. Honestly, pot and kettle on that one, but tonight, I'd let him have it.

"Oh, did you do it?" Dexter asked, craning his neck to get a peek at Gage's hand.

Lifting it up into the light again, nodding with a Cheshire grin on my lips, I showed off the shiny new band, earning a broad smile from my kid, along with two sets of bewildered looks from the twins.

Gage's voice cracked when he turned to look at Dexter. "You knew about this?"

Dexter rubbed the back of his neck. "It was... kind of obvious."

Gage shoved his face against my chest once more, heaving another watery exhale. He was so goddamn cute it was hard not to sweep him up into my arms and carry him back into the damn firehouse where I could find us an empty room.

"Wait, what's happening?" Greyson's gaze darted between Dexter and I.

"My dad proposed." Dexter held out a hand to him, curling his fingers twice. "That means you owe me."

What...

"Shit," Asher muttered, taking out his phone. "You do CashApp?"

The alarm inside of the fire station had us all jumping apart. Flashing lights, along with the piercing sound shattering the quiet of the street, had everyone around us bouncing into action. Two of Gage's coworkers grabbed at the garage door and lifted it open, the rest jogging inside to grab their gear.

"All right, you know the drill!" Captain Clarke called out, following them in. "Let's get a move on, night crew!"

Gage quickly wiped his face, his expression steeling instantly.

Pride bloomed in my chest. "Go get 'em, tiger."

His face faltered for a split second, a small smile tugging at his lips before he schooled it back down. He gave us all a tight nod before spinning on his heel and jogging back into the station.

Asher, Greyson, Dexter, and I kept toward the back with the rest of the plus ones that attended the party. It took the station no time at all to gear up and roll out, the skeleton crew being the only thing left behind after it was all said and done.

Once the door to the garage was pulled closed again, everyone let out a small breath.

While it was no surprise that the station was getting calls from people setting their shit on fire with homemade fireworks displays, I was a little disappointed to have Gage ripped away from me so soon after proposing to him.

A pair of arms wrapped around me from the side, causing me to look down to see Dexter hugging me.

"Congratulations."

Smiling, I brushed a hand over his head. "Thank you. You think he liked it?" I teased.

"I think you're probably in for another bit of waterworks when he comes home."

Oh, I have no doubt about that.

He pulled away from me with a small smile

that turned rather devious when he turned back to the twins. "CashApp you said, right?"

"Shit, he totally remembered," Greyson said, nudging his brother.

Asher nodded. "I was really hoping the fire truck stuff would distract him."

"Nice try," Dexter drawled.

I shook my head at them. "All right, you three brats, get in the car. You can sort out your betting pool when we get home."

CHAPTER 33

Gage

I ROLLED my thumb along the underside of my ring for the thousandth time, admiring the smooth metal that felt like silk against my calloused hand.

No matter how many times I touched it, it still didn't feel real.

He'd fucking proposed.

That's why he was acting so goddamn weird. He'd been carrying this ring around in his pocket for who knows how long and I bet it'd been burning a hole in whatever he'd stashed it in until tonight.

No wonder he'd been keeping me at arm's length.

I had to slap my hand over my mouth to keep myself from dancing and screaming as I carefully unlocked my front door and slipped inside. There was a single light on in the foyer to greet me as I came in; an adorable gesture that I had no doubt was from Xavier.

Kicking off my shoes and dropping my gear bag just inside the door, I headed deeper into the house and flicked off the light behind me. The living room was dark, as was the hallway.

Passing by the twin's room and the guest room that was serving as Dexter's room, I saw no light coming from under the crack of either door. Probably a good thing since it was pretty late.

The fire hadn't been horrible to get under control, but had taken forever to get the entire thing put out. By the time we were finished, all of us were exhausted and ready to call it a night.

As I got to my room, I happily noted that the light from under the door spilled out into the hallway. Seeing it made me smile. Xavier waiting up for me wasn't expected, but was appreciated, nonetheless.

While I wouldn't blame him for falling asleep from the jet lag, I also wanted to celebrate with him.

Getting engaged was a big fucking deal!

Popping the door open, I slipped inside as quietly as possible and then closed it behind me without a sound.

Xavier was sitting up in my bed with the covers laid out over his lap and his phone in his hand while he watched something. His head snapped up immediately the moment I stepped into the room, his phone getting tossed to the side in favor of focusing his attention on me.

"How did it go?" he asked, slipping out of bed to come over to me.

I folded myself into his arms, sighing when he pulled me into a tight hug. "Fine. No casualties."

"That's good to hear."

He ran his fingers through my hair, still a little damp from the fast shower I'd taken at the station to get the smell of smoke and sweat off me. Being stuffed inside of my helmet and gear for the past three hours after being brutally assaulted by the scorching heat of a house fire did not produce a smell that would be pleasant for our celebration.

"I can't believe you proposed to me." I still couldn't get any of it out of my head. The way he'd looked kneeling in front of me, how he held out the box to me with the ring inside just as the sky lit up bright with fireworks, or how earnest he'd looked as he'd asked me to marry him.

Ugh!

I was never going to get over it all. Of course, I didn't want to, either.

"Come here," he said, walking us backward to the bed.

I let him lead us, pulling him into a kiss as he turned me around to lay me down on top of my bed. He only broke it briefly to divest me of my clothes, tossing the material away from us and laying me bare before him.

A soft grumble rumbled up inside of his chest as his gaze roamed over me, and he looked pleased at what he saw.

I beckoned him forward with a single finger, loving how easily it was to call him to me. I wrapped my arms around his neck, dragging him down into another kiss.

His tongue rolled along mine, his hips bucking

until I spread my legs and wrapped them around his waist.

Fuck, I wanted him so badly.

Xavier was my damn addiction and I didn't even care if that was wrong of me to think.

He trailed his lips down my jawline, leaving wet kisses until he found the sensitive spot on my neck that always made me squirm whenever he sucked on it. He sank his teeth into my skin, sucking and licking as he did so, hard enough that I ground myself up against his hips and begged for a damn release.

At some point, he was going to have to stuff a sock in my mouth because there was no way I was going to be able to remain quiet.

Seeming to read my mind, Xavier's hand curled around my mouth, keeping it locked tight while he sat up. "You going to behave for me?"

I shook my head. I knew my limits too well to pretend like I was any good at obeying them.

He chuckled and took his hand off my mouth in order to tug off his t-shirt. Next, he shoved his sweats down his hips, his cock popping out and bobbing at me. Automatically, I grabbed onto the back of my knees and brought them up to my chest, exposing myself to him.

His eyes locked onto my hole immediately, his lips parting with lust. "Oh, Gage..."

"Hurry up and fuck your new fiancé. He's tired of waiting."

Xavier let out a soft groan. "Oh, I love the sound of that."

I watched him quickly slip off the bed to retrieve my lube out of the nightstand and then toss it next to me. He kicked off his pants before crawling back onto the mattress, one of his hands clamping down on the back of my thigh to hold me steady.

He drizzled a generous amount of lube over the head of his cock, stroking it downward once before tossing the bottle to the side. His head fell back as he exhaled deeply.

"Put it in me," I begged.

"Fuck," he gritted through his teeth.

Letting go of his cock, he ran two fingers around my puckered hole, teasing me with each swipe over it. I was desperate for more, *needing* more from him or else I was going to actually explode.

"Please. Don't torture me like this."

"You are the prettiest thing I've ever laid my eyes on."

Two fingers slid into me, pumping in and out so deep that his knuckles were breaching my hole with each thrust.

My lashes fluttered shut at the sensations.

Oh, that was good.

But not good enough.

I wanted more from him, I wanted him to bury himself so deep inside of me that I wasn't sure where he ended and I began.

I tightened my hold on my legs, readjusting just enough to keep me from accidentally letting go. Finally, after what felt like forever, Xavier's fingers withdrew from my hole, quickly replaced by the blunt tip of his cockhead.

He leaned over me, a hand coming down over my mouth while his other was still locked onto the back of my thigh. I groaned loudly, thankfully muffled, as he slid into me slowly.

Fuck he was so, so perfect. He stretched me in a way that I'd never had before, his shallow thrusts becoming deeper with each one, until finally, his hips were flush with my ass. His cock twitched inside of me in response to my walls bearing down on him.

My selfish body wanted to keep him inside of me forever. Letting him go was the last option I wanted. He rocked into me, grinding his hips into my ass a few times until I was panting against his hand.

"Ready, fiancé?" he teased.

If he kept calling me that, I wasn't going to last at all.

Nodding at him, I tightened my grip on my legs.

He started off slow, rolling his hips back all the way and then sliding himself home again. His cock glided in and out of me easily, each pass over my prostate had my toes curling and my body twitching.

I loved his cock. I loved him fucking me with it.

I mumbled incoherently against his hand, getting lost in the pleasure of our bodies coming together after what felt like two long decades of being apart.

We were getting married.

We were *actually* getting married and now we'd never have to be apart ever again. He was going to move here and live with me. Long distance was a thing of the goddamn past now.

My swirling thoughts made me feel giddy.

I let go of my legs to wrap around his waist, pulling him closer to me. His hand was soon replaced with his mouth when he leaned over me, curling his arms under my body to hold me close to his own.

This was what I loved—this closeness—and what I missed when he was gone. I could live in this damn bed forever with this man if given the chance to.

His thrusts became a bit more frantic while his hips slapped against me. I held onto him for dear life, my balls tightening with the need to come.

He reached a hand between us to wrap around my cock and stroke in time with his thrusts. I choked out a moan, bucking my hips up into his hand as cum leaked out of me, coating both of us in the process.

He ripped his mouth off of mine and slammed into me, his body stiffening, warmth filling me as he unloaded into me.

My arms wrapped around him again when he collapsed on top of me. He panted against my neck, sending a shiver skating down my spine.

"So good..." I mumbled.

Xavier kissed my sweat-slicked skin, flashing me a grin. "Happy New Year."

I laughed and held up my hand up in the light to admire my ring again, my heart filling with so much love that I felt my eyes beginning to water once more.

God, I loved this man.

And what an amazing year this one was going to be.

EPILOGUE

GAGE

I STOOD in front of the mirror, trying to adjust my tie for the tenth time. My fingers trembled slightly, making the task more difficult than it should have been. The room was filled with the hum of nervous energy, and I could hear Greyson and Asher chatting animatedly behind me.

The evening was surprisingly chilly, with a crisp, cool breeze that seemed to seep through the windows and had chased away the usual humidity. The sky outside was a deep, twilight blue, and I could feel the excitement of the coming evening pressing down on me. I'd looked forward to this day for three damn years and I couldn't believe it was finally here.

"I hate these things," I growled.

"Gage, you've got to calm down. You're going to strangle yourself with that tie," Greyson said, his voice filled with amusement as he stepped up beside me. His easygoing nature was a stark contrast to my current state and helped me breathe a little better. Right now, I needed all the help I could get to calm my jangling nerves.

"Here, let me help," Asher chimed in, already reaching out to take over, flitting his fingers at Greyson in a gesture that told his twin to move out of the way. He deftly undid my sloppy knot and started over, his fingers moving with surprising skill.

"Hey, I had it," Greyson whined, punching his brother in the shoulder even as he stepped back to let Asher take over.

How was it my brothers managed to have a knack for being both annoying and endearing at the same time?

Both grown men in their own right now, both with relationships, careers, and homes of their own, Asher settled in Texas and Greyson in Georgia, they still remained the same mischievous twins they'd always been to me. Don't get me wrong, their happiness made my heart soar, but seeing that little bit of the old rivalry tugged at my heartstrings, too. They were finally grown. I'd done it. Now it was my turn for a happy future and they were both here to support me. Nothing could've made me happier.

"Thanks, Ash," I muttered, sniffling back the tears that threatened behind my eyes and trying to muster a smile. My heart was pounding in my chest, and I could feel the nerves settling in my stomach like a lead weight. "I just... I want everything to be perfect."

"It will be," Greyson said firmly, clapping a hand on my shoulder. "Xavier loves you, Gage. Nothing else matters."

I nodded, trying to take comfort in his words. Xavier.

Just thinking about him brought a rush of emotions. Love, excitement, and a hint of fear all swirled together, making it hard to breathe. We had been through so much together, and tonight was the culmination of it all.

Our wedding.

The thought of seeing him as I walked down the aisle, of finally pledging our lives to each other, was almost overwhelming.

"You look good, Gage," Asher said, stepping back to admire his handiwork. The tie was now perfectly knotted, sitting neatly against the collar of my crisp, white dress shirt. "Xavier's going to be blown away."

"Yeah, well, let's hope I don't pass out before he gets the chance," I joked weakly, earning a laugh from both of them. Their presence was grounding, a reminder that I was never alone in this.

There was a knock at the door, and Ellie poked her head in, her eyes bright with unshed tears. "Gage, it's almost time," she said softly. "Are you ready?"

I sucked in a deep breath, letting it out slowly as I glanced at myself once more in the mirror. The sharp, tapered lines of my suit fit over me like a glove, the dark material soft against my skin and the burgundy pocket square providing a splash of color. For a firefighter, I had actually managed to clean up pretty well tonight. Not half bad if I did say so myself.

"Yeah, El. I think I am."

～

XAVIER

As I MADE my way to the ceremony, Dexter by my side and standing in as my best man, the cool December air hit me, calming my nerves slightly. The garden was beautifully lit, with fairy lights twinkling in the trees and candles flickering along the path.

Our guests, coworkers from Station Twenty-One and their respective spouses and plus ones, were already seated, their faces turned expectantly toward the front. Even Jackson and his husband, Ayen, who sat staring at his husband in awe, tears shining behind his eyes, had flown out to Baton Rouge from California for our special day. The fact thrilled me to no end. I hadn't seen the man since I left my teaching position at the aerial program, the very program responsible for bringing Gage and I together, and moved to Baton Rouge three years ago. So much had happened for us both in that time and he looked good. Happy. Married life clearly agreed with him. A far cry from the player I'd known for most of my career there.

Kate and Dan were the other guests sitting in the second row that really shocked me. I'd invited them out of respect for Dexter but, truth be told, I never actually expected them to come. They'd been tolerant of my relationship with Gage, polite and cordial even whenever we had to interact in any way for something for our son, but I never actually expected them to support my impending nuptials on account of their religious morals. Color me impressed at Kate's changes over the last three years where my relationship with my son was concerned; she'd come leaps and bounds since that day I confronted her about the abuse our son had suffered. This though, sitting in actual support of me at my wedding, this was a change I could never have predicted. I knew having his mother there would mean the world to Dexter, too, and the thought that one day, despite our bad history, that Kate and I, and our respective spouses, might truly be a blended type of family for Dexter simply brought tears of happiness to my eyes. I wanted nothing more for my son than for all the past tensions and hurts to be erased and his future to be the brightest it could be. Maybe, just maybe, Kate's presence here today would be the start of that.

Captain Clarke stood at the front of the garden, an imposing yet welcoming figure. His navy dress uniform was immaculate, each medal and ribbon perfectly aligned. A tall man with broad shoulders and a dignified bearing, he commanded respect with a mere glance. His presence added a touch of formality and gravity to the occasion, but his warm smile and kind eyes softened his demeanor.

Captain Clarke had been a firefighter for over three decades, a Captain at Station Twenty-One, for the last one and a half, and his experience showed in the calm, steady way he carried himself. He had been a mentor to Gage, guiding him and supporting him through some of the toughest times in his career and his personal life, one of the very few commanders-in-chief who ran his station as an all inclusive, all accepting company, and it seemed only fitting that he would be the one to officiate our wedding.

I took my place at the front, standing tall and trying to steady my breathing even as I brushed at the tears collecting in the corners of my eyes. Dexter flashed me a smile and gave me a quick, one-armed hug, his supportive presence a comforting force.

He'd grown into such a fine young man, his grades at LSU were in the honorary role all through his last three years there, and amazingly, he'd gone to a therapist and managed to deal with all the horrors of his childhood and come out an incredible person despite that past. He'd even met someone he really liked and their relationship, though still in the early stages, seemed to add a sparkle to his eyes and a lightness to his step.

Our father/son relationship had progressed beyond my wildest expectations, and we often spent time together just doing things normal families did. All the things I'd missed out on in his childhood. I couldn't be more proud of the man he'd become, and I told him that often

The music started, and my heart skipped a beat. This was it.

As Gage appeared at the end of the aisle, my breath caught in my throat. He looked stunning, his smile lighting up the night. All the nerves, all the fear, melted away in that moment.

All I could see was him.

My love, my future.

When he reached me, we joined hands, and everything else faded into the background. It was just us, standing together, ready to face whatever came next. I squeezed his hands, and he squeezed mine back, his eyes shining with love.

"Ready?" he whispered, his voice steady and sure.

"More than ever," I replied, my heart full to bursting.

And as we said our vows, surrounded by family and friends, I knew that this was just the beginning of our forever.

～

Gage

As Xavier and I joined hands and stood before him, Captain Clarke's deep voice resonated through the garden. "Ladies and gentlemen," he began, his gaze sweeping over the assembled guests, "we are gathered here today to celebrate the union of Gage and Xavier. It is an honor to stand before you, to witness and bless the commitment of these two remarkable men."

He paused, looking directly at us with a mix of pride and affection. "Gage, Xavier, you have chosen to walk this path together, to face the challenges and joys of life as partners joined in matrimony. Your love is a testament to your strength and your devotion to one another."

Standing just underneath a simple, yet elegant arch adorned with small white flowers, Captain Clarke's presence was both reassuring and inspiring. His words carried the weight of wisdom and experience, and as he continued the ceremony, I felt a sense of peace and certainty settle over me.

With Captain Clarke guiding us through our vows, just like he'd guided me through much of my life in the way that I thought a loving father would have, I knew we were in the best possible hands. His blessing was more than just ceremonial; it was a heartfelt endorsement from someone who had seen us grow and thrive together. Someone who I respected and cared for very much. His presence was a connection between our past and our future, and as we spoke the words that would bind us forever, his blessing falling over us, and the crowd cheering when we were pronounced husband and husband, I felt truly ready to take this next step in life with my man by my side.

Xavier was my heart, my everything.

He'd come into my lonely life and changed everything in ways I could in no way have imagined. My world would never be the same and I couldn't be more excited for our future together.

I pressed my lips to his when we were finally granted the leave to do so, and with his hand grasped tightly in mine, tears of happiness tracing down my cheeks, we turned to face our family. As they all roared their approval, we made our way down the aisle together.

This was just how I'd dreamed my life would be.

One big family.

Thank you for reading the continuation of Xavier and Gage's story.

Oh, and if you enjoyed this book, maybe you'll consider doing me a huge favor and leaving a review. Even a few words would mean the world to me, and it also helps other readers find the stories you love.

Watch for Greyson, Asher, and Dexter to star in their own books sometime in the future. Don't forget to follow me on Facebook to keep up to date on all things yuMMy and the crazy antics of all the bad boys inside my head.

In the meantime, why not check out some of the other books in my backlist. A handy list is on the very next page!

Love,
~*Evie Riley*

Cade

Dawson

Drew

Grayson

Riley

Mitch

From The Edge

Shattered

Runaway

Jaded

Rescue

Hidden

Tormented

Gray Vale Pack

His Fated Mate

His Wounded Warrior

His Healing Heart

FOLLOW EVIE

Facebook Author Page
https://www.facebook.com/AuthorEvieRiley

Blog/Website
https://authoreveriley.blogspot.com/

Goodreads
https://www.goodreads.com/author/show/39018597.
Evie_Riley

Bookbub
https://www.bookbub.com/authors/evie-riley

Instagram
https://www.instagram.com/authorevieriley/

LGBTQ+ Romance Books ARC Team
https://booksprout.co/author/25823/lgbtq-romance-books

ABOUT THE AUTHOR

Evie Riley is a prolific, neurodivergent author known for her captivating MM romance novels. She has gained a significant following and topped the LGBT+ action and adventure bestseller charts with her series.

Evie's writing style often explores dark and gritty themes where her men must overcome difficult obstacles in their search for love, but she has also ventured into sweeter small-town romances, incorporating tropes like enemies-to-lovers, friends-to-lovers, age-gap, and forced proximity. She is known for crafting engaging romantic suspense novels and has a knack for creating interconnected series worlds that keep readers invested.

Outside of writing, she enjoys spending time at the beach and has a quirky personality, described by her partner as ranging from cute to deadly, depending on her blood-chocolate levels.

Evie spends her nights writing bad boys in love, and her days wrangling the sweet boys she loves.

www.ingramcontent.com/pod-product-compliance
Lightning Source LLC
Chambersburg PA
CBHW061042210726
48294CB00001B/6